From Sky to Sky

From Sky to Sky

Amanda G. Stevens

THORNDIKE PRESS

A part of Gale, a Cengage Company

No Less Days #2.

Thorndike Press, a part of Gale, a Cengage Company.

Thorndike Press® Large Print Christian Mystery.
The text of this Large Print edition is unabridged.
Other aspects of the book may vary from the original edition.
Set in 16 pt. Plantin.

LIBRARY OF CONGRESS CIP DATA ON FILE.
CATALOGUING IN PUBLICATION FOR THIS BOOK
IS AVAILABLE FROM THE LIBRARY OF CONGRESS

ISBN-13: 978-1-4328-7906-8 (hardcover alk. paper)

Published in 2020 by arrangement with Barbour Publishing, Inc.

Printed in Mexico
Print Number: 02   Print Year: 2021

Now unto the King
eternal,
immortal,
invisible,
the only wise God,
be honour and glory for ever and ever.
Amen.

1 TIMOTHY 1:17 KJV

Prologue

"Someone had better be dying. Oh, wait, we can't do that. Maybe you forgot."

Zac clenched his cell phone tighter. Colm sounded annoyed and half awake, no different than any other time he'd been woken up this last century. As if nothing had changed tonight. As if he'd committed no sins tonight.

"I'm standing in the corridor of the Harbor Vale Family Inn." Zac kept his voice just above a whisper. They did not need mortal witnesses to this, however it went down. "Come on out and talk to me."

"The Harbor Vale Family Inn? Where on earth is that?"

"Harbor Vale, Michigan. David's town."

"Why would I be in Michigan?"

To kill someone. "You're here."

"Listen, mate, your perceived emergency can wait at least until dawn cracks. Maybe by then you'll remember which city I live in."

"Colm. Come out."

The call ended.

A minute later, fully dressed in jeans and a flannel shirt unbuttoned over a black tee — shoot, he'd even put his shoes on — Colm emerged from a room near the end of the hall. He was nearer the exit, and Zac rocked onto his toes, but Colm didn't bolt. Anyway, if he did, David was outside to tackle him and no doubt would do so with grim relish. Zac padded toward him. The corridor was well lit, with no shadows from which to stalk an unsuspecting guest.

He did another quick check of his surroundings. They were alone. "There's a dead mortal in town."

"I imagine there are a lot of them. Death is sort of their thing."

"A murdered mortal — strangled, David thinks — left under a pile of brush."

Zac tried to find something in Colm's eyes to show him the truth, but the man's face was no different tonight than it had been in the nineteenth century. No additional lines, nothing new in the expression. Colm's forehead crinkled upward, his raised eyebrows as pale red as his hair and mostly lost against his complexion.

"You think he's covering up the murder by pretending to find the corpse?"

"Stop, Colm. It's over."

"What's that?"

"Your career as a serial killer."

At last his face did change. A poise was discarded, a warmth dropped away. His smile was bland as usual, no teeth, but it opened a foreign well of cold between them.

"Why?" Zac said. "Tell me what's in your head."

"Oh, that would go well."

"Tell me, man."

"I'm thinking I can stop babying you now, you and Simon — I hope you've looped him in — and I'm experiencing the satisfaction expected when someone becomes aware of the magnitude of your life's work."

"Colm —"

"You asked."

Zac drew as deep a breath as he could, and ice seemed to flood his lungs. His thoughts tried to disintegrate, but he held on to them.

"Why did she tell you?" Colm said.

Moira. He knew. "She didn't intend to."

"We had an understanding."

"There's nothing to blame her for."

"Maybe you're right. I'll think on it."

He could have driven his fist into Colm's

face. He could have wept. "You're not going to deny it. You're not even trying."

"Sorry to disappoint."

"Disappoint?" Zac's voice bounced off the close walls around them, and he forced it lower. "You violate them — you extinguish them in cold blood."

"If that's how you want to see it."

They'd stood here long enough. He shifted his feet, ready. "David's outside."

A flash of Colm's teeth. "To take me into immortal custody?"

"Essentially." And David wasn't alone, but he would leave Moira out of this as long as he could. If only Simon were out there too.

Colm motioned to the side door. "After you."

Zac cocked an eyebrow. "So you can jump me?"

"Oh, please. What would be the point?"

"Escape," Zac said slowly as if speaking to an infant.

"Nah. I'm cool with seeing where the next bend in the road takes me. What's your plan? Restitution to society, rehabilitation?"

They began walking, Colm more or less beside him but a pace behind his shoulder. Zac's hands tightened, and his senses strained to catch the first movement toward him, but Colm continued to walk and talk.

The glittering chill between them had re-submerged, no trace left.

"Or maybe you'll want to find a way to end my life, payment for the ones I took. I can't argue with the principle, but I'm curious about the method."

"Shut up," Zac said.

"Think on it, mate. Because this much I can tell you: I'll never stop taking them."

"I guess it's a habit like any other, if you've been at it since 1907."

A low whistle over his shoulder made him bristle. "For not intending to tell you, Moira got good and detailed."

Zac stopped walking when they reached the door, turned his back to it, and faced Colm. "Tell me why."

"It's what I'm here for, and it's what I do best."

"Murder is what you do best."

Colm dipped a nod. "Amen."

The irreverence flayed Zac. He opened the door and stepped out into the night, and his lungs drank a gasp of pure air. He fast-walked to David's parked Jeep. Colm matched his strides, a shadow on his shoulder, the shadow of terror and death, pain and grief. The shadow of rot and blight on the human race, ego run wild with itself and abusing its ageless, undying power.

At the Jeep, Colm raised his hands, his surrender as flippant as the last word he'd said. "Thank you. I've waited a long time for this."

Moira stared at them with white-edged eyes, and David looked ready to pull his concealed weapon and shoot Colm in pure righteous anger. Simon would weigh in on Colm's fate from afar when they called him. And Zac understood the thing that had eluded him till now, the quiet lament in his soul that mattered so much less than protecting the mortals, than bringing justice for the ones Colm had slaughtered, than learning why Moira had kept the putrid secret so long and let the mortals die. It mattered so much less and yet it ripped him seam from seam, and deep inside he felt the hemorrhage begin that he would never be able to stanch, never be able to numb.

His family. Tonight had broken his family.

One

Nobody knew, as he strode through the propped-open doors of Harbor Vale Bible Church, that Zac had not entered a sanctuary like this one in more than a hundred years. Nobody knew his legs were trying to turn him around and bolt. After all, he was Zac Wilson, and nobody knew a thing about him he didn't want them to know.

He lagged behind a few others who dispersed with clear direction. The foyer was open, the west wall composed of windows from the floor up that faced a side parking lot and a row of elderly pine trees. Nothing about the space justified Zac's reluctance to step into it. Behind a desk stacked with programs and papers stood a blond guy maybe twenty years old. He looked bored, but his smile was real enough as he saw Zac hesitate.

"Hey, dude, are you here for the pack-a-backpack thing?"

"Yep," Zac said.

"Okay, see the hallway off to the right? All the way at the end, they're in room 38."

"Thanks."

His legs quit fighting him as he fast-walked that direction. He hadn't expected a lightning strike, but the wrongness of his presence here was permeating. God saw he wasn't here to worship or repent, knew the lost cause Zac saw in the mirror.

"Zac?"

He pivoted toward the voice. Tiana Burton stood, hands on hips, at the mouth of the hallway he'd just entered. Her smile was one of the kindest Zac had known in all his years. He stepped toward her to absorb more of its warmth. They stood eye to eye, she tall for a woman and wearing heeled boots, he five-eight-and-a-half in his shoes.

"Well, fancy meeting you — Wait a minute." He cocked an eyebrow. "This is your church, isn't it? Yours and David's."

"It is. Welcome."

"What are you doing here on a Friday night?"

"Service event. Somebody brought in a ministry for foster kids and matched donations, so we're . . . Oh my word. Was it you?"

He spread his hands in a gesture of cluelessness.

Tiana laughed. "Does your fan base know about this?"

"I started it online. I wanted to do something local, and then the foster organization told me the backpack event was being hosted here."

She sobered. "You wouldn't have chosen a church for the venue."

"Feels hypocritical." The hairs on the back of his neck prickled, as if bridled electricity did indeed hover over him.

"I respect that. But I'm glad you came."

"I initiated the thing. Figured I should show up."

They walked side by side down a gray-walled, gray-carpeted hall with a ceiling high enough that his brain fabricated no threats to his life. The smell of cookies overwhelmed the recent use of lemon cleaner.

"Where's David? Is this his idea of a date?"

She gave a quiet laugh. "He's home practicing."

He waited for the object of the sentence, but then he got it. "Piano."

"He's agreed to stand in as church pianist as long as Karen Scott is on maternity leave, and she's due sometime before Thanksgiving."

"They'll never let him quit. The man could play Liszt with his hands tied behind his back."

They reached the propped-open door, through which drifted the lively delight of human conversations. Zac stood to one side and studied the crowd. Sixty or seventy people mingled. At the back of the room, a long collapsible table was spread with plates of cookies.

"I wanted to come," he said. "Money's distant. Hands-on is more my thing."

"Will you be swarmed by Zac Wilson autograph seekers?"

He rolled his eyes. "I highly doubt it."

But when they stepped inside, more than a dozen occupants broke off their discussions and beelined for him. Guys and girls, twentysomethings, beaming.

"Zac!"

"It's Zac!"

Tiana shoulder-bumped him. "News for you: church kids follow you too."

He couldn't help laughing. "Hey, everybody."

As she moved away, Tiana squeezed his shoulder. A few of the girls watched her go, and he guessed at the things they would notice: the easy confidence and poise in Tiana, from her long-legged stride to the elegant black coils of her hair.

"Are you two . . . ?" one of the girls whispered to him. "I won't post it online if you are."

"Tiana's a friend," Zac said. When the girl gave a doubtful squint, he added, "She's also dating a friend. Maybe you know him? David Galloway."

"The piano guy."

"That's the one."

The voices around him continued. "Zac, I brought white chocolate chip cookies," and "We saw your fund-raiser online and thought maybe it's a sign you're moving here," and "Oh, I hope so."

He flashed back to the line of thousands at Marble Canyon, autographs and awed faces, their relief as he described his rescue from certain death at the hands of an angel. Irreverent fiction, but they had swallowed it because they wanted to, because he was the one spinning the tale. He squirmed inside at the memory.

Movement at the front of the room drew their attention. A brunette woman in her forties waved for silence, and the room settled.

"Hey, all, in case you don't know me, my name is Louise Pitts and I'm the ministry coordinator here."

Ah. She had called last week and invited Zac to their event.

"It's great to see so many of you on a weeknight. As you know, we'll be packing backpacks for foster kids who are going into new homes, sometimes with nothing but the clothes on their backs. We underestimated the donations, which is a great problem to have. There's a lot to sort and stuff, most of it purchased by Foster Gifts with the fund-raiser donations. We have a ministry founder here to tell us about them. Let's welcome Jim DeClerck to HVBC."

Applause rippled as a middle-aged bald guy took over. Louise caught Zac's eye and smiled. He dipped his head in gratitude: she hadn't given him away.

Jim DeClerck talked for fifteen minutes, his timing so precise Zac suspected a military background. Then the group split up. The twentysomethings who stuck by Zac decided to sort and stuff for ten-to-twelve-year-old boys and grabbed grocery bags labeled as such. On each table, someone had already stacked about a dozen back-packs. Their group upended bags of clothes and toiletries. Zac compiled and folded a wardrobe for one unknown boy after an-other — shirt, pants, pajamas, underwear, socks. Soft fabrics between his fingers, reds and blues, greens and yellows.

The shirt in his hands now would have fit his nine-year-old self the day he became man of the house, whether or not he wanted the job. The kid who would wear this shirt might have faced the same thing, might be entering an unknown family and calling himself a failure. Zac rubbed his thumb over the buttons before folding it and setting it on the pile. He picked up another, an Oxford shirt in orange and brown plaid, and smiled. To him plaid would always be a '70s style.

A ponytailed girl took the place across from him. Her purple graphic hoodie bore a giraffe design, and she looked younger than the rest of their group. "Hi, Zac."

"Hi."

"I'm Crystal."

He stretched his hand across the table. "Good to meet you."

"Same. I thought I'd add toiletries to your stacks. I've got shampoo and toothpaste."

"Sounds like a plan."

Most of the kids seemed to know each other well. At first Zac's remarks amid theirs caused moments of deferential quiet. Then without looking he picked up a grocery bag from the bottom, spilled travel-sized tubes of toothpaste all over his feet, and laughed at himself. The kids laughed too, and as if a barrier had lifted, they plunged into a dissection of biblical themes to be found in Tolkien's master works.

A grin split Zac's face. Kids who appreciated something older than they were. The phenomenon became rarer with every generation.

"What did you read first?" Crystal said, glancing around the group. "I started with *The Fellowship of the Ring* because of the movies. I didn't even know about *The Hobbit* until after."

Answers varied, and then one of them asked Zac.

"The Hobbit," he said, and a warm memory filled him: reading late into the night, squinting in the wavy light of the kerosene lamp to finish one more chapter.

"I'm sure he wrote that one after," said a guy named Greg who had expressed half of the opinions aired at their table so far. "You can feel when you read it, he was returning to write the backstory."

"Are you sure?" This from a quiet girl who had been adding notebooks and pencils to each backpack. She hadn't said her name. "I don't think that's right."

"Somebody look it up."

Phones emerged, and Zac waved them off.

"*The Hobbit* came first."

Greg gave Zac a smirk that made him wonder how annoying his own could be. "Bet me."

"Nah," Zac said. "But *The Hobbit* was published in 1937, and *The Fellowship of the Ring* was 1954."

The kids gawked.

Crystal went to her purse and returned with her phone held up. "I have to know if he's right." After a moment, she gave a quiet gasp. "You guys, Zac is a genius."

He wished he could tell them what the story of a dragon's defeat and a Dwarf-king's courage had meant in a decade when the poverty around him and the age within him had weighed so heavily. He wished he could tell them how thirstily he had imbibed the great epic seventeen years later, national prosperity returned after a war that had torn the souls of men and women, his included.

Instead he fielded their quizzing as they discovered what they thought was a mere penchant for dates. They went on believing he was only as old as his face, their senior by years instead of a century.

At last the backpacks were filled, and Louise thanked everyone. Zac's crew volunteered to load up. He sprang into the back of her van and took backpacks passed up to him. By the time they'd finished loading, the kids had invited Zac to Sunday morning service and Wednesday night classes and a book club that met monthly at the coffeehouse.

"I know where it is," he said when Crystal tried to give him directions. "I had this town memorized thirty minutes after I got here."

One of the guys laughed. "That's about it."

As they dispersed, Tiana jogged up to him.

"Hey," he said. "What's up?"

"I've got nowhere to be, and I'm guessing you don't either."

"Perceptive."

"I cannot go to David's and listen to another flawless run-through of 'The Love of God' and 'Holy, Holy, Holy' and 'In Christ Alone.' Or I will pitch the hymnbook at his head — the one he never opens because, 'It's not necessary, love; I looked at the key signature.' "

Her attempt at a Scottish brogue was thoroughly butchered. Zac laughed. "I'm honored to be your alternate."

"I thought we could get coffee and catch up."

"Sounds like a plan."

In the month since they'd met, Zac had seen her and David two or three times a week. Tiana was good company, and returning to his apartment held no charms. Three weeks renting a place did not make it home.

Halfway through their lattes, she set hers down and folded her arms on the table. "I want you to hear me out."

Zac motioned her on.

"I know what you've got planned for tomorrow. David told me."

He tried to take offense but couldn't. "No big deal. I'm not dwelling on it."

"Then you must be coming down with something. You ignored the cookies earlier, and you ordered nothing here but a drink."

"Watching my sugar intake. Have to maintain my stunt guy physique, you know."

"Chicago's an all-day trip at least. David wants to be your backup driver."

"Not necessary."

"At least think about it."

Shoot, even a flat refusal didn't faze her. "No need."

She rested her hand on his arm. "I know, Zac. Not just what happened in the park — David told me all of it."

Saber flashing in David's hand, blood on fallen leaves. Shovel turning in Zac's hands, dirt falling into the grave. His arm stiffened before he could block the reflex, and she withdrew her hand and sipped her latte. But

Tiana had known about Colm's execution long before now. This was something else.

Zac had talked to David in the first hours of finding out what Colm had done. Maybe talked too much. "What did he say?"

Tiana's voice dropped so low he had to lean in to hear her. "It wasn't only one murder. He was a serial killer."

Oh, that.

"Even with that I was . . . *Angry* isn't the right word. I was concerned — not just about the law but for you, for all of you, having to carry something like that. But David said there's no legal method of execution that would work on a longevite."

In a less somber conversation, Zac would have smiled at her ease with his pet word for them. She had adapted to the science-fiction flavor of his life and David's faster than any mortal he'd ever known in on the secret.

Her sigh was quiet, conflicted but comprehending. "And he said some of the murders were so long ago, the police would have asked questions — age and all that — dangerous for all of you."

"Yeah," Zac said.

"So the four of you had to carry out his sentence."

"Yeah."

She tucked her chin under the weight of her next words. "And his name was Colm, and to you and Simon and Moira, he was family. A hundred years of living as family."

His mask was slipping. He could feel the slide of it, down toward a rise of feeling he refused to indulge. Colm would win something if he did, and Colm had won enough.

"And David said sometime before I was born, Colm told Moira everything for some reason, and said he'd framed you for the whole thing, to keep her quiet. Which was a lie, but it worked."

Friendship and brotherhood thrown away. Zac himself thrown away, turned into an unknowing hostage. He had stood against a wall blindfolded while Moira and Colm took point-blank shots through the heart of his trust. Even now he wouldn't know what they had done if David hadn't joined them: a new brother with new eyes to see clearly.

Zac flinched. What a joke Moira and Colm had made him. But he was inconsequential. Colm had murdered innocent people. People who disappeared, were mourned by friends and family. This was the important fact. Not how it felt in Zac's chest to be thrown away by a lifelong friend.

He looked up from where he'd been staring at the tabletop. "David talked a lot."

"He thought I should know everything."

She still didn't, but neither did David. For the best.

"I'm really sorry, Zac."

"It doesn't matter." He wasn't letting it matter. "I'll be fine." He had to be.

"I know you will."

Good. He'd fooled her if not himself.

"But I think you're making my point."

"How's that?"

"David said you're going to Chicago to get Colm's things in order. That's a lot to deal with alone."

"Nah. He didn't own property, just rented."

She tilted her head at him, flinty challenge in the stare. "Zac."

"Tiana." He gave her a smile that held no cares. "It's only an apartment."

Two

It was only an apartment.

He hadn't been here in over a year, but he didn't have to think about the turns, the street names, the destination of the visitor lot. He turned the car down a quiet tree-fringed lane. Redbrick apartments lined both sides, built sometime around the country's bicentennial. He parked the car and got out. David did the same then shut the passenger door with force. They'd said nothing for the last hour of the six-hour drive.

Zac stared up at the eighth floor. At the unit in the north corner, the window blinds drawn and sun-faded, stark autumn sky reflected in the glass. He swung Colm's key ring around one finger. Not a care. Everything fine.

He marched up to the door and let himself inside, scaled the steps two at a time and ignored the lack of windows in the stairwell, the echo of their footfalls that reminded him how close the walls were. He tramped down the eighth-floor corridor to the other end. And stopped. A sour taste filled his mouth.

It was only an apartment.

David stood beside him, his back to the door Zac faced, observing the hallway as if they were on some military mission and every angle of approach needed guarding. Another second or two of hesitation and David would notice. Zac thrust the key into the lock and turned it. Pushed the door open. The place smelled of less-than-fresh produce. Zac stepped in and to one side, allowing David entrance, and shut the door after them.

It all looked exactly the same. The TV stand stood diagonal in the far left corner, the couch along the wall across from it. No other furniture, no adornments on the ivory walls.

"Bit sparse," David said behind him.

"Nobody came here." Zac shrugged. "Well, me and Moira, but not often. I think Simon hasn't been here in five years or more. And when Colm wanted to be social, he went out, found people. Casual, you know."

No mortal friends for the man who'd called himself a god. Zac shuddered and headed for the kitchen. David followed, not hovering but still making Zac's spine itch. He should have stuck to what he'd told Tiana last night. He didn't need company.

The kitchen was last updated in the nineties, faux oak cabinets and all white appliances, never redone again because the landlady didn't care and neither did Colm. It was a serviceable place for a bachelor to cook. It hadn't needed to be anything else. Zac wandered to the stainless steel sink. He turned on the faucet, turned away from the sudden odor of old vegetables. He flipped on the garbage disposal and scrounged under the sink, came out with a bottle of bleach cleaner and sprayed it down the drain.

"He never remembered to run it," he said as he shut the disposal back off. "Until the drain backed up."

David nodded.

Zac opened the fridge, and the spoilage emanated even stronger from there. He shut it again. They'd have to clean everything out. He left the bottle of bleach on the counter and continued his inspection.

The bathroom off the hall was mostly tidy, the spare bedroom empty as expected. When Zac and Moira had visited Chicago, they'd always spent the night in a hotel. One room remained. Colm's.

Zac crossed the hall with David a few paces behind. Colm's bed was unmade, one of two pillow shams fallen to the floor, the beige comforter and sheets twisted and kicked to the foot of the bed. The lamp on the nightstand had been left on, casting soft light over a pristine copy of some historical novel with a pirate ship on its cover. It was all so . . . personal.

"He would dog-ear pages, but he hated wrecked covers."

Standing to one side in the doorway, David nodded.

"Something isn't . . ." Zac linked his hands at the back of his neck, where the sense still prickled that something was wrong. Or missing.

He turned a full circle in the room. Bed, nightstand, a pair of black leather loafers against the wall, a few clothes strewn about. A small bookcase that held fewer than a dozen books Colm deemed worth keeping. And the only wall decor in the whole place: a shelf on the wall opposite the bed. It held a row of shot glasses, Colm's souvenir of choice when he decided to keep a souvenir, which wasn't often.

All the years, all the places, and he had something like twenty of the things. Zac strode over and picked up the one from Colorado Springs, a wraparound image of the state flag. He'd been with Colm when he got it from the gift shop at the top of Pikes Peak. Had their personal association made the place matter to a psychopath?

But then there shouldn't be the glass from Windsor. They didn't know anyone there. There shouldn't be the glass from Rome. Colm had been there only once, with Moira in 1957. There shouldn't be the glass from Montana. Zac counted. Eighteen. The number wasn't significant . . . unless it was.

His hand clenched the Colorado glass. Nausea welled in his stomach.

"What is it?" David said.

The sickness rose into his throat. He swallowed. "Eighteen."

"Shot glasses?"

"The places, the number . . . the true number."

"Of what?"

"Eighteen. Instead of eleven. Kills, David."

David's face blanked. Slowly he shook his head. "There's no reason to assume . . ."

Whatever else he said became a roar in the back of Zac's skull as he barreled into the closet. Red veiled his vision. He thrust his arms between garments on hangers, spread them, found only clothes and more clothes. He knelt and dug into an old wooden box, clearly no less than a century old, painted to resemble the texture of cowhide. He tossed the lid aside, heedless of the history or the fragility, and drew out the contents. Silver and gold coin proofs nestled in plastic holders. Dozens of them. The coins tumbled through Zac's fingers onto his knees, onto the floor.

Nothing else was here.

He looked up when a shadow loomed. David, standing in the doorway.

Blocking the doorway.

"Move, man." Zac nearly choked on the words.

David sidestepped, and Zac pushed to his feet and stumbled back to the living room. He unlocked the sliding door and escaped onto the balcony. Splinters of wood bit his hands as he gripped the railing. The sky and air opened his lungs, but his stomach still roiled.

Eighteen. The number of mortals murdered. Seven more than he'd known about before. As if his knowing made any difference. He saw them in his sleep sometimes. He saw Colm's hands around their necks. He saw his friend kill people, though he'd never seen it in reality.

David came to stand beside him, and the human presence helped as it always did. Zac shoved his hands through his hair, elbows propped on the rough wood of the rail. If he tried to straighten up, he'd vomit over the edge. He stayed there, doubled over and breathing through his locked teeth.

"I need a minute," he finally said. "Before I go back in there."

"We've all day to get it done," David said.

"They're mementos."

"Of his victims?"

"Of the places he found them."

"We'll never know that."

"He'd been to visit me dozens of times. Dozens. And one day we're in a touristy gift shop in Colorado Springs and he picks up that shot glass and says, 'It's about time I added this place to the collection.' "

"He was playing." Under David's calm snapped a band of tension. "As he played with Moira."

"It was the third day of his trip." Zac's hands shook on the rail as details came back. Meals they'd shared. Rock-climbing afternoons. Reminiscing about decades past. But the guy hadn't been with him every hour. "So the first or second day . . ."

"We ended it, man. We ended him."

I'm sorry. Zac didn't know whom he was

trying to talk to. Maybe the victim of that Colorado trip. Maybe all Colm's victims. Zac might have been typing a text to the man while he was ripping a mortal's life away.

He straightened slowly, a test, and his stomach didn't revolt into his mouth. He met David's eyes. "There's nothing in that apartment to tell me anything."

"Did you expect there would be?"

"No. Maybe. I guess I wanted . . . a reason."

David shifted on his feet, gazed out past Zac at the line of trees backing up to the blacktop.

"I wanted to know why."

"Boredom or pleasure," David said.

He knew that much about psychopaths, but he couldn't apply those motives to Colm without knowing for sure. He would never know. And it didn't matter.

The victims, they mattered. "I wanted to find their identities here. A list of names. Jewelry. Polaroid pictures. Maybe DNA that we could ensure got to the police. Something. Anything."

"He didn't own a computer?"

"No. He had his phone — that was it." And Zac had spent days trying to find data on it. There were no incriminating pictures, no password-protected notes . . . nothing.

"A Spartan sort of man."

"Yeah, he was."

"Souvenir glasses are less help than personal jewelry. If that's what they are."

"It's what they are."

David studied him a moment, nodded, and went back inside.

Enough of this. Colm would laugh and poke Zac's chest. *"Look at me, power beyond the grave. Look at you, all broken up."* Imitation laughter? Maybe nothing had been funny to Colm, just as nothing had mattered to Colm.

Zac would not be the broken one, not over this. He pushed off the rail and walked inside.

He grabbed a black garbage bag from the cabinet under the kitchen sink and stalked to the bedroom. David was already there, pocketing his phone as if he'd been on it. Texting Tiana, probably. Something like *Pray for Zac. He's a real mess.*

Well, they could both stuff that notion.

With one hand Zac held open the bag, and with the other he lifted the shelf from its props, balancing all eighteen shot glasses. All eighteen deaths. He dumped it into the bag, and the glasses crashed with a few cracking sounds but mostly clinking. Not good enough. Zac wielded the shelf like a shovel and smashed its rounded end down into the bag. A glass shattered. Then another. And another. And another.

When all eighteen were broken, he threw the shelf aside and hoisted the bag. It hadn't punctured. The shards jingled against each other as he walked back to the kitchen and doubled the bag.

He opened the refrigerator and pitched everything in on top of the glass. Greek yogurt cups, a bag of now-slimy deli meat, Styrofoam containers of takeout Chinese, a cardboard box of stale pizza. He didn't stop until the fridge and freezer were bare.

David joined him in the pitching process. Clothes. Shoes. Bedding. All into black bags. Some of this could be donated, a thought born of stuffing backpacks last night. But no. These things belonged to a man rightfully dead, and they must cease to exist too.

When Zac began chucking the paperbacks, David winced.

"What, you want to sell them?"

"No. Sorry," David said. "Involuntary reaction."

"It's not a bad idea. Mix-and-match sale on the serial killer's library. Could bring quite a crowd."

"Including the Harbor Vale police."

As usual, humor was lost on David. Whatever.

Less than three hours after they arrived, Zac was locking the door behind them, and nothing remained inside but the landlord's furniture. The antique box of coin proofs was tucked under David's arm. Foolish to throw those out, though Zac might have if David hadn't been here.

He gestured to the box. "A favor, if you don't mind."

"Of course."

"Do whatever you want with that. I don't want to see it again."

David gave him a measuring look.

"I typed a letter," Zac said as they walked to the car. "Management will get it in a day or so. I included a check to cover his breaking the lease. Couldn't find a copy of it anywhere."

"Some tenants walk away without a word."

"Yeah." Zac slid behind the wheel and started the car. "But I didn't want them going after him to collect a debt. This seemed a cleaner way to finalize things."

"As long as he wasn't behind on rent."

"He wouldn't be."

"Were there neighbors to ask after him? Anyone?"

Zac began to navigate the one-way streets back to the interstate. "He used to say he was a shadow among the mortals. He took pride in it, I think."

"I suppose it's all the better for us now."

"Right? Considerate of him to plan ahead like that."

Again the exasperating look of scrutiny.

Zac twisted his mouth into a smirk and shrugged one shoulder.

"Zac . . ."

Something about David's tone made Zac want to leave him here to find his own way home. "Might as well say your piece."

David turned his eyes back to the passing landscape. "Tiana told me to hold my peace."

A laugh burst from Zac, but it was wrong, a mirthless bark. "Too late now. Go on."

"We've noticed a toll on you, in your face."

"There's nothing wrong with this face. Ask the fangirls. Ask the modeling agencies I keep turning down."

"Tiana isn't one to waste concern."

He searched for a comeback to that and couldn't find one. He gestured at the city around them. "We did what needed doing. I never have to think about him again."

"Perhaps."

"Why would I?"

"Some ghosts aren't banished with action but with words."

"Words? Are you serious?"

The steadiness of David's gaze was nothing less.

"Right. Words, of course, because the pen is mightier than the sword — oh, and the tongue is a rudder on a ship, almost forgot that one."

He squeezed his eyes shut against an image of Colm's face, the widening of green eyes in the instant before Zac's uppercut silenced his mockery. Another image followed it. The body. The blood. The grave. He pressed his fingers to his eyebrows.

"Tell you what," he said. "If we find a way to bring eighteen murdered people back from the dead by talking, then we will talk."

"Very well."

A lot of things could be said for David. One of them was his respect for boundaries. Good thing, because the drive from Chicago to Harbor Vale, Michigan, was just under six hours. Would have been an expensive taxi ride.

They drove for a silent half hour, and then David spoke as if there'd been no tension. "Tiana's had an idea she wants to try. She calls it Blind Date with a Book. A display at the front of the store. If you'd care to help us wrap books in packing paper, we'd be glad for the extra hands."

Zac shook his head. Wrapping books. Quite the rogue he was becoming. The fans who tagged him online to ask for another shirtless photo shoot would be disappointed, but Crystal and Greg and their church cohorts would be all in. A smile tugged his mouth.

"Sounds intense," he said. "But I think I'm up for it."

David smiled. "I'll let her know."

As they merged onto I-94, Zac nodded his satisfaction. He'd done what needed doing, and now it was finished. Maybe he'd even sleep tonight.

"So in order to join my road trip, you left Tiana running the store for the day."

David shot a glance at him. "She's capable."

"Sure, but does she get time-and-a-half when the boss no-shows?"

"I no longer think of the store that way. Haven't since . . . well, since we redefined things."

Neither did Tiana, based on Zac's observation. She and David no longer behaved like manager and owner of the bookstore; now they were more like a single owner/manager unit. Either of them could tend to personal business without any hindrance to their bookselling, and both of them spoke of store decisions in terms of *we* and *us*. David's reckless devotion to a mortal was baffling yet right. They suited one another down to the ground, as far as Zac could tell.

David dug into the backpack he'd brought, which held more books than snacks. When he sat up, a new book in hand, Zac laughed.

"How many books can you get through in a day?"

"This is only the third, and we talked little on the way here."

"I guess we'll also be talking little on the way back."

"If we'd flown instead, we'd already be home."

Zac's shoulders tensed. He couldn't have forced himself onto a plane. Not today, not this week or this month, not even first class where the ability to stretch his legs helped to calm him.

"I like to drive," he said.

"If you change your mind, I'm still willing to spell you."

"Nah."

David opened his book.

"I'd swear the author of that book is still

alive," Zac said, "but you are reading it, so I must be mistaken."

"I like him."

"It's a Western." And Zac had seen the mass-market edition on grocery-store end-caps.

"Aye."

"Those are never accurate."

"Some more than others."

"Never shoot a man in the back? Solve our differences at high noon and ten paces? Oh, the loquacious stranger wears two guns, he must be an arrogant, overcompensating —"

David's laughter erupted.

Zac couldn't keep the grin off his face. "I'm right."

"You are." David tapped his index finger against the book's cover. "Yet I've returned to the genre for the last eighty years. The more mythological, the more I enjoy it."

"Blurry nostalgia."

David set the book on his knee and, to the degree that he could, stretched his legs under the dashboard. "Something like that."

Zac left him to the book for a time, until David remarked on the genius of John Ford and ignited a nonchalant debate on the greatest directors. At least they agreed to William Wyler's place among the top three.

When the topic waned, David returned to his book. Maybe he'd come along only to read, which was fine. Silence in company didn't hold the weight and mass of silence alone.

Traffic leaving the Chicagoland vicinity was no worse than it had been driving in, and Zac had driven this highway many times. So there was no excuse a few miles later when his brain began perceiving the cars around him as a shrinking box. No excuse for the cold sweat that broke out on his neck.

A Mack truck loomed up beside him, filling the driver's side window. The long silver hulk flowed past him as the left lane outpaced his, then cut over in front of him. Zac braked, and David's head jerked forward.

"Sorry."

"His fault, not yours. Although, in general, you drive with animosity for the human race."

"Do I?"

"Traffic has been cowering from you all day, and Michigan drivers don't cower."

Zac smiled, though the truck's back end filled his windshield. "Happened after I moved to Denver. Those people will put the fear of death back into you."

He relaxed his hands on the wheel. He was all right again. Until a second semi inched alongside him. In front and to the left now, he could see nothing but silver metal.

The sky was gone.

Three

Traffic stopped. In the lane to Zac's right, an SUV and a pickup truck formed a third side of the box around him. His rearview mirror showed him the bumper of yet another Mack truck, and his lungs began to seize. He hit the button for David's window, because rolling down his own would only reinforce the proximity of the truck. Without looking up, David hit the button on his side.

"Bit cold for open windows," David said as the window slid back up.

"I want it open." Thank goodness he sounded casual.

David looked up from his book. "What for?"

"Autumn's nice."

"When accompanied by the exhaust smell of a thousand sitting vehicles?"

Zac hit the button again, and David's window rolled down. "Doesn't bother me."

David shrugged and went back to his book.

Zac drew a breath of chilled outside air, and it eased his chest muscles. Proof this wasn't physical: cold would exacerbate the problem if he were an asthmatic or something. No, this was all in his head. The air outside helped by virtue of being outside. He glanced sideways and, curse it all, David was watching him. Well, let him watch.

"Hey," David said.

"Yeah?"

"Anything the matter?"

"Nope."

Zac gritted his teeth, grasped another breath but kept it silent. Nothing the matter. Once they got moving again, the control of driving would dispel the last of the stress.

David's cell began to ring like an old rotary. He picked it up from the side console and said, "Tiana."

Zac could have thanked her for her timing.

"Hi," David said. A pause. "On our way back. A few miles out from the city, at a standstill for now." She said something else, and David lowered the phone from his ear and changed to speakerphone. "All right, you have both Zac and me now."

"Hi, Zac," came Tiana's voice.

"Hey, Tiana."

"So, listen, something weird happened a few minutes ago, and I thought you both would want to know about it. This guy came into the store and asked to see David Galloway. Not 'the store owner' — he asked for you by name, David. I told him you won't be in today, and he said, 'What about Zachary Wilson, do you know how I could get in touch with him?' "

A reflexive glance between them, and David looked the way Zac felt — hackles up, ears attuned, despite being three hundred miles from the stranger.

"What did you tell him?" David said.

"Just that I didn't have the information he was looking for. I figured I couldn't pretend not to recognize Zac's name, or not to know he's been living in town."

Smart of her.

"Do you know where he is now?"

"He got lunch at Mongolian Grill. I saw him leaving when I went into the diner."

The restaurants were across the street from each other. "Did he see you?" Zac asked.

"Yeah, but he didn't approach me. Just wandered off, looking like a first-time tourist, you know? Sort of aimless. I haven't seen him since."

David's brow furrowed, and he tilted his head at Zac. Questioning.

"If he'd asked about only one of you," Tiana said, "it wouldn't have felt odd to me."

Zac grinned. "You get a lot of people asking about me?"

David cocked an eyebrow at him, and Zac held in a chuckle. The guy was so easy to kid.

"I think the grand total in the last month has been three," Tiana said.

Zac huffed loudly enough for her to hear, and she laughed. But some connection was nudging his brain. He flexed his hands on the wheel and popped his thumb joint a few times. "Tiana, what did this guy look like?"

"Um . . . just normal. You want a physical description?"

"Did he have black hair, dark eyes, maybe, um, five-foot-ten or so?"

A slight pause. "Yeah."

David nodded, general alertness replaced by recognition. "Sharp cheekbones, white guy but not too pale, more of a tan complexion. Slight ridge on his nose, probably broken years ago. Voice inflection flatter than the average person's."

"Whoa, yes. That's him. Who is he?"

"Well, his name is anyone's guess, since he didn't bother sharing it last month."

She drew a soft breath. "The guy who shot you?"

"The very same." A growl infused David's words.

"Why would he come back here?"

"Don't try to find out," David said. "Stay clear of him."

"Well, obviously."

David raked a hand over his hair, standing it up in black spikes, and his chest filled with a harsh breath. "Ach, Tiana, be careful, please. The man's unpredictable, and we don't know what he wants."

"To threaten you again?"

"I don't know, love. But . . ." He shifted in the seat as if the space were too small now for him as well as Zac. Three hundred miles from the woman he loved, and though Tiana chided him — and Zac — for it often, there was no way to detach from the fact that she was susceptible. To death.

"All right, listen, boys." Tiana's voice had softened. "I'm a grown woman and I'll be careful. Don't you dare start breaking traffic laws."

David chuckled. "Reading my mind again."

"I mean it, David. From what you've told me, he only risked a shot at you because he knew it wouldn't kill you. That doesn't mean he'd harm me."

David ducked his head and closed his eyes a long moment. Praying. Of course. Zac focused on the traffic, which had begun to trickle again, one car at a time, thawed rivulets in the great block of ice that was the Chicago highway. He swallowed a lump of gravel. God was nearby, no doubt, springing into action for the prayers of David Galloway. Must be nice. The thought drove a little hole through the center of Zac's chest. He blinked hard.

"If he comes into the store again, call me," David said.

"Okay. And hey, Zac?"

He cleared his throat. "Yeah?"

"I hope what you had to do today wasn't too hurtful."

More like freeing, he hoped. "Thanks. It's done now."

"I'll see you soon."

She always assumed he was coming back to them. Well, he did keep doing it. "You will."

"And you, David." Her voice took on a teasing lilt.

"Aye," he said. "See you soon."

Over the next six hours, the sun set in the rearview mirror and, once they passed the halfway point, the interstate traffic lessened.

They discussed David's book when he finished it; they discussed a dozen other things that didn't matter. Mostly they dissected the possible motivations of the stranger with the antique revolver.

Zac coasted the car down Main Street in Harbor Vale at twenty minutes to eleven. Earlier than he had anticipated, but they'd spent less time at Colm's apartment than he'd planned. At the next stop sign, Galloway's Books stood on the northwest corner, one of the larger buildings in town, gray brick from ground to roof. The windows were dark, but an old K-car sat in the parking lot, half eclipsed by the store.

"That's not Tiana's car," Zac said.

"No." David sat forward. "It's occupied."

They were sitting at the stop sign. No other cars on the street, but Zac got moving again. "You think it's him? Watching for us?"

"I'm guaranteed to show up there eventually." David frowned. "Make another pass?"

Zac drove down a dark neighborhood street and made three quarters of a square to set him back on Main Street. "I'm going to stop at the sign again, give you a chance to see."

He'd barely completed the stop this time when David said, "That's him."

"Want me to pull in?"

"Of course."

They were of the same mind, then. Might as well face the guy head-on if he planned to cause trouble. David motioned to Zac to keep the car running and together they got out, without discussion splitting up to approach the car from either side. The windows rolled down. David stopped at the driver side and Zac at the passenger side.

The interior of the car was dark, and the man had parked away from the floodlight. Impressive that David had been so sure from the street, but being shot point-blank had likely seared the details into his brain. Now that he was nearer, Zac could identify the man as well. His shoulders tightened. Their fellow longevite wasn't the only person inside.

In the back seat lay a woman. A purple blanket was tucked around her, a fold of it fallen aside to reveal the seat belt awkwardly fastened at her waist.

"You wanted us to leave you alone," David said. "Which we've done, yet you return here."

Way to set an amicable tone.

"For help," the man said.

Of all the possibilities Zac and David had come up with, that wasn't on the list.

Zac leaned nearer to the window. One of

the woman's arms rested outside the covering, her smooth skin bearing an age spot on the back of her hand. Her eyes were closed, her red-gold hair braided over her shoulder, escaped wisps framing her face, which also showed spots of age. She gave a quiet groan, seeming unaware of David and Zac.

The man twisted in his seat to touch the inside of her wrist with two fingers.

"Help? You want our help?" David was practically spitting the words.

"Not for me. For her."

"After you shot me, after you accused us of murdering your friends and threatened us with —"

"David," Zac said. "I think she's rejuvenating."

David straightened, stepped to the back of the car, and opened the door. He leaned inside and stared at her. The woman opened her eyes, but they remained unfocused.

"One of your people?" Zac said to the man.

"Yes."

"Why bring her to us?"

"She's aging permanently. Dying."

"How can we help?"

The man got out of the car, ignoring the stiffness of David's posture braced for defense. His attention had fixed on Zac like a laser. He stood before Zac with his shoulders loose, his hands at his sides, nothing aggressive in the lines of his body. He seemed to be trying to convey harmlessness, even surrender.

"You fell thousands of feet into that canyon." The man's voice shook, strange when emotion remained absent from him otherwise. "I saw it. The video. Not even one of us could survive that."

Not medically, no. Not scientifically. Zac's gut tightened.

"You have a secret."

Zac shook his head. "Nothing to keep one of us alive if the serum's expiring in her veins."

The guy surged forward so fast Zac had no chance of reacting, seized his shirt, and shook him. "You have to help her, you have to —"

Getting over the surprise took about one second, but in that time the grip was torn away. David hauled the man off Zac and hurled him to the ground. Rather than retaliate, the man remained huddled on his hands and knees between them, his head drooped low. David jerked the man up by the front of his shirt and shoved him against the car and patted him down. The man let him.

"He's unarmed." David released the man with enough force to make him stagger against the car.

"Okay." Zac tamped down his annoyance with both of them and coated the word with boredom instead. If David didn't pick up on it, he'd go with a direct approach.

But the single word seemed to work. David caught his eye, drew a deep breath, and nodded. He stepped back from the man, who caved against the car, hands braced on the hood behind him.

"She hasn't done anything to you." The man drew a ragged breath. "Please."

It was only rejuvenation. Age spots, aches, weakness, slushy lungs. They all knew this routine well, their bodies taking an annual break from the daily grind of keeping them ageless.

"Don't you go through this yearly?" Zac said.

"I'm telling you, she's dying."

"Have you done anything to treat her? And the others in your group, what do they think?"

The floodlight glittered in the man's eyes, reflecting desolation. "There aren't any others. Only Cady."

David stepped forward, his height making the move more aggressive than it might have been otherwise. The man flinched away. " 'Come after my people, and I'll expose yours.' That's what you said. Were you exaggerating your numbers, then? After a strategic advantage?"

"There used to be others."

"Used to be, three weeks ago?"

"Yes," he whispered.

"And now?"

"Now it's just Cady. And me."

A quiet groan drifted from the back of the car, and the woman called out, "Finn?"

He kept one hand braced on the car as he leaned inside. "Here."

"What's happening?"

"Don't worry about it. Just rest."

"How long?"

"Two days."

She seemed to drift again.

"Okay," Zac said to Finn. Good to know his name at last. "What makes you think this is more than rejuvenation? The cycle thing, I mean."

"I can't tell. So I came."

Forming simple sentences now seemed to require Finn's total concentration. Maybe something was wrong with him too. Maybe it was a contagion of some kind. A contagion that could cure immortality.

In which case Zac and David should

distance themselves.

David glanced across the roof of the car. Zac cocked an eyebrow at him. Were they thinking the same thing? He studied the woman again. The upturned nose, the slender fingers and fine wrist bones of her visible hand. The spotted skin. The shallow breaths rising under the blanket. Contagious or not, these two people were longevites. As such their kinship ran as deep as a mortal bloodline.

"We can take her to my apartment," Zac said.

David glared at him but, after a long moment, gave a sigh. "My place is closer. And more private."

Zac nodded his acknowledgment. He hadn't been about to volunteer the home of the most introverted guy he'd ever met, but he wouldn't turn down the offer.

"You'll save her," Finn said.

"I don't think she needs saving," Zac said. "I think she's going to be fine in a day or so."

Finn's grip tightened on the frame of the car door. "Okay. You're still young. Maybe you know."

"Can you drive?"

"I know where he lives." Finn tilted his chin at David.

Not what he'd been asking, but okay. "We'll meet there." They got back into the car, and Zac shut his door before blurting, "What is wrong with him?"

"I don't know." David cupped one hand around the other and propped his wrists on his knees. "He wasn't like this before — there's a kind of strain on him now."

"And it was there even before you threw him around."

David growled.

"He came in peace, man."

"This time."

"You're not doing much to foster civility."

"With the guy who shot me in the head."

"There is that."

"We'll help the woman, and I'll . . . avoid further antagonism. If he does."

More acquiescence than Zac had hoped for. He drove toward David's home with the K-car's headlights in his rearview. "Her symptoms look like rejuvenation. He should be familiar with it."

"Aye, I'd think so too."

Zac had been to David's house several times in the last nineteen days. New memories to dilute the old, to normalize the place. It hadn't happened yet. He stepped through the doorway and could hear Colm's voice over his shoulder. *"Lied to her. That's all."*

Lied to terrify Moira, to keep her quiet, to keep Zac clueless.

David led them to his bedroom. They passed the bathroom in the hall, and another memory sucker-punched Zac in the chest. Moira's hair in his hands, the sweat on the back of her neck while she knelt over the toilet and vomited. Her eyes when she looked up at him, brown depths glittering with exposed terror. And her voice, broken.

"I do want him dead."

His confusion in that moment galled him now. She had been afraid of Colm, not for him. And Zac had missed it.

Finn lowered the woman to David's bed. Her eyes were open now.

"Hello," David said to her. "Your name is Cady?"

She didn't seem to hear him as Finn took her hand between his. "Yeah. She's Cady."

"How long has she been ill?"

"Three days."

Zac stepped through the doorway, though the three of them inside shrank the room. "That's not an unusual time frame," he said as Cady turned her head and found Finn.

"Hey." Finn squeezed her hand.

"Hey." Her voice came hardly above a whisper. "Quit freaking out. I told you I'm fine."

"You're not." His voice broke.
"Relatively, immortally fine." She gave a quiet laugh that turned into a wheeze.
Zac's chest constricted in sympathy. Of all the symptoms of rejuvenation, for him the mud-in-the-lungs feeling was the worst.
Cady reached up and touched Finn's bicep, the gesture . . . familial? More? "I'm not dying."
"Okay." No conviction there.
"Heard from James yet?"
"No."
"Head?"
He sighed. "Bowling ball."
"Stomach?"
"Licorice."
They spoke their code language with utter nonchalance. Cady looked for the first time around the room. "You're Zac. Zac Wilson."
He nodded.
"Why are you here?"
"It's more like we're there," Finn said.
She frowned in confusion. "Michigan? You drove us to Michigan?"
"I had to."
"When? What day is it?"
"Friday. No, Saturday now, I think."
"You drove for a day and a night?"
"You got worse, Cade. I thought they could help."

She covered her face with her age-spotted hands, then lowered them to rest at her sides. "Okay. I get it. Now go lie down."

"When you're better."

She studied each of them, first David, then Zac, then Finn. She reached for Finn's hand and tugged it to her. "Train of logic."

Finn blinked. "Now?"

"You brought me here, which means you trust them."

"Yes."

"I won't be alone, and you can't do anything more right now."

"No," he said quietly.

"You've been awake for two days and two nights. Train of logic says it's time to rest."

"I . . ."

"Go on."

"Yeah. Okay." He turned to the door, shoulders slumped and head down. One step, two, and then the third dragged over the carpet and he nearly pitched onto his face.

Zac surged from the corner and caught Finn's arm. Unnatural warmth radiated through his sleeve.

Finn corrected his balance but did not pull away. "If she gets worse, you have to tell me. Right away."

"Of course." But she wouldn't get worse.

Zac shot a look over his shoulder at her. She was watching him, not Finn.

"We need to know what's going on," he said.

"If one of you will take care of him, I'll save the explanation."

One of them wasn't going to be David. The man still looked prepared to eject Finn from the room. Or the town.

"Right." Zac sighed. "Come on."

FOUR

Zac led Finn to David's living room, an open concept area with a wood floor and windows on two sides, one corner occupied by a baby grand piano. Before he finished gesturing to the sofa, Finn was sinking onto the middle cushion, hands gripping its edge.

Take care of him. That's what Cady had asked. "Hey, uh . . . anything you need?"

Finn didn't look up. "The lamp. It's bright."

Headache. The tightness around his eyes gave it away. Zac switched off the table lamp, and when the room became dark, Finn's sigh held relief.

"Thank you." The words were quiet. Spent.

"Anything else?"

"Cady. If she's wrong, if she's . . ."

If she's dying. Zac cleared his throat. "I don't think she is, man. I really don't. But I'm betting she'll rest easier if I can tell her

I did the best I could for you."

"Yeah." Another pause, another sigh. "If there's an ice pack. Or a frozen bag. Peas and carrots . . . peas *or* carrots. Or anything."

Zac went to David's freezer and dug around inside. The food of a bachelor — takeout boxes mostly, though David did enjoy fresh produce — had been joined by signs of deliberate meal preparation, Ziploc bags dated and described in Tiana's precise handwriting. A smile tugged his mouth as he moved items aside. Here in the back was a bag of frozen green beans. No less effective than peas or carrots, one could assume.

For his stuntman-variety injuries, Zac always had one or two gel packs ready — shoulders and knees, typically, but in the last several years he'd also managed to wrench his neck, sprain an ankle, and crack ribs. None of which threatened his life; therefore none of which activated the healing serum. He'd have to remember to stash a few gel packs in David's freezer. If Zac didn't need them in the future, Finn might. He and Cady seemed accustomed to this malady of his, whatever it was.

Right. Because the two of them had become a permanent part of Zac's life. He ought to learn caution with people, but he hadn't managed it to date, so his odds weren't great. He could at least take a page from David's library and require trust to be earned. For all he knew, Finn and Cady were a team of serial killers.

He returned to the living room expecting Finn to have drifted to sleep in the last minute. The man looked sufficiently wiped out to do so. But his eyes tracked Zac's path across the room to the couch.

"Here." Zac offered the bag of green beans. "Best we've got."

Finn didn't answer as he took the bag. He reached for a pillow at one end of the couch and lay down, his movements slow and smooth. Routine. He gave a hard sigh, positioned the bag against the base of his skull, and eased his head back to the pillow.

"I'm sure there's painkillers around here somewhere. I'll ask David."

"Had some before, but they don't . . . all the time . . ." He sighed. "Sorry, I can't . . . need quiet now."

If he was falling somewhere, it wasn't into sleep. More like confusion or agitation. Zac nodded and took a step back, but Finn squinted up at him.

"Tell Cady I said . . . tell you."

"Tell me what?"

His hand jerked at his side, an incomplete

gesture. "She'll know."

"Okay, man."

"Care of her."

"We will."

Finn draped his arm over his eyes, and Zac left him alone.

In David's room, Cady had propped herself on a few pillows. She and David weren't talking, but she sat up straighter when Zac entered.

"How is he?"

Zac shrugged. "Lying down in the dark with a bag of frozen vegetables on his neck."

A small smile formed. "Thank you for doing that."

"I think he's running a fever."

"Low grade is his norm for times like this. But thanks for letting me know."

David pushed away from his sentry station in the corner of the room. "Is he ill?"

"Not the way you mean, no."

She wrapped her arms around herself as if catching a chill. Probably she had. She looked small and withered, though her body bore no outward sign of aging except the spots on her skin. Her eyes held weary despondency. She had buried friends too these last few weeks, lost to her not through the necessity of justice but through a mysterious affliction.

"Finn said you should tell us."

Her gaze flicked up to his. "Tell you what?"

"He said you'd know."

"Wow. All right." She stretched her legs then drew them up to her chest, wincing.

Zac perched on the edge of the bed, listening and letting her know. David could go take a hike, or he could stick around and learn something about putting people at ease. He still stood with his arms folded, a soldier at attention, carved from stone.

Cady seemed unbothered by his granite stance, or at least unsurprised. "How's your knowledge of TBI?"

"Traumatic brain injury," Zac said.

"Yes."

A dozen questions spiraled into his head. How? When? Not fatal, or Finn wouldn't still be dealing with it.

"It's a complex condition with a variety of repercussions, including the headaches." Again that tiny smile. "And if he's letting you in on it, then he must be ready to acknowledge new family."

The word tugged inside Zac like sutures trying to close a wound.

"You might choose not to claim us," she said more quietly, maybe misinterpreting his expression. "But regardless you *are* ours, in a way."

"You don't know us," David said.

"Not yet. I guess that'll change, now that we're here."

If you didn't know him, you'd see only a scowl, but behind that David was cataloging, compiling a file in his head to process everything. Zac had seen him do it a dozen times in their three weeks of acquaintance.

"What else?" David said.

"I'm not going to lay out the whole story for you. That's his."

A reason to respect her. Zac said, "We don't need to know how it happened. But that code you were using . . . bowling ball, licorice."

"A creative pain scale. We tried numbers for a while, but everything was a three to him."

It was a strange image, the hard-eyed gunfighter with cognitive damage. But every person alive carried at least one thing you'd never guess.

"A few times he's said his head feels like a house. That's a ten, or at least that's the largest object he's ever used. *Licorice* stands for nausea. He hates licorice even when he's feeling well."

"Whatever works."

"Exactly. He's been dealing with this since

before . . . well, since before we became what we are. It's a long time to be . . ."

"Damaged," Zac said quietly.

She looked up quickly, as if she expected to find him sneering. "His intelligence is intact. Wholly."

"What's with the 'train of logic' thing then?"

"You're seeing him at his cognitive worst, and by the way, he knows it. When he's gone too long without sleep, sometimes he needs a nudge toward clear thinking."

"Cady," David said and waited for her to look up at him. "Does his injury have any bearing on his trying to put a bullet in my head?"

She looked away. "As I said, some things are his to tell."

"I've the right to be told now if I've brought a ticking bomb into my —"

"He is not a bomb." She pushed up in the bed and swung her legs over to set her feet on the floor. "Or a dog on a leash or a — He's Finn. He's always Finn."

As she tilted to one side, Zac set a hand on her shoulder and braced her up. "Hey."

"If this is how you see him, we'll go now. We can fend for ourselves just fine."

She said it while leaning most of her weight into Zac's support. He squeezed her shoulder. History rippled beneath her words.

"That's not necessary," Zac said, rather than point out how unfit either of them would be to drive right now. "Lie back, okay? You're looking shaky."

She gave in and shut her eyes. David's jaw still looked like a stone carving, but he said nothing. Cady opened her eyes again, but her voice was fainter, and she remained limp against the pillows.

"It wasn't an accident the bullet grazed you. He made sure there was a tree behind you to catch the slug. He only wanted to get away."

David angled the right side of his head toward her. The white scar line through his black hair was the width of a pencil lead. "Quite the risk."

"It was a broad tree, he told me."

A furrow dug between David's eyes.

"He's a crack shot, David. There was no risk. I'm sorry for the scar, though."

"There was no reason to assault me in any way."

"You had him cornered."

"In the middle of a public parking lot?"

"The place wouldn't have mattered."

"He was the one to approach — hurling accusations and threats, I might add."

"He told me."
"Did he also tell you he panicked for no ascertainable reason, that I did naught to threaten him?"
"Yes, he did."
They studied each other so long, they seemed to forget Zac's presence. At last David settled in the desk chair, and even the air around them seemed to ease.
"What is it you're asking of me?"
"That you judge him on more than one incident."
A month ago Zac would have been making the same case to David. He knew better now. But how many incidents, how many years, were needed to know a man?
"He believes you're dying," David said.
She sighed. "I'm not. But you have to understand, we didn't think Sean and Holly were dying either. And then I got . . . well, lost . . . in the memories. Does it happen to you all, when you're going through this — the memory fog?"
They both nodded. Cady seemed to absorb this, to grip it as a safety line or maybe a connection between them. And in Zac's dense brain, something clicked. He wasn't intimidated by David's scowl and grilling, but she was.
They were strangers. They were male.

They were healthy and strong. And she was lying on a bed looking like a bad Halloween makeup job, too weak to stand up, outnumbered, not knowing what kind of men stood staring down at her.

For all that, she defended Finn and betrayed not one wit of trepidation. Wow.

Zac crossed the room to the chair in the corner. Give her space. Help her feel safe. Weariness was pressing her to the bed like a flower petal to a scrapbook page. She sighed, and the age spots seemed to darken as her pallor sharpened.

"Shall we leave you to rest?" David's voice softened, chivalry reasserting itself.

About time, man.

"Actually, I'd like to keep talking." She gave a small smile. "Sorry it's in this condition."

"We call it rejuvenation," Zac said.

"I like that. We don't really have a name for it."

He wished Simon were here, able to offer her a transfusion of type-O blood that would refresh her body within a few minutes. But Simon was in Florida living his lab tech life.

"I do have a question, if you're up to it," Zac said, and she nodded. "Last time we saw him, Finn was convinced we'd caused your friends to age. Now he brings you here to stop your aging. Something must have changed his mind."

Her mouth crimped. "I guess he decided to listen to me. I told him the serum in Sean and Holly aged out, and you had nothing to do with it."

"He said you're the only ones left."

"What?" She shook her head. "James and Anna — we've been worried. They've been out of touch."

"Finn said there used to be others, but now there's only you two."

"You misunderstood him," she said. "They went somewhere and don't realize they have no cell service. Or something."

"How long since you heard from them?"

"If this is Saturday, then . . . eight days."

"Ah." Hardly long enough to assume catastrophe. Maybe that was another facet of Finn's injury.

"But I texted Anna five days ago, and she doesn't ignore my texts. Not for days, that's not Anna. And when I called, I got her voice mail immediately. Like her phone's turned off or dead."

"Maybe they're in some trouble," Zac said.

"I hope not." Her eyelids sank again. She rested against the pillows with the stillness of one who might be dying. If Cady could die.

David was nodding, no doubt adding to his mental case file. But Zac's brain had latched onto one fact and was chewing it now, down to the bone. If James and Anna had died, Finn and Cady were alone among the mortals unless Zac and David — and Simon, if the man could be bothered, and Moira, if anyone ever heard from her again — accepted them.

"There were six of you originally?"

Cady nodded. "Me. Finn. Sean and Holly. James and Anna."

One more than their own group had been, while Colm still lived. He imagined interactions, personalities and history melding. Maybe they'd even found love, given the way Cady spoke their names in pairs without a thought.

"I'm sorry," he said. "About Holly and Sean."

"Thank you." Her voice had hushed.

"Where are you from? I hear the slightest drawl."

She smiled. "Originally Oklahoma Territory, all six of us. But Missouri these days. Warrenton, a suburb outside St. Louis. James and Anna live there as well. Holly and Sean had been in Southern California for about four years."

Zac's own group had done that a few times — the four of them, before David. Lived in easy driving distance. The last time they'd moved away from one another had been the late 1970s. Could Simon be persuaded to move up here, or David to move to Florida? Probably not.

Cady pushed up on the pillows. "I wish Finn hadn't taken me away from home with them out of touch, but maybe it's for the best. It'll prove to him you're not cold-blooded, better than your online presence could do."

Zac sat forward. "He's, what, following my hashtags?"

"He thought we should monitor your whereabouts as long as there was a possibility you were behind . . . whatever happened. You haven't made it easy since you moved here, but he wouldn't give up."

Hiding away had been part of the point of moving. Zac's haunts in Denver were well known, though most people respected his space. It had never been an issue before the fall at Marble Canyon. Weird how a daredevil's failure made him a household name more quickly than safety and success could ever do.

David scrubbed a hand over the back of

his head. "So he didn't come to Michigan to mete out justice."

"Of course not."

"But there is a chance the deaths by aging were unnatural?"

"By *unnatural* you mean murder."

"Aye, of course." They were the most relaxed words David had spoken since spotting Finn's car. They slipped out unconsciously, and the *r* rolled a bit.

For the first time a hint of strain showed. Cady's lips pressed tight, and a tremor ran over her. She stared past him and whimpered.

"Cady?" he said.

"Where is he?"

A shiver ran down Zac's spine. She wasn't speaking to him.

"Cady." David leaned toward her. When she flinched away, he straightened. "You're in Harbor Vale, Michigan. It's the twenty-first century."

"He's dead." A whisper. Her hands clenched at her sides. "They've killed him."

Five

Zac got up and sat at the bedside, eye level with her, nonthreatening. "No, Cady. No one here has killed anybody."

Nowhere near the truth.

A tear squeezed from one eye as she shut them tight. "Oh no. What have they done?"

Zac reached for her age-spotted hand and slipped his fingers into hers. She latched on like a baby. Another tear fell.

"It'll pass," David said quietly, a reverence in him for the sacredness of a memory so old.

Which was crap. Remembering was hurting her. "Cady, if you can hear me, it's Zac Wilson. Everyone's okay."

"God help him." A quiet sob hitched in her chest.

He encased her clenched hand in both of his. "He's okay, Cady. He's okay."

She opened her eyes, and tears stood in them, magnifying their green depths and the hazel specks near their pupils. He wanted to wipe away the final tear that tracked down her cheek, passing over a small age spot, or a large freckle. She blinked at him.

"Zac."

"Hey, that's right. Are you back?"

"Finn?" She nearly crushed his hand.

"He's okay."

"Right. Of course." She gave a slow blink that seemed to force away the last of the memory, but her grip remained strong. "And we were talking about . . ."

"We don't have to go into it now."

Cady dug her fingers into her hair, mussing her braid and seeming not to notice. "It has to be the serum. The days of the Elderfolk are ending naturally. I knew we would someday."

"Elderfolk?" Zac said.

"Well, what do you call us?"

"Longevites."

Judgment pursed her lips, which for some reason brought heat to his cheeks.

"We're not something from Tolkien," he said.

"We're not something from the Red Cross disease handbook, either."

He laughed. Maybe inappropriate right now, but it burst out of him sounding like . . . himself. Not like the barking cynic whose best friend had been killing people.

"James and Anna," he said. "Is it possible they were taken?"

"For what, a ransom?" Her arms opened from her sides. "We're living obscurely. And I can't imagine there's a government conspiracy to nab us."

Zac shrugged. "For the sake of exploring options . . . maybe there's been an alien abduction, point-zero-zero-two percent of the population."

David cocked an eyebrow at him.

"I'm only half serious."

"That's not a reassuring percentage."

"Maybe it's the Rapture. No, forget that." He jabbed a finger at David. "You wouldn't still be here."

His friend crossed his arms. Zac almost grinned.

"Let's for a moment rule out science fiction and the end times," David said.

"We *are* science fiction, man."

"It isn't any of that," Cady said quietly. "Either they're all right, just uncharacteristically thoughtless, or . . . well, or their time ran out too."

Zac touched her shoulder. "We'll help you find out. Nothing more to talk about, okay?"

David's sharp glance said there was plenty

more. Zac shook his head. Later. Already Cady was sinking down on the pillows, eyes closing.

"You sleep for now," Zac said.

"I don't think I have a choice." She sighed. "I'm sorry Finn pushed us on you like this."

"No worries. Just rest."

She didn't respond.

Zac followed David from the room and braced himself for whatever the man was going to volley at him. David stalked through the dark living room, and Zac followed. Finn was silent, maybe sleeping as they passed the couch he lay on. David kept going, all the way to the garage. He moved to let the door slam, but Zac caught it on its hinges and shut it gently. David frowned.

"Migraine care 101," Zac said. "Light, sound, smell."

"Ah. Right." David leaned his shoulders against the garage wall.

"Well?"

"I don't think she's lying," David said.

Zac blinked. "Is that all you got out of what just happened?"

A deeper scowl. "It's what I need to determine before the rest means anything."

"They're wrecked, man. Detective Galloway can step off for a few hours, at least."

"What's this discrepancy in their stories? Cady believes the missing two are alive, but Finn clearly thinks they're —"

"Agh, David, stop."

Zac's throat was too tight to swallow; his chest throbbed with pressure. He stood in the chill damp of the garage and it rolled over and through him, all of it. Finn's fear that produced aggression. Cady's grief for lost ones, submerged in her concern for those still living, both reactions flowing strong and ocean-deep. She loved her friends.

"Hey," David said after a moment.

"They're hurting. Give them a minute to hurt."

With a sigh the man pushed away from the wall and sat on the stoop, long legs folding his knees almost to chin level. "Aye, you're right."

Zac rubbed his knuckles against his chest and looked around the garage. These walls, this house, the revelations it had held less than a month ago, the distress of strangers it held now — strangers who were kin nevertheless — he hit the door opener and strode into the night.

David followed. "Zac?"

Down the sidewalk, shivering without his jacket, hands thrust into the pockets of his jeans, shoulders hunched. As he walked, the pressure on his throat and chest lessened.

"I felt it," he said.

"Felt what?"

"What they're going through. It's sort of a thing with me."

"Empathy."

"Moira calls it an extra portion. Simon calls it oversensitive foolishness." Colm had called it a creepy talent and joked about its potential uses.

After a few minutes of wordless walking, somebody had to say something, so Zac did. "I know what you're going to do."

"Oh?" David glanced at him as they passed under a streetlight.

"You're going to pull a Marshal Dillon on them."

A chuckle. "I'm what?"

"This is your town. They have until noon to get out of Dodge."

Now the glance was sharp.

"Not in those words maybe," Zac said. "But they do make it crowded, in terms of longevite population."

"They've as much right to stay here as any mortal."

Zac stopped walking and looked out on the street for a minute. David did the same.

"Something isn't right," Zac said.

He wanted them to be trustworthy. The same thing he'd wanted of David when he first laid eyes on the man. The thing he would always want from a fellow longevite. He shook his head to dispel the sensation of Colm sneering at him. From hell.

They'd meet there someday, no doubt.

David turned to study him. "You think someone's lying?"

"No. They're both telling us what they know. Or what they think they know."

"So one of them is mistaken."

"And until we know which one, we won't know the true threat. If there is one."

David ran his finger along the scar at his temple. "We'd best keep them near until the questions are answered."

"Agreed." At least that long. Zac wouldn't turn them away in any case. Not family.

"Simon's been hoping to track Finn. I suppose I'll update him."

"Good idea." Zac turned and headed back for the house.

Walking beside him, David said, "Tomorrow they get a hotel."

Zac laughed, and the heaviness on him receded, like a tide washing out that would wash in again at some future time.

Back at his apartment, he noticed an email

notification on his phone. His pulse notched up. It might be Moira. He'd tried every address he'd ever known her to have to no avail, but maybe tonight she would reply. He tapped his way to the app, hoping for one particular subject line — *re: talk to me?*

It wasn't her, but his mouth tugged upward anyway. Lucas. He tapped again to bring up the message.

Zac,

So I read it. It's not perfect, but you were mostly right. It was good. I can't believe I made it through a book from the '60s. It's weird that things were like that when my grandpa was my age. I mean, yeah, he's old, but I guess he really is OLD.

He chuckled. "Thanks, kid."

I got to the last line and had to double check if that was the first line too. And it was, which is cool. I could tell a girl wrote it. Sorry, but guys don't talk about Gone with the Wind like that. And the poem. Except I actually liked the poem.

I watched your Warrior USA episode again and how you look like a ninja climbing the rock wall. I let it play while

I did my arm and leg weights. Not really heavy, but I have to do something or they'll turn into jelly and I'll never be able to climb a rock wall.

I wanted to ask you something serious. Sometimes I imagine the tightrope fall, the way you were just walking up there, not going to die at all, and then death was coming at you so fast.

His mouth dried. Death came up too often with Lucas.

I want to know if you were ready. Or if you even had time to be. Or if you had time for thoughts about what would make you ready.

The kid was okay. He wouldn't be weight training otherwise.

And then when the angel talked to you and caught you up. I want to know how that felt.

Later,
Lucas

P.S. Any other old books I should read?

Zac set down the phone and fetched his

laptop from the bedroom. Their email correspondence went to his dad Nate's account. If Lucas had his own address, Zac didn't know it. He settled on the couch and began to type.

Hey Lucas,

Told you so.

It is a cool book. Head and heart together is how I think of great books. You think and feel. This one makes you want to speak for someone who can't. At least it does that to me. And I got you liking Frost too, huh? Bonus level unlocked.

About your serious question.

He read the email again, and a knot formed in his stomach. Lucas was eleven years old, for crying out loud. Zac's most devoted fan. The kid could have gone anywhere in the world, and he asked the Make-A-Wish Foundation if he could meet Zac Wilson the stunt guy. He'd faced death more times than Zac had, and he had the careful thoughts and somber eyes that came with such experience. Zac couldn't give the kid a mask. He shut his eyes and searched for a middle ground.

I don't know if anyone can be completely ready.

As the words came from his fingers, he pictured David. If anyone could be ready to meet God face-to-face, it had to be this guy who had walked with Him for a hundred-plus years. But even David had Tiana. Leaving her for blissful eternity would rip the man's will down the center, temporariness of the separation notwithstanding.

People are pretty much never ready for the unknown, and you can't get more unknown than death. But you didn't ask about people in general; you asked about me.

He swallowed hard. He tapped the keys without pressing them, stared across the little apartment through the window at the night silhouette of the lone apple tree someone had seen fit to plant in the front yard. Probably without realizing they were sentencing the maintenance crew to a lifetime of picking up rotting apples every fall.

If I'm honest I have to say no. I wasn't ready. Not even in the ways I could have been. And yes, I had time to know it. As for how I felt when I realized I wasn't dead after all,

His fingers froze. A shiver traced his neck. He set the laptop aside, walked across the room to the window, and stared at the clouds past the apple tree. For a full minute he didn't move.

How it felt to survive. To know you always would.

He wandered back to the couch and the laptop. He set his fingers on the keys.

it was mostly disbelief. Then I guess it was some confusion and some gratitude.

He stared at the last word. It should be true. It might be. But it didn't feel true.

He left the word there because he couldn't tell any mortal, much less an eleven-year-old, the whole truth. The certainty that he should have been dead this time, finally, irrevocably dead. The throb of guilt that he wasn't, though he'd already lived more years than anyone deserved. The fear that sent ice creeping up his arms and legs as he surveyed the remains — his remains. His clothes mostly gone, and what looked like blood but was already dry, as if it had come from someone else, sometime in the past. And then the awareness. This wasn't luck, wasn't the serum.

When he had asked a hundred years ago, God hadn't spared him. Now, without his asking, God had.

He had thought about praying, there in the canyon surrounded by rock older than he was. He had stared at the blue sky above, squinted at the sun for a second or two, watched the clouds drifting past him above and their shadows drifting over the earth at his feet. Beauty from God's hand. Yet Zac couldn't manage one word to Him.

I don't know what else to tell you, Lucas. It's a hard question. If you want to ask more about it, you can. I don't mind, even if I don't have the answer.

Zac

P.S. That depends. What kind of book do you want?

Six

He flailed his way to consciousness with the weight of a behemoth on his chest. Pushed up in bed, but the weight bent him forward. His knees pulled in as his energy funneled to the single goal of drawing a full breath. He wanted to call out for help. *Please, anyone.* But there was no one to call out to. He knew that much.

He buried his face against his knees. Dark in the room, no whisper of dawn, a night-light down the hall that had done exactly nothing to ward off the dream. Never did. He shook like a child. Or perhaps like a man whose mouth and throat and lungs once filled with death while his body could not die. The dream grabbed hold again, a hawk and Zac the field mouse, crushed by a muscled foot, torn by talons and beak. His body rocked in place on the bed. He tried to breathe.

Please. Help.

The phone was in his hand before he knew he'd reached for it. Contacts. S. He stared at the screen. He knew what the voice mail would say if he called. Not that he ever did these days.

"Leave a message if you want."

Long minutes. Short breaths.

He cradled the phone. *Work through it. Not the first time. Not the last. Talk.* Words helped.

His first attempt sounded more like a sob. Simon would have something to say about that.

"Yeah," Zac said. "I do this to myself. Idiot. Get it together."

The screen darkened, and the disappearance of Simon's name increased the pressure on Zac's chest. He tapped his finger to bring the light back, and his lungs opened a little.

"Sorry." He spoke between breaths. "To bug you. Like this. Throw some snark at me. If you want. I'm listening."

No sound in the room but his cursed gasping.

"This is stupid." But he couldn't put the phone down, not while needles pricked his fingers and palms and his ribs seemed to be shrinking.

Stupid. An inconvenience to friends. Moira had told him so after years of shouldering this weakness alongside him. She'd finally been honest with him. Honest about this and lying about everything else.

Zac curled his fingers around the phone and rested his forehead against the back of his hand. He worked for more breaths. They entered his lungs like shards of glass. He curled his free hand into the bedsheets. He tried to cast his mind back to nights like this one, deepest trenches of night, when he had called and Simon had answered and recognized Zac's terror audible across miles. Simon stayed on the line making small talk until Zac could breathe again and never asked questions, though the interrogator in him had to be salivating for an explanation.

Zac's next breath came easier, more sandpaper than ground glass. The attack could last only so long. He uncurled to an upright position and stretched out his legs. Cold sweat soaked through his shirt at the chest, armpits, and back. He sat a few more minutes breathing. Then he stripped off the shirt and tossed it onto the floor and shivered, though the room was warm. His hands were like ice, but the tingling in his fingers was lessening.

"Okay," he said. This time when the phone went dark, he tossed it onto the bed. "I'm okay. Thanks, man."

Crying out loud, if Simon knew he did this . . .

In silence Zac got out of bed and threw on a clean tee. He pushed his bare feet into his running shoes, locked his apartment, and walked out into the floodlit parking lot. The waking birds were his companions as he paced the full length of the lot beneath a sky that turned gray at the edges. Paced and breathed. Eventually, around five, he hit his last lap. He'd worked the panic out of him. He could stop moving.

He halted under the canopy of the old maple tree, its leaves half yellow, half shed. He leaned his shoulder against its trunk and then rested his head too.

Another night exactly like the last twenty.

Purging Colm's apartment hadn't purged Zac's brain. That was annoying. And, well, a little unnerving. Something was still wrong with him.

Zac pushed his palm against the bark. Looked up into the branches that bobbed in the almost ceaseless lake wind. Through their rugged pattern the sky was turning pink. No telling why he loved this tree so much. Maybe because it was the oldest in the lot. It seemed to watch over him, mute witness to his struggles out here in the nights since Colm's death. An inane fancy, but a comforting one.

Okay, enough. Five in the morning, a good hour of the day. Past time to get on with it. He returned up the walk to his front door and let himself inside. As the door shut and the walls surrounded him, as the ceiling blocked the sky, his throat and lungs tried to close again, but the reaction washed over him without soaking in, receded instead.

He entered his unit, threw on some running clothes, and stepped outside again, into the bracing chill. He'd be sweating soon enough.

His five-mile run circled the town of Harbor Vale twice: shops and neighborhoods, hushed and drowsy, gray light turning to pink and then yellow as the sun rose. As he ran, he wondered what continent Moira slept on right now, if indeed she slept. She might be awake purely due to her time zone. She might be only an hour or two different from his but awake anyway. Painting maybe. Fingers brushed with yellow and blue, her favorites. Hair pulled back messily.

The image made him ache. Did she sleep as poorly as he did? Did she dream Colm back to life with blood on his hands?

After the run, he did some weight training

with a cheap set he'd bought at a department store in Traverse City, since Harbor Vale didn't have a gym. He showered off the good sweat of his workout and the cold sweat of his panic. He grabbed his wallet and keys and left the apartment. It was too small.

The drive to David's was more automatic than conscious decision. When Zac drove up, he was kneeling in his backyard under the oak tree, arms folded against the chill of the morning, head bowed. Praying.

Zac hunched against his car door. He pictured himself, scant hours before, grappling under the other tree. David might be grappling too, but he addressed the One who made the trees. When he rose, Zac approached with a loose stride, a swing to his arms that bespoke casual ease.

"Morning," David said.

"Best time of the day."

"Aye."

The K-car was still in the driveway. Navy blue in daylight, Missouri plates. Zac nodded at it. "No hotel yet, I see."

"Cady says that's not necessary."

"Oh, she does, does she? And what are your thoughts on that?"

"They're preparing to drive home."

Leaving. Just like that. "How's Finn?"

David shrugged. Really, he hadn't asked? Some host. Zac shook his head and headed inside.

Cady sat at the kitchen table eating cold cereal, her hair escaped from its braid in every direction. Sunlight fell on her through the bay window and deepened the shade of her hair to something like raw honey. She spooned a bite of cereal with a young steady hand, one that bore no age spots but, he could see now, was spattered with freckles. Like the wrist. Probably like the arm hidden by the sleeve of her hoodie. Like . . .

She lifted her head, and her eyes met his. Clear today. Bright. And so green he was reminded of a shed door he'd painted that color sometime in the 1950s.

"Hello," she said, her voice almost soprano. She tilted him a smile, freckles like confetti on her cheeks, nose, and forehead.

"Hi." He smiled as he sat across from her. Far be it from Zac Wilson to lose his words around a lovely woman. Now that her skin had lost its age, that loveliness was easy to appreciate.

She was still looking at him, spoon halfway to her mouth, dripping milk into the bowl. Her cheeks warmed to pink.

"David says you're leaving," he said.

She took her bite of cereal and swallowed

before she answered. "Still nothing from Anna and James. I have zero experience with missing persons, but I'm about to learn."

She didn't mean a report to the authorities, not when they might have aged eighty years in eight days. "Where'll you start looking?"

"After their usual places? I have no idea."

"I'll help if I can. And once we find them, you can all come up here to visit."

She took a few more bites. "To visit, of course. You don't have to worry about overpopulation."

"David said something to you." The misanthrope. Zac planted both hands on the table. "Well, he doesn't own Harbor Vale."

"So far he's said 'Good morning' and 'You seem well' and 'Please feel free to eat any yield of the cupboards.' He slept in the tent out there" — she gestured to the door that opened onto the deck — "and I think he came inside only to make sure we were okay. Then he went back out again."

Providing for those in need, yet avoiding unexpected company. Predictable. The man could close his bookstore and spend a year walking up and down the aisles, as happy among his books as most people were among, well, people.

Zac sat back in his chair. "He actually said 'yield of the cupboards'? Of course he did. I can hear him saying it."

Cady grinned, but it faded. "He's settled here. We wouldn't interfere with that. It's not about ownership; it's about respecting boundaries."

"And if I ask you to stay? I mean, I'm living here too."

"This isn't your home, Zac."

He looked away, then met her eyes again. "That's what I keep telling myself, but I'm still here."

"You came less than a month ago. I'd hardly call that permanence. And Finn told me someone died here. The memories can't be easy."

Zac scrubbed a hand through his hair. "No."

"David's home, David's boundary, if he chooses to draw it. Though I appreciate your invitation."

Movement at the open entry to the kitchen drew her gaze as well as Zac's. Finn stood staring at her, rumpled with bloodshot eyes, but the strain was gone from his mouth. A deep breath rose in his chest.

"Cade."

She rose. "On the mend, just like I told you."

Before she'd finished her sentence, Finn was halfway across the room. They engulfed each other in a hug, his hand cupping the back of her neck, her arms squeezing him around the ribs.

"I'm okay, Finn."

"Thank God."

"Sorry I scared you."

"Just — the timing."

"I know." She squeezed once more and then they both let go.

They hadn't kissed.

Cady ran her palms over her messy braid. As if only now noticing him, Finn locked eyes with Zac.

"Hey," Zac said.

"I owe you an apology. Or more than one."

"We're good, man."

"No. I was . . . I've been . . . ready for war." He grimaced. "And yesterday was a bad day."

Zac stood and offered his hand. Finn gave a half squint that seemed to be his version of raised eyebrows, hesitated another moment, and then clasped Zac's hand with a firm grip.

"Let's start over." Zac shook his hand. "Zac Wilson, born 1855, stopped aging thanks to a mystery serum in 1887."

The man smiled for the first time in Zac's

presence. "Timothy Finn. Born 1863, aged until 1891."

"Young whippersnapper." Zac grinned. "Timothy, huh?"

"Don't use it," he said without a hint of levity.

Zac pointed at Cady. "Next."

"Cady Schuster. I was born in '70 and stopped aging in '96."

Physically, those dates made her six years younger than he was — even more negligible for them than for mortals — but his mind didn't stop at math. He mentally replaced her hoodie and jeans with a slim-waisted dress of pale green that accented her eyes. Her fuzzy yellow house socks became dark stockings, and — He halted the picture of the rest of her wardrobe, the pieces he couldn't see. Okay, he tried to halt it.

Time to say something, help himself out. Ages. Right.

"David was — changed, turned? Whatever word I use, we sound like vampires. Anyway, he was the first of us."

"Our first was James," Cady said.

Footsteps sounded from the hall, and David stopped just outside their gathering. His eyes warmed, though his posture still held a wire-fine tension.

"Even among ye, I'm ancient," he said,

the vowels lilting with his true accent. "1848 here."

"This old man" — Zac jabbed his finger at him — "served in the War between the States."

"Oh my." Cady's eyes widened. "You could be my father."

He crossed his arms. "We'll measure the gap in physical age, not calendar age. So I'm thirty-five and no one's ancestor."

"Seems fair," she said, not bothering to squelch her smile.

"I disagree." Zac sat back down and propped his feet on the chair opposite. "If we're only as old as we act, you could be our great-great-grandfather, man."

A gentle laugh chimed from Cady, but Finn didn't crack a smile. Zac must be off his court-jester game.

Before David could offer a retort, Finn took a step toward him, face still bland as candle wax. Zac would have to learn the tells that worked in place of facial expressions.

Finn offered his hand to David as he had to Zac. "I've wronged you. Attacked you without cause. Thought you murdered not just that man but my family too. I had no right to come here again."

"You came to save her life," David said,

arms still crossed.

Finn did not lower his hand. “Yes.”

“Fear drove you.”

“Yes.”

David nodded and grasped Finn’s hand. “We’ll speak of it no more.”

Only as the man’s shoulders relaxed did Zac realize the tension that had gripped Finn. He shook David’s hand. “Thank you.”

“Aye.”

“So, David,” Cady said, “you were given a mystery serum too?”

“Just so,” he said. “I wasn’t conscious, and after recovering I returned to my home in another town. Not until last month did I meet the others.”

“Last month — of this year?”

“Indeed.”

“Oh, how terribly lonely.”

He smiled. “No longer.”

“We had a file on him,” Zac said, “left behind by our doctor. We knew he was out there in the world.”

“A doctor who treated you for something mortal, right?” Cady said. “I tore my arm on some barbed wire and developed an infection.”

“Same here. We should compare notes. See how similar we are biologically, how similar our stories are.”

"Do you think that might help us understand what happened to Holly and Sean?"

He hadn't been thinking of Holly and Sean, only of knowing the stories of the two in front of him. "It's worth a try."

"The present solved by the past." Cady gave a heavy nod. "It's a good idea."

"But first . . . Finn, the man you saw, the — the body." Zac met Finn's eyes and glimpsed the deep wells behind the flatness. Words were clotting in Zac's throat, but it was time to end their suspicion for good.

"You were right," David said when Zac couldn't continue. "He was executed according to our unanimous decision."

"Why?" Finn said.

"We took his life to pay for those of the mortals he had taken. And to prevent further murders."

"He was Elderfolk?" Cady said.

"Aye."

"And he killed mortals?"

"For pleasure. Evil in him grew with the years. He did not know remorse."

David's words were a slug to the stomach, their truth notwithstanding.

Cady's voice took on a hush. "How did . . . I mean, what was . . . ?"

"The method? The only effective one, unless you know of another. He was drugged unconscious and then . . ."

Hesitation didn't suit David, especially for Zac's sake. Zac met his eyes and nodded.

"An old saber of mine," David said. "Guillotined."

Of course David would use the most polite verb possible.

"You were close to him." Cady's words were gentle.

She was addressing Zac, not David. The bite of gall rose in his throat. "And I never guessed."

"Nor did Simon," David said.

The new barking laugh escaped. "So?"

"So would you censure him as you do yourself?"

Agh, David, shut up. Zac rubbed a hand over his face. No, he wouldn't blame Simon. Simon wasn't the resident lie detector. Zac looked away from them all. David's words had pierced like a hot poker straight to the festering sore inside.

His knee was jumping under the table. He tried to be still, but all he wanted to do right now was find a gym mat and throw himself into a few handsprings. Instead he had to find the edges of the mask and slide it back into place, the mask that seemed ready to crack down the middle if he said a word.

"It means a lot," Cady said, "your telling us."

He didn't want it to mean anything. Or ever to have happened. Stupid to bring it up. The relevance of a moment ago felt lost.

"Yeah," he said to keep them from studying his silence. "Well." He cleared his throat. "Cady, if you're like us, you need more than cold cereal to finish recovering. We could keep talking over breakfast."

Breakfast with strangers while they grieved friends. After Colm died, Zac spent two days ranging the streets and sand dunes around town like a tethered spirit. He'd wanted to book a flight home. He'd ignored David's texts. All the while he'd known he couldn't seal the gaping hole with solitude, that solitude only ever made devastation worse for him. But the knowledge hadn't strengthened him enough to reach out. Not until, days later, David sent another text asking if he'd left town. The second it lit his screen, Zac had recognized the lifeline for what it was. Had finally texted back.

In those days at the bottom of a chasm, a meal with a stranger would have been the last thing he said yes to.

Finn, however, was nodding.

"I guess we could," Cady said.

"I can't," David said, facing Zac. "I've a

store to run. I'd be unfair to leave Tiana alone again."

"Sure."

"I'll try to join you this evening," he said to Cady and Finn, "if you're still in town."

Cady blinked as if she thought the words an underhanded dismissal, but David would have told them straight out if he wanted them gone. Zac would clarify later.

He recommended the diner. Sure, he'd eaten there yesterday, but he wouldn't choose an inferior restaurant simply because he was wearing a rut with this one. Cady and Finn followed him, Finn again behind the wheel. Cady would be feeble for another day or so and needed to sleep through most of it.

As he parked, Zac glanced down at the floor on the passenger side and swore. Colm's box. The coins. He shoved the box under the back seat, invisible to anyone who might peer into his windows, though they'd have no way of guessing the fortune inside something so dilapidated.

When he locked the car, he seemed to be securing something dark and dirty.

SEVEN

They entered the diner by nine, two steps ahead of the breakfast rush. Everyone in town seemed to come here on weekends. Zac offered his best photo-shoot smile to Luann, and she rolled her eyes and laughed. Within a minute, she was motioning them across the cozy restaurant to a booth.

"The perks of fame?" Cady said as Luann left to fetch three menus from behind her hostess podium.

"They know how I tip." Zac smirked.

They were shrugging out of coats and claiming seats as they spoke, but before Zac slid in on the opposite side of Finn and Cady, someone approached over his left shoulder. He turned.

At first he saw only her hair. She'd colored it silver with an underlayer of charcoal. It looked trendy and, framing her lineless face, kind of weird. Her eyes were violet blue, a color no more real than that of her hair.

She might be of legal drinking age, or she might not. She was staring at him as if he'd hung the entire solar system.

That look never felt right. He enjoyed signing slips of paper, glossy photos, even T-shirts for grinning fans. Guys who called him "dude" and asked technical questions about the stunts he'd performed, girls who prattled about being nervous and then asked some human interest question — his favorite book, his favorite band. Sometimes he was ogled, which he didn't mind. Sometimes he was moved by stories of struggle, victory, loss. Sometimes, after they'd gone, he had to walk off the pressing ache of their emotions as they'd told him how much his fund-raisers meant to them, what one or another organization had done for their own family in time of need.

All of it, he wouldn't trade for the privacy Simon and David preferred.

But then there were fans like the gray-haired young woman in front of him, whose fixation ran so strong she couldn't hide it. Not that she was trying. It made his skin itch. It made him want to turn her away, tell her to find a worthier idol.

"Hi," he said and smiled.

"You're Zac."

"That's right. And you are?" Cut to the

chase. Move her along.

"Rachel."

"How're you, Rachel?"

"Well, I'm talking to Zac Wilson."

She wasn't digging in her purse for a pen and paper. She wasn't moving at all, unless he counted her shift from one foot to the other. He didn't offer an autograph because she might not want one. She might be nervous because she'd approached to tell him off about something he'd said online. Or not said. It had happened before, though rarely.

"Just a normal guy here."

"Yeah." She pointed to herself. "Same."

Before the pause could become awkward, she glanced past him to the booth and saw Cady and Finn. Her lips parted, the only outward giveaway of a viscous discomfort that rolled off her from nowhere. It might be an aversion to intruding on his private breakfast. It might be something else altogether.

She met his eyes again. "Why do you do it?"

"Do what?"

"The stunts. The tightropes and the free climbing — all of it. Did you want fame or something else?"

He'd been asked the question before but

never so bluntly. She was holding her breath for his answer. Zac weighed the truth and the veneer and gave her a measure of each.

"Fame was the last thing in my head when it all started." Truth. "I wanted to challenge myself physically, that's all." Veneer. "But when my video channel blew up, I decided fifteen minutes in the spotlight could be fun. And then I decided I should try to do something helpful with it, as long as I have it."

"You've had more than fifteen minutes." The words were matter-of-fact, but curiosity lay underneath them as well as something more somber.

"It'll end." Was already starting to, and would continue when his followers got no more stunts to watch.

"Why challenge yourself? What was behind it? I mean — I'm not sure if that question makes sense, but . . ." Another glance at the booth behind him, and her face flushed, emphasizing the colorless hair framing it. "I'm sorry. I'll go. I've just been wanting to know, and I saw you —"

"Hey." He said it quietly, because she looked ready to bolt or cry. "You're not intruding, Rachel."

"Oh." Barely a whisper.

Who knew what she had experienced, was

experiencing even now — emotional neglect, he would bet on, if not something worse. He pictured her leaving the diner and going home to lovelessness, and he swallowed and peeled one more layer off his veneer. Just one. Maybe it would help her.

"We've all got some tough things, right? Part of living."

She nodded.

"The stunts were a way for me to challenge my tough things."

The idolizing look had melted into something truer. She was quiet for a moment.

"Hope that makes sense," he said when she didn't seem inclined to move away.

"Oh, yes." A decided softness held the words.

"Good."

"Thanks, Zac."

"My pleasure."

"I'll let you get back to your friends." Her face filled with a naked, artless longing that heightened the pressure in Zac's soul.

"Good to meet you," he said.

She hurried from the restaurant with her head down. He sank into the booth across from Cady and Finn, both of whom were watching him.

"Perks of fame?" Cady's question came quietly.

"Doesn't happen often. And when it does, it's not usually that intense."

"You were kind."

He scoffed and picked up his menu, though he knew it by heart. Just then their server came for drink orders, a merciful distraction.

Kath looked at each of them and deadpanned with wide eyes, "Why, hello, Mr. Wilson."

He rolled his eyes, and she laughed.

"You really do know everyone in town, don't you?" Cady shook her head and opened her menu.

Zac pointed at Kath. "No messing with these guys, okay?"

"Now, Zac, you know I only mess with celebrities." She set water glasses in front of each of them.

"We're safe then," Cady said. "Utterly unknown."

"In that case, what can I get you to drink?"

Cady ordered cranberry juice; Finn, grapefruit. Zac went with coffee, which wasn't his usual daily choice but had become necessary to brain function. Stupid freaking night attacks.

"What did she mean about messing with you?" Cady said as Kath walked away.

"Oh, that. The first time I ate here, she

told me I was the second most famous person ever to walk through the doors, after a soap opera star. I agreed that I paled to any soap opera star, and she burst out laughing."

"So there's never been a soap opera star here?" Other than ordering his juice, it was the first time Finn had spoken since they sat down.

Zac shrugged.

"You didn't ask her?"

"I guess it didn't matter."

Finn's brow furrowed. "What was the point then?"

"Baiting me. Seeing how seriously I take myself as an internet celebrity."

"Oh. Right." He shrugged and returned to his perusal of the menu but after a few seconds looked up again. "Social subtext. My brain misses it sometimes."

Zac hadn't intended to comment further, but if Finn was inviting him to . . . "And here I am taking it for granted."

"Hang around me long enough and you won't."

The guy was so different when he wasn't feeling cornered. Or terrified for his friend's life, or bowed over with a migraine. Shoot, Cady was right. Zac had no experience with Finn except at his most desperate.

David had said they'd speak of their first encounter no more, but Zac wanted to know. He'd back off if Finn took this wrong, but he seemed open now. Zac folded his arms on the table and leaned toward the man. "So about that time you shot David in the head."

Cady's bristling could have been felt from across town. Across the table, Zac let her glare jab him like porcupine quills. He couldn't say he didn't deserve it, but thus far Finn had preferred the direct approach.

Finn's gaze was level. "Yeah, about that."

"You wanted to talk to us, and a blink later you wanted to escape us."

"Yeah."

"I'd like to know both of those whys, if you don't mind."

" 'Course," Finn said. "I thought you knew how to survive anything, even age, after you lived through the canyon fall. I wanted to know how you did it in case Sean and Holly weren't the only ones of us to start aging. Wanted to be prepared."

"But?" Zac said when he paused. Might as well get through all of it now that they'd started.

"I watched you for a day, just caution at the time, but then I saw you with that man Colm." He hunched his shoulders. "It's why

I was sure you'd somehow killed Holly and Sean."

"And why you resorted to gun violence?"

Finn missed or ignored the sardonic levity in Zac's tone. "Mostly, yeah. And sometimes I feel cornered, whether I am or not."

The place wouldn't have mattered, Cady had said. There might be more to it, but Zac knew when to back off.

"Thanks," he said.

" 'Course." Finn shrugged. "Your right to ask."

The three of them sat quietly, somehow more settled with each other than they had been before Zac pushed the question.

After a minute Cady said, "Recommendations for the out-of-towners?"

Zac huffed a laugh. "I was one myself the other day."

After Kath came back and left with their orders, Cady said, "All right, let's try it, solving the present with the past. Do you think our ages make a difference?"

"If the serum's expiring, David should have aged first." Zac poured one creamer and two sugars into his coffee and sipped it. Still too bitter. He added another packet of sugar.

"So individual physiology must affect it, right? David's an entire generation older than we are. Than we were, I mean. Than they were." Her chin trembled.

If he could do something to help them, he had to find it. For now he would let one of them break the silence.

"I don't fully believe it," Cady said at last. "That they simply grew old, after all these years. It's the reasonable explanation, but I don't believe it."

"Not believing it doesn't change it." Finn's voice was flat.

Zac couldn't look at them without putting himself in their place. Imagining if he had lost Colm this way, not an execution but a mystery. Not a killer but a true friend. If Simon and Moira were dead right now, he didn't know how he'd stand it.

Cady sipped her water and cleared her throat. "Finn's right. Let's compare histories. Let's see if that leads anywhere."

Strange how difficult it was to believe they were his age. For so many decades there had been only one missing longevite on his mind, and finding David had completed the family. Now here across from him sat two more who had been moving and breathing, thinking and talking in the world all this time.

"You said you were dying of an infection, and the serum healed you."

Cady ran one finger around the rim of her juice glass. "Fever broke, redness and swelling disappeared in a few hours, and then the wound did too. Within a day, it was as if I'd never torn my arm at all."

"Sounds familiar." A shudder ran down his back. To this day he could press his hand to the exact place the bullet had entered his body, though he too bore no scar.

"You were healed in a day?"

"More like two, but that makes sense."

"Bad injuries?"

"Ambushed by some robbers." He forced a smirk. "Pretty much a John Wayne B-movie. Doc took a bullet out of my stomach, but I wasn't going to make it."

"Oh."

"And Finn? What's your story?"

Finn looked at him a long moment, and the depths behind his eyes seemed to bottom out. "A mob beating."

"A . . . gang? Outlaws?"

"Townsfolk. Law-abiding men. Thought I killed a friend of theirs."

"But you didn't."

Finn gave a slow blink. "I didn't."

Not a painless topic, but if he wanted to change it, he seemed the type of man to say so. As long as he was willing to talk, Zac wanted to listen. A hunger had opened in him to know them. Really know them. Maybe they could see it, but he didn't care.

"Wasn't there any law around?" Zac said.

"By the time Doc was called, I was mostly dead."

Right. Let him tell it in his own way, his own sequence. Zac shut up.

"They broke both my arms. And there was lots of bleeding, you know, internally. They left me after a while, and then somebody brought Doc, asked him to give me morphine." Finn shrugged. "He gave me the serum too."

"Both your stories fit with ours." David's injuries had been accidental, but his body had been as broken as Finn's.

Finn nodded. "And once a year, we deal with that resetting process. Rejuvenation, you called it."

"For a few days?"

"Or longer, depending on the person."

"And it varies for the women," Cady said. "The month, I mean. The men are predictable, but one year it happened to me only seven months apart, and then the next year it was more like fifteen. We told the guys it must be something to do with our blood. You know, female . . ."

She blushed, and Zac hid a smile. Apparently David wasn't the only one who clung to some of the antiquated proprieties.

"I get it," he said to spare her, and she nodded. "We only have one chick, Moira, but now that I think about it, she's kind of like that. I remember one year she rejuvenated in the spring and one year it was fall."

So far, so similar. Zac waited a moment, gave them time to ask their own questions, but they were quiet.

So he kept on. "Okay, say you stub your toe and fracture it. Healed in a few days?"

"No," Finn said. "It's not a mortal wound."

"Right." This was incredible. They were biologically, medically alike. "You get sick?"

"Sure," Cady said.

An exception glared at him in the form of Finn's flat expression. "Wait a minute. If you were given the serum when . . . Why didn't you . . . ?"

"The brain stuff was an old injury by then," he said. "That happened when I was nineteen."

Zac tried to measure his comfort with the topic, but nothing could be read in Finn's face. No way to tell if this was the boundary line or not.

Cady pushed her glass away and said quietly, "Zac."

"No, it's fine, Cade. Family can know."

Zac leaned back in the booth and nodded him on.

Eight

Finn watched over Zac's shoulder and lifted one finger as Kath came with plates that steamed, their aromas making Zac's stomach rumble. He claimed his meat-and-egg scramble and side order of chocolate chip pancakes. In this moment, with these new people who were growing to matter to him faster than his head could keep up, Zac took a few bites before noticing the absence of Colm's voice in his head. *"Breakfast doesn't need dessert, mate."* It hadn't left him, but it had faded to the background. It would be back, of course. But he'd take the reprieve while he could get it.

Finn started on his fried eggs and hash browns with the enthusiasm of a trail hand who'd subsisted for months on watered-down coffee, biscuits, and beans. Might have been his reality at some point. Cady ate too, the fork wobbly in her hand at first, aftermath of rejuvenation. She'd ordered eggs, turkey sausage, and ham; the whole-grain muffin sat on the edge of her plate like an afterthought. Protein overload to refuel, or simple preference.

For a few minutes, they didn't speak, and the quiet was more or less comfortable. Then Finn sipped his juice and set down his fork.

"Some men from a ranch near town had some horses stolen," he said. "They decided I was the thief. In the course of attack, one of them hit me full in the head with a shovel. I woke up from a coma nine days later." He gestured to his head. "I was pretty bad off at first. My brain's had a hundred and twenty years to heal where it can. In the beginning I'd lost reading, writing, short-term memory. All that's back now, and the headaches aren't so often."

Zac pictured himself chafing at the inconvenience and ache of injuries sustained during stunts and sports. Things he had done to himself. And the man across from him sat sipping fruit juice and speaking with tranquility about cognition loss.

"I don't get it." The words burst out with an edge he hadn't known was there.

Finn shrugged. "Life, right? Like you told that girl."

"And you're cool with it." With two separate acts of savagery committed against him. With pieces of his mind missing for the rest of his life.

"Not always."

"But mostly?"

"Mostly. Yes."

"How?"

"I didn't get here alone." Finn took another bite of hash browns and washed them down with more juice. "I've had God."

Pancake lodged in Zac's throat. He cleared it and sipped his coffee. He looked up; both of them watched him, and Cady's eyes held curiosity and challenge.

"I get it," he said.

It made sense that God would stick by someone like Finn, someone who had suffered such injustice. No doubt Finn served Him with devotion.

"David has Him too, the way you do." He nodded to Finn. "I think David talks more to God than to any human, maybe every human combined." *Okay, shut up, Wilson.* At least until he could steady his voice.

"And you, Zac?" Cady's voice was quiet as she cut her sausage patty into quarters.

Oh, shoot. Cady too.

This had to be irony. Zac had lived for a century with three agnostics as his closest friends, and now in the course of one month, he met David and Cady and Finn so they could shove scripture in his face.

"I'll tell you guys what I told David." Good, steady voice now. A bite behind it to let them know this topic wasn't to be explored. "I know what He wants from me, and I can't give it to Him, so I'm not going to pretend. I'm not the submitting type. That's all there is to it."

"There's always more to it than that," Finn said, still munching his breakfast as if they were discussing preferred ice cream flavors.

"There isn't." He shook his head and tried to stop feeling so much. "We're way off topic."

"You asked." Finn pointed his fork at Zac.

"I'm withdrawing the question." Zac tried to smirk, but neither of them were buying casualness, not now. His attempt felt like an insult. He dropped it. "I understand your concern, given the condition of my eternal soul . . . and all that. Now back to comparing biology."

"You wanted to know the story of my brain damage."

"The biological aspects of the story."

"Okay," Finn said.

He should move them on, but curiosity

won. “The murder — did someone set you up?”

Finn didn’t shrug this time. “No. My father was Apache.”

At first Zac didn’t see it. Finn’s skin was white. But as Zac studied him with different criteria, his hair, his cheekbones, his nose . . . Yes. In the late nineteenth century, in the grand old suspicious West — no more or less suspicious than now, though prejudice molded itself a new face for every new generation — Finn would have been noticed. *Half-breed.* No doubt a name he’d lived with.

“Half Apache. So of course you stole some horses and murdered a man.”

“I told you I didn’t.” He hadn’t so much as blinked, but sudden hurt radiated from him like a shock wave.

Which made zero sense. “I’m not saying you did.”

“That’s exactly what you said.”

“No, I . . .” Ah. Social subtext. Zac held up his hand. “No, man. Sarcasm.”

Finn frowned.

“Yeah, I’m an idiot. Sorry.”

“That was supposed to be funny?”

“More like bitter.”

“What?” Finn looked to Cady, confusion furrowing the space between his eyes.

"On your behalf," she said.

He rubbed his forehead and sighed. "Okay, I'm not going to catch up with this one. Just move on."

Quiet wormed in between them, and the soft drone of conversation from other booths and tables filtered back into his awareness. Zac focused on his food and pondered.

He donned masks so often — masks of fun, frivolity, self-absorption, carelessness. Simon and Moira and Colm had occasionally known what he was doing and let him do it, respecting it as a boundary. The rest of the time, they'd taken those masks at face value, at which point the masks became a true, rather than perceived, defense. The balance was delicate, but it had become unconscious.

Until now.

David got along with him unless Zac relied too much on his persona. But David was too serious for his own good. Finn, on the other hand . . . He could alienate Finn. And Cady. He wouldn't earn her respect by wounding her family.

He couldn't be flippant with them. The realization made him quake inside. With these two he had to be himself. All the time.

His screwed-up, thin-skinned, irredeemable self.

God help him.

The sardonic thought rammed headlong into his inner dam, and behind it the words turned into a silent cry.

"Should we switch gears a bit here?" Cady said. "What about the microscopic level? Have you been able to observe that?"

They finished their food while analyzing their discoveries within their own blood cells. They were able to conclude that, in this too, the science was the same for all of them.

"Good thing we had some crazy innovative doctors back then," Cady said as they were waiting for the check.

"Yeah." But her words tugged at old beliefs in Zac, maybe old assumptions. "Did your doc ever tell you about the organisms, where he found them?"

"Some lake," Cady said. "A long distance from Oklahoma Territory, he told me. He had a limited store of the stuff because he'd only ever found them in that one water source. Fisher Lake, Illinois."

Around Zac the restaurant seemed to grow still. Finn and Cady stood out in their booth as if they were the subjects in a stereopticon — or a 3D movie, if he wanted to be current about it. The shock must have thrown his mind back in time to . . . then.

"Zac?" Cady said.

"It was more pond than lake."

"Um, what?"

"It's where I'm from, where all of us are from. Fisher Lake."

Cady's hand froze around her juice glass.

Facts caught up with him, memories coated in the rust of decades. "But he didn't go west. He went east. He thought he had TB. He left his notes to us. Not just on David — he took careful notes every time he used the serum."

"What was his name?"

"Dr. Leon."

"We knew him as Dr. Noel."

A chill ran down Zac's arms. He nodded slowly, though it was impossible. Had to be impossible. He glanced at Finn and tried not to be obvious about it, but the man caught his eye and gave a grim nod.

"I can pick out a four-letter anagram."

Zac turned his hands palms up. "Sorry."

"It's cool. Figuring out my head takes longer than a morning." He gave a half squint. "Is it medically possible, what we're talking about?"

"Maybe," Cady said. "TB's prognosis is unpredictable."

"And we don't know what he had, not for sure. It might have been cancer. It might have been something else, something that wasn't terminal."

"But he said he was going east." As if a man couldn't lie or change his mind. Zac sounded obtuse. But he couldn't grasp what they were saying, the upside-down flip of his view of Doc and the longevites and the secret of Fisher Lake. "He said he wasn't going to practice medicine anymore, was going home to die among family."

"He never said anything of that nature to us," Cady said.

"Did he tell you the serum cured all mortal conditions including age?"

She shook her head. "When he was with us, he thought it worked only on mortal injury. Not illness, not age."

Even in this, Dr. Leon and Dr. Noel matched. Zac scrubbed a palm over his hair. "I just don't think he took it."

Or he couldn't imagine Doc traveling the country making more longevites, half a dozen here and there. It was impossible. Simon had scoured medical media for decades looking for a similar discovery, and not a hint had ever surfaced. Then again, across from Zac sat two people who had existed all this time without showing up in any search of Simon's.

Finn sat back in the booth and folded his arms. "If he got sick enough, maybe he figured it couldn't hurt. Didn't know he'd be making himself like us."

Maybe. Okay. "So . . . let's say he's alive. For the sake of discussion."

"We have to find him." Cady's voice began to shake. "And Anna and James. Now, right now. Anna would have called me by now if she could, and if they've started aging — started dying — if Doc can save them —"

"No." Finn choked the word so faintly Zac barely heard it, but Cady broke off as if he'd shouted it.

"No what?" Cady said.

"He can't save them."

"We won't know until we ask him. He's a doctor, a scientist. His research must be ongoing. Maybe he's still in practice."

"No."

"Finn, it's worth trying."

"There's something I haven't told you. I couldn't when you were . . . when I thought you were . . . but now I have to."

"What are you talking about?"

"Not here, Cade. Finish your food. You need food."

"I need to know Anna and James are okay."

"After you eat."

"I can't eat now."

Finn folded his arms. Gazed at her with the flattest expression Zac had seen on him yet. After a moment, Cady ducked her head and took a bite. After a sip of juice, she said, "You've talked to them?"

Finn's Adam's apple dipped below his collar. "After a fashion."

"And they're all right?"

He took a long breath that shook as he exhaled. "After a fashion."

"Meaning what? Are they in danger?"

"No."

Cady pushed her plate away, stood, and stepped out from the booth. Without another word she marched out of the diner. Finn watched her then met Zac's eyes.

"Remember what I told you."

"That you and Cady are the only ones left." A weight was growing on his chest. A sense of suffering from Finn that left Zac feeling blind; he still could see no hint of concern on the man's face.

"Will you stick by us while I tell her? She loves Anna."

"You think I can help?"

"Well, I can't. I don't grieve."

He couldn't mean that literally, but he seemed to mean everything literally. "I'll do what I can."

"I'll be obliged," Finn said.

Nine

Cady was pacing the sidewalk in front of the diner when Finn and Zac stepped outside. She spun and faced both of them with her hands tucked behind her, soldier style.

"Finn, whatever it is, just say it."

"Not here," Finn said. "It needs to be private."

"We can go back to David's," Zac said.

"We don't have to go anywhere. Inside a car is private." Cady marched to her car and got in on the passenger side and motioned them in after her. Finn got behind the wheel, and Zac slid into the back. He took a deep breath as he shut his door. A bigger car would be helpful.

Cady swiveled in the seat to face Finn. "Come on, Finn. Talk."

"I've been to their house. The first day you were laid up, before you got bad."

She clenched her hands in her lap. "You

found . . . ?"

"They weren't there. But this was."

He shifted in his seat to thrust a hand into the front pocket of his jeans. It came out with a sheet of white stationery, adorned with burgundy scrollwork around the edges. Cady reached for it, and Finn's fingers tightened on the paper.

"You have to be ready, Cade."

"Give it to me."

He did. She unfolded the sheet and began to read. At last she handed the letter back to Finn and sat there, lips parted, chest barely rising and falling, looking like a cast of herself, eggshell thin.

Zac expected Finn to break the silence, to reach out to her somehow. But in a few minutes, Cady collected herself and met his eyes.

"They're gone," she said.

Finn stared down at his hand clutching the letter, crinkling it at the center fold. He nodded.

"Let him see." Cady's voice had become as flat as Finn's. "He needs to know."

"Only if you want me to," Zac said.

"It's your right. As Elderfolk."

Zac accepted the letter from Finn's hand. Its edges were crumbling to softness, though it had been found only days ago. Finn had handled it enough to age it. Cady turned her face away, staring out the side window, as Zac began to read.

To our loved ones, Finn and Cady.

We hope to be able to say these things to you in person, but in case something goes wrong as it did for Sean and Holly, we leave this letter to speak for us. We've agreed to maintain the anonymity of the person who has offered us hope for a natural life span, brought into contact with us through Holly's facilitation. Said individual does not know of this letter. If you find this, if you find our shells after we have abandoned them for spiritual eternity, please do not lament too long. We made a careful decision, reached for this chance to join the normal world again. We refused to do it except together.

If we don't meet you here again, please forgive us. We know we could lose. No, I mean to say we know you could lose. We will gain, however this ends.

Dearest Cady, you know of my (Anna's) yearning for a child. You have witnessed my tears and my petitions to our Lord Jesus that He cure this thorn of timelessness in me that others might see as a blessing, but I cannot. Cady, you know; now please believe. I made this choice, and James is doing it for me. He won't allow me to venture into this uncharted place alone.

To both of you: if we are separated from you now, we ask you to show your love by remembering us with kindness and letting us go. Remember always we will see you again. Deepest love to you, our kin through lifetimes.

Anna and James

Zac swallowed past the stricture in his throat and looked up from the gentle script. He handed the letter to Finn and clasped his hands at his knees. Their despair was flooding the car; already he felt up to his armpits. But neither of them demonstrated a hint of it.

"I am so sorry," Zac said.

"I was wrong. They didn't age out." Cady looked into his eyes and seemed to find support in them to continue. At least he could offer that. "Someone did this to them."

Zac shouldn't be here. The devastation didn't belong to him. He couldn't do a thing for them. Yet he couldn't abandon them either.

"Anna did want a baby. Whoever he is, he

knew details about them."

Finn gave her a squint. "What are you saying?"

"I'm saying this letter is nonsense. They didn't want to die."

"It's not that they wanted to. It was a risk; she wrote that." He lifted the letter. "They accepted the risk."

"After it killed Holly and Sean? No way."

"This is proof." Finn jerked the letter in her direction.

"Or not." Cady looked to Zac. For an outside perspective. For backup.

Zac shook his head. "Not following."

"Anna didn't choose the cure, and she didn't choose to write the letter."

Finn rested his arms on the steering wheel. "This is why Anna asked you to believe her. She knew you wouldn't want to."

Her fists were balling in her lap, ever tighter as they argued. "Or the cure-maker doesn't want us looking into things."

"Cady, we have to accept it."

"No, I don't!"

"Okay," Finn said. "I'll go back to Warrenton and go through their house for evidence. If force was involved, there'll be signs. If I'm wrong and someone did this to them, I'll deal with him myself."

She pressed a fist into her stomach. "I'm going to be sick."

She got out of the car. As she doubled over with one hand braced on the hood, Finn watched her. Not grieving was one thing; staying in the car while she grieved was another. Zac got out and rounded the car to stand beside her. A wave of hurt rolled into him. Her bent body heaved once with a quiet gagging sound, but she didn't throw up.

Zac placed his hand on her back, between her shoulders. She stood with hands clenched, turned and almost walked smack into him, as if blinded. Her forehead would have collided with his nose, so he took a step back and set his hands on her shoulders.

"Anna," she said, eyes unfocused. "Anna's gone."

"I'm sorry."

"Someone killed Anna."

Maybe. "I'm so sorry, Cady."

After a long silent minute, she pressed her palm to his flannel shirt as if just noticing how close they stood. Her eyes met his, filling not with tears but with an anger that lifted off her like smoke.

"Someone killed Anna."

On the other side of the car, Finn opened

his door and got out.

"I'll come with you, Finn," Cady said.

"You'll sleep the whole time. As long as you're still recovering, I'll move faster without you."

She glared. "He has to pay for what he did."

"If you're right, I'll make sure he does."

"What would be this guy's motive?" Zac said. Someone had to talk some sense. "Why take their lives?"

"I'll know that when I catch up to him," Finn said.

When, not *if.* They couldn't be expected to think straight right now. Zac held his hand out for the letter, and Finn gave it over carefully. Zac reread.

"I don't care why." Cady's tone took on a harsh frustration. "Maybe he likes killing and figured out we're a bigger challenge."

Colm.

It was impossible. But Anna hadn't dated the letter. Suppose they'd been dead a month? *No, stop. Think.* "You talked to Anna. Eight days ago, you said?"

She nodded.

Zac's chest emptied in a sigh. Not Colm. The man had been dead for weeks. And that left . . . "It's Doc."

"But he's —" Cady's voice broke. "He's a

doctor. He cared for our town, Zac. He cared about us."

"Us too."

Her voice dropped to a whisper as if the alternative would be to scream. "Now he's rescinding that care? Now he deceives his patients, his friends? Not Dr. Noel."

"If someone did coerce them into this . . . Who else but Doc would know us for what we are?"

"All right," Finn said. "If it's Doc, I'll find him."

Zac held up his hand. "How? He's going to have to find you two."

Finn frowned. "He should have by now, however he found the others. Four of us lived in a ten-mile radius. How'd he miss Cady and me?"

Zac shook his head. "And if he thinks he's doing right by us, he shouldn't be hiding his identity. We're missing some things."

He leaned against the car and looked up at the sky and wished he understood it all. He shut his eyes for a moment. Maybe he could ask David to pray. For all of them.

"I'll grab a flight into St. Louis," Finn said.

"Finn, I'm telling you as her best friend, Anna would never do this."

Time to give them privacy to talk. Zac touched his palm to Cady's shoulder. Her eyes glittered with defense, desperation, but no accusation. He wasn't an intruder to them. Well, he wouldn't cross that line if he could help it. He crossed the blacktop and paced the length of the diner.

He imagined Finn hunting Doc down, the odds long on finding him, but if he did . . . The man who shot David in an open parking lot because he felt cornered would not wait to hear explanations, not while mourning four family members. Heck, in his place anyone would have difficulty with that.

After a minute Finn ambled over. "Thanks."

"Want a wingman?"

"Why?"

Zac shrugged. "Looks like you could use one."

"Cady." Finn glanced back at her as she got back into the car.

"David and Tiana will keep an eye on her. Tiana is kindness personified, and —"

"It's not just that. I don't see what she's saying, Zac. I really don't. But she did know Anna better than anyone else did, maybe even James. And if Doc or someone is after us, then he could get to her while I'm gone. She could be dead before I . . ." Finn covered his eyes with one hand.

Wavering objectivity there. "Hey."

After a moment Finn lowered his hand and met Zac's eyes, his expression still flat.

"Once he decides he's on your team, David is a first-rate guardian," Zac said. "We'll fill him in."

Finn frowned. Looked back at the car, where Cady still huddled in her seat. "I don't know."

"Okay, listen. You saw us leave the park that night. After."

Finn nodded.

"Who was carrying the saber?"

"David was."

"I couldn't go through with the — the execution. So David did, as" — Zac cleared his throat — "as my friend, and because it had to be done. He doesn't flinch."

Finn swallowed hard. "She'll be in good hands."

"Some of the best I know."

"You're sure."

"I'd never leave her here otherwise."

Zac held out his hand, and Finn shook it with a firm, callused grip. "Thank you."

"Let's go get this done and come back to her as soon as we can."

Zac didn't say the rest: come back to stay. Somehow he already knew he wanted them to. It was a need with a scope that felt larger than his own. It would have felt like a nudge from God Himself, if those still happened to him.

TEN

He had told Cady, "I'm going along," and she'd reached for his hand and squeezed it. He'd given the same news to David, recounted everything they'd pieced together so far, and received a scowl and a "mind your back." David might have meant generally, or he might have meant vigilance against Doc, or he might have meant lingering suspicion toward Finn. Whatever.

The fastest means would be a flight from the tiny Traverse City airport to Detroit and another flight from Detroit to St. Louis. But the limited departure times from Traverse City meant a delay of almost twenty-four hours. Finn declared they would drive to Detroit, where the next flight to St. Louis departed at 4:35 that afternoon. To make it they'd have to break a few speed limits.

Carry-ons stowed in the back seat, Zac began the drive while beside him Finn tapped his phone to book the flight. Zac swallowed a few times, or tried to. Just yesterday he'd acknowledged his current incapability of getting on a plane. At least he didn't have to get on two.

"First class."

" 'Course," Finn said, thumbs still tapping.

"Are they —" His throat closed. He cleared it. "Are they letting you choose seats?"

"Nah. Too close to departure."

Zac kept his grip relaxed on the wheel. He wasn't driving toward actual danger, only perceived danger. In the matter of low ceilings, his brain was unreliable. Was a major screw-up of tsunamic proportions. All he had to do was refuse to listen to his brain. He was fine. He had an Ambien in his carry-on, which he'd take before they boarded.

"Booked," Finn said and set the phone aside.

"You know, Simon would be good to have onsite. He was a cop, retired in 1976."

Finn rested his hands on his knees and continued watching out the windshield. "Walked a beat? Or detective?"

"Both. He was in homicide when he quit. Might see something we miss."

"If you think he'll come, I'd be obliged."

Another surprise. Figuring this man out was going to take a while. Zac brought up Simon's contact just as he had this morning while battling to breathe. This time he went through with the call.

"Hey," Simon said.

"You got a minute?"

The hesitation was slight. "Yeah. What's up?"

"Did David call you?"

"About our gunman who's not dangerous after all?" Predictable skepticism dripped from the words.

Zac told him everything that had happened in the last day, and Simon responded with a few grunts along the way. Finn never looked from the highway in front of them.

"We've got to solve it," Zac said. "Confirm it's Doc. Figure out why he's doing this. Stop him."

"Stop him how? Sounds like it was voluntary."

"Cady doesn't think so." Still no glance from the man beside him.

"But Finn does."

"Yeah."

"And you're running off to Missouri to investigate."

Zac shrugged. "Nothing else to do."

"I guess you want me to join you."

The tone told him all he needed to know. "This affects all of us, man."

"Not arguing the point."

"But?"

A long sigh, maybe a little strained. "Zac, I can't leave right now. Some things here are . . . time sensitive."

"More so than someone hunting longevites and curing them to death?" The guy defied explanation. Zac shook his head at the silence on the other side of the call, free hand tightening on the wheel. "They're family."

"Maybe so."

"But you won't come."

"If I can, I will."

It didn't deserve a response, but they were about a century past petty temper, so Zac said, "Okay. Thanks," before he hung up.

Finn said nothing.

Zac gestured, phone still in hand. "Time sensitive. Are you kidding me? He works in a lab now. Blood work et cetera. Normal mortal job, no reason he can't call in for a few days."

"He doesn't know us," Finn said.

"Not the point."

"Sure it is. He'd come if you were dead." The glance was the first he'd sent Zac's way since they started driving. "Did I blunt that?"

Zac laughed. "Well, you made it blunt."

"Right."

They'd be driving long enough for Zac to hear the man's entire life history, if Finn wanted to tell it. Twenty wordless minutes suggested he didn't. And this silence wasn't the easily occupied current that buoyed Zac and David toward confronting Colm's place. This silence was held by a man who didn't find release in words.

The hours dragged. Halfway down the state, Finn shifted in his seat.

"It's strange," he said.

Zac flicked a glance at him. *It* could refer to a lot of things at the moment.

"Going off on a mission, the guy next to me is always James. Once we were at a concert, and this guy grabbed Cady's purse and took off. 'Course we took after him. Got her purse back. James clocked him a good one, but we didn't hurt him. One time some raccoons got into their chimney, and he called me yelling and cussing at like four in the morning with Anna in the background telling him to stop cussing — and I came over and we were up on the roof after those coons."

Stories. Life lived. Sacred ground. Zac

drove and kept quiet while the torrent of words continued to cascade from Finn.

"He made me come with him to buy her ring. I told him, 'You're the one marrying her, you pick it out.' He said sure he would, he just wanted me at his shoulder while he did it. Like we were heading into battle or something."

Zac chuckled. "He sort of was."

"Y'all were in civilized country, I guess, back in the old days. Not Westerners."

"No," Zac said. "Illinois."

"Right. You said that before."

"Little prairie town. I worked at the mercantile when I came of age, bought it out when I could. Worked at that until our faces forced us on, but we never went far."

"Me and James, we rode herd together until the twentieth century came along. He was the best man with a rope I ever saw. Don't think he ever really got over the end of open range, even to this day."

Zac nodded.

Finn looked out the side window for a few minutes then out the windshield again. "I keep thinking it ought to be him driving. Him helping me solve this thing. Only it's him I'm putting to rest, and it just don't seem right."

"It isn't right."

Finn ran a hand down his face. "Death isn't right."

He said not another word until they had parked Zac's car in the airport lot. Now that Zac wasn't driving, he dug into the side pocket of his backpack for the pill.

"What's that?" Finn said.

"Ambien." Heat crept up Zac's neck.

Finn's brow furrowed.

Shoot. He had to tell him. "Keeps me chill."

"Fear of heights?"

"No, um, closed spaces." His face grew as hot as his neck. "Should kick in by the time we board."

"Going to knock you out?"

"Nah. Just keeps me from . . ." Trying to claw his way through the side of the plane.

Finn nodded as if this were a normal conversation. Then his brow furrowed. "We don't see doctors. For anything, ever."

Zac chuckled. "Same here."

"But it's . . . Oh, right, cheap on the street."

"You're quite the law-abiding longevite."

"When I can be." His mouth pulled up, as if Zac had contributed to an inside joke. Then he hoisted his backpack. "Come on, look at the time. We might have to run."

And that was it. Finn knew the thing that

could cripple Zac, and nothing changed. Zac took a breath, and it came deep and easy.

They did run. Their gate was on the other side of the building, and Zac's experience flying in three weeks ago had educated him on the labyrinth that was the Detroit airport. The exertion, such as it was, ensured he was nothing short of alert as they stepped onto the boarding ramp. By the time they found their row, cold sweat had beaded on Zac's neck.

"Here," Finn said. "You want the window or — ?"

"Aisle." He all but choked on the word. Finn didn't seem to notice.

Given Zac took only one or two a year, a pre-flight sleeping pill usually helped him. Usually. If this was one of the exceptions, he had to deal with it now while he could. Checklist time.

Deep breathing. Tactile anchor: he curved his fingers around the arm of his seat. Visual anchor: he studied his hand, familiar and his, creases in the knuckles, a slightly raised vein across the back, stubbed nails. The scar on his thumb, 1883, left by the broken chimney of a kerosene lamp. The scar on his little finger, 1958, left by the top of a can of diced tomatoes. He glanced away from his hand, and his breath caught at the sight of the ceiling and the microscopic window. *No. Calm down.* He visualized himself relaxed in a La-Z-Boy at Moira's, black leather upholstery that felt enough like the vinyl pressing his palm now. He was sitting in that chair. He was watching Moira paint one of her square canvases. Crazy what people would pay these days for a fourteen-by-fourteen stretched canvas. She laughed when he said so: *"Crazy what people will pay for anything these days."* Her hand on the brush, the little strokes creating light on water and tufts of grass around the edge of the lakeshore. The crackling in her fireplace across the room. The smooth taste of wine on his tongue as he sipped from crystal so old he couldn't believe she still used it. But that was Moira. Nothing serviceable should be enshrined simply because of age.

"And if it breaks?" he'd said once.

"Then its time is ended."

The memory kept his lungs open until a chime sounded over his head and drew him up from the past. He blinked. His grip eased on the arm of the chair. The sweat had dried on the back of his neck. Finn was watching something on the airline TV. At Zac's glance, he turned his head but left the earbuds in his ears.

How much longer? Zac swallowed the pathetic question. He gave a thumbs-up, and Finn nodded and returned to his movie.

Zac risked a look around him. Above him the seat belt light had come on, and the turbulence warning was finishing over the speakers. He felt okay, a hint of lethargy in his limbs, nowhere near the verge of hyperventilating. So the drug was doing its job after all. He stretched his legs. Checked his phone for the time. They'd been in the air about thirty-five minutes. One-third over, two-thirds remaining.

He'd survive. He always did.

ELEVEN

The people for whom Ambien lasted four hours were using it to sleep, not to impede traumatic stress response; such was Zac's reasoning for why he could disembark wide-eyed from a plane regardless of the duration of the flight. They rented a car, and he offered to do the driving again.

The suburb of Warrenton sprawled about an hour from the airport, and the longevites had lived another fifteen minutes past it, rural outskirts where everyone owned at least five acres by ordinance. Finn navigated, the only words he spoke until Zac coasted the car up the gravel driveway he pointed out. Dusk was falling, darkness delayed here by the depth of the sky unblocked by buildings or trees. They could see without need for flashlights though seven had come and gone, daylight saving time still in effect for the next few weeks.

The house was a beige Cape Cod with

blue shutters. Behind it stood a small pole barn. Zac shut off the car and waited for Finn to move first. Long minutes they sat there, still and silent.

"Finn," Zac said at last.

"They could be inside."

"You were here a few days ago. The letter was all you found."

"They might've come back sick with the cure. Or he might've brought them here, after."

"Well, you've got a wingman for a reason." Zac's hand went to the door.

"I'm no coward." With the bitten words, a spike of emotion singed the air in the car.

Zac opened the driver's door but didn't get out. At last Finn rubbed his nose and gave a quiet, lost sigh.

"I have to do it," he said.

A near echo of the words Zac had spoken at Colm's grave, preparing to send him into it. But David had pried Zac's fingers from the saber hilt, had shouldered the burden of executioner. A kindness Zac could never pay back but could, here and now, emulate in a small way.

"I'll go first if you want. So you know what you're walking into."

Finn swallowed, nodded, but didn't wait in the car. When Zac headed for the porch,

Finn waved him to the two-car garage and entered the code, and the door rolled up. Inside sat a black pickup truck and a gray two-door, both dusty from the unpaved road.

"James's truck, Anna's car," Finn said as he swiped a key on a leather fob from a pegboard on one wall. "My first warning. We'd been thinking they were off somewhere."

"Anything else strange?"

"Just the letter." He opened the door into the house, shut the garage, and nodded Zac inside.

Zac stepped into an immaculate laundry room. He inhaled through his nose but caught no odor other than a hint of vanilla and caramel room freshener. He stepped through to the kitchen. No dishes in the sink, no crumbs on the counter. He opened the refrigerator. Mostly empty, no leftovers in glassware, only reasonably long-lived items: plastic bottles of salad dressing, coffee creamer. Jars of pickles and pesto sauce. Nothing that would spoil in the next few days.

"You cleaned out the fridge?" he called to Finn, a question he might not have thought to ask if he hadn't just done the same at Colm's.

He wished he knew how long his thoughts would relate things to Colm. When they would stop. If there was a way to hurry them up.

"No," Finn called.

Odd, because somebody must have. Zac passed into the living room. Not a throw pillow out of place. Had they resisted Doc, surely something would be overturned, displaced. Unless Doc had tidied up. After all, he hadn't wanted his role revealed. Zac circled the lower level, peeked into the guest room. It was more of a study, with desk and bookshelves and upholstered rocking chair. Nothing amiss here either. He called back down the hall to Finn.

"Lower level is clear."

Finn's hikers scuffed over the kitchen tile. "Okay."

Zac jogged upstairs, peeked into the bathroom and two small bedrooms. Nothing. He stepped into the master bedroom and froze. The comforter was stripped to the bottom of the bed, the sheets thrown aside. Zac's gaze darted around the room. Ghosts were fictional, yet a chilled breath seemed to sigh on the back of his neck. If they were indeed dead, they might have died here side by side. And someone had taken their bodies from the bed and left it disheveled.

Or they'd left the bed unmade the last night they slept in it, and his deduction was a long leap. Simon would probably be able to reconstruct the whole story if he stood here.

Finn's steps halted at the bottom of the stairs. "Anything?"

"Not really."

Finn met him in the bedroom doorway and looked past him.

"Only room that isn't spotless," Zac said.

"Doesn't mean anything."

"Well, what sort of housekeepers were they?"

"Like this." Finn gestured to the rest of the house. "Order."

Then it did mean something.

"Maybe they never made the bed. Not like anyone saw if they did or not."

Unless his lack of expression concealed it, the man wasn't spooked. Zac shouldn't be either. He watched Finn stop in the doorway of each room, satisfying himself, nodding, moving on, until he was ready to follow Zac downstairs.

"They haven't been back here," Finn said as they exited onto the back deck. "Not since I was here and found the letter."

"Did you go upstairs then?"

"No. But the lower level, nothing's been touched that I can see."

"Did you . . . ?" Zac's fingers curled as the chill again found his neck.

Finn stopped halfway to the red pole barn to face him. "Did I what?"

"Did you call out to them? I mean, call their names?"

His squint might indicate annoyance. "They obviously weren't home."

Then he plodded to the barn, and Zac followed. The barn too appeared undisturbed, mostly empty other than a John Deere lawn mower and a collection of garden utensils. Out the rear doors, past yard and field beyond, the view ended in a dense forest.

"Where's their property line?" Zac said.

"Along the back of the field. And this direction . . ." He turned ninety degrees to point. Then he went still.

"Finn?"

Finn headed toward a small hill past the pole barn, not much of a rise but picturesque and planted with a single oak tree. His stride lengthened, and Zac hurried to keep pace.

On the hill lay two mounds about six feet long. A thin carpet grew over them: grass, petite wildflowers, taller weeds. A deliberate distance from them, two more mounds, similar in length and width, but coverless. Fresh earth. Finn stumbled to the new mounds and dropped to his knees between them. His arms stretched out to lay a hand on each grave.

Zac knelt where he was, fifty feet back from the mounds. Finn's people. No, *their* people. Dead in the ground. Finn bowed his head. Zac looked out over the land, eyes open for the appearance of a neighbor, but the nearest houses were acres away. After a few minutes he approached and crouched on the other side of one of the mounds. Finn's face was an utter blank.

"Finn."

Finn closed his eyes, and his words slipped into each other, his tongue seeming to shuffle them. "God be here please now close by."

The rockslide of a prayer seared Zac to his core. His own eyes closed, reflex or reverence, he couldn't tell. He gripped his knees.

After a little while Finn pushed himself up from the ground, the rawness of the prayer gone from his eyes. Zac blinked at the shift in the man.

Finn gestured to the other graves, the two that might have been weeks old but no more. "Sean. Holly. We buried them. The four of us together."

"You didn't see this before? The others?"

Finn pressed his palm to his head. After a moment he turned back to the house, his eyes catching the bright white beam of the barn's floodlight, activated by the waning day.

"I didn't look."

Not even after he'd found the note?

They trudged down the hill to the house. In the laundry room, Finn removed his shoes and then gave a fractured laugh.

"Guess it doesn't matter anymore if I take my shoes off."

Some door in the man swung on a precarious hinge, neither open nor closed, but he seemed to want to keep it open. Well, Zac would be the doorstop. He removed his shoes too.

"Anna?" Zac said.

"She was ridiculous about dirt. Clutter. All of it."

Yet she hadn't made the bed.

They hadn't eaten in hours. Zac didn't expect Finn to be hungry, but he was the one to suggest dinner. The fridge empty, they ordered delivery pizza with the toppings preferred by the carnivorous sex, which included every guy Zac had ever met until the asparagus-and-mushroom-craving David Galloway. The food was halfway eaten when Zac set his current slice aside. Time to talk.

Finn spoke before he could. "Doc ought to be lurking; he hasn't finished the job."

"Something's off about this," Zac said. "A lot of things, actually."

"What do you mean?"

"The scenario doesn't work. He killed them in cold blood, and then he cleaned out the fridge. He forced the cure on them, and then he carefully buried them beside their family."

"Maybe Anna cleaned."

"Before or after he forced her to write the note?"

Finn shook his head.

"We have to consider everything."

"So my friends chose the serum, knowing they'd probably die."

Ouch. The stone face had just experienced a tremor. "It's what you've believed the whole time."

Finn stared down at the remaining pizza. "Cady being so sure . . . she made me wonder."

"Well, Doc has answers. But I don't know what to do about that. Not like we can inquire at the hotels."

"There's a dozen hotels in Warrenton. Could be in any one. And it's been two days now since we left."

"How old was he when you met him?" Zac said.

"Somewhere in his forties, I guess."

That fit. Doc had been no more than five years older than Zac, in his thirties when he left Fisher Lake. So he hadn't taken the serum yet when he went west instead of east. "Did he live there long?"

"Sure," Finn said. "Ten years or so."

"And he got older."

"His hair grayed a lot. And he got thinner with the illness, so if it was terminal, the serum wasn't in him to cure it."

Yet at some point he must have taken it. Not that Zac had expected to discover Doc's trail if the guy was trying not to leave one, especially in the age of privacy rights, but if they couldn't offer a description, that ended all possibility.

He kept working on the pizza. He'd been ignoring food too often lately.

Neither of them spoke for a while, and then Finn said, "I'll have to tell the neighbors there was an accident."

"Okay."

"And I want to see the Wisters, friends of ours from way back."

"How far back are we talking about?"

"About thirty years."

Zac's shoulders tensed. He tried to nod, but the motion was stiff.

"We've been trusting them a long time." When Zac didn't answer, Finn tilted his head. "No mortals like that with y'all?"

"Not currently. There's Tiana, David's girl, but I've known her only a few weeks."

Zac got up, stretched, and moved to the window. All this uncertainty, and now Finn wanted to go talk to some mortals who knew their greatest strength and vulnerability. His limbs itched for some kind of exertion, some way to shed the last day.

"They don't have to know you're Elderfolk," Finn said.

"Definitely not." Zac ran his thumb along the window frame. "Simon's wife, Beth, died a few years back . . . shoot, eleven years now. It doesn't feel that long. Anyway, until Tiana, she was the last mortal in our circle."

He glanced over his shoulder. Finn was watching him, studying.

"I'm friendly with mortals, neighbors in my Denver apartment, a few friends I camp with, you know. Online I interact with strangers all the time. But . . ."

"I get it," Finn said. "And I guess it's different for you, being sort of a celebrity. That whole thing is weird to me."

"My typical day doesn't include paparazzi."

"But hasn't it shifted things for you?"

"How so?"

"I don't know. Just seems it would."

"I'm having a great time with it, honestly." A smile tugged Zac's mouth. "And I've seen ways to do good with it. Trying to fulfill that as long as people still want selfies with me."

"Guess it doesn't make them any younger. Or us any older."

"We're not so old."

Finn huffed. "Depends on the day."

Zac shut up. He was wrong to talk about age to a guy who'd seen it blow into his friends like a north wind and steal their souls from suddenly crumbling bodies.

"The Wisters have a condo about twenty minutes away," Finn said. "We meet for dinner once or twice a month. We moved here a year after they did, figured we'd stay as long as they lived."

Zac nodded.

"Sure didn't figure on . . ." Finn ducked his head and pushed the pizza box across the table.

Over the next hour, the pizza disappeared. Finn cleaned up, waving off Zac's move to help. Not much to do, but he was meticulous about it. As he threw away the pizza carton and hand-washed the plates, the sense took hold of Zac again that Finn's expressions and body language would never reveal his real self. The heaviness on him weighted the air, and something else lurked too. Something unique to Finn, something that left an occasional buzz, like an electrical current with a short.

Zac paced. A problem was poking his brain. He couldn't fall asleep and let Finn witness a night attack.

"I'll keep watch," he said. "In case Cady's right."

Finn frowned. "She never said he broke in and injected them in their sleep."

"Might as well play it safe."

A long sigh, a palm to his forehead. "Stay up all you want. I can't."

Fair enough. One of them might as well be rested in the morning.

Twelve

They packed a few things from the house, including James's laptop, which Finn said held all the information they'd compiled on themselves. Unlike Fisher Lake, Doc didn't leave his second group of ageless patients with the research journal pertaining to them. Maybe he'd started to realize how powerful his serum was, wanted to protect it from the wrong hands.

They also packed a few items Finn said Cady would want. To the car Zac carried a handmade quilt from the guest room bed, squares of ivory and pink and orange bordered in yellow. Under one arm Finn tucked an oatmeal-colored throw pillow from the couch, embroidered with a pine tree and script that read GET OUTDOORS. In his free hand he held a framed cross-stitch square. The design was a brown bird sitting on a nest and above it carefully stitched words: FEAR NOT, THEREFORE; YOU ARE OF MORE

VALUE THAN MANY SPARROWS. MATTHEW 10:31.

They stowed the items in the back seat, and Finn drove down the gravel driveway.

"Did they believe too?" Zac said.

"In God?"

Zac gestured at the cross-stitch lying on the dashboard. "In the whole scripture. In who Christ is."

"Yeah. They did."

"What about Holly and Sean?"

Finn was quiet until they reached the nearest neighbors, a couple named the Rooneys. As he pressed their doorbell he said, "No."

No one came to the door. As they left, Finn said, "Sean was the most confident atheist I ever met. Holly called herself a spiritual person. Whenever it came up, she told me to relax. She said she loved the people and animals of the world, and at the end of our lives, whatever gods exist would see that."

The second house belonged to a woman named Nicole, who Finn said had known the four longevites for a few months, just moved up from Florida. She came to the door with her phone in her hand and her purse on her shoulder.

"Oh Finn, hi. You just caught me on my

way out the door. Got an interpreting job in an hour."

"You have to go?"

"I have a few minutes." She adjusted her purse strap and held out her hand to Zac. "Hi, I'm Nicole."

Zac shook her hand. "Zac. We won't keep you, but we do need a few minutes."

"Are you a police officer?"

What on earth made her ask that? Their somber expressions probably. "Just a friend."

"What's going on?"

"This past Monday," Finn said, "James and Anna were out in California, visiting friends of ours. They were in a car accident."

"Oh, that's awful. Are they in the hospital out there? Let them know I can water Anna's flowers until she's back. I have once before — I know exactly what to do."

Finn blinked as if her words left him lost, but his voice didn't waver. "They died, Nicole."

"They . . . what?"

"They're gone."

Her purse slid down her arm and dropped to the porch. "I . . . I . . . they're both gone?"

"Yes." If his expression could flatten further, it was doing so now.

"Finn, I'm so sorry. When is the service?"

"I'm flying out there with Cady. Nothing's sure yet. I just wanted you to know why they're . . . why you won't . . ."

One second Finn was carrying the act without a flinch. The next his words seemed to stall. Zac stepped nearer.

"There's something you can do, Nicole."

She picked up her purse and fingered the strap. "What's that?"

Zac pointed to the house between. "Those are the Rooneys?"

"Yeah, Jimmy and Jill."

"We're flying out today. Would you let them know what's happened? And any other neighbors who need to know?"

"Oh, of course. I'm so sorry for your loss, Finn. And Zac — you knew them?"

Best to keep it simple. He nodded.

"I'm so sorry."

"Thank you."

"Their lights were on last evening. Were you there late?"

"That was us. You didn't see anyone lurking the last couple days, did you?" Zac feigned a shrug. "I'm just concerned about the house being vacant. I expect it will be for a while."

"Oh, there's been nobody that I saw. I didn't even realize they'd gone anywhere, but now that I think of it, I guess I didn't see them come home the last few days. The garage has been shut too. But crime out here is minimal. Let that be the last thing you worry about right now."

"That's good to know. Thanks."

"Thanks," Finn said then turned and walked down the porch steps back to the car.

"What a terrible loss," Nicole said, watching him. "It comes in waves, I know. I lost my brother a few years ago."

"I'm sorry," Zac said.

She blinked, tears surfacing. "They were good neighbors."

They said goodbye, and Zac went to the car. Finn had put the key in the ignition but sat in the passenger seat this time. Zac got in behind the wheel.

"Drive," Finn said.

Zac obliged. With no other destination, he began to turn into James and Anna's driveway.

"No," Finn said. "Keep going."

Zac drove to the end of the road and stopped at the four-way sign. "Where to?"

"I don't care."

Okay. Zac rolled down his window and took a long drink of the air outside. He turned left and drove down a wide blacktop road, corn and soybean fields on one side, widely spaced houses on the other, autumn's crispness in the cloudless blue expanse above him. The gas tank was full, so he let the miles roll away.

A quarter hour later Finn said, "Nicole won't see them anymore. And I won't see them."

He'd see Anna and James. Eventually. Zac knew that as surely as he knew he would see Colm again. These people had the hope of glory. Zac had thrown it away.

"I forgot we could ever leave," Finn said. "I still knew, but day to day I forgot."

Had Zac done the same before Colm forced him to remember? Maybe.

Finn pressed his palm to his head. "It's a little late to ask, but what do you think of the odds? Of tracking him?"

"I never thought they were great."

"But you came anyway. On a wild-goose chase."

Zac shrugged.

Finn gave him a squint that might have held suspicion. "You wanted answers too."

"Sure."

"And I'm too unreliable to get them myself. Is that it?"

Zac gave a sigh that came from the depth of sleepless nights and the need to scale a dune or two. “I didn’t know, man. I don’t know you, not really, and this thing is . . .”

“Yeah,” Finn said, then after a minute, “I want to see the Wisters. And we’ll grab some things from Cady’s place. And I guess then we’ll go back to her without a lead on Doc.”

“Maybe she’s had time to process all this. Accept what Anna wrote to her.”

“Without proof? Don’t count on it.”

THIRTEEN

"Why, it's Finn."

The door opened wider to reveal a man in his seventies, his face crinkling with a smile that brightened his eyes and gathered wrinkles in their corners. He was about Zac's height, and he'd beaten baldness by shaving his head, probably long ago. He motioned both Zac and Finn inside, shut the door, and offered his hand to Zac.

"Matthew Wister."

"Zac Wilson. Good to meet you." Matthew's grip was feebler than Zac expected given his sharp gaze.

"Any friend of Finn's. But what brings you over here at ten in the morning?"

Finn's fingers curled into his palms. Matthew noticed the gesture, glanced from him to Zac and back again.

"Something's happened, Matthew." Finn's voice had hushed.

The room seemed to draw in its breath

and hold it. Matthew gave a slow nod. "I'd better get Ruth. I think she's out feeding her birds."

"I'll get her," Finn said.

He disappeared toward the back of the house, his stride easy, his way sure. With a slower gait, Matthew led Zac to their kitchen and offered him a seat at the table. He turned away to rummage in a cupboard.

"Coffee? Tea? How long have you known Finn?"

"No, thanks. And long enough to know he's got one of those faces that never seems to age."

Matthew took a tea tin from the cupboard and shut the door but kept his back to Zac. "I hadn't noticed."

"Finn says differently."

Tension gripped the man's shoulders, straightened posture that had a moment ago been comfortably hunched. Zac should have realized before — would have, surely, if his thoughts weren't submerged in the sludge of sleep deprivation — that he could not reveal his knowledge without causing suspicion. A man Finn had never mentioned knowing, a man with a face as young as Zac's, should not have the knowledge.

Too late. Besides, they couldn't have discussed anything as long as Matthew and his wife thought they had to protect Finn's great secret.

Stiff now, Matthew turned to set the tin on the counter between them. "Sir, the man we're speaking of is very dear to my wife and me. If you mean him any hurt, I'll do what I can to stop you."

"I get why you don't trust me. But Finn will tell you —"

"Maybe I should try digging something up on you in return. These days secrets are uncovered on the internet; what would I find?"

A social media following of nearly a million individuals. A video of a tiny figure falling from a tightrope, flailing its way down toward death until it disappeared behind rock outcroppings. Zac forced himself not to look away as he gestured to Matthew: *Go ahead; look me up.* In the quiet, the cuckoo clock on the wall behind him piped the half hour. A faint bubbling noise that must have been an aquarium sounded from a nearby room. A door slid open and shut, and a woman's voice reached them.

"Let me make you some green tea."

"Maybe later," Finn said as they entered the kitchen.

"Finn," Matthew said. "What's going on? Who is this person?"

Finn glanced at Zac long enough to convey a promise: he wouldn't reveal what Zac had asked him not to. He shrugged. "He's Zac. We covered that."

"Why is he here?"

"He's here as a friend."

"Since when?"

Finn frowned. He didn't put it together — the significance of the query. "Since a few days ago, I guess."

"But you told him."

Ruth drew in a quick breath. "Told him what?"

"Yes," Finn said. "He knows we're old. Me, Cady — all of us."

"All of you?" Matthew folded his arms over his concave chest as he turned on Zac. A giveaway gesture. Fear for his friends.

Zac could assuage it. He had only to disclose his own birthday. He kept his mouth shut.

"Later," Finn said. "Right now I've got to say what I came for."

Matthew carried the tea tin to the table and sat, the stoop returned to his shoulders. "All right then. We're listening."

Each of them moved to join him. Zac sat with his back to a corner, facing the cutaway wall. Finn sat across from the Wisters, folded his arms on the table, and told them the story. Ruth was in tears before he finished. Matthew sat trembling, his lips parted as if he would speak, but he didn't.

"Oh Finn," Ruth whispered. "All four of them?"

Finn nodded.

"I miss them already."

Another nod.

She palmed the tears from her cheeks, but they continued to fall into the corners of a smile that drew her face into bunches of wrinkles. "But oh, James and Anna. Sweet Anna meeting Him at last." Her veined hand lifted in a gesture at herself. "Any day now, for Matthew and me."

"I know." Finn bowed his head.

"Oh Finn. I'm sorry."

"No. You're right. I haven't been able to see it . . . that way. Not yet. And with Sean and Holly, it's . . ." He looked up to meet her eyes again. "You know."

"I do. I have regrets with them."

"So do I."

"But they chose long ago, Finn."

"I know."

She reached across the table to set her spindly fingers over Finn's broad hand. "Have there been any signs for you or Cady?"

"I don't think so. We don't feel different.

But . . ."

"You said it hit fast. How fast do you mean?"

"Sean said something to us at lunch that day — that his heart felt strange, like the beats were slowing down. He asked if we'd ever felt anything like it, and none of us had. And then within a few hours, his hair was graying, and . . ." He gave a long sigh. "There's something else though. This didn't just happen to them."

"What do you mean?"

He pulled Anna's note from the pocket of his jeans. The edges had tattered further in the day since Zac had seen it. Finn handed it to Ruth, and Matthew leaned in. As she read, Ruth nodded, sighed, touched the lines, then looked up with new tears on her cheeks.

"You old children. What've I told you about turning out like Matthew and me? It's nothing to envy." She ran her thumb over the signature. "But I see Anna had to find out herself."

Finn took the letter back. "Cady's questioning it."

"What is there to question?" Matthew said.

He explained her theory, named Doc as their suspect, but before he'd finished Matthew and Ruth were shaking their heads.

"Maybe I can see it because of something James told me," Matthew said. "They missed being parents, grandparents, part of the raising of generations. Anna especially. To me this makes sense for them, for who they were."

Ruth nodded. "And as she says, they weren't risking much. Hard even to tell which of the possibilities would be worse."

She was crying as she said it, yet her eyes held no heartache. Zac studied every movement of her face, muscles that tightened and relaxed as she spoke. He must be staring, but he couldn't look away from her. The tears were for herself. The quiet radiance in her was for Anna and James. Ruth Wister's heart seemed to overflow into Zac's, a waterfall under which he stood frozen, feeling the pure depth of her feeling. He tried to find the word for it as she folded her hand again over Finn's.

"Finn, we can't let this eat us up. They're walking with the King, lifetimes of trouble fallen off them for good."

"I'm trying," Finn said.

She bowed her head over their hands and without transition said, "Almighty King Jesus, we wish we could see them once more here on earth. We weren't ready; we didn't know we needed to be. But You were ready to receive them, and for them I rejoice."

That was it. Ruth was rejoicing.

And her joy was flooding Zac's chest and rising all the way into his eyes and he had to get out of there.

He pushed to his feet, his chair skidding back over the tile. The three of them jolted at the noise, and Zac held up his hands, hoping to distract from his face. "I'm sorry. Please excuse me."

He fast-walked out the front door, down the porch steps, down the sidewalk. He dug his knuckles into his chest. Stupid. Of all the things he picked up from other people, joy in eternity should be a relief not a wrecking ball.

Someone was near. He glanced over his shoulder. No, nobody around. He lengthened his stride as if outpacing a pursuer. Creating distance from Ruth had stopped the overflow, but he was still filled with it. He stopped in front of a house with a wrought-iron fence running parallel to the sidewalk. He curled his hand around some pointed decorative thing and hunched under the weight of Ruth's joy, the weight of the way she'd spoken to Him. He squeezed the edge of the fence until it left an impression across his palm and he heard his own voice.

"God."

"He's here," David had said that night out on the dunes. Sure He was. He was everywhere. Didn't give Zac the right to speak to Him.

"I — If I could just —" He pushed away from the fence and broke into a run as the words continued pouring from the overflow of joy that was drowning him and souring in the pit of his own soul. "God, if — No. I can't, I won't, no."

The wind took the words away as he ran faster, words he didn't need, didn't want, didn't deserve to say.

Fourteen

By the time Zac had run himself out and returned to the Wister residence, Finn should have been waiting annoyed by the car. Instead Zac sat on the porch for at least fifteen minutes while their three voices drifted through the screen, too quiet for him to make out many of the words.

He did hear his name. Twice.

He gritted his teeth. Rudeness wasn't his way. He had to get a grip and stop escaping from people he would have embraced a month ago. He stood to rejoin them, but Ruth's joyful eyes were a memory too near. He caught himself pushing his knuckles to his chest, but it was an absent gesture now. The run had emptied him of everything he'd felt within the walls of the house. He'd stay out here until Finn emerged.

When Finn did, he was alone. He gave Zac the indecipherable squint and nodded to the car, and Zac got behind the wheel before Finn had the chance.

They drove without a word. For directions Finn let his phone do the talking. Soon they were pulling up the driveway of Cady's home, a gray-green bungalow decked in white trim and wrapped halfway around with a porch. Flower boxes and hummingbird feeders all around the house, a purple bike in the garage. Zac smiled at the female touches everywhere. Cady's vehicle was a compact pickup truck, salsa red. He smiled at that too.

"What are we taking back?" he said as Finn unlocked the door from the garage to the mudroom.

"Clothes and toiletries. Some other stuff."

"You plan on checking a bag?"

"Yeah. One of hers."

This time Zac hung back and Finn traipsed through the house as if he lived there. The possibility snagged Zac like a snare around a rabbit's neck. He paused between the mudroom and the kitchen and looked around the lower level as far as his line of sight would allow. A flannel shirt was tossed over the back of a chair, unisex buffalo check, and he waited for Finn to disappear upstairs before stalking to it and snatching it up. He held it out by the shoulders. A woman's cut and size. He sighed.

The living room held a small TV and a big sound system. One chair, one couch. Everything decorated in pleasant earth tones. He wandered everywhere but upstairs and had to chuckle at himself. He accused David of old-school piety, yet he couldn't walk into Cady's bedroom lest he feel like a cad.

Finn looked unfazed by the intimate environment he was leaving as he lumbered down the stairs dragging a wheeled suitcase.

"Finished?" Zac said.

"Got clothes for her, and this pink thing she keeps makeup in."

The latter was a waste of suitcase space. Cady didn't need makeup. "What else does she need?"

"Her laptop. For work." Finn wandered into the living room, frowning. "She probably misses her vinyl collection, but it's not like we can take her turntable and all. Anyway, we'll be home soon."

Zac's jaw tightened, but he had to expect this. Harbor Vale wasn't their home yet. Shoot, wasn't his home yet either. Well, mission to find Doc or no mission, that was going to change. As soon as they got back. He wanted to stay. He would stay.

"Did you call and ask her what she wants?" If so, he should have heard Finn's voice from upstairs.

"Right now I don't think she cares."

"Pick something nonessential. You know, a comfort item."

Finn tilted his head as if Zac were some escaped zoo animal.

"Come on, she's a grieving female in a strange place. She needs something from home."

"That's what the 'Get Outside' pillow is for. She got it for Anna and James as a housewarming present when we moved here. And I think it was also a joke."

But that belonged to Anna. Cady needed something of her own. Zac turned a slow circle, trying to see the decor from Cady's point of view. The wall art, the double-stacked bookcase, the retro record cabinet with frosted glass doors. Over the back of the couch was a folded blanket, a few strings pulled through and dangling. Its faded mauve clashed with the room's color scheme. Zac strode to the couch and picked it up. The thing had been worn so soft he feared ripping it.

"This," he said.

Finn seemed to appraise him. "She's had that since the fifties. I don't know how it hasn't fallen apart yet."

"Definitely this."

"Okay. And . . . maybe a book or two."

"She have a favorite?"

"She's into music biographies and vampires."

Zac's mouth must have fallen open. He shut it. "Vampires."

"Yeah, you know, immortality? She can't get enough of it." Finn nodded to one of the shelves.

Cady had shelved teen paranormal romances — a few so famous even Zac recognized them — beside *Dracula* and *'Salem's Lot.* He laughed.

"She has search term alerts sent to her email. Vampires, immortals, age reversal, fountain of youth. You'd think she'd have her fill from looking in the mirror." Finn shrugged.

"No, I get it."

"You do?"

"Sure." He couldn't explain it though. With nothing else to go on, he chose based on the condition of the book spines. The most battered were *A Nineteenth-Century Vampire Anthology,* one of the notorious teen novels, and a biography of the Bee Gees. "These."

"Whatever you say." Finn unzipped the

suitcase and stuffed the blanket and the books inside.

When they left Cady's, they had nowhere to be until their flight departed in six hours. Finn stated no need or desire to check on his own house, so Zac headed for the nearest town. Maybe they'd run into Doc while walking the streets.

Right.

They'd been driving in simple silence for maybe fifteen minutes when Zac's phone pinged from a cup holder in the middle console and, simultaneously, Finn's did from somewhere on his person. Zac glanced aside as Finn fished his phone from a front jeans pocket and tapped a few times.

"Well?" David or Cady. They were the only people on the planet who had both Zac's and Finn's phone numbers.

"Hold on, I'm —" All the breath seemed to gust from Finn's body, as if someone had punched his chest in with an armored fist.

"What?"

"Cady."

Zac's pulse spiked. He grabbed his phone and pulled up the text. THIS WAS WAITING FOR ME AT THE HOTEL. A photo attachment. He kept his hand steady on top of the wheel. The picture was of a handwritten note.

Cady, please forgive me for my grievous errors. I never intended what happened. I am so sorry. Please forgive me if you can.

Unsigned. The handwriting was an obvious mask, careful printing as if from a penmanship textbook, back when the art was still taught. A tremor ran down Zac's arm, and he put the phone down and replaced his hand on the wheel.

"He's there. He's after her." Finn's voice was strangled.

"He's there," Zac said. "Doesn't sound like he's hostile though."

"She was right all this time. It's a ploy like he pulled on James and Anna. He's going to kill her."

"Finn, we do not know that."

Finn palmed his forehead and closed his eyes. "God, please."

"Pull it together, man. Call her."

Finn didn't seem to hear him. He caved forward, straining the seat belt.

Okay then. Zac snatched up his phone and did it himself.

Her line barely rang. "Zac?"

"Yeah. Hey. You okay?"

"I'm a little freaked out."

"Where was the note?"

"Someone left it behind the guest counter."

"Someone like a skinny middle-aged scientist who's been middle-aged for a while?"

"They couldn't tell me. One of the clerks spotted it already sitting there in a sealed envelope with my name. They didn't think anything of it."

"Are you at the hotel now?" His pulse thrummed as he pictured her alone and Doc surveilling the place, surveilling her, a needle full of anti-serum within reach.

"Don't worry, I'm not going to stay here. I'll find a mall or something and keep in view of lots of people."

"No. Get to David."

"He's not any less vulnerable to this particular threat, Zac."

"Doesn't matter. He's a soldier and he was fairly paranoid before this threat ever showed up. And he's a six-foot-whatever male who works out and you're —"

"A five-foot-five female who works out."

"Cady, come on."

"All right, I hear you. I'll call him and ask if I can join him wherever he is."

"It's a weekday. He's at the bookstore. Win-win: public place and battle-trained bodyguard in one package. Okay?"

She sighed, and it came out shaky. Her voice did too. "Okay."

"You're fine to drive?"

"I've been sleeping since you left. I'm good as new."

"Stay on the phone with me until you get there."

"That isn't necessary."

"It is one hundred percent necessary. Don't hang up until you're with him."

She didn't respond, but she didn't hang up. After a minute she said, "We might be misjudging Doc's intentions. The note is asking me to forgive him, after all."

"I'm not taking chances with you."

That might not have come out right. She didn't speak for a few minutes, and he didn't either, picturing her now behind the wheel of her car, both of them driving toward each other in a way yet too distant for him to do a blasted thing if Doc appeared like a specter and drove a needle into her arm. He glanced at Finn. The man hadn't moved.

Noted. Finn could go from proficient to useless with one blow of bad news.

At last Cady's voice came. "Parking at the bookstore. Can I hang up now?"

"Do you have the note with you?"

"Yeah. I'll see you tonight."

"Go inside first."

This sigh was steadier, maybe exasperated. The chime of the bell over the door came through the line. "All right, Sir Guardian, I'm inside. Hi, Tiana. Can I talk to David?"

Tiana's voice, too distant for Zac to make out.

"Awesome, thanks." A brief pause then David's voice as he greeted her. "Zac? I'm hanging up now."

She'd asked no questions. Maybe because no answer would bring her family back. "If you'll put me on speaker, I'll fill you both in."

"Oh."

A moment later David's voice came. "Zac. What have you found?"

"Not much."

Other than two more graves. Heck, what a lousy way to tell Cady. No wonder she hadn't asked. But Zac told them everything he knew in the kindest wording he could find. Cady said almost nothing until it was her turn to inform David about the apology note.

When all had been told, David said, "All right. I'll not let you out of my sight. We can't assume Doc is stable or sincere."

"Agreed," Zac said. "We'll be back tonight."

"Good. See you soon."

Distant room noise disappeared; Cady must have turned the speaker off. She said nothing but didn't hang up.

"I'm sorry, Cady." There had to be something more, something better to offer her, but whatever it was he lacked it right now.

"We still don't know how it happened." Her voice quieted. "But thank you, Zac."

The call ended. She hadn't cried. She hadn't screamed or raged or denied it could be true or reacted in any way. Maybe she'd do all those things now that she was off the phone, but Zac's instincts whispered that she wouldn't.

Zac hung up and looked at Finn. "Hey. She's fine." Physically anyway. "She's at the bookstore."

Finn didn't move for a few seconds. When he sat up, he seemed stiff. Old. "Thank you."

"You good?" The guy did not look it.

"Was praying."

"You couldn't have prayed and acted simultaneously?" The bite to his voice wasn't planned, but it wasn't out of line either.

"Thanks for checking on her."

"I guess that's a no."

Finn said nothing for a while, and in the

meantime Zac cooled down. Peevishness didn't benefit the situation.

"It takes more for me to feel a thing," Finn finally said. "But when it happens, I don't get warnings; I mean, I don't get the low level of a thing, like most people do. Instead I . . ." He shook his head.

"Instead you're an emotional fault line."

Finn's brow furrowed. "What?"

"You know. All's quiet underground for years, and then out of nowhere the earth starts heaving."

"Guess that fits."

"Noted." And shoot, he ought to cut the guy some slack.

"You said she's with David?"

"Yep."

Finn sighed. "Going to be a long six hours."

Zac didn't deny it.

Fifteen

They arrived in Harbor Vale by eleven that night, a short flight and a long drive and little talking between them but little tension either. Finn took Cady's luggage and both computers and joined her at their hotel. Zac walked the streets near his apartment until the small hours of morning, avoiding the behemoth in his bedroom and daring Doc to approach a less defenseless longevite than Cady. He couldn't decide if he'd start pummeling the guy immediately or, in light of the apology note, allow a conversation first.

At some point he did have to sleep, which went as well as expected: three hours interrupted by an extended attack that, when it ended, left him pounding his fist into his pillow. He couldn't hit walls he didn't own with a satisfying amount of force, and his neighbors wouldn't appreciate even pulled punches.

True dawn eventually came. Running

pants. Fresh shirt. Socks and shoes. Keys in pocket. Go. Walk it out. He crossed a four-lane road to reach Harbor Vale's downtown. Maybe he'd breathe easier here, passing the bookstore and the bakery, shambling down Valerian Street all the way to the water. Had to be better than watching the sunrise in his apartment lot yet again, fingers digging into the bark of that patient tree until his lungs opened.

A woman in black-and-yellow workout clothes passed him at a clip, jogging pack around her waist, earbuds trailing their cord to the tiny iPod strapped to one pumping arm. The strawberry-blond braid down her back brought recognition through his distraction. It was Cady. As the thought flickered, he took in the rest of her. When she wasn't rejuvenating, Cady Schuster was in great shape.

She turned three strides later. Jogged in place as she said, a little winded, "Hey, Zac."

"Morning, Cady."

"Mind if I join you?"

Someone to walk beside him. It would help him breathe. "I'm not planning to match that pace right now."

"Few match my pace." She tugged the earbuds from her ears and twined them around the iPod's armband. "Especially when I'm messed up."

"I get you."

"A little low on stamina, thanks to the Elderfolk reset." She slowed to power-walk shoulder to shoulder with him. "No more notes behind the counter."

"Good."

They walked in silence awhile, and his chest began to open. Slowly.

After a few minutes he said, "You probably shouldn't be out here alone."

She glared at him outright.

"Just saying."

"Finn isn't the early bird type, and this is how I deal with things. Anyway, I have pepper spray in my pack."

More quiet. More air in his lungs. They'd hit the hour of the morning when the birds all seemed to wake in the same minute. Or maybe one woke and began its chirp and woke the birds in the surrounding trees, a ripple effect of song. A pleasant image either way.

"Finn's one of those people who can get in a run or a workout in the evening and still sleep soundly. It's kind of disgusting."

He tried to tell if she was talking to talk, feeling awkward. She didn't seem to be. "Have plans after this?"

"Some long-distance work from home. I

flip houses in Missouri. Most of it can wait, but I should try to straighten out a few things — scheduling and stuff."

"You have a crew?"

"Two guys work for me sometimes if it's a real fixer-upper. If it's just refacing, I do it myself. Finn likes to pitch in but never lets me put him on the payroll."

"You make money?"

"Usually."

Her smile, a mix of self-deprecation and contentment, held him for a moment. He wanted to touch her — her arm, her back — and fisted his hand to keep it still. They walked awhile, and the weight eased off him and his chest relaxed. He drank the brisk air into his lungs and held it there before letting it out.

Cady turned her head to catch his eye. "How are you doing?"

He gritted his teeth against the gentleness of the question, but she couldn't know. Could she?

"I'm not asking for details. Just seems clear I'm not the only one trying to outpace my troubles."

Outpace troubles. Okay. But his trouble was his own weakness, and he wasn't letting her in on that.

"You already know mine," she said. "In

vivid detail. If you want to talk yours out, you can."

The smirk came out, ever ready. "And then what? Pray for deliverance?"

She looked away. Well, he wasn't going to tell her any of it, not on a walk in the morning air, he unprepared for disclosure and she fitting perfectly into her workout clothes.

"Cady." He jolted at the plea in his voice. "I'm sorry."

"I wasn't trying to pry."

He was stupid.

Or smart. He didn't *want* to tell her about this crap. He really didn't.

She scanned their surroundings. He'd hardly noticed when they turned down Valerian, and now they stood at the end of the blacktop, a straight seam that met the sand in a little dip. She stepped off the pavement and headed for the water, a slow, thoughtful pace as she gazed up and down the beach. Zac stayed on the street and watched her go. Only fifty feet or so. She stood letting the gentle waves brush the toes of her shoes. Then she walked back to him.

"Finn told me the book selection was your idea. And the blanket. Thanks."

"Sure."

"How did you pick?"

"I figured anything in very used condition must be a go-to."

"Wise man. I saw the Bee Gees in concert seventeen times."

He danced forward a few steps, disco hands and sliding feet, impersonating Barry Gibb's falsetto through the last line of the "Stayin' Alive" chorus. Cady's laugh rang spontaneous and sweet.

"You've got perfect pitch," she said.

"Yep."

"And you're so humble about it."

"Well, it's not my doing."

"Any vocal training?"

"Nah. I worked at it on my own, you know, strengthening the muscles. I sing all the time." Or used to. He couldn't remember even breaking into a hum in the last month. He couldn't figure out why he was telling her this.

"My only talent is my ear," Cady said. "I never stuck with an instrument long enough to know what I was doing."

"Me neither. Some guitar dabbling, but I always fall back on having time to learn it later."

Sadness shadowed her eyes. They walked the rest of the way without words, but an ease worked its way in to replace her seeping sorrow. He didn't want to, but at last they reached the street where she'd first caught up to him.

"Thanks for checking your pace for me," he said.

"My pleasure."

He hoped so. She lifted her hand as their paths split. She power-walked away, and he enjoyed the view, but more than that, he looked forward to the next time he would hear her laugh.

He went back to his place, showered, and put on jeans and his old favorite pullover hoodie. Then, in the absence of a better plan, he drove into Harbor Vale and prowled the town. Maybe he would ask some of the store owners if they'd seen a white male tourist of uncertain age but no younger than forty.

While he prowled, shoulders hunched in the charcoal-gray hoodie, he pondered. When he passed Cousin Connie's Bakery, a new HELP WANTED sign was propped in the window, and he halted in front of it.

If he was going to live in Harbor Vale — and he was — he had to stop loafing.

Tiana would love it. And maybe stop worrying about him.

No, now wasn't the time for frivolity, but . . . well, maybe he needed something frivolous to break up the life-and-death monotony.

A bell tinkled above the oak door as he pushed it open. Two customers stood in line; one more browsed in front of the glass cases of cupcakes, pies, cookies, and fritters. He waited to one side until all three were gone, each with a brown cardboard box in hand, then approached the counter and the bakery's proprietor standing behind it. Connie Mazur was a tall woman in her late fifties, hair gone salt-and-pepper, hands broad, the skin on her knuckles worn thinner than one would expect for her age. She wore a green apron over a white collared shirt and jeans. As her customers ambled outside, she picked up a pair of plastic tongs and began turning fritters under a heat lamp. She set the tongs aside when she saw Zac.

"How can I help you?" She gave him the genuine smile of an artisan businesswoman who melded profits and passion every day.

Zac gestured to the sign in the window. "I'm hoping you'll give me that job."

She studied him a long moment, clasped her hands together, and leaned toward him. "No, I don't think I will."

He felt the muscles in his face slacken. He looked at the sign again, then back to her, trying to remember the last time an interaction with a mortal had swept his feet from under him.

"You're that celebrity who's been moseying around town the last few weeks."

"Well, quasi-celeb—"

"Movie stunt double or something, right?"

"No movies." She was still frowning at him. He pushed a hand through his hair. "Daredevil stunts, mostly."

"A YouTube celebrity."

"Accurate."

His honesty did nothing to soften her scowl. "And you were on that TV show with the obstacle courses."

"Right. *Warrior USA*."

"You don't look like much of a warrior to me."

Dusty memories tugged at him. The feel of his rifle in his hand, the heaviness of the helmet on his head, the popping of nearby guns and the rumble of distant artillery. His mouth went dry. He hadn't been a soldier, a true warrior, in seventy years. If ever.

"Fair enough," he said. "I still want the job."

"You don't need the money."

"Nope."

"I need somebody dependable."

This was getting ridiculous. "I'm dependable."

"For the time it takes you to find yourself while you hide out here in my town. That's why you're here, isn't it? The stunt that went wrong? Ducking the public eye for a bit. And then ten days from now you come in and say, 'Guess what, Connie, I found myself, and here's my notice.' And I'm back to putting the sign in the window and whoever would have wanted the job ten days ago has found another one."

So she was practical. He could work with that, and he wanted the job more now than he had when he walked in. A solution for both of them. Hmm.

"Okay," he said. "How about this: You leave the sign in the window. Somebody else comes along wanting the job, you replace me on the spot, no hard feelings."

"And if somebody doesn't?"

He spread his hands. "You're going into a busy season, aren't you? Thanksgiving and Christmas? You might as well have me while I'm here."

"Salesman at heart." She jabbed a finger at him.

Now the memories touched him with warmth. Standing behind his mercantile counter, laughing and chatting with his customers, nudging them toward one item or another. Quality items he knew they could use but wouldn't think to want. A smile spread over his face.

"Why this job?" Connie said.

He shrugged, an exaggerated motion. "I like cookies."

Her laugh was broad like her hands, tugging a grin from deep inside him, the place that had stopped singing.

"And people," he said.

"That I believe." She offered her hand across the counter, and he shook it. "Welcome to Cousin Connie's, Zac Wilson."

"Thank you, Connie."

"And who knows, maybe that celebrity face of yours will help me sell some pastries."

"You never can tell." He couldn't stop smiling.

"The job is mornings, eight to noon or maybe one if there's a line out the door, especially closer to the holidays. I have a college girl who works the second half of the day, after her classes."

"I don't want to take anybody's hours," he said.

"Be here at seven forty tomorrow morning and we'll get the paperwork processed."

"Yes, ma'am."

As he left he checked his phone notifications. His superfan Lucas had emailed him.

Zac, can you call soon? I have to talk to you and I can't type it.

His knees trembled. He leaned against the brick wall of the bakery and cradled the phone in one hand while his other hand made a fist. *Okay, chill out, no use getting scared.* The kid might want to talk about anything. But his heart was pounding. Something Lucas couldn't type. Only one thing that could be.

Zac tapped the screen to bring up Nate's contact information. He hit the Call icon. The phone rang.

"Hello, this is Nate Giordano; if you want a call back, please leave a message."

Zac cleared his throat before the beep ended. "Hey, Nate, it's Zac Wilson. I got Lucas's email just now, asking me to call. Please let me know if there's anything new going on or just, you know, how he's doing. Thanks." He ended the call, stood up, and thrust the phone back into his pocket.

Legs numb. Dread overflowing him like a cup held too long under a faucet. Nothing to do. Nate might call back in an hour. A day. His legs went from numb to twitchy. He began to pace. He envisioned himself out on the dunes, nerves working out of him in the strong stride of his legs carrying him upward, in the pumping of his arms and the sweat that would break out on his back if he climbed far enough. Everything that had happened in the last few days felt heavier with this final brick laid atop the rest.

He was overreacting. The kid wasn't prone to overstatements, but that didn't rule out the possibility. Zac didn't know anything yet, and he wouldn't until he got word on his boy.

No, not his. Only sometimes Lucas reminded him. Not *of* his sons — he didn't know the kid half well enough for that. But of the fact of his sons. The fact they had lived, grown old, and died, and on the day their hoary heads went to their graves, they remained his sons.

Nate Giordano should not face a grave like those. But all medical statistics promised he would.

Zac paced the parking lot and pumped his arms as he walked. He couldn't talk this out with anyone. None of them knew about Lucas.

"I did."

The smugness in that voice — Zac had heard it a thousand times in life. And he couldn't contradict it now. Colm had thought Zac crazy to continue contact with the family after his Make-A-Wish obligation was fulfilled. He shut the memory down and lengthened his stride. Colm was irrelevant.

Maybe one day he'd believe that.

He tried Nate's cell again, got voice mail again. He sank to the curb of the parking lot and cursed cancer, cursed mortal bodies that sickened and suffered and died. Once the outpour started, he kept going, folding his arms on his knees and spitting words no one heard. He cursed the cure that had taken Cady and Finn's family, never mind their eternal destinations. And he cursed himself for not knowing how to make any of it right.

Sixteen

At the bakery the next morning, Connie beckoned him in with a smile and a quick arch of her eyebrows. He would lay money she hadn't expected him to show up. He breezed through the paperwork, and then Connie gave him a quick tour of the baked goods and the idiosyncracies of the cash register. By then opening time had arrived, and she unlocked the doors.

Zac hadn't forgotten that he enjoyed selling things. But he might have forgotten how deep his enjoyment ran.

Muffins, donuts, and fritters were the hot morning items, breakfast for workbound folks. Connie told him cookie and cupcake sales would rise after lunch, and suddenly Zac wanted to be there for that shift too, to compare the inventory demand. Okay, so he might be getting into this a little more than he planned to. But it was fun.

He'd been there less than two hours when

a twentysomething woman walked in wearing jeans and tennis shoes and a pink hoodie that read I CLIMBED THE DUNES AT HARBOR VALE, MICHIGAN. She looked up from the donut case, saw him, and gasped.

"Whoa."

"Hey, what can I get for you?"

"You look exactly like Zachary Wilson."

"No way."

"I swear, you do." She gave a bounce on her feet that had to be involuntary. "You're him. Aren't you? I saw online somewhere, now that I think about it. You were touring the Great Lakes or something."

"Hmm." He pretended to ponder.

"Oh. My. Squee."

He laughed.

"This is unbelievable. Would — would you mind a selfie? If you don't mind. You can totally say no."

A lull had fallen over the bakery a minute before she walked in. He wasn't shirking other customers. He stepped out from behind the counter, they posed in front of the donuts, and he held the phone at her request when she denigrated her "stubby little arms," which appeared no shorter than average.

She was grinning as she took the phone

back. "Best souvenir ever. Thank you so much."

"No problem." He might be grinning too.

"Oh, and can I get a custard donut?"

"Sure thing."

As he wrapped it, her smile fell away. "Does this mean you're retiring?"

He laughed at the word, so meaningless to him. But concern gathered lines in her face. She cared about his answer. He handed her the brown bakery bag. "On hiatus, that's all."

"And selling pastries?" Red pushed into her face. "Sorry. Way too personal."

"When it's time for me to retire, I'll be public about it. Fair enough?"

"More than fair. Thanks. Wow. Um, thank you."

He nodded. With a last smile she left, nearly bumping into the next customer, whose artificially silver hair was the only identifier he needed.

"Well, hi," he said.

Rachel from the diner stood staring at him. "Hi yourself."

She stopped a few steps past the doorway. Zac smiled, but she didn't return it. The pause became awkward while he tried to figure out how to dispel it — treat her like a fan? Like a customer? She seemed like neither at the moment, ignoring the baked goods and somehow looking equally displeased with him.

"How can I help you?" he finally said.

"You work here?"

He gestured at himself behind the counter.

"I don't understand. Are you secretly broke or something?"

Nothing remained of the Rachel from a few days ago. No melancholy, no vulnerability. Today she was studying him like an entomologist recording the habits of a newly discovered insect species. Time to erect some boundaries.

Which was just as well. Today he lacked the emotional energy to offer a listening ear. Even his smile felt plastic.

"Thanks for your concern, Rachel, but —"

"I mean, if you've got a job here, you must be planning to stay. For a while, at least?"

Information she didn't have the right to, but the matter was self-explanatory. Zac shrugged.

She approached the counter, but now her focus was on the case of muffins. As she scrutinized them, she said, "You must be crazy overqualified to sell baked goods."

She stepped the length of the case and he wondered, as he had last time, if someone abused her. But maybe she was the abuser.

Maybe a tar pit of hatred boiled at the core of Rachel; maybe nothing did, no feeling at all. But no, that last wasn't it. Even now she fizzed, a shaken soda bottle of uneasiness.

"Can I get one banana nut and one cranberry orange?"

"Sure." He grabbed a pair of tongs and placed each carefully into its own small box. "Would you like a bag?"

"That would be perfect."

He nestled them inside a brown paper bag and handed it to her, hit keys on the cash register, and told her the total before the machine had finished ringing.

"Good math skills," she said.

"Old-school education." One-room schoolhouse, to be precise.

She paid him cash, exact change. "I guess I'll see you here again. I like this place."

"Welcome anytime."

"I'm a photographer. Sort of itinerant. There's so much beauty in this area, I might stay too for a while."

He nodded. She seemed to be making more than small talk, offering him a piece of personal information to make up for her earlier forwardness.

"Have a favorite subject in the area?" he said.

Her eyes brightened. "There's this gorgeous abandoned barn off the highway a few miles from here. Getting dilapidated but still majestic somehow. Maybe majestic because of the disrepair. But I wish someone would restore it."

"Do you mean the one off French Road, about halfway to the national park?"

"Yes! You've seen it."

"I've driven by a few times." His time exploring the old structure felt suddenly private.

"I think I've captured every angle by now, every nail and wood grain. It's such a neat old place."

She looked over her shoulder as several people stepped up behind her, forming a line. The unsettled carbonation in her spurted everywhere. Zac tried not to wince.

Without one giveaway, she lifted her bag and moved aside for the others. "Hey, I'm all set. Go ahead."

She walked out without another word, and customers began giving Zac their orders. He tried and failed not to analyze her as he boxed up a dozen cherry white chocolate chip cookies. People mattered; life mattered because of people. He couldn't trust the human race, and he couldn't renounce them either. Where did that leave him?

For the rest of the day, he served customers when they came in and paced behind the counter when they didn't, hands latched behind his neck. He punched out at 1:15 and got his keys and phone from a corner nook on the kitchen counter. He'd missed a call.

Nate Giordano.

SEVENTEEN

No voice mail. Zac's heart pounded as he let himself out of the kitchen, waved to Connie, and headed to the lot behind the bakery for his car. He got inside before hitting Redial.

No answer.

He clenched his eyes shut and saw three gravestones. His sons.

Months ago, Lucas had given himself a stress fracture while working his leg weights. He had freaked out on his parents, pleading with them not to let Zac know about his weak bones. Thinking Zac, stuntman extraordinaire, would be disappointed in him.

Curse that stupid TV show. Curse the serum in his veins. Curse a world that brought pain to kids. He'd done a lot of cursing lately. He tried the call again. No answer.

Even when Lucas's leg had fractured, Nate had answered Zac's call. Twenty-four hours had now passed. He could tell himself to wait for news. He could tell himself this might be no worse than a fractured bone. But he knew.

He dropped the phone into the center console and started the car. His eyes blurred. He blinked away the tears before they could fall. Lucas. The cancer in his body was on an assault mission, and Zac could do nothing for him.

Or maybe he could.

The thought flashed in his brain like the original camera flashbulbs that blinded and popped, dazzled and smoked. He could do something. He could save his boy.

He started to drive. One block over, he parked in the lot of Galloway's Books.

Through the door he charged. Behind the counter, Tiana was ringing up a group of customers, but she glanced out of habit at his entrance. She went still for a moment as he barreled past her.

"David?" he said. Maybe snapped.

"In the stockroom."

"Thanks."

He rushed at right angles down aisles of bookshelves, toward the room in the far right corner of the store. Past rare hardbacks and well-read picture books and supermarket romances. Past the aisle of David's adored Westerns, in which men knew what they had to do and did it. In which men preserved the lives of people who mattered to them, regardless of the cost.

He pushed open the stockroom door. David knelt before a few boxes, carefully turning the pages of a nineteenth-century hardback, no doubt inspecting it for damage or foxing or whatever else he looked for. He lifted his head, and his eyebrows arched.

"Zac."

"I have to talk to you."

"Of course." David set the book aside and stood. He looked around the room with a frown that said he hadn't evaluated its appearance in a while. "No chairs."

Zac gestured a dismissal. "I won't be here long. Just want you to know I'll be gone for a day or so."

"Where this time?"

"About a year ago, I did a thing. You know what the Make-A-Wish Foundation is?"

David nodded then tilted his head. "You were someone's wish?"

"His name's Lucas." The words seemed to turn a valve inside him, release the torrent of the rest. "He's twelve, has osteosarcoma, they found it in the long bones of his legs but he's been well for months now, they said cancer free but if it ever comes back or shows up in his lungs . . ."

The torrent dried up. He couldn't speak the words.

"And now it has?" David said.

"He asked me to call. I have. Four times. I can't get any —" He pressed his thumbs into his burning eyes. "I can't get any news, which means there's something wrong with him. Something really wrong."

"I'm sorry."

"No, that's not why I'm — I'm going to fix it, David. I'm going to fix him."

Caution smoothed the furrow of David's brow. "How?"

Zac's jaw tightened at the man's willful obtuseness. "I'm going to give him blood. My blood."

David folded his arms and studied him as if Zac had just proposed to fall off another tightrope. "I thought our blood was no good to the mortals."

It wasn't. Zac knew. Simon had tried to heal a mortal once. A long time ago. The woman had died anyway. But Zac's blood had never been tried, and each of them was different. Simon's blood could speed up the rejuvenation process for others; Zac healed faster from mortal injury than the other longevites did.

"They live in Ohio. I'll start driving now,

and by tomorrow he'll be a healthy kid again." If only Lucas would hold on until Zac got to him.

"He's in a hospital?"

Stupid question. Zac huffed.

"So you'll go in and offer them a blood sample. And they'll run the usual tests and wonder about the altered nuclei."

As if he hadn't thought of that. "I have to risk it."

"What will you tell his parents? His doctors?"

"I'll tell them my blood can make him well and they'll give it to him."

"And you'll tell them his body will stop aging from that day on? That he'll be trapped with an adolescent physiology for the next hundred years?"

"We don't know that. Maybe he'll mature to adulthood and stop aging then."

"Would you experiment on him without their consent, or the child's?"

"It's not an experiment." His pulse began to pound in his ears. "I'm going to save him."

David took a step closer, and his arms lowered to his sides. "You can't do it, Zac."

Zac was breathing as if he'd been out for a jog. He stepped up too, and David didn't flinch as Zac closed the gap, invaded the man's precious space bubble.

"You're not going to stop me."

"Revealing your blood chemistry holds risk for all of us. And not telling the mortals the whole truth would be an immoral use of —"

"Immoral?" He pushed closer to David. "Lucas will live. There's nothing immoral in that."

"You're wrong."

Not about this, he wasn't. About a thousand other things, but not about this.

"I don't care what you think of it," he said. "I'm going to do it. I'll be back here in a few days."

David pushed him against the wall and held him there by the shoulders. "You'll not do this thing to a child. You will not."

The shock of the physical aggression broke something open in Zac. Something that had been waiting to break. He swung a fist, and David blocked him, and Zac swung again and despite his shorter height connected with David's jaw. David staggered back into a stack of boxes, and the top one tipped and spilled books to the concrete floor.

David came at him again. Tried to pin him again. Zac dodged, and David raised his voice as if he knew the pulse in Zac's ears might otherwise drown him out.

"It's not your problem to fix."

"Yeah?" Zac swung his fist again but pulled the punch in time to spare the drywall. "I don't see anyone else fixing it."

They stood in silence, breathing hard.

"The mortals don't need to be fixed, my friend. Their role has been set."

"Some role. Dying of cancer, getting murdered —"

A quiet choked sound.

David turned away and knelt before the spilled books. One had landed facedown, splayed open, spine cracked and pages falling loose. David set his hand on it, the gesture mournful. He lifted it gently though it was ruined. An old, old edition of MacDonald's *Dealings with the Fairies.* As he set it aside on top of a tape-sealed box, his shoulders hunched.

"Supposing we found some way . . ." David cleared his throat. "I'd never do it to her, Zac. I'd never ask her to carry this."

Tiana. "Even if the alternative was death — I mean, imminent, premature death?"

"Even then."

"Maybe she'd want it." Maybe Lucas would. Maybe his parents would.

"We've talked about it at length. She wouldn't."

"She'd rather die?"

"You speak of death as though it's the last page of the story."

Zac shook his head against the image of Ruth Wister's tearful jubilant face. "I can't go there right now."

"It's —"

"David, please." He turned to go. He had to move, take action. "I can't."

He yanked the door open and left the room, began navigating the narrow aisles, working his way toward the front, walking under bare lightbulbs and ducking their trailing string pulls. His path ran into the returns cart, and he turned around and headed for the next aisle. A man and his young son were browsing the picture books. The man offered the kid a bottle of water, which David would object to had he seen it. As Zac neared them, the boy tipped the bottle to his lips and gargled water in the back of his throat.

Zac staggered. Gripped the corner of a shelf. His vision tunneled, gray around the edges, as his chest closed up.

"Hey," the man said. "Hey, man, are you sick?"

Breathe. Breathe. Breathe.

"Danny, go get Miss Tiana."

"Where?"

"Behind the front counter. Go get her now."

Pattering footsteps receded.

"Hey, can you hear me? Are you okay? Do you want me to call an ambulance?"

Can't get a breath, not a single breath, someone please help.

"Zac." Tiana's voice. Static on a walkie. "David, I need you, aisle three."

More static. "Be there in a moment."

"Now, David. I need you now!"

"I'm calling 911."

"No. Please don't do that."

"He's having a heart attack."

"He isn't. Please, I know him, and —"

A third voice. "Ach. Zac."

"Mr. Galloway, I really think I should call —"

"Thank you, but it isn't needed."

Hands fit under Zac's arms and lifted him from his bowed posture.

Another voice, this one female. A stranger. "Is that Zac Wilson?"

And David, snapping, "Please move aside. Thank you."

The hands guided him to the back room where he'd just been, but now the closed space, no windows — he balked, and something like a whimper escaped his throat.

"It's okay, Zac." Tiana's voice, not David's. "We're just going to hang out in here for a minute to keep you out of sight. I know you don't want the customers gawking."

She propelled him forward as she talked. The door shut behind them, further shortening his breath.

"If you can give me a sign, that would be great. But if you can't, I'll keep talking until David gets the store cleared out and then we can figure out what you need. Sound good?"

She squeezed his hand. He clung in return. Tactile anchor. *Thank you, Tiana. Please don't let go.*

"You can hear me?" she said.

He squeezed again.

"Good. Let's talk about . . . um, I guess the topic doesn't matter as much as my voice? How about the weather; there's a classic. It's sunny today. The trees don't have many leaves left, but their branches are sort of pretty. I always picture them shivering though. Wishing they had their coats back. Or how about the dunes? I know you're partial to them."

She talked on about the beautiful dunes. About the water of Lake Michigan that washed up on the sand at the end of Valerian Street. He tried to see it in his head, but his inner eye kept glitching on mud and night and blood and bodies pressing in on him.

"How is he?"

"I've never seen him like this."

"Let's get him outdoors."

"O . . . kay?"

"He's claustrophobic, Tiana."

"Oh. Oh Zac."

"Come."

"He's never reacted like this in the store before."

The air changed. Chilled. Zac tried to drink it in, but his lungs refused to open. They were holding him up, a hand under each of his forearms. He could see the parking lot and his own car, the naked trees and the sky, but he'd fallen so far into the panic he might never claw his way back out.

Claw his way. Through the mud and the bodies.

They grew hushed, the voices of the friends he knew were here with him. Friends who hadn't been there in the mud, so he wasn't in the mud either. Except he was.

"Jesus, please be close to us right now. Please let him breathe."

"Place Your hands on him, Lord God. Bring Your peace to the war in his mind. Bring him back to us now."

Their voices overlapped, murmured agreement with one another. The terror and the memory receded, inch by inch, and Zac felt hands on both his shoulders, his arm, his back. They were hemming him in with their touch and their prayer. He leaned, he didn't know into whom. Exhaustion left him limp. The past still pressed so close. If he opened his eyes, he might see the trees and the sky and his friends. Or he might see the pit and the corpses, the pools of blood soaking the earth around him. He shuddered and drew a gasp. The hand on his back began a slow circular rub, so that was Tiana.

"Zac?" she said.

He opened his eyes.

He was slumped against David. They had seated him on a bench behind the bookstore and were sitting on either side of him. He tried to straighten, but he was so tired.

"Sorry." He shut his eyes. Somewhere in Ohio, Lucas might be dying.

"What happened?" Tiana said.

"Um, panic attack."

"Uh-huh." Her hand moved from his back to his shoulder and squeezed. "We noticed."

"I'm good now."

"Zac, *why* did you panic?"

"Does it matter?"

"Of course it does."

He planted his palms on the bench and

sat up, away from David's support. Tiana watched him, while David gazed off across the street. Zac drew in a full breath and let it out, and his chest didn't lock up. In a minute he'd have his legs back, and he could get out of here.

"Something's going on with you," Tiana said.

"Well, life's been stressful lately."

"Do you know what I do when life stresses me out? I watch too much Star Trek."

"Is that a prescription?"

"That's a compare and contrast."

"Try surviving a world war or two and maybe we won't contrast so much."

Silence. He met her eyes. She was gazing right at him, right into him. "I'll keep it in mind."

"I'd rather you didn't." He bent and planted his elbows on his knees, scrubbed his hands through his hair. "I'd rather forget this fiasco and leave you guys to reopen the store. David, what do I owe you for that book?"

"I hadn't priced it," he said.

"Let me know when you do."

"Zac, why are you claustrophobic?"

He lifted his face from his hands. David asking too. "Look, I'm working on it. I don't see why the *why* matters."

"Who does know?" Tiana said. She hadn't removed her hand from his shoulder.

"Simon and Moira, obviously."

"They know you struggle with your war experiences?"

"Experience. Just one really, relating to — all this." He gritted his teeth. *Shut up, Wilson.*

"Okay, then they're the ones you need to talk to. I get it. We're still getting to know each other."

He ducked his head. Let her assumption stand. Continue with the deflection he excelled at. The idea of getting up and walking away, the memory still locked inside him, felt like the safest thing he could do. Safest and loneliest and maybe most terrifying. He shuddered, and Tiana's grip strengthened on his shoulder.

"What is it?" she said.

"I —" The single word shattered against his mask. He looked down at his hands. They were shaking. They hadn't been a few seconds ago.

A minute passed while he sat there. Mute. Caught in the web of every attack that had hit him in the last three weeks. He didn't know how to start. If only she would say something else, nudge him toward the words he couldn't reach, but no, of course he didn't want that. Better she was quiet now.

David stretched his legs and folded his arms and leaned back against the bench.

"What're you doing?" Zac blurted. "Waiting me out?"

"Aye."

That word was the nudge. It came to Zac in the deepest place of his soul. The place that had curled up and withdrawn when he realized how his struggle had burdened Moira, how she had resented shouldering his weakness. The place that had frozen up the next time he tried to call Simon for help through a bad night. The place that had known better than to call Colm, ever, because best friend or not, the man always mocked fear.

"In 1917," he whispered, "I was mortally shot."

Eighteen

The six words sounded as new to him as they would to David and Tiana. He groped for more, unsure which ones his mouth would speak until he heard them emerge.

"Through the throat. Blood and — the sound, it was that sound. In the bookstore. That kid gargling his water. I — I didn't think about it at the time, but that's what it was. The trigger."

David sat utterly still beside him. On his other side Tiana watched him, but he couldn't meet her eyes. He kept his gaze, like David's, trained across the street.

"I regained consciousness as they dragged me to the grave. Mass grave. Hundreds. Of bodies. I stayed quiet while they — while they buried. Us. The corpses and me."

A soft breath came from Tiana. He couldn't look at her and keep talking. The danger of what he was doing filled his chest. They might not want this once they knew.

They might go inside and reopen the store and tell him they'd see him later, only to call and say they'd thought it over and needed a break from his brokenness. From him. If he kept the brokenness to himself, he'd more likely get to keep Tiana and David.

"Zac."

Not the first time Tiana had said his name, he was sure. Concern drew her mouth down, and David now studied him too.

"That's all," Zac said.

"How were you rescued?" Tiana said. "Your troop found you?"

"No one found me." Not God, despite his pleas. Not anyone else either.

"Then how . . . ?"

"It had rained for weeks, everything was mud. I dug myself out. The second day was sunny. That was my mantra. Find the sun. Keep breathing and find the sun."

"Zac."

He risked a look at her.

Tears stood in her eyes. "I am so sorry this happened to you."

The emotion in her words hit like a summer downpour on his parched soul. She wasn't retreating. He wasn't inconvenient. He didn't have to silence how it hurt to lie beneath the dead, some of them his friends, to breathe the stench of their decay and taste their blood in the mud that filled his mouth. How it hurt to scream for God to save him, please save him from this grave, and to be left to dig his own way out.

But he had to be clear so they understood. He wouldn't continue to be the burden he was now.

"It's been okay for a long time. I mean, there's a bad night once or twice a year. But I don't live like this."

"Right now you do."

Her gentle words clobbered him. Heat flooded his face. "It won't last."

"When did it start?"

"The night after we buried Colm."

She nodded as if that meant something to her. And shoot, David was nodding too.

"What?"

She said, "Don't you think there were things to remind you? Sounds, smells?"

Turned earth's rich scent. Dark hole he helped deepen. Shovels clinking. Zac forced his legs to hold him as he stood and paced. A little wobbly, but he had to move.

"What do you think?" David said, watching him.

"The man is dead. He was dead when we put him in the ground. I don't see why there's some connection in my head."

"But perhaps there is a connection?"

He stopped and pushed shaking fingers through his hair. "I . . . yeah. Maybe."

No maybe about it. For proof he needed only take stock of his body right now. Adrenaline spiked his pulse, and his legs began shaking like his hands. As if all of him had been waiting for his stupid brain to put the pieces together, and now . . . He sank back onto the bench between them and gripped his knees.

"Knowing the source might help you through it," Tiana said.

"How?" If being on the outside of the mess let David and Tiana see clearly . . . "What do I have to do?"

"I can't answer that one," Tiana said.

David's eyes were steady on him. "You know the answer, friend."

His fingers curled into loose fists, but he had no inclination to use them now. "This has nothing to do with God."

"All things have to do with Him."

"So if I don't repent and surrender, I spend the rest of my life like this?"

"That's not —"

"You're not listening, David. I just said I've been fine for the last hundred years."

"And has it been so long since you've

walked with Him?"

Zac was on his feet without a conscious decision to get up. He met David's eyes and let his mouth twist into the hint of a sneer.

"To the day," he said.

Tiana laced her fingers together and wrapped them around her knees. "The day . . . ?"

"If He would ignore a prayer like 'Please don't let them bury me alive,' then He clearly wasn't going to hear anything else I said."

"But Zac —"

He paced away from them. He'd said too much. "No. Just stop. I mean it, Tiana. Stop."

She was silent while he paced. He swiveled to jab a finger at David. "I'm going to talk to Cady and Finn about Lucas. See if they've ever done it, and how old the mortal was."

"And if they have?" David said quietly.

"Then I'm going to make him well, David. And no one is going to stop me."

David held his gaze, and Zac stared back, until David shook his head. "It's a terrible mistake you'll be making, friend."

Don't call me that. He almost said the words aloud. He didn't know where they'd come from, only that David's dogged use of the word made him want to hit things.

"Whatever," he said with a flippancy that was the last thing he felt. "I'll go now. I know you two can't wait to start praying for me to come to my senses."

When Tiana flinched, the remorse nearly choked him. He kept his face impassive and left both of them sitting on the bench. He got back into his car and texted Cady.

ARE YOU AND FINN AROUND TOWN? WANT TO ASK YOU ABOUT SOMETHING.

She responded after he'd driven no more than a block. WE WENT TO THE DUNES. ABOUT HALFWAY UP ONE AT THE MOMENT.

CAN I CALL YOU?

GIVE ME FIFTEEN MINUTES.

He could drive out there. He'd prefer to talk to them face-to-face. On the drive he could breathe deeply and absorb the country around him. But he didn't have time. He needed the answer now. He needed to start driving to Ohio. Now.

He gazed out the windshield across the street. The maples lining the sidewalk were bare or holding on to a few dry leaves. Just as Tiana had described for him.

Friends. That's what they were. They deserved to be treated as such.

Or he might be wrong about them too. He'd known them a month.

And what he'd just told them was something no one else knew. In the years after the Great War, a soldier didn't put his memories into words. But the last few decades had birthed an oversharing culture, and these friends hadn't known him in those days. Was that the only reason Zac had spoken of it at last?

Didn't matter. As long as he didn't blunder like that again.

After eighteen minutes, Cady had not texted again, but customers were beginning to fill the bookstore lot. David must have turned the sign back to OPEN. On faith, Zac went to a gas station and filled up. He pulled away from the pump and parked in one of the spaces in front of the little snack mart. Then he texted Cady.

IS NOW A GOOD TIME?

After less than two minutes, she responded. Sure.

He dialed, his mouth dry with the possiblity of hearing from them what he'd just heard from David.

"Hi," Cady said.

"I need some information."

"What's up?"

He stretched his back, tipped his head up to stare at the sky, tinted by his moonroof. Didn't need to close his eyes to see Lucas in a hospital bed and Nate ignoring his phone because the kid was . . .

"Zac?"

"Yeah." He cleared his throat. "Are we talking, um, privately?"

"We're sitting on one of the stone benches at the top. I've got you on speakerphone, but nobody else is coming over here because we're occupying the only bench."

He could picture their exact location; he'd climbed there often enough. They were safely secluded. "I need to know if you've ever turned anyone before. With your blood."

In the quiet, a gust of wind over the phone roared in his ear.

"No," Finn said.

"Have you tried it?"

More wind. Zac fidgeted in his seat.

"Zac, you can't just make more of us." Cady's voice held a new edge.

"That's not what I'm trying to do." And how she could think him that callous . . . Well, she didn't know him yet. He threw open the car door and got out. He slammed it shut. They'd heard that, no doubt. He paced the length of the front bumper. "Just tell me what happened when you tried it."

"Nothing," Finn said. "They died anyway. Our blood's ineffective."

"Whose blood was it? The same person's? How many times — ?"

"Sean tried it once, and I tried it. Once."

"And?"

"They died anyway, Zac." Cady's voice was downright frosty now. "Our blood has no healing properties. None whatsoever."

He bowed over the hood, braced himself up with one hand, and held the phone away from his mouth as a ragged breath left him.

"I'm sorry," Finn said.

"Yeah." His voice sounded like some other guy's. Some guy who'd just lost his footing and landed at the bottom of a canyon. "Thanks."

He hung up and shoved his phone into his jeans pocket.

He paced and tried to think. There had to be another chance. Another hope. He tugged his phone back out and called the only person left to call. The phone rang twice.

"Hey," Simon said.

Zac leaned into the bumper and ducked his head. "Hey, man."

"What's going on?"

"Did you ever try again, after Melissa? To change someone?"

This pause was longer than Cady's had been. So long Zac checked to see if the call was still connected.

"One other time. It doesn't work."

The recipient wasn't the problem then. "Maybe your blood doesn't. Maybe mine would."

"It didn't work for Moira either."

The air around him seemed to thin. "What?"

"She gave her blood to Prudence, Zac."

Prudence. Zac shut his eyes. Moira's daughter had been ten or eleven when cholera took her, so being young didn't help. "She never told me."

"I was with her when she did it. She could never talk about it after."

"Yeah." Maybe he could understand that.

"What's this got to do with Finn and Cady's people? You think Doc used — ?"

"Nothing. This is something else. A mortal."

"Like you needed one more thing to overinvest in. Who is it?"

"A kid I know. Eleven years old. Cancer."

"You want to take chances with a kid?"

Not one of them understood. "I think he's sick again. Really sick, dying, maybe gone already."

"You think? You don't know?"

"Forget it. Just forget it."

"Hold on a minute, you idiot."

Zac bowed over, free hand gripping his knee. Hope drained out of him like blood, left him weary deep in his bones, in his cells maybe, where the serum continued giving its nontransferable gift.

"You're close to this kid."

"I know, big mistake. The fool who can't walk away, who latches onto mortals like —"

"Shut up."

"It's what Colm told me."

"Screw Colm. If there's a hell, I hope he knows he's burning."

The words cut the air like razor blades. Zac felt sliced by them too, but in a way that released him from something he hadn't known was binding him. He stood upright. He grasped a long breath, more able to now than when he'd hung up on Cady.

"Don't you ever assume I'll say what he said. Don't you dare."

"Yeah." Zac's voice was hollowed out. Humbled, as he deserved. "I hear you."

"I'm sorry about the kid." Simon ended the sentence there. No *however, get over it.* No *however* anything.

Zac nodded at the ground. "Yeah."

"If I thought my blood might work, I'd give it. If I thought we could do it without sentencing him to an immortal life in an immature body. I know you'd want to try it anyway, and we could argue about that if there were a chance. But there's no sense arguing, because there's no chance. I'm sorry."

Simon hadn't apologized to him this many times for anything in the last century and a half. "Thanks, man."

"Sure."

He hung up. He tried Nate's phone again. Maybe it had been dropped into a toilet or a lake or something. Maybe Nate didn't know Lucas had asked Zac to call. Maybe the kid wanted to talk about weight training techniques.

Voice mail.

Zac got into his car. Drove laps around the outskirts of town until the answer finally came. The last shot he had.

Doc.

The man had a cure for the serum. He must have more of the serum itself. Zac only had to convince him to give a dose of it away. And if he'd penned an apology to Cady yesterday, he should still be in town. Should also be aware of Zac's presence here. After all, whose face had been on the news lately linked to an impossible survival story?

Problem was Doc still didn't want to be found.

Maybe Zac could offer something to make exposure worth it. Doc was a scientist. He'd know Zac should be dead, serum notwithstanding. Bartering was high on Zac's skill list. He would exchange details of his survival for the serum. He'd make them up if he had to; and he would have to. If that failed, he could demand it as part of the restitution owed. Convenient of Doc to acknowledge his guilty conscience.

Zac turned the car toward his apartment and his laptop. He didn't maintain social media apps on his phone, didn't want to be tied to them, but from his computer he could reach out. Surely Doc would see a public post from Zac.

Yes. This could work. He could still save his boy.

Nineteen

Zac had been tagged more than seven hundred times in the last hour, which was rather excessive, but he ignored the notifications tab and clicked instead to compose a new public post. Good thing he couldn't die, because Simon was going to kill him for this.

The wording had to be right. Plenty of people would pop up online claiming to be whomever Zac Wilson said he wanted to talk to. He'd have a lot of filtering to do, but he'd know the real Doc when he found him. He started typing.

If you see this, Doc, I want to talk. On behalf of Anders. Contact me.

No one but Doc Leon would know Zac's birth name, and without a surname no stranger could dig up his original mortal self. This assuming traces still existed of Anders Eklund. He stared at the words for a moment. He tried to predict any reason he might regret this later, but it seemed the only chance Lucas had.

He posted it.

Now to check out who on earth was chattering about him. This traffic didn't match that of his original rocketing into the public's notice after the airing of *Warrior USA*, or that of a month ago when he fell. But it was runner-up to those two events for sure. He clicked.

A picture of him. Grainy, a phone zoom. Wearing the clothes he was wearing now, gripping the edge of a bookshelf to stay on his feet, mouth open and eyes glazed. The caption read, *He went bat crazy in the middle of a store where I was shopping. Owner had to ask us all to leave. Don't want to speculate, but something's weird with this guy.*

Zac scrolled down, and a dull pain bloomed in his chest.

I'll speculate for you. That's drugs. Totally 100% drugs. SMH. I really thought Zac Wilson was one of the cool guys.

Agree with @Running4Princess, looks like he's high to me. Wow, so, that's really disappointing.

That must have been kind of scary, @JameyZ! Glad he wasn't violent or anything but whoa.

Maybe it isn't drugs, you know? Maybe he's

still dealing with the Marble Canyon thing. But dude, go get some help if you're losing it in public.

LOL @MissTeaMorning did you see this? still want to have his babies? LOL sorry gurrl.

There's more to this, ppl. Come on, it's Zac. Something's up and he needs our support. What kind of fans are we going to be? #StandByZac

@WinnieTheBoo If he wants support, he needs to tell us what's going on. It's been two hours and there's been no response from him whatsoever.

It went on for seven hundred tags. For every *awww* and *poor guy, that's sad* were two or three others calling him a wreck, an embarrassment, a washed-up flavor of the month whose time in the spotlight was thankfully ending. He ought to stop reading, but he couldn't. A few people upbraided the poster of the picture for publicizing it. A few said they were praying and hoped Zac would feel better soon, as if the picture suggested the flu or allergies. A few said they would be Zac Wilson fans until the day they died whether he was on drugs or not.

This is so weird, you guys, I saw him in town the other day and he said he was on a hiatus. Now I'm wondering what that means. What if there's something really wrong with our Zac?

A row of terrified, weeping, and heart-eyed emojis followed the post.

Zac stared at the user's profile picture. It was the selfie he'd taken with the girl from the bakery.

He couldn't swallow past the stricture in his throat. They had caught a glimpse past the mask, and this was what they did with it. Assumed, mocked, trivialized, disowned. No, not all of them, but so many of them. They wanted the Zac who signed their shirts and photos, who posed and grinned and made them feel at ease. Made them happy. They had no use for the person with flaws and fears like their own.

Since he'd been scrolling, another eleven mentions had pinged in his notifications. He jumped to the bottom.

Did you guys see this, he's looking for a doctor?

I volunteer as tribute!

No for real what if it's about that pic from earlier?

Who's Anders? Anybody know? Anybody? C'mon, Wilsonites, who is Anders???

@ZacWilson Ignore these stupids, I can hook you up <wink> message me, babe.

He shut the laptop and pushed it away. His stomach was a hard, burning knot.

He should delete the post. But he

couldn't. Lucas needed Doc's response.

He paced his apartment room by room, twitchy agitation growing in him. He cartwheeled down the hallway and moved into a handstand at the doorway of his bedroom. When he lowered his feet to the floor and stood upright, his humiliation cracked open, and the hurt at its center spilled through him. He shuffled to the kitchen and sank to the floor in a corner, knees up, forehead resting on them.

He sat that way for an hour, and when he got up the clock had barely ticked past five. This was going to be a long evening. A long night.

He could go climb the dunes. He'd done so in the dark plenty of times since that first night climb with David. But his body felt weighted. Zac Wilson, stuntman and daredevil and gymnast, couldn't force his limbs to lift him from his seat on the floor.

After a time he got up to check his phone, though he knew it hadn't rung. No calls, no texts. He opened the computer, and his social media accounts were all exploding with new notifications. That picture was getting around fast. His gut burned. Coward. Broken, scared joke of a man. Not a warrior; Connie had known before she met him.

To Colm too, he'd been a joke. Someone

to mock. Someone to fool. Someone to use.

But he could do this. He opened the thread created beneath his last post. And watched.

The comments wrapped around him like barbed wire. Even the kind ones. He watched them add up, reading every one. The sun set in the window over the kitchen sink, and still he read.

Zac jolted up from the floor, and his computer skidded a few inches as his knee bumped it. He'd fallen asleep. He pushed to his feet and found the clock. The digital numbers blurred until he blinked a few times. 7:38 p.m. He'd slept over two hours.

He snatched up his laptop and checked the thread. New notifications: 264. He groaned.

Okay, fine. He had work to do.

A pounding came at his door, and then his phone vibrated with a new text. Simon.

LET ME IN. I SEE YOUR CAR.

What? Zac strode to his front door, which opened not onto a porch but into the apartment foyer. He peered into the spyhole. Nobody there. Yep, that would be Simon, standing to one side as if he were still a cop and Zac's place were the residence of a suspect. He shook his head, unlocked the door, and swung it open.

"Hey," Simon said as he stepped inside.

"Uh, hey."

"I've been knocking for five minutes."

"Sorry. Was asleep."

Simon wandered the living room, then the kitchen, then stood at one end of the hallway to survey the bathroom and bedroom from a distance. "Cozy place."

"I'm cool with it."

"Mm-hmm."

Yeah, definitely Cop Simon. The guy would be a pit bull with a bone, jaws clamped until death on whatever problem he was gnawing at the moment.

"Simon, what are you doing here?"

Simon grunted, crossed back into the living room, and sat on the couch, stretching his arms over the back. He appraised Zac with an old look. A look from the days when Zac still called him on bad nights.

A dangerous look. It had always made Zac feel not that he wanted to talk but that talking was inevitable, so he might as well get on with it. David had waited him out at the bookstore, would have sat in silence as long as necessary. Simon didn't wait. Simon nudged and needled until you spilled your guts hoping he would go away.

"Simon, what are you doing?"

"You're the one who asked me to show up. Be part of the family crisis and all that."

"In Missouri. Four days ago."

"Couldn't get to Missouri. Figured you could use me anywhere." His teeth flashed in a grin.

"Okay."

Simon nodded as if that settled it. Right.

"Well, we know Doc is in town. Or was yesterday. He left a note for Cady at their hotel."

"Oh?"

"Asking for forgiveness."

Simon's eyes lost focus as he mulled the puzzle. "Interesting."

"Not what we expected."

"No, I expected a threat. Instead he kills four of them and then apologizes to the survivors. He's all over the place."

"Maybe before we age out we get senile."

"Huh."

Then Simon sat in silence broken only when he began to crack his knuckles. Zac continued to watch him. At some point the guy would say more. When he was good and ready.

"What'd you find when you went to their homes?"

"He buried James and Anna. Family plot. Respectful. We went to Cady's and packed a suitcase for her, brought her some clothes. No sign of forced entry there. No sign of anything. The neighbors were informed there was a tragic accident, so they won't expect to see Anna or James; the other two lived in California and only came to visit. Really there wasn't much, man. I guess the graves confirmed we have four dead, not two."

"Okay."

"There was an old couple Finn went to see. In on their secret. I kept mine."

Simon folded his arms and leaned back in his seat. Nodded Zac on. Shoot, he could interrogate without saying a word. Zac rolled his eyes. *I know your tactics, moron.*

Simon nodded. *Darn straight.*

Zac sighed. Whatever. "They believed that James and Anna accepted the serum. Informed consent. Cady's now the only holdout on that."

"Anything else?"

"Nope. Well. A somewhat unrelated matter."

He got up and retrieved his laptop from the kitchen. He opened the thread, scrolled to the top to view his original post, and handed the computer to Simon.

"What is . . . ?" Simon read a few lines down. "You have got to be kidding me."

"I had to try it. For Lucas."

"You used your old name on a public . . ." His eyes widened as he kept reading. "You have over a thousand comments on this and you posted it four hours ago."

"Perks of popularity." The words came out flat.

Simon didn't seem to hear him. His finger was moving down the touchpad, his eyes scanning the words that Zac had absorbed over the last few hours. Zac got up and folded an afghan from the back of the chair. An already folded afghan. At last Simon's eyes met his, grayer in their coldness.

"They turned on you like a pack of dogs."

Zac smoothed his palm over the afghan and swallowed the sour lump in his throat. "Some of them were concerned. Genuine."

"Too few."

"Aren't you going to complain about the post that set them off?"

"First I want to know what picture they're talking about."

"No, you don't." Should have thought of that, though, because Simon was tapping and reading, tapping and reading.

The moment he found the photo was betrayed by a faint inhale and a fainter curse.

"That's a decent summary." Simon would

know it all now. "Look, what matters is Doc might respond to my post. Might have a way to save Lucas. I have to monitor the thread as long as it's active in case he —"

"He made a cure. Before he was remorseful, he was eradicating us. If he had any of the original serum, he probably destroyed it."

The simple logic seared Zac's brain. His legs folded and dropped him into the big stuffed chair across from Simon. "I . . . I didn't think . . ."

"Of course you didn't." But no judgment resided in Simon's tone. "A child you love might be dying. And you've heard nothing?"

He shook his head.

"So you posted this thing to Doc and you still don't know if the kid's even sick."

"I'm not going to wait for confirmation when every hour could matter."

"Right, okay. I don't expect you to be rational about any of this. If he still wants to take us out, maybe this will help us catch him."

Simon pushed to his feet, folded his arms, widened his stance. It was his Action Hero pose, which Zac had ribbed him about for the last hundred years, the nickname evolving to reflect the slang of the times.

"I missed dinner," Simon said, "and you

probably did too."

The suggestion alone prompted a growl in Zac's stomach. He'd ignored lunch as well, hadn't even snacked. He nodded.

"I passed a Mexican restaurant just off the highway, maybe ten minutes."

Of course Simon picked Mexican, but the last thing Zac had energy for was a restaurant debate. He pushed to his feet.

He broke his rule about social media apps on his phone. Installing and logging in took only a few seconds. Simon was scrutinizing him again, so he shrugged.

"So I can check the comments while I'm out of the house."

"Best thing you could do right now is step away from that for an hour or two."

"Not if Doc responds in the next hour."

Simon sighed. "Suit yourself."

Zac's eyelids were heavy as he drove up to Salsarita's. He got the enchilada plate and Simon got his beloved beef tacos. While they waited for their food, Zac checked the comments on the Leon post, then checked once more when the food came. Simon made no remark. Nothing posted could be Doc, though several replies hoped Zac would believe they came from a doctor who was "deeply concerned about Anders" and "prepared to help him in any way." The rest were expressions of best wishes or sharp mockery.

He and Simon ate in a silence that chipped away at the barrier between Zac and exhaustion. They were waiting for the check when Simon spoke for the first time since they'd ordered.

"Moira."

"Yeah?" Zac rested his arms on the table.

"Have you talked to her?"

"I've tried every contact I know. The phone numbers are disconnected and the emails are undeliverable."

Simon's Adam's apple dipped. "Same."

"You're looking for her."

"It's been futile so far, which I expected. But I had to try this time."

If ever there had been a time to track her down despite her wishes, this was it. Zac kept emailing, kept calling, though he didn't know what he'd say the next time he saw her. They fell into quiet again as they drove back to the apartment.

"I'll see you later," Zac said as they got out of the car. "You staying at the Best Western again?"

Simon stood on the other side of the car and studied him.

"What?"

"Well, now that we're face-to-face, I've

made a decision."

"Great."

"I'm going to crash on your couch."

Um . . . what? "No, you're not."

"Going to cut to the chase here, okay? Okay. You look like a wreck, brother. Not so a bystander would notice. But you've lost weight, and you have circles under your eyes like freaking makeup, and I don't know or care to know all the inner workings of Zac Wilson's sentimental brain, but I can tell when a man is in trouble. And right now you are."

Zac tried glaring, which bounced off Simon like rubber off steel. "I don't need a nighttime babysitter."

"Yeah? You're sleeping sound. Eight hours, no problem."

Zac fought the need to dash off down the street. Away. "I'm dealing. I know how to deal."

"Good. You can deal with me sleeping on the couch."

Zac crossed his arms, clenched his jaw. "I mean it, man; go get a hotel and leave me —"

"Fine. I'm calling a Life Buoy."

Zac's arms lowered. Oh.

He wasn't always the mess, though he had been the first to hold that position and through the years seemed to hold it more often than the others. It had been Simon a few times, Moira a few other times. It was never Colm; if he got involved at all, it was to join a vigil alongside someone else. Made sense now. Colm hadn't had the emotional capacity to become a mess.

Eleven years ago, the last time the family had called a Life Buoy, it had been for Simon. His wife's passing had wrecked him in a way Zac had never seen his friend wrecked before, left him stranded in grief that made him erratic and mean. Zac had arm-locked him more than once to keep him from tearing his own house apart, destroying her things. Simon had yelled curses at him, fought like a baited bear, and finally collapsed in blank weariness. In the first days, Zac hadn't allowed Moira to spell him. Simon was shamed by that later, when she joined the rotating watch over him and he realized why she'd been absent. But they had absorbed his shame as they absorbed the rest: his violence, his rage, his loss. They had made him safe, carried him through it, and after a long time had brought him out of it into life again.

And the code was simple. You couldn't refuse a Life Buoy called on your behalf.

"It's not that serious," Zac said through

gritted teeth.

"Not your call."

"Simon, go and —"

"No."

The word was quiet. Inflexible. Zac had lost.

He had to keep it together now that he was stuck with Simon, but regardless, Simon couldn't walk away as long as the Life Buoy was in effect. Zac pressed his fingers to the corners of his eyes and shook his head.

"Come on," Simon said and went to the foyer door.

Zac trudged up to the door and let them inside, trudged to his front door and opened that one too. When he locked it for the night and turned around, Simon was already hunting in the linen closet across the hall.

"Your pillows suck."

"Pansy."

Simon came to the couch with an armful of sheets. "It's, what, ten? I'm wiped. Good night."

Zac stood there a moment while Simon draped the sheets over the couch. When he started pillow-fluffing and grumbling to himself about cheap millionaires, Zac headed for the bedroom.

Maybe having someone else in the house

would convince his subconscious the walls weren't closing in. Maybe he'd sleep through the night and wake up to news from Nate or an answer from Doc.

TWENTY

"Zac."

The behemoth was back. Planting one foot on his chest and pressing, leaning, crushing. But a hand was there too. On his shoulder. Shaking him. His eyes opened to a view of the ceiling. Simon sat to one side, out of Zac's space, hand clamped on his shoulder.

"Zac."

His voice garbled a meaningless syllable.

"Right, okay."

Relief swelled in Zac's throat, cutting off more of his air, not helping the panic. He tried to talk. It sounded more like a sob, but he couldn't care about the weakness revealed in the noise. Simon was here. Zac wasn't alone.

"Okay, man, we've got this. It doesn't last forever, remember. It's going to pass. Try a longer breath, long and slow."

Zac tried. The gasp was harsh, loud.

"Okay, that's something. Now again."

Zac curled his fingers into the bedsheets, and another breath filled his lungs.

"Good job, buddy. Can you say something?"

"Yeah."

"Aha, there he is."

"Here."

"Yep, me too. I was watching *A New Hope* on TV, so that's kind of ironic."

Zac blinked. "Ironic?"

"Last time, it was right after *Return of the Jedi* released and you were put out that I hadn't seen it yet."

"Last time?"

"Last time you called me with this stuff."

Zac shook his head. A squabble over *Return of the Jedi* didn't sound familiar. Granted, he'd been in distress at the time. He uncurled into an upright position and stretched out his legs.

"And now here we are." He spoke around breaths. "In a world of endless sequels and remakes."

"Erosion of creativity, audience astuteness, and general culture. Not that I'm in a mood or anything."

"Nah. Just your normal disposition."

Simon gave a snort.

Eyes shut, Zac took a few more breaths.

He let the hand on his shoulder remind him he was okay. Would be anyway, in another minute or so. But when he opened his eyes, the walls seemed to cave in, the ceiling to lower. At his renewed gasping, Simon's grip tightened on his shoulder.

"Need to get out," Zac said or tried to say.

"Outside?"

"Yeah."

Simon braced his arm around Zac's back and guided him to his feet. He stood on his own, legs shaking but in no danger of collapse. He staggered, hand on the wall, and made it barefoot out into the floodlit parking lot. Simon walked beside him as he paced and breathed. Paced and breathed. They didn't talk.

After a while, Zac's lungs stayed open. He wandered over to the tree that had seen him through most nights of the last few weeks and leaned against it. Pink had begun to fill the sky, stretching upward from the eastern horizon.

"What time is it?"

"Not quite six," Simon said.

Almost eight hours. Wow. "And Star Wars was on TV?"

"Yep."

If the guy was as wiped as he claimed, he

shouldn't be awake watching a movie. But Simon was doing what any of them would do after calling a Life Buoy. Zac's role was to accept the help. It galled him and left him more grateful than words. Funny how that worked.

"*Return of the Jedi.* That's been a while."

"Yep," Simon said. No rancor there, just fact.

A snippet came back, cobwebs draping the memory.

"If I were going to spend two hours on a film, I'd go see that other new one. The gangster one. Not some fantastical epic space thing with puppets."

"One puppet."

"One's enough."

"I'm not telling you how Solo gets out of the carbonite."

They returned up the walk to the front door, and Zac let them inside.

Simon cocked his head. "Good?"

"Yeah."

Simon sighed.

A rusty knifepoint pricked Zac's chest. "Sorry. I thought with you here, maybe I'd be — I mean, maybe you wouldn't have to deal with —" He spread his hands, head ducked to hide his heating face. "Sorry."

"Oh, shut up." Simon's tone was equal

parts annoyance and . . . warmth?

Zac looked up. “What?”

“So that’s what happened. You got it into your head you’re a bother.”

Of course he was, when he was like this.

“For a while I hoped you didn’t call because you didn’t need to. But that wasn’t it. All these years, you’ve kept this crap to yourself.”

“Not often. About like before. You know, a trigger every year or two.”

“What about now, recently?”

Zac leaned on the wall. This conversation was making him tired again. “Every night.”

Simon went still. “Every. Night.”

“Since Colm died.”

Simon gave a quiet curse.

“Yeah,” Zac said on a laugh that broke. He crossed the foyer and let them inside his unit. Flopped onto the couch, his limbs rubbery.

Simon stood over him. “You’re an idiot.”

“Probably.”

“You think it’s just going to stop?”

“I was hoping soon.”

“And it never occurred to you there might be a cause you had to deal with first.”

“Um . . .”

The cop’s gaze sharpened to a glare. “Life Buoy.”

Right. Second tenet of the code: no lying. He was too tired to hedge, and it was time for Simon to know. "They thought I was dead. So they buried me."

Simon stared as if seeing him for the first time.

"You knew it had to do with the war. I mean, that's when it all started. No genius deduction required."

Simon nodded. Speechless? That was disconcerting.

"Well, we buried Colm, and it started over. Like it had just happened. I got left in a grave and took a while to get out, and now every night I'm back in that grave again."

"You have to deal with this."

"I would've by now if I knew how, man."

Simon rubbed his thumbs under his eyes. "Fair enough. I want one thing though, going forward."

"Okay."

"Life Buoy or not, you have to stop faking us out. If I hadn't gotten up here, and you'd kept on like this — I've seen guys deteriorate over this kind of stuff."

Zac snorted.

"I mean every word. Guys on the force, way back, years ago. How many hours' sleep were you averaging before tonight?"

"Three."

"Okay, for the record, for the rest of our distinguished life spans, if it gets this bad again, don't you dare try to cope almost a month without calling me. Or Moira if you want."

"Moira doesn't want any part of this." Zac flinched. Those words had come from nowhere.

Simon shook his head. "You know her better than that."

"She told me. And before you go all *you inferred wrong,* I'm telling you. She said it straight out."

"Colm could've been messing with her."

He'd considered that, but it didn't fit. Colm wouldn't have cared if Moira had stayed with him through two bad nights in 1985 — truly bad, worse than this, flashback dreams that trapped him until his screaming got loud enough to wake him. He could count on his fingers the number of times in the last fifty years that these nightmares had come after him. Could count with fingers to spare. Moira had witnessed the unusually brutal trigger episode of 1985 and known as well as Zac what would happen to him the next few nights. Always before, when they knew it was coming, she would be there to wake him up, to free him from the trauma playback in his head. This time she had looked him in the eye and said, *"This is inconvenient."* She'd caught a flight to Europe the same day, and he didn't hear from her for two months.

He would never argue the inconvenience of his mental scars. Still, her words, her leaving, had torn him up worse than the nightmares had. To this day he couldn't tell if his hurt was unfair to her or not.

"It is what it is," he said.

"Or it's not that at all."

"Really, Simon, let it go."

Simon shrugged. "You going back to bed?"

"I won't sleep." He tugged his shirt away from him where it stiffened with drying sweat. "Anyway, I have to be at work in less than two hours."

"Work?"

"The bakery in town. I sell desserts." He grinned.

Simon didn't roll his eyes. Instead he chuckled. "Nice."

"It's fun."

"Whatever you say."

He arrived at Cousin Connie's at 7:42, was into the mental zone of customer service and sales by 8:00, but he kept his phone nearer than usual and checked his post once an hour in lulls between customers. He didn't hide the minute it took to do so, and Connie seemed not to mind. The replies to the post were trickling down, fewer with every hour. And none of them were Doc.

At 10:15, his phone vibrated on the back counter. He finished ringing up a customer and snatched up the phone. Email. Lucas.

Zac,

I figured out you're probably calling Dad's phone. Here's Mom's instead. I hope I can talk to you.

A phone number followed. Nothing else.

He looked up at Connie, and her mouth puckered. "What is it?"

"I need to make a phone call. It's important."

"Something going on today?"

"I'm waiting for news about someone. Health news."

"Go on break." She waved him to the back kitchen for privacy.

"Thanks," he said, already thumbing the number into his phone.

"Hello?"

Not Lucas but his mom. "Dana, hi, it's Zac Wilson. Lucas asked me to call him at this number."

"Oh."

He couldn't swallow, could hardly form words. "Is he — He emailed me, asked to talk. Is he — ? I've been trying Nate's phone for two days, and —"

"Nate's gone."

"Gone?"

"Left."

For a second or two, Zac's brain refused to process. Gone left — he pictured Nate driving the family's SUV and making a left turn under a green arrow. He pictured Nate sleepwalking down the sidewalk with a suitcase, because no way would he leave his family if he were awake and aware.

"He's divorcing us. That's how Lucas keeps saying it. But of course I'm the only one he's divorcing." Her sigh was quiet, depleted.

"I — Dana, I'm so sorry."

"Thank you."

The formality was clearer than words. She was finished with this call. Of course she was. "I — Lucas —"

"He just fell asleep for the first time in two days. I'm not waking him up to talk to you."

The emphasis on the last word was subtle. "No. Of course not. I'm sorry. If there's anything —"

"There isn't. He needs his father."

Not a guy who emailed him every other week. Understood.

She sighed again. "I'll let him know you called, and he'll talk to you when I think he's ready."

"Of course."

She hung up.

Zac's legs gave out. He slid down the cabinet to the floor. His phone fell from his hand and hit the tile with a quiet clack. The fear of the last two days drained out of him. Fear for a mortal's life that had never been in imminent danger in the first place.

He couldn't help worrying about their physical safety. Any of them could stop breathing any minute. Meanwhile his heart beat in his chest as young and strong as it had been in 1887, incapable of wearing out. But he'd worried wrongly this time. Maybe the deaths of longevites he'd never met were messing with him.

Feet came to the door in his peripheral vision. He drew a long breath, held it, and let it out.

"Sorry." His voice was mostly steady. "I'll be out. Just need a minute."

No response. The feet approached, and those weren't Connie's clogs. They were black-heeled boots. He looked up.

Rachel. Gray hair in a messy bun, eyes hazel today and filled with compassion.

Zac scrambled to his feet and shoved his phone into his pocket. "You're not supposed to be back here."

"Connie said you were on break. She's dealing with a bunch of kids, so she didn't notice me sneak back."

"Rachel, you're not allowed —"

"Did they die? The person you were scared for. And you just found out?"

"The person I was . . . What are you talking about?"

Her brow crinkled. "Your post, of course."

He'd go into his app right now and delete it and with it all the replies that had pierced him. He swept out his arm and pointed at the EMPLOYEES ONLY door Rachel had walked through.

"You need to go."

"I know what you were trying to tell me in the diner. All the stunts you've done, even that fall — you're testing your body, but it keeps surviving. You must be so frustrated."

A chill traced down his spine. "What?"

"I should start over." She took a step nearer. "Doc's gone, Zac, but I'm still here. Doc was my father."

Twenty-One

"Doc's gone?"

Not possible. He'd been moving and thinking and talking in the world just days ago. Zac shook his head. That wasn't the most outrageous thing she'd said.

"You . . ."

Rachel folded her hands as if in petition. "I was born Rachel Leon in 1901."

He glanced at the door shut against the public, against Connie. Against mortals.

"I didn't know Finn and Cady were here. I saw your story online. To survive what you did, you had to be ageless. And the bookseller — he's one of us too, isn't he?"

"Why do you say that?"

"I've seen you talking to him. His eyes are old."

Zac shook his head. He was missing something in front of his face. Something . . . From the inside out, he went still.

"What did you do?" he whispered.

Her face turned as pale as her hair, and if yesterday she'd been a shaken soda bottle, now she was a geyser.

"Rachel . . ."

No. He couldn't talk to her here. Connie would poke her head back to check on him any moment. No mortal could overhear a word of this.

But she was answering him. "When Doc died, I inherited his research. And the product of it."

He drew a long breath. The strain pulled tight across his shoulders.

"I thought you would want it," Rachel said. "Like Anna did: on any terms."

He was mostly keeping up, but she kept throwing monkey wrenches. "You thought I want to die."

"Isn't that why you fell?"

"I fell because the wind changed. I fell because my foot didn't land where I wanted it to."

"You don't want mortality? An out?"

"I'll take another few centuries, if I can get them."

"But I was so sure." She covered her face and spoke into her hands, seeming to shrink into herself while she stood there. "Someone I could really help. Someone with the question to match my answer."

The geyser showered him in cold despair. He had to steady himself, steady her.

"There's no matching question though, is there? So I've got nothing to offer to anyone."

"Hey. Rachel. Look at me."

She lifted her head, and the emptiness in her eyes was a punch to his chest. "I'm so sorry, Zac. Please tell them I'm sorry."

She bolted for the employee exit onto the back parking lot, threw her entire body weight into the crash bar, and dashed outside.

"Rachel!" He barreled after her just as Connie appeared in the doorway between the front area and the kitchen.

"Zac?"

He didn't slow his pace, ducking through the doorway before the door could shut on him. Rachel was already halfway to a gray SUV.

"Rachel!"

She flung the driver's door open and threw herself inside. Seconds later, while Zac still hurtled across the lot toward her, she swung the car out into the street with a squeal of rubber and a revving of the engine. The driver behind her honked but braked in time to avoid her. Zac ran to his car. He couldn't lose her.

Connie's voice chased him from the back of the bakery. "Zac, what's going on? Do you want me to call the police?"

The possibility spiked his pulse. He swiveled to face her across the lot and shook his head. "No. Please. This is personal."

The concern in her eyes made him want to holler at her: she was mortal and useless to every one of his predicaments. A flicker of anger joined her sincerity, which he deserved. He was about to leave mid-shift after less than a week on the job. And he didn't care, and she could probably tell.

Nothing else to say and no time to say it. He reached his car and started driving. Rachel couldn't be far ahead of him, not the way the traffic lights turned in this town. But the SUV was nowhere to be seen.

Five minutes later, he spotted it. He followed it another five minutes and frowned when it pulled into a gas station.

The woman who got out was the right height, but her hair was blond.

He had lost Rachel.

His fist beat the steering wheel, and something in him cracked, as it had when he hurled a punch at David yesterday. He punched the wheel a few more times, shouted a few curses, and none of it lessened the pressure in his chest or the knowledge he was failing. Again. Wrong in everything he knew. Powerless in all he did. He had been since the night he learned Colm was murdering mortals.

No. He had been wrong, powerless . . . lost . . . since the sunny, windy afternoon he had fallen to his death. And then woke up alive.

Cold terror gripped him, the ceaseless cold of the grave he should be occupying right now. He curled his hands around the wheel. He had to find Rachel. A woman ageless like him, lost like him, terrified. Like him.

Go. Find her.

His thoughts came together. Okay, a gray SUV. Not helpful. A gray-haired young woman. Slightly more helpful. If only he could know where she would go, a hotel or . . .

The barn. Old like them. Susceptible to entropy, unlike them. She felt the same kinship to it that he did. Would the feeling drive her there, to say farewell to a place that had mattered the way the subjects Moira painted mattered to her? It was a ridiculous long shot, yet it was where she would go. He didn't know where the certainty came from, but he couldn't ignore it.

Or maybe he should. One more opportunity to be wrong and no reason to believe he was about to break his streak.

No other ideas, though. Nothing else to try. He straightened behind the wheel, drew a long breath, and began to drive. The winding two lanes of blacktop calmed him. Twenty minutes later he turned onto the gravel path that had mostly eroded away. He parked near the road. If she heard his car, she'd try to run again. But he didn't see hers. He got out and walked around the building.

She had parked behind it. His heart pounded. He'd found her. Now to talk to her, though he didn't know what he would say. He stepped through the big sliding door in the back, which she had left gaping. The floor was dust, small puffs forming around his shoes with each step, though the ground beneath was hard. No wind inside but still cold. He hunched his shoulders, thrust his hands into his coat pockets, and looked around. Three stalls on one side, swept out and empty. In a corner, a rusted pitchfork and rake had been left behind, old wood handles rotting away for at least a few decades. The rest of the barn was open space to the far wall. No Rachel.

Zac tipped his head up to the ceiling. No cutaway to see into the hayloft, only a small square opening at the front of the barn, to one side of the center where the loft doors would be. Dangling through the square opening, a rope swayed. He walked the length of the barn, studying. No one should be walking up there. Over one of the stalls, he could see up into the loft through several holes. The floor was rotting away.

Steps sounded overhead, booted feet but a light tread. She must know where to step.

He walked over to the rope and nudged it with one finger. Brand-new, smooth and bright white, nylon fibers. He tugged it then shimmied up.

As his head cleared the floor, Rachel screamed.

"Hey." He pulled himself into the loft. "It's just me."

"What are you doing here?"

He stood and looked around. She had spread a red-and-orange beach towel over the old boards dusty with hay and dry with age. Beside a professional camera case, a white plastic bag appeared to hold trash from fast food meals.

She was still staring at him. Her breaths heaved through her jacket.

Maybe a trivial question would calm her. "How'd you get the rope up here?"

"I climbed on the roof of my car."

He gestured to the things she'd brought up. "You're not living up here, are you?"

"No, no. I just like the environment. I came up here a few times with lunch."

"And you came back to say goodbye."

A faint blush. "On my way out of town."

"You live nearby?"

She pointed out the loft window at her car. "Home. I roll with the highways. I stop and take pictures. You know, to remind myself I was there."

Or to prove it to herself. To the people who never saw her and never had seen. Right now her emotions were spurting over the whole place, the terror and loss as she'd run from the bakery, but not only that. Zac's chest grew tight with the abandonment he'd picked up the day they met.

"We need to talk, Rachel."

"I'll pay my debt. I promise you, I'm prepared to do so."

As she said the words, he was hit by a spray of something new and cold and dark. His stomach knotted.

"Now please go," she said, "so I can return to solitary confinement minus the confinement. It's not a bad way to live really."

The tone was a poor attempt at casual. She had lived as David had, a century alone.

It had left David . . . well, old, in a way that Zac and Simon weren't. Longevite humor wasn't only lost on him; it seemed to wound him in a way Zac could not understand. He tried to remember not to joke about death, or imperviousness to it, around David.

Behind Rachel's eyes lay a hollowness that was different from David's quiet hurt, but it occupied the same place.

"You thought you were helping the others."

"I was healing them," she said quietly. "I was curing our cancer."

He blinked and saw an image of Lucas, the last scare they'd had, a year ago. Eleven-year-old child hooked to wires and machines, burning with a fever the doctors couldn't combat, tests for tumors in his lungs that mercifully came back negative.

"No," he said. "It isn't anything like cancer."

"It is a disease." She held out her hands, fingers spread, as if showing him a deformation. Her hands were whole, the fingers straight and young, the skin blemish free. "A disease that keeps us stuck here. I would give my right arm to find a true gray hair on my head."

"And Anna would have too?"

She lowered her hands to her sides. "I told

her I needed more time to rework, or the odds were at least fifty percent she would die like Sean and Holly. I needed a year, maybe two. Anna came back eleven days later."

"To die?" Zac's voice rasped.

She dropped to her knees and curled her hands into her thighs.

Zac started across the loft to go to her. "Hey."

She put a hand up. "Please stay back. The floor's dangerous." She looked like painted glass kneeling there, her hair stark and colorless, her shoulders quivering. "She said a whole year was out of the question. She said, 'I can't stand one more barren day.' "

"Rachel, listen. I can't let you go explore some more highways while I pretend I don't know you." He couldn't drag her before the others, either. If she refused . . .

"I never should have left that letter for Cady." Tears broke her voice. "They could have gone on thinking Anna and the others finally got old."

He knelt where he was. He braced his hands on his legs, mirroring her pose, and said as gently as he could, "No."

She looked up. Tears stood in her eyes.

"Anna left a letter, Rachel. Before she died."

Her lips parted for a harsh, panicked breath.

"She didn't identify you. That's why I thought — they still think — your father was the one who administered the cure. But we've all known it wasn't natural."

"It was supposed to be. A natural life span, that's what I was trying to give them."

"Cady believes they were murdered."

She groaned and covered her face. "Then you have to tell them. It's only — I didn't want to be hated at the end."

A sob shook her whole body, and he couldn't sit here watching her break down. He stood and stepped toward her, his strides loose and easy, trying not to look threatening. He would stay an arm's length away and —

A crack echoed through the barn as the floor fell away beneath him and he fell along with it into darkness.

Twenty-Two

He opened his eyes to an unknown roof, barely glimpsed through a jagged hole in the ceiling. What on earth . . . ?

The barn.

He had fallen. Becoming a habit. Crap.

"Rachel?" His voice was hoarse, his throat dry. Hay dust had drifted into his mouth while he lay there. He coughed. "Rachel. Are you okay?"

The only sound was the wind passing through the building, under the eaves that didn't need to be airtight and wouldn't be by now, in a building this run-down. She might be unconscious. He tried to get up.

The attempt at motion brought sudden awareness of his body. His legs and torso didn't rise when he told them to, but he wasn't paralyzed; he felt the muscles gather and execute the commands of his brain, but they weighed too much. He blinked a few times, dust on his eyelashes too, and then cast his gaze down the length of himself.

Buried.

His chest began to squeeze. No, not now. No time for that. He had to push this wreckage off himself and get up. He shoved at the slabs and beams pinning his torso and left arm. His legs were trapped too. Only his head and right arm were free. He strained against the wreckage for long minutes while the behemoth prowled around him, closing in. He yelled wordlessly as if he could scare the beast into leaving him alone. But with the sound of his cry, it pounced and landed squarely on his chest, weighing more than the debris piled on him.

"No. No, no, no."

He couldn't walk it off. He couldn't get outside. He couldn't find the sky.

His voice continued in his ears, screams he could not stop. He was buried again. He was suffocating in blood and mud and corpses. He was crushed under the barn's collapsed floor. They were both happening to him at the same time. Words filtered into his mind, words his mouth was making.

"Get me out. Don't leave me here. Please."

His throat was raw. He couldn't speak anymore, but he couldn't breathe either. His back arched in the tiny space he occupied between hard ground and debris. He tried to buck the weight off him. He tore at the unmovable beams until his right fingers bled.

When he had exhausted himself into stillness, the afternoon had come on. His lungs eased open, adrenaline so far spent the behemoth had to get up and go away.

He tried, for the first time since waking, to think. At first his mind glitched on panic the moment he directed his thoughts to his situation. He lay still and numb, drawing shallow breaths, and in time the pins and needles in his hands and arms withdrew. He tried to find any injuries. Bruises seemed to be everywhere. His left side twinged every time he drew breath, something he should have noticed before. Likely a fractured rib. A surface lick of pain crossed the outside of his left hip, sharp but probably a flesh wound. Nothing mortal as far as he could tell, but it didn't matter. None of it mattered if he couldn't get out. Panic flickered and popped in his system like faulty wires; his heart skipped beats, and his breath caught.

He shut his eyes so he didn't have to look at the ceiling and the walls, then opened them again and studied the view above him. The perimeter of the floor was intact. Rachel could have kept to the edges, lowered herself down the rope, and escaped. He lifted his head off the ground and angled his eyes as far as he could in every direction, but she wasn't lying trapped beside him. She was gone.

He lay for hours. Shoving at the beams and big flat sections of floor, shifting a few things but never moving enough weight to leverage himself up. He wasn't going to get himself out of this. The thought came to him as dusk was seeping into the barn through the door she'd left open.

"Someone will come," he whispered into the air that was growing colder every hour. He shivered. His breath was visible now, and he was wearing only a fall jacket, and the wood keeping him trapped ate his body heat.

His shift had ended hours ago. David and Tiana had closed the bookstore by now. Someone had texted him, called him, wondered why he wasn't responding or picking up. He'd left his phone in his car. The fact chafed, but he had to wait here for them to come. No choice.

In the meantime he worked to keep his breathing steady, his mind clear. His adrenaline would burn out eventually and send him crashing, but it hadn't happened yet.

Instead his system kept rocketing deeper into fight-or-flight whenever his brain registered the confined space as if it were news. Shoot, maybe this would cure him altogether.

He was okay. Coping. Dealing. Take that, Life Buoy.

He was suffocating. Mud filled his mouth and the weight of the bodies reminded him where he was, how deep the grave was turning out to be, and he had to keep digging. But the mud was solid now. Rough. With splinters. He gasped and writhed, and a board clattered somewhere over him. The barn. Not the grave. Deep night, moonlight filtering in from somewhere, temperature near freezing, trapped.

Trapped.

"No."

Sparking, fizzing panic. Heart rate out of control. His muscles trembled with cold and fatigue, and the cracked ribs had progressed from an ache to a stabbing pain. But he was okay. He was dealing. He lay there an hour or more, shivering and straining his eyes to focus on the one beam of moonlight through a small hole at the peak of the roof. Okay. Dealing.

Someone would come.

Another hour. And another. No tracking them to the minute, but the sense of them creeping by was a skill he'd retained from the years when a pocket watch was used by railroad men, not teenage freighters. Time was instinctive to him then and now. It was past midnight, perhaps two in the morning. Clouds rolled over the moon, and the little silver light above him went out, and a cry escaped him.

"Someone."

Long, dry sobs heaved from his gut. Alone and in the dark. Alone and unable to move. Maybe they would never find him.

He should be able to dig himself out. He'd done it once before. But he couldn't move the beams, and his right hand was too raw now to keep trying. He was as powerless in this as he was in everything else: couldn't figure out Colm was killing people, couldn't maintain the mask of the affable celebrity for the fans who now mocked and mistrusted him, couldn't save Lucas's family from a loss very much like a death. Couldn't keep Cady and Finn's family from being accidentally slaughtered by a desolate woman who sought death for herself too. It all gushed out of him like so many mortal wounds.

When he thought he might be able to

catch his breath, the last of the wounds tore open. Couldn't place his foot on the tight-rope, couldn't keep his balance against the wind, couldn't stop the plummet to earth and the explosion of pain and death and the waking up from both in his undamaged body that he *knew* had not been undamaged, had not been alive, had not been a body anymore except that here he was inside flesh and bone that had not perished, had not even broken.

"What did You do to me?" The words were hoarse, raw. "What are You doing to me now? I know You're here."

He bucked in the trap.

"You don't make any sense. Why won't You let go? Why won't You let me go?"

Be still.

He thrashed again. "In the grave I tried to find You. I begged You — don't You remember I begged You to get me out?"

Be still.

"No!"

Zac fought the rubble for an hour, teeth locked against more words. When at last he stopped, his breaths were ragged gulps of cold air that left him coughing. He tried to keep wrestling, but he had no strength. He closed his eyes.

"I don't understand." The words rasped

in his shredded throat. Shredded like the skin of his right hand. Like the soul that twisted inside him.

For as the heavens are higher than the earth, so are My ways higher than your ways and My thoughts than your thoughts.

"You woke me up," he whispered. "At the bottom of Marble Canyon, You put me back together and woke me up."

Be still, and know that I am God.

Zac lay motionless beneath the weight of the timbers and shivered, not only with the cold. The quaking began within him, in the soul whose rage and pain were morphing into something else. He had laughed as he told the fawning fangirls an angel had caught him. He had signed autographs in the place where Jehovah Elohim had restored his life although he had run as far as any man could run, a distance of one hundred years. He had made the canyon a mockery rather than admit what God had done there.

A week later, thinking he'd regained his grip on the world around him, he had learned Colm's true nature, presided at his execution, and turned shovelfuls of dirt onto the monster he had believed was his best friend through lifetimes.

"I've been wrong," he whispered, shaking

hard now. "About too many things."

Know that I am God.

"Yes." Zac covered his face with his raw right hand. "You. I AM WHO I AM, You are God."

Be still.

"I don't know how. But I know I've sinned against You." His voice shook so hard he almost couldn't speak. Oh, how he had sinned. "You have to judge me. You're just to judge me."

But when he was yet a great way off, his father saw him, and had compassion, and ran, and fell on his neck, and kissed him.

"Wh–what?" Zac lowered his hand to the cold ground and looked up at the hole in the roof. The clouds still hid the moon.

The words had been set into his soul from a source other than himself. True, he'd memorized them long ago, before the serum. But he hadn't been thinking of that parable at all. That son hadn't run from the Father for a century.

"I don't get to go home. I don't expect You to let me do that."

Bring forth the best robe, and put it on him; and put a ring on his hand, and shoes on his feet.

"Not me, that's not for me."

And bring hither the fatted calf, and kill it;

and let us eat, and be merry. For this my son was dead, and is alive again.

"I was. I was dead."

He was lost, and is found.

If only he could be found. The yearning for it broke out of him in a groan. "Oh God, find me. Forgive me. Please, please, come and find me, God."

This my son.

"Father?" The name he had held most in awe for Him. Zac had thought never to speak it again. "You'd let me be Your son again, Father?"

My son.

Two tears squeezed from the corners of his eyes and trickled into his hair, into the dust.

Twenty-Three

He lay still as the sun rose, no longer struggling to move when the panic crept up on him, but the repeated spikes of adrenaline left him battered and frayed. He was drifting in his mind, cold and bruised and queasy with hunger, trying not to focus on anything in particular, when a noise brought him fully awake. Gravel crunched under someone's feet. He tried to call out, but his throat could make only a feeble, rasping croak. If they didn't come into the barn, they'd never hear him. His scabbed fingers scrabbled at the dirt, as if somehow the person's presence would lend strength to his own limbs.

The big front door slid and squeaked in its track. Now light poured in from there as well as the back, fell on Zac's face and warmed him. He lifted his hand, and a female voice gave a cry.

"Zac?"

Cady. She dropped to her knees beside him and enfolded his hand in both of hers, which were blessedly warm. Her green eyes and red-blond ponytail caught the new sunlight. She had a lot of hair. It was kind of beautiful.

"You're freezing. Are you badly hurt?"

He tried to answer. Drew a breath that ended in a cough that brought fresh pain to his side. Cady let go of his hand, a true loss, to dial her phone. She put it on speaker and set it on the ground beside her as she surveyed the heap of lumber pinning him.

"Well?" came the snapping voice from the phone.

She'd called Simon. But she didn't know Simon. What . . .?

"I found him. Out on French Road, I just happened to see his car."

"He'd better be recovering from something mortal or I'm going to kill him."

"He isn't talking, but I think he's all right."

"It's Zac. If he's not talking, then he's not all right."

"Simon, listen, I need you and David here. He's pinned under a bunch of rubble, and I don't think I should move it without someone else's help. If he's injured, I could —"

Zac pointed to his throat. "Hoarse. But

I'm fine."

"Did you hear that?" Cady said to the phone.

"You said he's pinned? As in buried?"

"Other than head and shoulders and one arm, yes, as in buried."

"Zac," Simon said. "Buddy, tell me how you're doing. And remember what I said."

Life Buoy, no masks, got it the first time, Simon. "Breathing through it."

"Been bad," Simon said, not a question.

"Why I can't talk."

"Shoot, I'm sorry, man. We looked all night at the dunes. David said it's where you go to get away, and I thought you'd heard bad news about the kid."

They had missed him. He could hug every one of them, but his gladness sharpened to an ache. No one was missing Rachel. No one but Zac.

"I'll be there in five," Simon said. "David's farther, closer to the dunes."

"I think two of us can free him," Cady said. "I could eventually, but I might shift something and hurt him."

"No, wait for me. If Zac can wait."

"I'm okay," Zac said.

"I'll call David and Tiana." Simon hung up.

"Tiana too?" Zac rasped as Cady pushed

her phone into her pocket.

"And Finn until around midnight. He had to go back to the hotel for some sleep."

While Rachel drove farther from them, unlooked for. To keep back tears he said, "Is there any water?"

"Not with me. I'm sorry."

"No, it's okay."

Cady reached for his hand again and froze when this time she noticed the torn flesh of his palm and fingers. "What was Simon asking you?"

"Closed space. I'm not a fan."

She looked over his trapped state and set her hand on his shoulder.

"Change the subject? Until I'm out of here."

"Are you injured anywhere that you can tell?"

"Broken rib, maybe two. I think that's the worst of it."

"I'll keep talking until Simon gets here."

"Nothing's really going to help except getting me out of here." Then he remembered Tiana's words in the bookstore. "Well, maybe if you would talk about the sky?"

Whoa. The unmasking thing wasn't supposed to happen without his permission.

For some reason Zac's request seemed to move her. She set one hand on his head, and as worn out and beat up as he was, the gesture felt intimate. He closed his eyes to the dim, dusty confines around him and tried to imagine the sunset Cady painted with her words until Simon's tromping feet sounded on the gravel outside.

He burst into the barn like a roused bear, growling the moment he saw the rubble and Zac beneath it. He stood over Zac and shook his head.

"Buddy, you look like —"

"Lady present." Zac jabbed a finger toward Cady, and she laughed.

Simon was already moving. Circling the wreckage and tilting his head this way and that, calculating.

"Simon, do you have water?" Cady said. "I finished mine."

"Black sports bottle in my car." He tossed her his keys without looking up from the puzzle in front of him.

Cady jogged out of the barn jingling them in one hand.

"Guess you've met," Zac rasped.

"I like her. Can't make heads or tails of Finn."

Zac chuckled then swallowed a moan.

Simon stood back with his hands on his hips. "Nice work."

"I don't plan these things, you know."

"Uh-huh."

Cady returned with an industrial-sized water bottle and knelt beside Zac. She held his head in one hand and the bottle in the other. The taste of water hadn't been so dear to him in a long time.

She helped him drink his fill and then rested his head on the ground again. "No pillows on hand."

"Just get me out." His voice was a little stronger. Good.

Simon beckoned Cady to a long beam pinning Zac's legs. "Come on. This guy's been stuck here long enough."

As they lifted it, a portion of the weight on Zac lifted too. Because David wasn't here, Zac grinned and said to Simon, "If the damage is worse than we expect, you can shoot me through the heart. Should speed things along."

Simon didn't pause in his work. "I came here with a carry-on backpack. Weapons stayed home."

"Too bad. I'll have to heal up the old-fashioned way."

"Stop tempting me."

Cady's gaze darted back and forth between them as if she'd never heard longevite jokes in her life. Well, maybe she hadn't. Finn would take them seriously.

Twenty minutes later they had moved enough of the debris to see down inside the pile to Zac. Cady gripped Simon's arm as she stood on tiptoe and leaned past the tipping point of her balance, peering down.

"Can you move your legs now, Zac?"

"It'll all cave in again." The possibility choked him.

"Just try it, little movements. If you can, then there's just one more timber and this big slab of flooring — if we pull this off you, you should be able to slide out from under the rest."

His mouth dried as he wiggled his feet. Bent his knees the slightest bit. Shifted his hips and blinked away the slice of pain across the left one.

"I'm good if the rest doesn't move at all."

The section of flooring had been the heaviest weight on him, he realized as it lifted.

"Can you slide out?" Cady said.

He tried to prop himself on both elbows to shimmy backward, but his left arm wasn't there. He gasped. No, it was there. Dead and numb and useless. Had it been sheared off by something in the fall? But his shoulder joint was attached —

"Zac," Simon said.

"It's asleep." He laughed, coughed,

laughed again. "My arm's asleep. Can't move it. One second."

"One second's about what you've got, man."

He rolled toward his right side, propped up on the elbow he could feel, and dragged the rest of him out from under the rubble. As his feet cleared, he said, "Free."

They lowered the slab as he flopped onto his back. "Thanks."

"Yeah, well, try not to fall through another floor, if you don't mind." Simon sat next to him and mopped sweat from his forehead with his coat sleeve. "You're bleeding."

Zac pushed up on his elbow and surveyed himself. He was filthy, coated in dust. And yeah, his jeans were sliced at the hip, dark with drying blood.

"Can you stand?"

"Uh, in a minute. Might need a hand. Legs feel stiff."

"So what were you doing out here?"

"I'll tell you in a minute."

"Is it your boy? Something happened to him?"

The man had no patience whatsoever. "His dad left his mom."

Simon folded his arms across his knees. "Not sick again?"

"No. Just stunned. Hurt. Too young for

loss like that."

"Like you were."

One of those things he rarely thought about anymore. "He's a little older than I was, but still too young."

"Why'd that send you out here?"

"It didn't." Zac glanced at Cady, who was listening without comment. They all needed to know as soon as possible, but he wanted to start with Simon. "It's a long story. Help me up."

Simon stood and bent to grip Zac under the arms. "Ready?"

"Here, let me help." Cady moved to Zac's left side as Simon got him halfway to his feet, and Zac lifted his left arm to drape it over her shoulders.

The ribs stabbed straight through to his back. He sucked a hard breath and doubled over, spots filling his vision. He tucked his left arm close to him.

"Right," Cady said. "Simon, if you'll drive him to his apartment, I'll follow in his car, and then you can bring me back here for mine."

"I can drive." The words gritted past Zac's locked teeth.

"You are not driving right now," she said. As if the decision were hers. As if she had known him for years, not days.

"I'm fine."

Simon nudged Zac's side with one finger.

"Agghh." The pain buckled his knees.

Simon caught him and lowered him to sit on the ground. "Idiot."

"Moron."

"Someone needs to look you over," Cady said.

"I'm not dying."

She rolled her eyes. "If there's something nonlethal wrong with you, you'll have to heal at mortal speed. Do you want a grinding rib for the next hundred years because you were too stubborn to let someone set it right?"

"What're you, a nurse?"

"I'm a female who's lived through both world wars, who wanted to serve her country, who wasn't interested in joining Rosie the Riveter. So yes, I was a nurse. Additionally my best friend has a closed head injury and can't be treated by a doctor. I'm all he's got. I have to know my stuff."

"Finn breaks ribs often, does he?"

She glared at him. "Finn ignores pain until it puts him prostrate on the floor. I see male giveaway behaviors before you guys even know you're broadcasting them."

He could keep protesting, or he could relax in the passenger seat while Simon drove him home. He'd wanted to talk to the guy alone anyway. He allowed his body to double up as he sat there on the ground.

"Okay," he said. "Uncle."

He told Simon everything and concluded with, "We have to locate her."

"Good luck," Simon said. "Her home is her car, and you have no way of predicting her."

"No detective tricks to help me out?"

"You've got nothing, Zac, not even a surname. Social media might give you a shot, but only if her account has interacted with yours. She's probably just watching you anonymously from a browser."

"I have to try."

Simon's mouth tightened. "You think saying she has nothing to offer makes her a danger to herself."

"And she's prepared to pay for the deaths she caused. And she didn't want to be hated 'at the end.' "

"You're also assuming she kept aside some of the cure for herself."

"The way she was talking, I'd be shocked if she didn't."

"Hmm."

"I have to try, man."

But by the time Simon pulled into the

apartment lot, Zac's body was demanding immediate sleep. Then he'd have to refuel with some good food. Then, maybe, he would let Cady examine his ribs.

Before he could tell Cady the order of events, she followed him into the living room and scrutinized his movements as he lowered himself to the couch and closed his eyes.

"Shirt off," she said.

"But we just met."

"I'm serious, Zac. Let me look at you."

He cracked an eye open and cocked an eyebrow and tilted his mouth. She bit her lip, which was cute. Then she rolled her eyes, and he had to admit his game at the moment sounded less Freudian quip than usual, more high school cheese. Turning on the smolder was a nonstarter when he couldn't keep his eyes open.

"You don't get to sleep until I check your ribs," she said.

Nurses. So freaking dedicated to their calling. He pushed up from his slouch and tried not to wince. He undid the first few buttons of his shirt and was thankful he'd donned a button-down yesterday. He jolted at the thought.

"What time is it?"

"A little after eight."

"Oh no. The bakery."

"Bakery?"

"I got a job this week."

Her mouth twitched. "Well, you can call in and explain in a minute."

"David said he would when I called him," Simon said from the kitchen. "He knows the owner."

Zac sagged against the couch. Whether Connie would accept the excuse of broken ribs was anyone's guess. He should care about her deciding he was undependable after all. But it was a ridiculous trivial job working for mortals, and she could fire him with no repercussion to his bank accounts, and . . . and he was a jar with a thousand cracks, energy leaking out of him everywhere.

Cady sat beside him on the couch. "Adrenaline crash?"

"Sucks."

"Yeah." She nodded to his fingers, gone still in the act of unbuttoning his shirt. "Come on, let's get this done."

Too drained to keep arguing, he eased out of the shirt, and Cady made a humming sound of sympathy. He looked down at his torso. The purple and black bruising was darkest along his side but reached all the way to the tattoo on his pec. The ship braving waves, challenging tides. Zac himself, sailing his own way through this ageless life.

He knew what Jehovah Elohim would say to that.

Shame surged into him, and he closed his eyes. *You can't possibly want me for Your son. Not after a hundred years.*

"Zac?"

He blinked. "It's not as bad as it looks."

"Can you lean forward for me?"

Not a problem. Eased his side a bit. She set her hand on his back, to one side of his spine, and her palm pressed carefully. Ow. A pathetic yelp burst out of him.

"Contusions on both sides of your spine. You might have fractured a rib here too."

"I don't think so."

"Do you have ice at the ready?"

He nodded toward the kitchen. "Always. Stunt injuries."

She felt each rib beneath the bruises, front and back, and he kept as quiet as he could.

"Two fractures, but they're not displaced. They should heal fine."

He managed a nod, still catching his breath.

Cady got up, returned with a frozen gel pack, and offered it to him. He winced at the cold as he held it to his side, but it brought a slow relief to the sharpest of the pain.

"Do you want help with whatever's bleeding?" She gestured to his hip.

"It stopped. I'll deal with it later."

She gave him a dubious squint. "I've seen worse. And more."

"I don't need stitches." And wouldn't be getting them even if he did. "It's fine."

"Moving on, then: Motrin. When did you eat last?"

"Breakfast yesterday."

"Your blood sugar must be bottomed out."

He couldn't make himself care.

Simon wandered into the living room and sat in the chair across from them. "We can go out for food after you've slept a bit."

Go out. The girl who'd taken the picture at the bookstore — she might snap another shot of him. This time he would look adrenaline-fried and exhausted. Anyone he ran into might recognize him right now, the way those posts had been gathering notice yesterday. Anyone might wonder if he were high or shiftless or a fraud.

He was a coward, because he couldn't face their judgment. Not today.

"I'll just . . . order delivery later. Or something."

For a moment, Simon's frown seemed offended. Then his face lit with a deep understanding and he nodded.

"Dinner in. Sounds good."

"You guys don't have to stay." Zac kept the ice pack against his ribs and lay back on the couch. He had to find Rachel, but sleep had found him. He was powerless to hold it off.

"Whatever you say, buddy."

Simon's voice faded in Zac's ears, but nonetheless he recognized the sarcasm. When he woke up, his family would still be here, and then he'd tell them everything.

Twenty-Four

Once or twice, he surfaced briefly from sleep. Their voices came to him hushed, thoughtful. Sometimes in the room with him, sometimes not. The apartment was too small not to hear them wherever they were. Strangers cautious with each other; longevites instantly connected. When he fully woke at last, he lay quietly, eyes closed, not ready to talk yet. The ice pack had gone lukewarm against his skin, and the ribs were stabbing again in a way that didn't let him feign deep breathing, but he didn't have to. Simon and Cady were in the kitchen.

"Most accident-prone human being alive."

"I watched the canyon footage."

"A week after that, he got himself stabbed by a crazed fan."

"Well, that's not an *accident* exactly —"

"And now here we are a few weeks later, and that's just the last month of his life. You want to talk about the last hundred and fifty years, I've got stories."

A quiet laugh. "But they're his stories, so you won't tell them."

"Oh, I don't know about that. When I'm the one who patched up his reckless hide, I think I get to tell my version."

"Hmm. I like this concept. It would give me a world of blackmail material on Finn."

"There you go."

"So what can you tell me? About him."

"He's an idiot."

"That's not very helpful."

"Should be all you need to know."

All she needed to know? A stone seemed to sink from Zac's chest to the pit of his stomach.

"Maybe it would be," Cady said, her voice somehow both softer and firmer, "if I thought you meant it."

"I mean it. One hundred percent."

Zac's fingers curled loosely into his hands. He should get up and go in there so they'd talk about something else.

"Okay, I don't know you guys yet at all, so maybe I'm way off base. But I don't think you'd be here if Zac were nothing to you but a careless fool."

"Well, he's my brother. No matter what else he is."

The deepest truth between him and Simon. It shrank the stone inside but didn't disintegrate it altogether.

"But what else is he?"

"He's got the caution of a toddler and the humility of a peacock."

"And?"

"And he invests himself into everything. A friend's personal crisis, a chocolate chip pancake — to Zac, everything is equally vital and equally vivid."

A clanking of mugs, and then one of them was pouring coffee. The scent wafted out to Zac, but he was too hungry to enjoy it.

"I think that's admirable," Cady said.

She did?

Simon made a scoffing sound.

"No, I really do. After we've lived so long, how does he still do it? I know I don't anymore. I'd like to get some of it back."

"Hang around him long enough and you'll see him tear up over the beauty of nature."

Cady's quiet laugh warmed Zac as he lay there. "I wouldn't mind a bit, for the record."

"Females usually don't."

"Envious?"

"Not a chance."

"But see, you're proving my point. He's much more than an idiot."

This stretch of quiet lasted longer. At last

Simon said, "We're just different, you know."

"I get it. Holly was a woman of pedicures and designer purses. She designed greeting cards for Hallmark. Give me hiking boots and a backpack; give me a neglected house to flip. My favorite part of the work is hands-on restoration."

Like David and his bookstore. The zeal in her voice rang strong.

"But even when we disagreed about the big things, which we did often, Holly was family."

"Yeah."

"Her . . . absence . . . their absence." Her voice broke. "They saw so much history, it's surreal to think those memories have passed away from the world. But more than that, they were a piece of *me*. For so long."

"I hear that. Zac . . ."

Zac nearly sat up, but Simon wasn't addressing him. He lay still and waited for the man to finish the thought. The stone inside him had eroded to a tiny pebble now.

"You'll keep this to yourself."

"If you like."

"He's the best man I've ever known, and that's a fact."

"Why should I keep it to myself? A guy should know his brother feels that way about him."

"He can figure it out."

"Haven't we lived long enough for you two to outgrow that taciturn macho thing?"

A grunt. "DNA doesn't change."

She gave a soft laugh. "I'm going to call Tiana and see what their ETA is."

Their . . . what?

"Great. I'm famished."

"Want to wake him?"

"When the food gets here. He should sleep as much as he can."

"Simon . . ."

"Yeah?"

"I — I didn't want to pry earlier, but he . . ."

A sigh. "Now that is his story."

"I'm sure he wouldn't tell me."

"Won't know unless you ask him."

"I couldn't. Not yet."

"Suit yourself."

A presence entered the room, and then Cady's voice drifted from the kitchen. "Hi, Tiana, it's Cady."

He opened his eyes. Simon was standing across the room from him, gazing out the front window. Zac shifted, and the ice pack slid down his side and dropped to the floor. Simon turned.

"The others are bringing lunch. We got to

you around seven and it's a little after eleven now."

Zac pushed up to a sitting position and tried to wince as little as possible.

"You might want to shower before they get here." Simon cocked an eyebrow at Zac's bruised chest and dusty jeans.

"Is Finn coming?"

"Cady said he was."

"I need to tell them about Rachel."

Action Hero pose. Simon crossed his arms over his chest and gave Zac the assessing cop stare. "They might not take it well."

His throat hurt more now than it had when he'd fallen asleep, and his voice sounded like sandpaper. He was so exhausted he wasn't sure he could handle their reactions right now. All inconsequential details.

"They need to know. Then I'm going after her." He got to his feet, wobbly but okay. "Crap, she might have gained another three hours' distance while I was asleep."

Or taken the cure by now. The thought brought physical pain to his chest. He shook his head against it. He had to work with what he knew, cradle hope as long as he could.

Simon sighed. "Go clean up. Eat something. Then we'll work the problem."

He hated the delay, but he did need food. And Simon's plans were usually reasonable.

Before he stepped into the shower, Zac examined the horizontal slash across his hip. About two inches long, deep enough to scar though he couldn't see down to bone. He irrigated it with antiseptic and sealed it with two Band-Aids so he wouldn't have to keep dealing with it. Not that infection would kill him, but it would be a nuisance.

He showered away layers of sweat and grime, fear and flashbacks. He stepped out of the steam feeling clean deep down. His mouth watered and his stomach growled at the smells coming in around the door, and he dressed as quickly as his ribs would allow in jeans and a red zip hoodie. The Band-Aids on his hip had withstood the shower.

When he stepped out into the hall, conversation enveloped him. Tiana spotted him first, came straight to him, and wrapped him in a careful hug. He returned it, keeping protective distance between her and his ribs.

She patted his shoulder the way one might touch a butterfly, and he grinned.

"I'm not going to crumble into dust."

"Simon told us everything."

"And made it my fault the floor caved in."

Her crooked smile didn't deny it.

"I owe you an apology," he said. "I was a jerk recently."

"Oh, that."

"Yeah. I . . . ah, if you wouldn't mind . . . I would appreciate . . ."

She waited. Making him say it. Or maybe she didn't know where he was going with this. Even after the last day and night, the words didn't want to come. He had a long way to go, if a path did exist for him. A path to being a son again.

Before he could force himself to ask for something he didn't deserve, Cady called from the kitchen.

"Hey, Tiana."

Tiana's eyebrows lifted, her attention remaining on Zac.

Not the time for this conversation. He motioned her into the kitchen and followed her.

"Here," she said to Cady.

"I've distributed most of the sandwiches, but there's also an order of spaghetti and meatballs." Cady held up the plastic container, steam obscuring its clear lid, a Sharpie scrawl naming its contents.

"Oh, that's Zac's."

A grin split his face. "Spaghetti, huh?"

"You were asleep; I couldn't get your order. I went for classic and filling. From this place, it's more like meatballs with a side of pasta. Their sauce is homemade and delicious, and there should be a breadstick too."

Cady handed him the container. "Enjoy."

"Definitely." He touched Tiana's shoulder. "Thank you."

"This talk isn't done," she said.

"No."

"Good." She took a sandwich from Cady and meandered out to the living room to join the others.

"How do you feel?" Cady said, unwrapping a battered fish sandwich that released the tang of tartar sauce into the air.

"Starved."

Zac popped open the lid on his meal and dug into one of the takeout bags for a plastic fork. He balanced the container on one hand, twirled the fork into the spaghetti, and tasted a bite. Tiana was right. This was delicious. Then again, at this point, instant ramen would be delicious. Or army rations from the nineteenth century.

Cady was watching him eat. "What about the . . . well, do you have to deal with an aftermath? When you've been trapped that way?"

He gestured to the vaulted ceiling in the living room, the windows in the kitchen that were set close together to create a sort of panorama on that side of the apartment. "Why I picked this place."

"I see." She was studying him, looking for something. "I don't think you're putting me on."

Ah. "Too wiped at the moment."

"So honesty is temporary with you."

He shifted on his feet and forked a bite of meatball. He'd never thought of it that bluntly before. Not a thing to be known for. "I don't want it to be temporary."

"Only you can carry that out."

He nodded.

She glanced down, stalling with a bite of her sandwich. "Steamroller remarks. I'm famous for them."

"I've made a few lately. Such as yesterday when I called making demands and didn't bother to explain myself."

She met his eyes, faint challenge in the set of her shoulders. Yeah, he had offended her with that call. With good reason.

"I'd never try to replace them, Cady."

Her lips thinned. "You couldn't if you tried."

"I know. I should've said so."

She gave him a long look, and something in him, muted by current crises, hoped she found what she was looking for in his face.

No smile in either of them today, but at last she nodded.

"Okay," she said.

He gestured her ahead of him into the living room. David and Simon remained on their feet, and Finn and Tiana had claimed the chairs across from each other. Everyone seemed to be balancing caution and curiosity in varying degrees. The small talk was quiet. Anticipating. They hushed when Zac eased himself onto the sofa.

He looked around at the people who had formed his search party. "So . . . thanks. Everyone."

Everyone but Moira. Her absence felt like a hole in the air itself. They were not complete.

"Simon might have told you, I have information."

Nods around the room.

Zac cradled the spaghetti container in both hands and met their eyes, each in turn. He swallowed the memory of Rachel's fear-stricken face as he told her he knew what she'd done.

He nodded at Cady, at Finn. "I know who it was."

"Not Doc?" Finn said.

"Doc is dead."

The news rippled through the group, rattling them like a gust of wind through exposed leaves. Even Simon. Zac hadn't mentioned this detail before. David and Simon each took a step back, nearer the wall where they stood, guards over the room, opposite one another. Zac would lay money they'd positioned themselves that way unconsciously. Finn's and Cady's faces had gone still and grim, dread in their eyes. Only Tiana looked fully composed, listening and waiting. Her stake in this was less, being mortal, but then again, maybe not. She was watching David, not Zac.

"Doc Leon has a daughter who took the serum. Her name's Rachel." At Cady's surprised inhale, Zac nodded. "The gray-haired girl at the diner. When Doc died, she continued his research."

For the second time he recounted his encounter with Rachel, how he'd ended up pinned in the barn.

"She's gone," he said at last. "Unless we go out and find her."

"Why would we do that?" Cady had finished her sandwich while Zac was talking, but now she looked sick. "Doc's daughter killed our family. There. Now we know."

"And you know she didn't intend to kill them."

"If she's telling the truth," Finn said.

"She is."

"She's one of us; we've all learned to lie."

"I'm telling you, Rachel isn't lying."

"He's probably right," Simon said from his corner. "Zac's been a natural lie detector since I've known him. I don't know how he does it."

A fact that had caused Simon no small amount of annoyance over the decades. Zac nodded his thanks for the backup and tried not to think about the one person who'd succeeded in lying to him for most of his life.

"All right, say it's true," Finn said. "Maybe in a few months, she changes her mind. Stalks Cady in a grocery store and sticks her with a needle."

"No way. I can't prove it, but I'm sure."

Simon stepped out closer to the middle of the room. "So you don't want to apprehend her for trial."

"Trial?" Zac said.

"Manslaughter."

Of course Simon would ask. "She's not Colm. She's nothing like Colm."

Simon made a gesture of acknowledgment. "Hence manslaughter."

The guy could have mentioned this in the car; no doubt he'd been thinking of it. "Simon, no. This is about putting the mystery to rest. For them especially." He gestured to Finn and Cady. She looked away.

"Why did she do it?" Finn said.

"She sees us as diseased," Zac said. Quietly, but Cady flinched as if he'd shouted. "She thought the cure would give them a normal life span. Immediate death was an accident."

"Not that it matters," Cady said.

Finn looked across to her. "Of course it does."

"What, that her motives were pure? I couldn't care less."

Zac rested his still-full spaghetti dish on his knees. "She intended to fix it, make it into a true cure for us. And she's had no one. She compared her life to solitary confinement."

"Solitary confinement is where she belongs," Cady said. "Someplace she can't *cure* anyone else."

He wouldn't contradict words spoken from so much pain, but he wouldn't ignore pain like Rachel's either, invisibility to the entire human race. He didn't know how to ignore it.

"I'm not looking for a consensus," Zac said. "You each do what you want to do."

"What'll you do?" Finn said.

"I won't let her live in isolation for another couple of centuries, and if I can, I'll keep her from the cure in its current form."

"Indeed, you'll have to keep her from it," David said quietly.

He'd been so still so long, his presence had all but melded into the wall behind him. He was a simple read most of the time, but now Zac had to work at it. Behind David's veiled expression, desperation swelled. His voice held a deep hush.

"She's seen us now. Knows who we are." The brogue thickened with every sentence David spoke, *r*'s rolling and vowels morphing. "That knowledge will deepen her loneliness. She will end her life."

The room was quiet a long moment until Cady whispered, "Then let her."

Twenty-Five

Let her.

No one spoke for a long moment, as Cady's words settled around them like shed feathers drifting to the ground.

Finn stared at her as if he didn't know her. "She's a human soul."

"And if Zac's right, she's innocent of malice," Simon said.

Cady thrust her fingers into her hair as if to ease a headache. "So leave it up to her."

Simon looked to Zac. "We might have to. You still have no way of contacting her."

A low buzz of power was rising in the room, a decision coalescing between him and Simon, readiness to carry it out. The protector and servant in Simon was rising too. He might voice his certainty of failure, but he'd never refuse the mission. Zac thought through the impossibility of it. Rachel had wanted to be seen and heard the first time he met her. Even in the bakery, she had demonstrated that.

He pushed away from the wall. “I might be able to get her to contact me.”

Cady made a quiet choking sound.

“Look,” Simon said, “if she’s emotionally stable, it’ll be her choice. Permanent distance from us if that’s what she wants.”

Fine. The rest of them could let her go. Zac would stick by her regardless.

“No.”

The word was faint, hoarse, ragged to such a degree that Zac didn’t realize it was David’s voice until Tiana swiveled in her chair to look up at him. The man stood in his corner, tall frame seeming to have shrunk in the last few minutes, shoulders bowing as if they carried a world’s weight. When he met Zac’s eyes, the veil had dropped, and his expression had twisted into one of desperation.

“David,” Zac said.

He intended a ceding of the debate floor, but David seemed to take Zac’s speaking his name as a reproof. He looked from Zac to Simon, then to the others, his gaze coming to rest on Tiana. She nodded encouragement.

“She cannot distance herself from us,” David said. “She must not.”

“Why not?” Zac said.

"She must finish her work." His brogue had grown so thick, Zac's ears had to work to adapt. "The cure — she must finish it."

"For us?"

"I know you don't want it, Zac." David looked around at them. "I venture to say none of ye want it, not today and perhaps not ever. But I —" His voice splintered into a rough inhale.

Tiana stood and went to him. She circled her arm around his waist and stood close to him, her eyes petitioning the rest of them. Maybe for compassion. Yes, her stakes were high in this room of ageless folk. She loved the man who now leaned against her.

"I need my years to begin counting again. I need my days to be numbered. Aye, Leon's daughter has done great damage." David looked to Cady and Finn with a nod of deference. "Indeed, it's damage to all of us. But I ask that she not be punished with isolation."

"All this is moot if we can't find her," Simon said.

David wrapped his arm around Tiana's shoulders, and they seemed to face Simon's words together.

"I'll come with you," David said.

A muscle twitched in Simon's jaw. Any moment he'd go Action Hero on David.

"Three people aren't needed."

"Zac can remain behind and recover."

"No, I can't."

The tensions around him were pulling tighter: Cady's hostility, David's desperation, and Simon losing patience with both of them in his drive to stay on task. Zac drew a breath and forced his shoulders square, his posture straight.

"If I'm not there, she's going to run again."

"Then you and I will go."

Simon crossed his arms, spread his feet, and glared.

Despite the vaulted ceiling, despite the sunlight spilling through the windows, the room began to close in.

"I have experience dissuading people from harming themselves." Simon's voice was a cool wall of stone against which David was welcome to bang his head. "And if she's dead, I have experience making the scene clean and undetectable."

David took a step away from Tiana to match Simon's posture. "I need her research."

"If we can't bring her back, we'll bring her work."

"Neither of you will make that your priority."

"No, David, I'm making the woman herself my priority, and if you —"

"Well, Finn?" Cady rose to her feet, wrapping her arms around herself as if she stood against a winter wind. "Why don't you go too? The whole lot of you can go rescue her from herself, and I'll go home and hold a one-person memorial for my *manslaughtered* family."

The vise in Zac's chest clamped down hard. He pushed to his feet, pushed past all of them toward the sliding door.

"Zac," David said.

His fingers wrestled with the lock. He slid the door open and staggered onto the deck, into the bitter bleak afternoon that spit drizzle at him. He braced his right hand against the railing and the sting of the square wood edge against his palm reminded him of the torn scabs there. His left hand pressed tight against his side. He didn't dare try for a deep breath, the kind that cleansed him of other people's hurt.

The guys' animosity was stifling enough, but Cady, what had flowed out in her words just now . . . Zac bowed over the rail and shut his eyes against her anguish. It wasn't a word he used lightly, but it was Cady right now.

He forgot to regulate his breaths, gulped

the cold air recklessly, and his tight lungs reacted with a cough. Zac sagged against the deck rail. Wretched, undying body that still cracked and snapped and tore and bruised.

"Zac."

He couldn't straighten. "Yeah."

David stepped outside. "Are you with Simon in this? You want to prevent me from —"

"Stop."

"I must be —"

"Stop talking."

David approached, studying Zac now, a crease forming between his eyes. "What is it you need?"

"I need you to shut up."

David stood at his side as Zac sucked breaths through clenched teeth. He kept his eyes shut until the pressure in the room behind them released its grip. When he could, he raised his head.

"That thing Moira calls extra empathy."

"Aye."

"It doesn't hit this hard most of the time, but I . . . I haven't been sleeping, and I'm . . ."

David nodded. "Worn down."

"Would you pray for me?" The words he'd hoped to say to Tiana left him now without forethought.

"I do so often."

Zac tried to smirk and failed. "I need a lot of it."

"Everyone does."

"I spoke to Him last night."

David grasped the deck rail in a gesture that didn't try to hide his investment in the topic.

"But I don't know where I go from here," Zac said. "There. Wherever."

"He'll show you."

This my son.

"He might be trying to. I can be a little willful." Zac's mouth tugged on one side, but again the mask refused to fit. "I don't know, man. I'm . . . I'm uneasy, I guess."

"About what?"

Uneasy was hardly the word for the quaking in the core of him when he imagined himself standing before Jehovah Elohim without excuse. One more example of Zac's cowardice, especially compared to David's confused expression at the idea of a man's uneasiness before the Almighty. Well, David Galloway had probably never feared anything in his life. Zac forced his posture straighter and ignored the stabbing of his ribs. Couldn't have this conversation bowed over like a weakling.

"I broke a hundred-year silence, you know?"

"Aye, and He heard. 'Tis a good thing."

"Yeah, maybe."

"How can it be other than good?"

So much faith in this guy. Zac wouldn't mind borrowing a tenth of it. "I had the gall to knock on His front door last night after a freaking century. He should cast me out of His house forever."

"But He won't."

Bring forth the best robe, and put it on him.

Zac propped his forehead in one hand, all out of words. His head buzzed and ached, his back and hip throbbed, and none of it hurt half as much as his ribs. He tried to gather himself, but his legs turned to rubber and let him slide down toward the waiting floor of the deck.

"Zac."

David gripped his forearm. Zac drooped forward, and David caught his other shoulder.

"Sit, friend."

"Okay."

David frowned at the reply. He propped Zac against the deck's half wall and crouched beside him. "Your strength is sapped."

"Fair summary."

"You didn't eat."

"Oh, right. Guess not." Two bites didn't count in a metabolic sense.

"Wait here."

Zac looked down at his limp hands, his legs stretched out in front of him, and chuckled. Groaned. No more laughing for the next six weeks.

David strode into the lit house, disappearing around the corner into the living room. He returned in minutes with Zac's food, a bottle of water, and Tiana. She held a pill bottle.

Tiana knelt beside him and offered him the dish of spaghetti. "I can microwave it, if you want."

"No, this is fine." He forked a bite, chewed slowly. "How's Cady?"

"She went out. Said she needed some space."

"Oh." Zac leaned his head back and closed his eyes.

"Zac," Tiana said. "How many hours since you had pain meds?"

"Haven't yet."

She huffed and popped the top open on the ibuprofen. "Get these into your system while you finish eating."

He accepted two pills from her hand, then the water bottle. Tiana watched him swallow the pills.

"I'm all right," he said, and when she rolled her eyes, "I have to find Rachel. I can't worry about trivial stuff right now."

She gave a slow nod. "I guess it's trivial from your perspective. From the mortal perspective, it feels like you almost died again."

He smiled.

"What?"

"Was picturing Simon's reaction to that."

"Because he cares."

"More like he relishes my humiliation."

But the words he had overheard warmed him. It was stupid to cup those words in his hand and keep them. He'd known the man would call him brother just as Zac would say of Simon. Still, though.

Maybe he was just too tired.

"Well, allow me to say as your friend and former fangirl, I'd love it if you would stop ending up hurt."

"Former?" He grinned, and this felt real too.

She shrugged. "They're mutually exclusive terms. Obviously *friend* wins out."

His eyes burned. Yep, definitely too tired.

"Feeling steady yet?"

"I think so."

He'd eaten the meatballs, the buttery

breadstick, and most of the pasta while they sat there. He set the plastic dish aside and planted his palms on the floor to push himself up, but David had already moved to his uninjured side and offered his arm. Zac gripped it and let David take most of his weight. On his feet, he breathed as deeply as he dared then took a step on his own. His legs held him up, and the headache was fading, though the pain in his ribs hadn't eased yet.

"Thanks," he said to both of them.

Tiana squeezed his arm then looked from him to David. "I'll be inside."

Right. They hadn't yet begun to argue.

"Okay," Zac said. "Bring it."

"I'm going with you."

"No matter what Simon or I have to say."

David's jaw hardened as he turned his head away. "I'm not a liability."

"Not typically, no. Right now you are."

"What are you talking about?"

"She's a means to an end for you."

"That's not true." The brogue was back in force.

"What did you imagine when you theorized her suicide? Was it loss of the woman or loss of what the woman might be able to produce?"

Shock smoothed the fury from David's

face. He backed a step away from Zac, bumped into the patio table, and sank into one of the plastic chairs.

"She might have stopped at some hotel along the highway last night and injected herself. Have you even wondered about her soul?"

David bowed his head.

"So no, David, you don't come with us. Because she'll see the way you're viewing her." Zac made no attempt to steady his voice. David had to hear the urgency, had to understand. "And that might be enough for her to go through with it."

"Lord God forgive me."

The man had gone from bullish to penitent in three-point-two seconds. He covered his face with one hand and sat a long moment. When he looked up, his eyes were glossy.

"A day or two ago, Tiana joked about how much she reads, that she'll be blind at forty."

Zac nodded. "And it reminded you."

"I didn't need reminding."

"No, I guess not."

"You don't understand."

"No." Zac sighed and pressed a hand to support his ribs. "I don't."

His wife had died so young, before he'd known he couldn't. And then there had been Moira, only Moira. When she wasn't in his bed, he slept alone, despite every recent rumor to the contrary. Not because of moral fortitude, he knew to his shame. Because he couldn't share his body with a woman and not share his soul. He wasn't capable of detachment.

And he couldn't endure the kind of grief David would endure.

"It's nearer every day." The words broke. David turned his face away. "She is sweet beauty to me, warmth and kindness. She is home, and when she leaves me I'll be . . ."

"Hey." Zac came near and set a hand on the man's quaking shoulder. "Is something wrong? Is Tiana sick?"

"Aye, she's sick with mortality, man. She's dying daily, and I cannot stop it, and I cannot join her journey."

His friend's burden settled onto Zac, dragged at him like sodden clothes on a man overboard. He tried to shed it, to keep hold of the necessary focus.

"I hear you, David. I do. But Rachel is at risk right now, this minute."

"I know it." David swiped a hand under his eyes. "I'll not lose sight of it again, God help me."

"We have to do something."

"What is there to do?"

"I have an idea." An idea that galled him, but to save her life he would do it.

Twenty-Six

The last thing he wanted to do was go online, but it was the only way he might find Rachel. Cursed media generation. Then again, twenty years ago he'd have had no chance of finding her at all. First things first: get rid of the desperate post reaching out to a dead man. But as Zac's cursor hovered over DELETE, he froze.

Simon joined him, David, and Tiana, taking the last empty chair at the kitchen table. "What's going on?"

"She saw this." Zac turned the laptop to face the others, though the stupidity of the post now brought heat into his cheeks. "She knew I'd tried to contact Doc."

They were nodding but slowly, failing to follow his line of thought.

"Suppose she's one of my followers."

"One of the million?" Tiana propped her elbows on the table and her chin in her hands.

She looked young but not ageless. Zac swallowed. If she lived to be ninety, her time on earth was a third over.

He cleared his throat and hoped they would think he was simply still hoarse. "Slight exaggeration."

She gestured to the screen, and he turned it back around. Shoot, she was right, which meant he'd garnered another fifty thousand in the last two days. Since the snapshot in the bookstore.

"Okay, but maybe she liked the post to Doc. There's only a few thousand of those."

"You want our help trying to find a profile that fits?" Tiana's eyebrow was cocked with a tinge of skepticism, but she was pulling out her phone.

"Yeah, or . . ." Zac kneaded his forehead. Had he bruised his head too? Felt like it. "Maybe I have to post something *to* her."

"And hope she replies," Simon said.

"Yeah."

"Does that sound like something she would do?"

"I don't know her, man. I just know we might be against a clock, and if she already . . ." He couldn't say it.

Simon was already nodding. "If she's cured, we have about thirty hours from that point."

Bless the man, Simon understood. Thirty hours to find her and ensure she didn't die alone. The tide of it rose inside Zac. He would do this for her, if he could do nothing else.

"Okay," he said. "Anyone who wants to help, let's look at the post likes first. Just in case."

"On it." Tiana's thumbs blurred over her phone.

David tilted back in his chair and crossed his arms.

Zac rolled his eyes. "Yeah, you'll be useless to me, you troglodyte."

"My apologies." He seemed to mean it.

For a silent twenty minutes, Zac and Tiana searched, she starting from the most recent and he loading the whole list to start from the bottom up. Simon and David wandered out of the room.

The number of unread notifications ticked upward while Zac scrolled. He huffed, blinked to keep his eyes from glazing, and it had increased by five. He huffed again.

Tiana glanced up from her phone then back down at it. "I've seen the current gossip."

"Doesn't matter right now."

"We can talk and search simultaneously, you know."

"I didn't want my moment in the spotlight to end like this. That's all." He shrugged, but his shoulders felt heavy. "It's not like it's an altered pic, you know? I can't deny I lost my crap in a very public place."

"Not for the reasons they're spreading around."

"Ah, what difference does it make? No, it had nothing to do with Marble Canyon, but it *was* a panic attack."

"Well, you're not doing drugs."

"You think they'd believe me if I said so?"

"Yeah, I do."

He glanced up from his scrolling. She did? Tiana's head was still bowed over her phone. "Your fans follow you because of you, Zac. Not because you looked sexy in a black T-shirt while conquering obstacle courses on *Warrior USA*."

He chuckled, winced, motioned her to continue when she looked up.

"I'm just saying, yeah, of course a lot of these followers are into your looks and what you can do with your body. You're dang attractive and you don't need anyone to tell you that."

"Has David heard you describe me as *dang attractive*?"

"Stop that." Now she did meet his eyes. Hers were darkest brown, like polished walnut wood, and deep with conviction as she dared him to look away. He didn't. "We're past that, and you know it. If you don't want to talk about this, just say so. Don't smirk at me."

"Sorry." He looked down, scrolled another page, and when he looked back up she was still watching him. "It's habit, Tiana. Since . . . well, since before you were born."

"Then I'll be patient while you break it."

"I appreciate that."

"Back to my point." She resumed scrolling. "It's the video you made eating white chocolate chip cookie dough while answering fan questions. It's the ways you find to help underdog charities keep their doors open. You treat your fans like human beings, and they see you as one too. I would say the majority of them do. And they'll listen if you decide to respond to the bookstore pic."

"Hmm."

"I know, not something you can deal with now. Rachel comes first. Cady and Finn come first."

"Yeah."

"One more example then. About a year ago, one of your fans asked you to wish her friend a happy birthday, because life had been getting her down. You didn't just say

'Happy birthday, Jayde!' You responded with three posts because you kept running out of characters."

"I did?" He had met Jayde a few weeks ago when he was new to town and she still worked for David. But he didn't remember the post.

"You told her to keep fighting on through whatever tough things were trying to knock her down. You told her *she* was worth the fight. She cried. Because that day no one had made her feel seen, all day long, except you."

"Me and the friend who tagged me."

She smiled. "You see where I'm going with this."

"I do. Thanks."

"You're welcome. And for the record, the most attractive man I know is my boyfriend."

This laugh made him groan, but it was worth it.

"Are you going to keel over?"

"I promise I'm not," he said. "Come on, I'm almost to the midway point."

"Same. I don't know if . . ." She fell silent, leaving the thought to dangle as she focused on the list. For another few minutes neither of them spoke, and then Tiana gasped. "Zac."

"What?"

"Whoa. Look at this." She tapped a few times, and her lips parted as she read. "Zac, look."

She handed him her phone. On her screen was a user named OldSoulPics. The profile picture was a vintage barn. No way. Zac clicked to enlarge it, and his heart began to hammer. The Harbor Vale barn, an exterior shot with the sun peeking around the roof on one side, the grass a fading green that hadn't died to brown yet but was on its way. A recent picture. The bio was shorter than character limits required.

Photographer. Old before my time. Or is that after?

"It's her," he whispered.

"It has to be, doesn't it? She's leaving you clues."

"It's her. It's Rachel." Her last post was a close-up of flowers. Chrysanthemums mostly, a fall arrangement in orange and rust and brick red, the leaves a vibrant dark green. But the foreground filled only half the shot. In the blurred background was a sign. Zac clicked on it, zoomed in, stared at the fuzzy letters until his eyes watered.

"Bed-and-breakfast," he said. "What's that other word?" He handed the phone back to Tiana.

"Oh!" With only a glance at the picture, she looked up at him, eyes alight. "I don't even have to read it. I've seen the place. It's in Leahy, north up the pinky finger. Maybe an hour and a half with traffic."

"Pinky finger? Oh, right." Michiganders and their mitten-hand directions. He checked the posting time. Yesterday at 1:17 p.m. His breath grew short. "What if she's waiting for me to come? It's been twenty-four hours, Tiana. I've ignored her all this time."

"You were incapacitated."

"She doesn't know that."

"She did see you fall, right?"

His chest squeezed. He couldn't help seeing Rachel lying on a generic bed in a generic room, a needle puncture in the crook of her elbow and her skin gone gray as her hair. Her heartbeat silent and her memories gone from the world.

"Zac." Tiana's hand rubbed a circle on his back. "Calm down, okay? She left a trail. She wouldn't have done that if she didn't want us to find her."

He tried to remember everything Rachel had ever said to him. Every clue she might have spoken. Maybe the post meant nothing. Maybe it was her final post.

He found David and Simon in the living

room. He thrust Tiana's phone into Simon's hand. "We found her. Tiana says this place is about ninety minutes away."

"Let's go," David said.

"Just give me a minute."

Zac stepped out onto the front porch. Finn sat on the stoop, his hands dangling between his knees, his unfocused gaze directed at the street. His mouth tightened when he spotted Zac.

"Where's Cady?"

Finn shrugged. "Took off around the block."

"We've located Rachel."

"Okay."

Certainty fell on Zac's shoulders as if from a great height. "You two want to leave."

"There's no reason for us to stay here while you go after her."

"We think she's only an hour or two away."

"Go ahead. Maybe we'll meet up again later, when this stuff isn't so . . ." He shrugged.

They needed a Life Buoy. "One of us will stay."

"What for?"

"For whatever we can do. Even if it's just bringing takeout to your hotel."

Finn scrutinized him as if Zac had offered him a million-dollar check they both knew was forged.

"Look, Cady told me you talked about family."

A cautious nod.

"So this is me agreeing with your conclusion. And trying to live up to it."

A long moment of stillness before he nodded again. "Good enough for me. I'll let Cady know when she gets back."

Zac returned to the living room and motioned David to one side. "I need a favor."

Twenty-Seven

"I'll not be a liability to you or to Rachel. My perception is clear. I know our priorities."

"That's not why I'm asking," Zac said.

"Why then? Speak plainly, man."

"Cady and Finn shouldn't be left right now. One of us should be with them."

David frowned. Zac relayed the words he'd had from Finn, and the frown deepened.

"We can't stop them if they wish to leave."

"They wish to leave because we're choosing Rachel. All of us. Unless someone stays here to show them otherwise."

"Have you asked Tiana?"

Zac shoved his fingers through his hair. "One of us, David. From their perspective, Tiana's not one of us."

"I don't see why it must be me."

"You'll have wisdom and scripture for them, and you know how to avoid wielding either like a club."

Zac couldn't keep him here short of hogtying the man, which wouldn't help Cady and Finn anyway. The stubborn, straitlaced imbecile clenched his hands and walked to the window to stare outside as if the matter held no urgency.

Something stirred within Zac with a wordless prodding sensation, something he was missing, something in front of his face. He was trying to see Rachel. Trying to see Cady and Finn. He was not trying to see David.

Well, the guy was slowing him down for no reason.

And he was a friend.

Okay. See David.

"Can we accelerate this at least?" Zac said.

David turned from the window. "What?"

"Tell me why you won't stay here and trust Simon and me to bring back the . . ." There it was. The clearest vision of David Galloway. "You don't trust us."

"Of course I do."

"I get it now." Zac held up a hand. "You've been on your own twice as long as you've had someone to trust. When you wanted something, needed something, you did it yourself."

David crossed the room to sink onto the edge of a couch cushion, fisted hands between his knees. "Aye. I did."

"And this matters to you too much to let someone else deal with it. Even fellow longevites."

David's mouth twitched at the name. "You could be right."

"Well, do you want to live like that for another century, or do you want to give us a chance to prove ourselves?"

He bowed his head over his clenched hands, and slowly they opened. In the silence, his prayer seemed to pour through the room like light. When he looked up, his face still held turmoil that dug furrows around his eyes and mouth. But he nodded. "I'm not at rest about it. But perhaps I won't be until I've learned again how to do it."

He pushed to his feet. On impulse Zac thrust his hand out, and David lifted his eyebrows as he shook it.

"You are coming back," he said, more an order than a question.

"With the information to make you mortal again, if it exists." And with a woman who needed a family.

"Very well." His shoulders squared, and he gripped Zac's hand one last time before releasing it. "I'll remain here. And as I'm able, I'll minister to the others."

David would be able, Zac knew down to his gut. The question was whether Zac would be equally so for the task set before him.

Simon was sitting on the hood of Zac's car, feet flat to the metal, watching traffic through the wrought-iron fence that, along with a low hill, separated the complex's parking lot from the main road. Drizzle pattered his black jacket and bits of sleet collected in his hair, but he seemed unbothered. He glanced away from the passing cars as Zac approached.

"No third man?"

"I told him to try trusting someone besides himself for a change."

Simon grunted and slid off the hood. "Guess it's a big change for him, after all that time."

"Yeah, but he has to learn."

"Impressed he's willing to."

They nearly collided on the driver's side of the vehicle. Simon held out one hand, palm up.

"Oh, right." Zac tossed the keys underhanded, and his ribs seemed to shift. He pressed his lips tight.

Simon pretended not to see as he slid in behind the wheel, and Zac walked around the front end to the passenger side as upright as he could manage. Simon entered the Leahy Bed-and-Breakfast into his phone and silenced the voice directions.

As they began the drive, Zac woke his phone and opened Rachel's profile. "I should message her."

"Okay."

Trying to make eye contact with Simon only worked when he wanted it to, and right now he was focused on the road with absurd doggedness. Something was brewing in his head. Well, whatever. He could stew for the next ninety minutes if he so chose.

Zac opened the app's messenger tab. If he didn't message her, and she was waiting . . . but if he did message her, and she saw it and ran again . . . He paused. Stilled himself. Thought. A message confirmed he'd found her profile, which he was pretty sure she wanted him to do.

Okay.

RACHEL, I KNOW THIS IS YOU. LET ME KNOW YOU'RE OKAY.

Without context he sounded rather like a stalker, but he sent it anyway. Depending on her response, he'd decide whether to tell her he was on his way to her location. He leaned back in the seat and closed his eyes.

Less than five minutes passed, and then

Simon gave a grunt.

"What?" Zac didn't open his eyes.

"Oh, nothing. You just lounge away. Never mind I was the one up all night searching and rescuing."

Zac gave half a smirk with his eyes still closed. "Rib fractures. I win."

Another grunt. A long quiet. Then Simon's voice, oddly hushed. "Was thinking about that solitary camping trip when I got rained out and fell in the mudslide and broke my leg."

"I remember."

"Yeah." His voice gained normal volume, plunging them into the retelling. "I was remembering it for other reasons, but then I got to thinking . . . must have been tough for you. The mud was awful. I remember it was all over us by the time we got back."

Zac sat up. "You mean as a trigger."

"Right." Simon kept his eyes on the road.

"It wasn't too bad as long as I kept moving." No masks. "But yeah, I was glad to get out of it." He grinned. "Man, I kept thinking I'd drop you. You're a heavy cuss."

"Nothing but muscle, brother."

"And poor Moira, holding you down while I set that leg. Kept her eyes closed the whole time, and you weren't even bleeding."

" 'How have you boys lived so long and

still not learned self-preservation?' " Simon's inflection and raised pitch sounded fairly like her.

Zac gave a truncated laugh, and then his eyes were burning. He pressed his thumbs into them. "Shoot, man. What'll we do without her?"

"It's been less than a month."

"But what's happening to her? You know? Where is she, how's she getting by?"

"She's getting by in style and effortlessly, and you know it. You're not worried about her physical safety. You're worried about her state of mind."

Simon willing to talk about someone's state of mind. What was the world coming to? "What if she's never the same again?"

"She won't be."

"Don't give me that 'none of us will' crap. I'm serious."

"So am I."

"Well, now what?"

"I don't know."

Zac blinked at him, but he kept his eyes on the road. Those three words sounded as foreign from Simon as modern slang would sound from David.

"I protect people. I get justice for them. The aftermath, road to healing stuff — that's never been my expertise."

Zac nodded. All true. He hadn't thought of himself as needing to heal, though. More like needing to process. To get past it. To learn from it. Of course Colm had hurt Moira, but the idea he'd also hurt Zac . . . it felt itchy. Wrong to dwell on, dangerous to touch.

A subject change was in order.

"Why were you thinking about a camping trip from over forty years ago?"

Simon huffed. "Tables turning and all. This time it was me out looking for your stranded butt."

"Oh, right."

"Literal payback."

"Yeah. And thanks. In case I didn't say it before."

"You did. Of course you did. The second you were clear of the debris, you thanked Cady and me."

"Okay."

The quiet held a strange new edge. Beside him, Simon seemed tight and strained, the seams of him overfull of something that wanted escape. Zac sat up again and watched Simon drive.

"You don't even remember, do you?" The edge had entered Simon's voice. Something hard and brittle.

"Nope."

"It took me a year to thank you. A year. I couldn't say it at first because I'm a proud old fool, and then I forgot to say it. And then one day you noticed the limp was gone, and I realized — I still had never said it."

"Well, did you say it then?" Zac wanted to laugh. Had this been bothering Simon for forty years?

"Yep, I did, and you said, 'You would've done it for me.' Just casual like that. Like it wasn't anything."

"It wasn't, Simon. It was just what we do. Like you coming here this week and declaring a Life Buoy on me."

"But what if you were wrong?"

"About what?"

The car sped up at least five mph. Simon merged into the left lane and passed a few cars. "That I would've gone after you. That I would've pulled you out of the mud and carried you home on my back while reliving a war."

He made the thing sound heroic, which was ridiculous. "Look, man, you would have come for me. Heck, you did. Yesterday."

A long sigh poured out of Simon, a partial release of the tension in the car. "I know what Colm said to you, the night you brought me back."

Colm. Again. "Which part?"

"Moira said you asked him for help, and he refused. Told you I shouldn't have been out there if I couldn't handle a storm on my own."

"Well?"

"I told Moira he had a fair point, and you could have listened to him. And she said, 'If Zac had listened to him, you'd still be out there in the dark, in the rain, with a broken leg.' "

The man had to be going somewhere with this. He didn't draw out a story, didn't include details without meaning something.

Simon smacked his palm against the steering wheel. "Don't you get it? I as much as told her Colm's reaction made more sense than yours. I sided with the serial killer."

Aha. Now they were getting somewhere. Zac shrugged. "You were just talking."

Simon rubbed one hand over his face. "I thought about it a lot, the week after his death. I thought . . ."

"What, that you're like him?"

"God forbid." He passed his palm over his mouth. "I mean that, Zac. If there's a God, I'd want Him to strike me dead before He let me become another Colm."

"There is a God. And you're — shoot, Simon, you're worlds different from Colm.

Can't believe you need someone to tell you that."

"We've all got darkness, man."

"You've never deliberately brought harm to an innocent person. Never. I don't care that you got some grim pleasure in tackling a guy to the concrete and kicking the gun out of his hand before he could shoot a bunch of mortals with it. I don't care that part of you misses law enforcement and hasn't found a rush to match it in all this time. None of that equals psychopath, Simon."

"I hope you're right."

"He brought home souvenirs."

Simon stared at Zac a second longer than was safe while traveling at eighty mph.

"Yeah," Zac said. "Shot glasses, bought in souvenir shops from every place he made a kill. I found them in his apartment."

"Where are they now?"

"Some landfill, I guess."

Simon grimaced.

"If you try to talk to me about evidence —"

"No. We couldn't have identified them from that alone."

They were quiet a few minutes. Simon's shoulders rose and fell a few times, long, cleansing breaths that seemed to settle him back into himself, to relieve the strain that had been building in him.

"You were actually worried about this," Zac said.

"There are things you don't know about me, Zac."

"But a shelf of trophies from the places you've murdered mortals isn't one of them."

"No."

"And you've never taken innocent life."

"Well, the wars."

"In the wars, we did our best. We tried to protect the innocent. When we failed, we mourned."

"Yeah."

"You've never looked at a helpless civilian and lusted for that person's life."

"Never."

"Well, there you go."

Simon shot him a sidelong glance, shook his head, but his mouth twitched at the corners. Then he sobered. "So many things he said to me. Like they're all echoing back at the same time."

"Yep."

"I've been wondering if any of it was true. His life in Fisher Lake, his blacksmith shop, his wife, and then Rose after her — what were those things to him? Cover? Toys?"

"I don't know." Zac gazed out the window

at the patchy clouds. "We never will, I guess."

A small voice rose inside him. Needing to know. Ready to know. He cleared his throat. "He told me once . . . a long time ago. I mean a long time, maybe the twenties." He had to clear his throat again. A lump of tears rose in it, ancient tears that had been swallowed so many times they'd become petrified somewhere in his gut. Now they began to melt. "He told me you couldn't stand me. But you did, for Moira. Since Moira wanted to keep me around."

Simon was silent.

Crap. Okay. The last few weeks had made Zac hope, given Colm had turned out to be pathological . . .

"Buddy, I can't believe you thought . . ."

The hope inside lifted its crushed head.

"I don't stay in touch with people I can't stand." Simon's voice had hardened. "I don't share a table with them at Thanksgiving. I don't answer phone calls from them in the dead of night. And I don't go out climbing dunes all night looking for their pathetic accident-prone —"

"Yeah, okay."

"You never challenged him on it."

"No." And that was on Zac. "I figured I managed to grow on you over the years, at least a little."

Simon huffed. "Can't believe this stuff's been lurking all this time. He messed with both of us."

"I think *you* messed with you, man."

"No, I'm talking about — He told me you talked about going off with Moira someplace. Cutting ties. When I said you'd never talked that way around me, he said of course not, I was a cop, and you knew I'd track you down. I told Colm he was full of crap, and he never brought it up again. But I wondered about it for a few months, maybe a year. Until it didn't happen."

"Because I never said it."

"He wanted us ill at ease with each other."

"What are we, high school girls?"

"Well . . ." Simon's mouth tipped up. "He succeeded, at least partly."

"But why bother?"

"Maybe it was a game. Or maybe he found it easier to fool us separately."

Zac propped his head in his hands as it throbbed afresh. "Right. Well. If you still need evidence you're nothing like him, there's some more."

"Hmm. Yeah."

"You know, I told David he was the one that kept us together. The glue of us. That we might drift apart forever without him."

"Where'd you get an idiotic idea like that?"

"What I'm trying to tell you. It was something else Colm said, fairly often over the years. It was the place he saw himself."

"Or wanted you to see him."

"Or that."

Quiet settled around them again, but it held a restfulness now. A shedding of old things. Simon checked his phone map, and Zac checked for a response from Rachel. Nothing.

"Anything else?" Zac said. "I mean, while we're at it."

Simon grunted. "Moira would be proud."

"Fact."

Someday soon, they would tell her about it.

Twenty-Eight

Zac jolted awake hard enough to jostle his ribs. And his head. He winced and turned his eyes to the clock. He'd slept about forty minutes. Simon looked wide awake at the wheel, which seemed unfair.

He stretched his back, one hand pressed to support his ribs, and checked his phone again. Still no response from Rachel. He gazed out at the endless water on his side of the car, nothing between him and the sparkling expanse but a guardrail and the occasional dock. Then the road veered inland a few hundred feet, and here were rows of waterside houses, their backyards a Lake Michigan bay.

"We're driving right up the side of the peninsula."

"Yep," Simon said.

Rachel had taken this road, maybe thinking she'd stay here a while before moving on. Maybe thinking she would never move on again.

At last Simon left the mostly empty two-lane highway and ended up on the main street of a town no bigger than Harbor Vale. He glanced down at his phone and said, "It's right up here."

Zac's mouth dried as Simon pulled into a tiny lot, bordered by a split-rail fence. He checked his phone once more as they got out of the car. "Nothing."

"Well, we'll know in a minute."

On one post of the covered porch hung a white sign painted with red letters: WELCOME! PLEASE ENTER HERE! They ascended the three stairs together. A screen door, old but kept in good repair, was unlocked and led into the home's foyer. A round oak coffee table stood in the corner of the spiral staircase, adorned with a doily and bearing several manila envelopes. Simon picked up the top one of the pile.

"Williams." He picked up a second one. "Armstrong." A third. "Reddy." He pushed the others around. "No Leon, no Noel."

"Are those keys?"

"Looks like."

"And they leave them here on the table, unattended?"

"Small-town trust."

"Maybe we can find the proprietor and

ask if she's been here."

"Mm, even small-town trust has its limits these days. And if they ask for our friend's last name, we're done." Simon set the envelopes down.

"Can I help you?" said a female voice from the far doorway.

She was somewhere in her seventies, hair dyed a light brown that allowed silver highlights to shine through. Smile lines bordered her eyes and mouth, and she wore a loose red sweater and jeans. Her hands were clasped in front of her, a welcoming pose.

"Would you be the owner?" Simon said.

"That's right, young man. Do you have a reservation?" She looked from him to Zac with the first seeds of suspicion in the furrow of her brow.

"We don't, but a friend does. Just wondering if she's checked in yet — young lady with long gray hair."

She blinked once. Yes, she'd seen Rachel. "I think you should call her on your cellular phone. Or send her a text message. Don't tell me you don't have a cellular phone."

Simon didn't hesitate. "I understand. I'm glad you have safety measures in place here. We'll get hold of her. Thank you."

Zac met her eyes long enough to nod his

own thanks.

The woman said, "Wait just a minute. You."

Zac tried not to look like a guy about whom a fan base was speculating. "Yes, ma'am?"

"You're Zachary Wilson."

Well, crap. "Yes, ma'am, that's me."

"I can't believe it." She stepped forward slowly. "You see, Rachel said that if a man named Zachary Wilson were to come here asking for her, I was to tell you. Only you." She flicked a glance at Simon.

"I'll wait outside if you'd prefer," Simon said.

The woman straightened to her full height, which might have been five foot even. "I would."

"No problem." Simon strode out onto the porch and shut the door.

"Is that man trustworthy, Mr. Wilson?"

"Entirely."

"Oh, all right then. Rachel showed me a picture of you yesterday, but when she left she said she hadn't expected you to come and wasn't the least disappointed."

A knot rose in his throat. He swallowed hard. "Where was she headed?"

"You seem on the level to me." She held out her hand, and he shook it. "Florence

Olheiser."

"Good to meet you." *Now talk already.*

"She didn't say where she was going, but she left a little after noon."

"Thank you, Florence."

Rachel had given him twenty-four hours, and he hadn't come. Outside on the porch Simon stood in a corner, leaning against the side of the house, arms folded.

"She's not here." Zac didn't pause in his rush down the steps. His heart pounded along with his feet. "She left almost three hours ago."

Not until they both were back in the car did they stop to look at each other.

"Now what?" Simon said.

Zac pulled out his phone and checked his app. "Nothing."

His fingers clenched around the phone as he returned not to his page but to hers. Maybe another clue lurked there, something they hadn't noticed.

The B&B was no longer her most recent post. Two new ones showed above it. The first was text only and had gone up not long after he and Simon had set out for Leahy. He read it aloud." 'After tonight this account will be permanently closed. I'm signing off with a final cavalcade of beauty. Stay tuned.' "

"Is that to you?"
"I think she's given up on me. I think this is for herself." Leaving a mark, unseen though it might be.
"What does she mean, cavalcade of beauty?"
No surprise the phrase would baffle Simon.
Rachel's most recent post was a picture. *Beauty* put it mildly. The vantage point was a porch, white columns in the foreground striating the shot. Beyond them a fountain caught the midafternoon sunlight with diamond-like sparkles, and a faded green lawn stretched all the way to the lake. A few Adirondack chairs nestled in a half circle on a red stone patio just off the porch. Rachel's eye had placed them poetically off-center.
"You have something?"
Zac held up a finger and ignored Simon's huff as he read her caption. *Almost didn't stop here but glad I did! A historical fountain, who'd have thought? And the grounds are lovely as you can see.*
"A historical fountain," he said.
"A what now?"
"We have to find a historical fountain. That's where she is." Zac's thumbs flew over his screen as he typed in a search. *Leahy, Harbor Vale, Traverse City, historical fountain.*

There couldn't be many of them.

The first resulting image showed the same building, facing the porch where Rachel had stood. The fountain was an artesian spring that had been flowing since the 1850s. The building had been erected in 1887. He brought up driving directions.

"She's thirty miles north. It's a straight shot up the lakeshore if we stay on the state highway." By the time he finished speaking, Simon had put the car in drive and was heading for the road.

Zac refreshed his phone. A cavalcade, and the fountain an unplanned stop. Her itinerary was fluid at best. He refreshed again.

"Hey, knock it off."

He looked up. "What?"

"Just be still. All your fidgeting's making me jittery."

He forced his knee to stop jumping and refreshed the app again.

"We're doing the best we can, Zac. But if she keeps ahead of us and we can't —"

"Shut up."

"I need you to be prepared, man."

"She said *cavalcade.* More than one. She's not going to — to do anything there. We just have to get to her before she leaves."

"And talk to her."

The lazy cynicism in his voice made Zac

want to deck him. "Yeah, talk to her. She thinks she's got nothing but solitude and her camera, but she has us."

Simon shut up. In the next forty minutes, Zac refreshed his phone app no less than eighty times. When they pulled into the gravel lot beside the weathered white bungalow, he was out of the car before Simon shut it off.

"Hey," Simon said as he got out at the pace of David's pet turtle. "You said she drives a gray SUV."

"Yeah."

"Then she's not here."

Zac scanned the lot. Not many vehicles, none of them Rachel's. "I want to look around. Just in case."

"Look for what?"

He didn't know, so he ignored the question.

Green signs informed him he was on park property owned by the township of Valerian; the historical house and the fountain's grounds were open to the public, but vandals would be prosecuted. An ordinance vehicle was parked at one end of the lot. Simon caught up to him, and together they strode around the building to the back porch. Zac mounted the steps and stood where she had stood, shifted his feet until the chairs and the fountain occupied the same spaces in front of his eyes that they did in Rachel's picture.

He looked up and down the long porch. A couple sat at one end, feet on the steps, watching their kids run around the fountain. Zac walked out onto the lawn, all the way to the water. He paced one way then the other, gazed back at the house and the fountain and the parking lot. She wasn't here.

If he could see the place through her eyes, find some clue to her in the beauty she had chosen to capture: a fountain of sun-wrought diamonds, a wide expanse to the lake and the sky. And porch pillars like prison bars, standing between her and all of it. Still a prisoner to her body.

She hadn't taken the cure yet.

His pulse jumped with relief, but he steadied himself. Only theory. Maybe a complete misinterpretation of her art. He wouldn't know until he reached her.

Simon had disappeared but now emerged around the side of the house. He shrugged. "Not much inside. A few roped-off displays. Nowhere to hide."

Zac approached the couple, hoping this didn't backfire and get the cops called on him. "Excuse me."

They looked up. “Yes?” the woman said.

“This is going to sound weird, but . . .” He brought up Rachel’s picture on his phone. “Am I in the right place?”

They both looked at the picture and nodded. “Taken from right here on the porch,” the guy said.

“That’s what I thought,” Zac said. “We’re following this online photo chase thing. Someone’s posting shots of landmarks, and we’re trying to catch up to him before he posts the next one, but we keep missing him, which is eventually going to cost me twenty bucks. Did you see anybody around here within the last, I don’t know, half hour?”

“We’ve been here about that long,” the woman said, eyes on her kids again, her interest in Zac waning. “No one else has come by, so your photographer must have left ahead of us.”

“Thanks.” He shrugged. “On to the next, I guess.”

He motioned Simon to follow, and they got back in the car.

“Him?” Simon said with a twist of his mouth.

“If I’d said *her* they might think I was a stalker.”

“And they’d be so far off the mark.”

Zac leaned back in the seat. The ache in his ribs was building again. His phone rang, and his pulse leaped, everything in him strained and straining, forgetting Rachel didn't have his phone number. It was Tiana.

"Hey," he said.

"Zac, are you watching her account?"

"Yeah. We're at the fountain now, but she's gone." He cringed. Not that word.

"What about Fishtown?" Tiana said.

"Huh?"

"Her newest picture. It went up three minutes ago. She's in Fishtown."

"Fishtown," he said to Simon. "Go."

Simon fiddled with his own phone while Tiana said, "Okay, I'm mapping."

"Us too," Zac said.

"If you're at Fountain Arbor right now, you're about an hour behind her. When you get off with me, check out her path now that you have three stops. You'll see she's going to run out of state highway if she doesn't deviate. There'll just be public beach and Lake Michigan."

"And how long will that take?"

"From Fishtown, maybe another hour."

"Okay. Thank you, Tiana."

Simon began to drive, and Zac hung up. This had to be it. *Please, God, let this be it.*

He could keep her there if He wanted to. A flat tire if nothing else.

"We're going to make it," he said.

Simon didn't reply.

TWENTY-NINE

No surprise Tiana had recognized Fishtown: the shops and hotel were built on docks, two strips of buildings that comprised the historical section of the village. Between the docks lay a cove fed by a dammed river. Rachel's picture had captured the ambience at a quirky angle, her focus on water falling over the dam. The background wasn't too blurry to pick out the weathered fishing shanties: wood siding, muntins in the windows, dock posts rising high in the picture. She'd crouched for a low angle to give them stark vertical prominence, but this time she was closer to the water than to the prison bars. If that's what they were.

He was overthinking. She'd captured a moment of beauty. That's all.

Simon parallel parked along a storefront, leaving the longer lot spaces open to the many vehicles towing boats. Zac checked for an updated post. Nothing yet.

"Let's split up," Zac said. "I'll take the near dock; you take the far one."

"If I spot her, I'll call you."

"Yeah. Okay."

"Back here in thirty minutes."

Zac hustled off, but action didn't calm him. They were running out of time and highway. Over the next half hour he walked the dock, river and boats to his left and shops to his right. He ducked into places selling jewelry, candles, souvenir shirts, stonework and metalwork and glasswork. He returned the smiles of shopkeepers and managed a sentence or two of small talk, but he couldn't recall a word he'd said after he left one store for the next. The sun was lowering, shadows stretching away from the lake. This time of year, once dusk fell, it would drop fast. By the time he returned to the rendezvous point, Rachel's post from this location was almost ninety minutes old.

Simon wasn't here yet. Zac checked her page. Nothing new and no response to his message, though she had to see it every time she posted.

He gripped a dock post and wasted energy trying to shake it loose. Maddening woman. Why wouldn't she stop running? He stared down into the rippling cove and tried to plan.

"Hey," Simon said from behind him.

Zac turned. "She isn't here."

"Don't think so. We could do another sweep, in case one of us missed her."

He hadn't missed her. But until she posted again . . . "Might as well."

They did. Twenty minutes later the sky was seeping colors toward the lake horizon, orange running down, dark blue trailing behind. Cars started. Headlights swept over the dock and backed away. Stores closed.

Zac returned to the same dock post, and this time Simon was waiting for him.

"Nothing new?"

"Not two minutes ago." But he checked again anyway.

And his chest closed up.

Rachel had posted a sunset over a beach. He stared a moment at the radiant colors. Then he read the caption. *"Old age should burn and rave at close of day." Or choose not to.*

"Oh God." He gripped the post as his knees threatened to buckle. "No."

"Zac."

He couldn't say more, not to Simon or to God. He thought he could feel his soul in his chest, crying out for Rachel's life. He handed the phone to Simon, and his hand shook so hard he nearly dropped the phone into the water.

Simon read, swore, and shoved it into his pocket. "Come on."

Zac followed him, words turning and striking one another inside him like rough stones in a tumbler. None of them would form in his mouth.

Rachel. Believing no one saw the last rays of her as she faded forever from the world. The storm in Zac whipped up and beat down until he could hardly see.

"There's still a chance," Simon said as they reached the car. "But it's getting dim, buddy."

"I know."

"All we've got left is that she stuck to the route."

"So we keep driving until we hit the beach."

Simon was already putting their half plan into action. Already joining traffic on the highway, which had become sparser as they journeyed north.

"Give my phone back," Zac said.

Simon handed it over with a grunt.

Zac texted Tiana. BEACH PICTURE. ANY CLUE?

In a minute she responded. NOTHING, SORRY. JUST LOOKS LIKE A BEACH.

His thumb hovered over the screen then

went ahead and sent his thought. PLEASE PRAY FOR RACHEL.

"Zac, what I said before about being prepared."

"And what I said before about shutting up."

"I just don't want to see you . . . you know."

"Well, shoot, Simon. Let's worry how the suicide of a woman who's all alone and broken with remorse affects *me*. Brilliant prioritizing there."

"You've been calling her family."

"Yeah, so?" But through the inner tempest he glimpsed memories, the ones he did not approach. Ever. "The — the boys?"

Simon glanced away from the road to meet his eyes. Concern rested heavy and dark on his brother. Mournful.

Zac shook his head. "That was different. My boys — It was different."

"Family's family to you. And love of heaven, Zac, you latch on so dang hard."

Not true. Or . . . was it?

"I don't get it, but I get it. People are your oxygen, especially close people. But longevite or not, Rachel isn't close. Might never be."

He didn't want to agree. Wasn't sure he could. He shuddered as the months of the first Life Buoy stirred in his memory, the months after his youngest son was killed in a car accident at fifty-two years old. And two subsequent vigils over him — when his eldest boy was lost to cancer, his middle boy a decade later to old age and Alzheimer's. To this day Zac's grief remained a monster, slumbering at the core of him, possessing claws and fangs and fiery breath, still capable of brutalizing him if he crossed near.

His phone buzzed. A text from Tiana. WITHOUT CEASING, FOR YOU TOO.

He pressed the phone to his chest and drew a long breath that stabbed in his side.

"What?" Simon said.

"I asked Tiana to pray."

"Hmm."

They drove. Road rolled away, miles added up, minutes ticked toward sunset and then kept ticking. Dusk turned dark. The reinforcement of Tiana's prayer faded. Zac's knee began jumping again. He messaged Rachel: PLEASE ANSWER. Beauty was gone from the sky now, from the landscape they passed. All was shadowed.

The road ended.

It had ceased to be a highway at some point and become a two-lane asphalt strip. It terminated in a pull-off complete with drinking fountain, restroom, locking bars for bikes, and of course parking spaces. None of the vehicles was a gray SUV.

Shoulder to shoulder, they struck out for the beach.

"Going to be freezing with that lake wind," Simon said.

The wind came in harsh off the water, watering Zac's eyes as they walked into it. At the end of the street, they peered into the night. Other than the streetlight under which they stood, the beach was left to the darkness, but as they cleared the first incline toward the water, orange lights glowed at random to their left and right.

"Fire pits," Zac said. "Come on."

As they padded down the beach, Simon's strides seemed longer than usual. Oh, right — Zac was setting the pace, practically running. The fires flickered against the young night, illuminating hunched backs on the near side of each circle and faces on the far side. Four pits in total, and three of them thronged with noisy, cheery groups. At the fourth, a single figure huddled, back to them, pale hair cascading halfway to her hips.

"There," Simon said.

Adrenaline surged into Zac's system. "Stay here for a minute."

He headed across the sand without taking off his shoes. He might have to chase her, and at this point, hang it all, he wouldn't hesitate to do so in front of witnesses.

She was crouched close to the flames, feeding them. Sparks popped and rose into the night to die over her head. Zac approached her from the side, but she didn't catch sight of him. Beside her lay an accordion file folder. Two more were succumbing to the fire, only seconds ago set atop the kindling wood, writhing and shrinking and falling apart into ashes. Papers within them began to scorch. She threw the stack in her hand onto the rest.

Not rushing her took all his willpower. Instead he called out. "Rachel."

She grabbed the folder and jumped to her feet. Past the circle of firelight she couldn't see him. "Zac?"

"It's me."

"What are you doing here?" She clasped the folder in her arms.

"Did you take it?" He dropped his voice. The water would magnify echoes. "Rachel, please, the cure, did you take it?"

"Soon." She spoke the word with the purest grade of hope and relief. "As soon as I've finished with my pyre."

THIRTY

Zac fell to his knees in the sand and stared at the heaps of ashes in the bottom of the pit. She had been burning paper for a while. He gripped his legs and leaned toward the fire as if he could find pages to save.

"Zac?"

"Tell me this isn't your research."

"Of course it is." She reached for another stack of pages.

"Wait." Zac jumped up between her and the fire.

She startled like a rabbit, didn't run but began to tremble. He might be trembling too. Her lips pressed into a thin line, her shoulders quivering, Rachel scooped up another stack of pages and held them over the blaze.

"Stop." Zac's hand darted for hers. He snatched the pages and held them to his chest. The paper was hot, and a page cracked in his grasp.

A veil fell over her expression. "You changed your mind. You want the cure."

"No."

"Then why come?"

"You said soon. That means you didn't take it yet."

She held out her hands, fingers spread. "Not yet."

At his other side, Simon entered his line of vision and crouched close. "You two are attracting attention."

"Copy that. Rachel, come on."

Her eyes widened at the sight of Simon. "I don't know you."

"Simon. I'm a friend of Zac's. Born in the nineteenth century." He smiled.

She drew a ragged breath. "I'm 1901."

"We need to go," Simon said.

"My notes must be burned. Well, mine and Doc's."

Simon drew a slow breath, exchanged a long glance with Zac. Rachel missed neither.

"Please, Zac, just leave me."

"So you can kill yourself."

"I told you I was prepared to pay."

Zac stepped nearer to her, and a wave struck him — a wave of Rachel's inner screaming. He nearly staggered.

"Sorry," he said. "You're stuck with me."

Her thin frame shook harder, the tremors

violent in her hands, arms, shoulders. "You know I deserve to die."

There it was. *Deserve.* That was the loudest of the screams. "No, Rachel."

She stood there. Shaking. Holding on to the accordion folder stuffed with papers. Simon and Zac tossed sand onto the fire, and she made no move. When it had smothered enough to leave it, Zac touched her elbow. She jolted though he had been standing in her line of sight the whole time.

"Don't touch me," she said, and the wave that drenched him now was sharp animal terror.

He lifted his hands. "Okay. But we're leaving now. All of us. Where did you park?"

"Up the beach." She pointed. "A cottage there."

Zac motioned her in front of them. "Lead the way."

She kept distant by more than an arm's length as they padded up the beach a few hundred feet, then climbed a slope of sand and walked down a sand-and-gravel pathway to a cluster of cottages, old but maintained. Hers was sea blue with white shutters, one room. She dug a key from her pocket and let them inside.

"I had planned to die at Florence's. The

bed-and-breakfast — did you look for me there?"

Zac nodded.

"But I couldn't let her find me in her own house. She'd never get over that. A cottage for rent isn't so personal. I'm sorry mortals will have to find me at all, but it's unavoidable."

"Rachel," Zac said.

She looked from him to Simon. "Restitution, is that it? I'll be dead by sometime tomorrow. Is there something additional you require?"

"Will you listen to me? I came to keep you from doing this."

She seemed to absorb his words with effort despite the fact he'd already said them. She looked past him at Simon, who was standing against the door, silent.

"Why did *you* come?" she said.

"Because he's not up to driving after that fall yesterday."

Zac was fine to drive, and Simon knew it, but *in case we had to cover up your suicide* was hardly something to say to her.

"Zac? You're hurt?"

"A little," he said.

"It didn't look like too much weight on you. I thought you'd be able to dig yourself out."

"I'm mostly fine."

"Oh. Good." Confusion creased between her eyes.

"But you wouldn't have been, if we hadn't come in time."

"I thought about leaving a note for the mortals, telling them I was much older than any of them, and this wasn't suicide, just natural death. But it wouldn't have made sense to them. Do you disagree?"

"I disagree with your whole plan, and I'll keep repeating myself until it sinks in."

She grabbed hold of the ends of her hair in both fists. "Don't be ridiculous. No matter what else happened, I was always going to leave one dose of the cure intact, for myself."

"For a natural life span, not death in a day."

"And then I killed four people. Changed the moral equation."

"Rachel. Where is it?"

She thrust her hand inside the folder and withdrew a collection of tiny vials. Three of unidentified liquid and two that had to be . . .

"That's blood," Simon said.

Rachel nodded.

The blood was labeled. One with a *J,* the other with an *A.* The other vials must contain the cure. Zac held out his hand.

Her hand closed around the vials. "You have to respect my choice, Zac."

"When your choice is to murder yourself, no, I don't."

She backed into the corner where a low metal table stood and placed the vials in a row. She took a step away from the table. It seemed an effort.

"Happy?" she said.

"Not the word I'd use," Zac said. She needed a distraction from those things before she tried to bolt with them. He picked up the folder and peeked inside. "It's all handwritten."

"I didn't do anything on computers. I recopied sometimes, just in case papers were damaged somehow."

"So this is your research to correct the cure? To make it what it's supposed to be?"

"I'd have to look at what's left. I wasn't paying attention, I was just burning it all."

David's hope, a pyre on the beach. Zac sank onto the daybed in one corner and dropped the folder next to him. He sagged.

"I don't understand," Rachel said. "You told me you don't want the cure."

When Zac didn't answer, Simon said, "He doesn't."

"Do you?"

"No, but another of us asked that we preserve your research and bring it back to him."

"And that's why you came."

Zac gripped the side of the mattress in both hands. "No. If you had no research to share, I still would have come."

"For me," she whispered.

"We want you to live. I'm not sure how many more ways I can say it."

"You want me to live," she whispered. "Me."

"Yes, you."

Standing in the middle of the single-room cottage, in the middle of the braided rug, Rachel wrapped her arms around her middle and gave a long moan. The sound fell from her like a morning rain, rose like a soft mist. The sound rinsed the room in penitence, in disbelief, in loneliness.

Zac went to her. He placed his palm on her shoulder.

"I can't be touched," she said, the words more like a cry.

"Why not?"

"Because no one touches me."

She didn't try to evade him though. She stood still. He stepped closer, and she shuddered, but he wasn't holding her there. She could have moved, made distance. She didn't.

He'd broken his spiritual silence last night. Now for the next step. He prayed for help, for wisdom.

It might be wrong; it might heighten her anxiety; but he thought it would be right. He hugged her. Her arms continued to clasp her middle, and another moan came from her, this one drenched in fear. He closed his eyes and prayed, this time for her. Slowly Rachel's arms loosened and fell to her sides. She leaned her head on Zac's chest.

"See, Rachel," Zac whispered. "You can be hugged."

"This isn't how the night was supposed to go." Her voice came as quietly as his, siblings telling secrets into each other's ears.

"You're supposed to live, kiddo," he said.

"I don't think that's right."

"I know. That's why I came."

"For me."

"Yep. Just for you."

She raised her arms inch by inch and touched his back with a graze of fingers, as if he might prove to be a phantom. Then she returned the hug so tightly his ribs gave stabbing protest. He bit his lip and kept quiet.

After a minute he guided her to the daybed and pushed her shoulder down until she sat. He sat beside her, and the years of Rachel's despair wrought their ache in him. The room had been small; now it was shrinking. He wrapped his arm around her shoulders and let her lean on him.

A look passed between him and Simon: *No talking yet. Let's give her a minute.* Rachel was silent. Not even her breathing made a sound. She slouched against Zac as if she might fall asleep with her head on his shoulder.

Minutes passed. Ambient sounds filled the time as Zac became aware of each: first the ticking clock on the far wall, then the leaves in the cottonwoods outside the door, then the far-off swishing rhythm of Lake Michigan's waves. He focused on that rhythm and tried to let it lull him, let it wash Rachel's fear and dejection from his spirit, let it convince his brain he was sitting on the beach under a blue sky canopy.

But the behemoth was in the room now. It prowled the perimeter, eyeing Zac, sniffing and tasting the air and catching the whiff and tang of his distress. Liking that scent, that flavor. Inching closer.

He had to get outside.

Simon stood and crossed to the window

nearest Zac and shoved it open. Brisk night air flooded in, chilled Zac's cheeks and nose. He drank it with mouth open. Rachel sat up and moved over on the daybed to watch him.

The behemoth didn't leave, but it backed off.

"Yeah," he said to Simon's interrogating stare. "Better. Good."

"What's happening?" Rachel said.

The stripping of the masks had to be an act of God. Only He worked with such thoroughness. By the time Zac posted a public explanation of the degrading photo, not a soul would be left to believe in his flippant persona.

Anyway, Rachel was family.

He rubbed his arms against the chill. "I'm not big on close spaces."

"I guess it is small." She frowned at the walls.

"It's okay. I just need a minute."

He didn't expect it to be that simple. He didn't expect the behemoth to sneak close, press against him for a few seconds, and then slink out of the cottage. But tonight it was that simple. Didn't mean the affliction was over; Zac had lived with it too long to be naive. But tonight he felt a gentle hand touch the old war wounds in his mind and soothe their scars. Maybe only for tonight. Nevertheless, it was grace he hadn't earned.

He gazed out the window at a streetlight filtered through the silhouette of tree branches. *Father. You're still my Father.* A tear slipped down his cheek. *Well, okay, here I am. Use this mess of ego and panic and pain for whatever You will.*

"Zac?" Rachel whispered.

He didn't swipe the tear away. "It's all right, Rachel." A smile tugged his mouth, and he fixed his eyes past the tree on the shining light. "In fact, it's kind of glorious."

Thirty-One

"Three people, two cars," Simon said.

"I have to drive." Rachel stood with her arms folded, not crossed in defiance but an X over her chest, as if attempting to keep her heart inside.

"You'll follow us to Harbor Vale?" Simon said.

"I'm agreeable to that."

"Will you be agreeable for the whole drive?" He planted his hands on his hips.

Rachel shrank from him though he'd made no move toward her. "I'll try. I am trying, really."

"Okay," Zac said, "we know you're driving. We know Simon's driving. I'll ride with you instead of Simon."

Her arms tightened over her chest. "I don't have guests."

"I promise not to leave your home a mess. Won't even put my feet on the dash."

"A passenger," she said as if tasting the

word. Slowly she nodded. "Only because it's you, though."

"Of course." He grinned.

Simon rolled his eyes, but his mouth twitched. "So if you're driving a passenger, you'll follow me?"

"Well, otherwise I'd be abducting Zac." Her arms lowered to her sides, and she studied Zac, searching his face for something. "You understand panic. What it does to a body."

"Everyone's afraid of something," Zac said.

"But not to the same degree. You looked like how I feel."

"Okay."

"I'm telling you because I might need help when we get closer to Harbor Vale. Closer to the people. They're my close spaces."

Oh . . . man. "I'll help you however I can."

"I'll do my best to fight it down. I usually can when it's weekly things — you know, grocery shopping, pumping gas, stopping at the bakery. But I don't know what'll happen with Finn and Cady."

"We'll get through it together. Okay?"

She clenched her eyes shut and stood there for a long moment. Then she opened her eyes, nodded, and motioned to Zac. "Let's go."

To make room for Zac in the passenger seat, Rachel had to move a stack of mass-market paperbacks and CDs, a lavender zip hoodie, and a cardboard display box filled with protein bars. Each item, even the hoodie, was re-homed somewhere deliberate on the back seat, which also held two piles of folded laundry, more non-prep food, and her camera case. On the floor of the SUV behind the front seats were two pairs of casual shoes and two duffel bags, one stacked atop the other.

"When was the last time you got a hotel room?" Zac said as he watched her re-arrange.

"Before Leahy? Oh, goodness, I have no idea."

"So in Harbor Vale, you were living . . . ?" He gestured to the vehicle.

"Yep. It's so comfortable, having one's very own space. Hotels are itchy in comparison."

"I see."

"I know it's not normal." She stood up and shut the door then walked around to the driver's side. "But I enjoy moving, Zac. I never wish for an apartment or a house."

"Fair enough."

He eased into the passenger seat and shut his door, leaned back and gazed out the side window. Simon had brought his rental sedan to the entry of the cottage row. He pulled onto the street first, and Rachel pulled out after him.

Zac waited a few minutes for her to relax into the routine of driving. When he wasn't discussing an emotional topic, Simon was a laid-back, defensive driver; but Zac expected Rachel's presence on the road would be downright grandmotherly.

How wrong he was.

In minutes she was practically tailgating Simon. Not close enough to hit him in an emergency stop, but close enough to let him know he was driving only a mile over the speed limit, and she had places to be.

"He's cussing at you right now." Zac held in a chuckle.

"What, my following distance?" Rachel scowled. "He drives like a woman."

"Please tell him that."

"I just might."

Of all the wonders of the modern world, Simon increased his speed by exactly four mph. Rachel widened the distance between them and sighed her satisfaction.

"He learns fast."

"Tell him that too."

A smile curved her mouth, slow and tentative. Then it faded, and she drove in silence.

Zac let her. After a few minutes, he closed his eyes.

"Usually I sing in the car," Rachel said as he was drifting into a weary doze.

Sacred information. A glimpse into her home, her life. Zac opened his eyes and sat up. "You can now, if you want."

"Oh no, I couldn't."

"Okay."

A return of the quiet. Was she trying to tell him something? He watched her drive for a minute, the calm focus on her face, the easy sureness of her hands on the wheel.

"Want to talk?" he said.

She swallowed hard. "Yes, please."

"Any topic in particular?"

"I want to hear about your life. Your history."

"Sure."

"I guess you'll want to know mine too. You and Simon and the other one — is it your bookseller, the one who wants to be cured?"

"That's the one."

"What's his name?"

"David Galloway."

"Oh, that's a lovely name. Don't you agree?"

"I've never thought of a name as *lovely* before, but sure, if you say so."

"Galloway," she said, the softness in her voice lending the syllables a kind of poetry. "Scottish, meaning 'way of the stranger.' "

"You're a fount of knowledge." And Zac had underestimated David's bookishness, which he hadn't thought possible. He grinned, and Rachel turned to study him.

"How old are you?" she said.

"Physically or literally?"

"Both, of course."

"I stopped aging at thirty-two. This year I'll be turning a hundred and sixty."

"Oh my."

"What about you?"

"I'm twenty-four forever, turning one hundred sixteen this coming March." One hand left the steering wheel to cover her mouth.

"What's wrong?"

Slowly her hand returned to the wheel. She turned her eyes to him, and they were fever-bright. "You're the first person ever to know my real age."

He couldn't respond to that without some form of condolence. "David's going to be a hundred and sixty-eight."

She turned her attention back to the road, shaking her head. "A long time for someone who wants the cure. How has he endured it?"

"You should ask him."
"I hope I get the chance."
"No reason you shouldn't."
"Well, there are reasons, of course. But while this lasts, I could tell you my story, and you could tell me yours."
Her eagerness filled the air to bursting, hungry and pure. He wondered what she had been like in her twenties, in her thirties and forties. Before decades of isolation.
"Sounds good to me," he said.
"Oh, I wish the drive were longer."
"Hey." He held out an open hand to her, wanting to squeeze her shoulder, but that wouldn't be wise when she was driving. She might startle and steer them over the median. "I am not going anywhere."
"I want to talk and listen. But it feels dangerous. Not — not like *you* might be dangerous. I know you're not. It doesn't matter, though."
Like his knowledge that rooms without windows were no less safe than the outdoors, not inherently anyway. "Want me to start? You can ask me questions."
A long pause then a shake of her head. "You ask me. Anything you want to know."
Later he would take a walk outside. Breathe and let go of all this brokenness. For now . . . he'd start with something

small. "What color is your hair?"

"Red."

"Cool."

"Not really. It's the bright orange that fades with age, except mine doesn't of course, so people comment on it constantly. Mostly compliments, but I couldn't stand it. I get fewer remarks on the gray, and it reflects my soul more accurately."

If she had this many words to say over the color of her hair . . .

Under normal circumstances, he'd be all ears for hours. Nothing was more fascinating than a human being's life story. But tonight his body throbbed and his head was foggy with exhaustion. Well, he'd do his best, listen as well as he could. And then, after he'd gotten some sleep, he'd keep listening to her for as many days or weeks or years as Rachel needed him to.

"Zac?"

"Just thinking."

"Oh, I'll be quiet then."

"No, go on."

"About what?" As if the color of her hair were the measure of her.

"You choose now. Something you want me to know."

She was quiet a long time, driving with checked aggression behind Simon. Her mouth pursed then relaxed. She glanced at Zac then quickly away when their eyes met.

"Were you dying?"

He didn't need her to clarify. "Yeah."

She nodded. "I'm pretty sure all of you were."

"We were," Zac said.

Strange that he was the only one of them who could tell her that, the only one who knew every longevite story. Eventually, if the family stayed together, they would hear each other's lives told; but it hadn't happened yet.

"I wasn't." She tapped her thumb on the wheel. "Doc didn't give me the cure to save me. Didn't give me the cure at all. He was dead by then. TB, did you know that?"

"He told us he had it, before he left."

"I inherited his experiments and his notes and his IQ. I didn't inherit his way with people, but I wasn't like this either. Just for the record. I had a fiancé and a future. I was a normal twentysomething woman of the twenties. Do you believe me?"

"Any reason I shouldn't?"

"You've only seen the anthropophobic version."

Her shoulders heaved in a silent fortifying breath. Her thumb tapped the wheel again. She needed more from him than blind acceptance.

"Used to be, I had no trouble with tight spaces."

Rachel met his eyes and, this time, held his gaze a long moment.

"You believe me, don't you?"

"Of course," she said.

"We've been hurt. All humans have; we've just lived long enough to collect a lot of hurt. I'll never judge anyone's fear, Rachel. But especially not the fears of my family."

"You shouldn't call me that."

"If you don't want me to, then I won't."

"It's not about what I want." She was quiet as she followed Simon in passing a row of three slow cars and a slower van. As they accelerated and merged back into the right lane, she said, "I probably won't be acceptable."

He had no response. He could promise acceptance from no one but him.

"I fell from a horse," Rachel said. "Not a bad fall, as those can go, but I landed on my arm. Compound fracture of the radius."

"Ouch," he said when her pause lengthened.

"Hmm? Oh. Yes. I'd never experienced that level of pain before, and I was quite the coward about it."

Starkness filled him. Rachel hadn't needed

the serum. Could have lived a normal life.

"I was irate when it didn't work. I had to recover on my own. I thought Doc must have made a useless batch of the stuff and never realized it. I nearly poured out the last doses."

"When did you realize what had happened?"

"Not for decades. Complete denial on my part. I enjoyed my youthfulness, but I waited for my age to catch up with me."

"You had no one to compare notes with."

"It sank in over time," Rachel said. "I thought this was my comeuppance for using the serum when I didn't truly need it. I could have saved a life with it, and instead I was selfish. So now here I was, stuck with this young face and this bright hair. I never guessed the agelessness happened to everyone. I thought if the serum prevented death, then its power was spent and you all went on to live normally."

"How did you find out differently?"

"I just started to wonder if I'd jumped to the wrong conclusion. I needed to be sure. I had your faces and your old names, but that was all, and it did me no good until recognition software became commonplace. I found Holly online and began to track her social media posts. She was constantly checking in at locations in Southern California, so I knew she lived there. I recognized Sean too, when she posted pictures of him. And then one day this past June . . ."

Minutes passed while Rachel drove, alternately biting her lip and clenching her hands on the wheel. At last her voice came again, the quietest yet.

"I saw them. Cady, Holly, and Anna. All faces I knew from Doc's notes. A picture of them in Missouri together, at a county fair. They were eating a giant cinnamon roll. They were laughing."

Her breathing grew rough.

"Hey," Zac said. "It's okay."

"I saw the picture and thought, *I won't be selfish again. I won't take this cure and not give it to the others first, and now I can find them, find them all.*"

"Rachel."

"And I did find them. And I did give it to them. And I killed them." The vehicle weaved.

"Hey, hey. You're driving, Rachel. Keep calm."

"It will never be okay."

He reached across the console and put his hand on the wheel to steady it. "Rachel, you're going to hurt someone mortal if you don't keep calm. You hear me?"

"Yes," she said after a moment, and her grip eased. "Yes."

"Tell me something else about you, something unrelated."

For a minute she said nothing, which was fine if she needed the quiet, but he guessed she was choosing what to reveal.

"I've been hiding for a long time," she finally said. "It started with Robert."

"Who's that?"

"He was going to marry me until he found out what I am. Then he was going to kill me."

Thirty-Two

She said her fiancé had wanted to kill her, and then she said nothing for at least ten minutes. But unlike Simon, Zac was a patient guy. He watched the nighttime landscape pass out the window, facing the peninsula's interior this time, wide stretches of fields and trees in variations of black beyond the highway's streetlights. Cady and Finn might be driving too, if David had failed to convince them otherwise.

Around the time Zac decided Rachel wasn't going to disclose further details, she began tapping her thumb on the steering wheel.

"Yeah," she said as if he'd asked a question. "Robert who loved me, until he knew me."

Quiet seemed the best response for now.

"We were together only a year, and then . . . well, it's stupid, but I used to keep a diary. He found it and didn't tell me, just put it back."

Curiosity conquered. "What year was this?"

"1949. I was almost fifty, but I looked like this, so I knew by then. My diary was brimming with angst."

"You said the twenties before. A fiancé and a future."

"Oh, Charles. Yes. He died before we could be married. Robert was my second chance. Then one night in bed he suffocated me with a pillow. When I revived, he was terrified. Wanted to know *what* I was. Started talking to me like I was someone else, someone he didn't know."

Suffocated by her fiancé. But these words didn't seem to ache in her. Not like her isolation, not like her guilt. These words didn't squeeze the vehicle from the inside out. Zac breathed them in, and they were weightless.

"I took what I could that was mine, and I left before he could try something else. I saw then how it would be for the rest of my life. No one could find out."

At that, the strain surfaced in her voice. "Rachel, I'm sorry."

"I burned the diary, of course. The funniest part is, I was going to tell him. I mean, that week, that month — I don't know when, but I was polishing the words. I was ready."

He had no answers for her, but she was speaking to herself now. Or so he thought until she met his eyes. No, she didn't need answers, but she needed to be heard. Zac nodded, and she sighed.

"Would you talk now?"

"Sure," he said.

The hour slipped away while he told her stories. Light stories, easy days, adventures to make her laugh. Every time, she jolted in her seat, as if the sound of her laughter startled her. He joked at his own expense and asked questions she could answer without thought, without caution. Her favorite color was green. Her favorite smoothie flavor was peach, and she laughed at his mock gagging noise. She collected fossils and seashells.

They were laughing at the time Moira had dragged Zac to a Bananarama concert without telling him who the artist was, when Rachel went silent and bit her lip.

"Everything okay?" Zac said.

"You've known Moira since the beginning. When both of you were mortal."

"Yeah."

"Are you lovers?"

No conversational caution with this

woman. He should mind, but he couldn't somehow. "Moira's husband was lost in a flash flood a few years after the last of us got the cure. About ten years later, typhus took my wife."

Rachel nodded, eyes on the road. She wanted the full answer.

"We got together about two years after that." One year and ten months of wrenching loneliness.

"So why isn't Moira here?"

Shoot, he had no idea, not really. "Some things happened recently that were . . . well, painful. I think she had to get away from what this place means now."

"But you didn't."

"David and Tiana, they have a life here. They can't uproot easily."

"And they matter more?"

It was so much more complex than that. He could say Moira had fled without a word, had given him no chance to choose her. He could say, since they were being frank, that he and Moira had not shared a bed in almost two years. But there was more he wouldn't say. That if Moira came back to him tonight, stood in his bedroom and disrobed, he would pray for strength to look away because the ship of his life was no longer his to steer but his Father's. Not that it had ever been his. But the century of nights with Moira had been, in addition to pleasure and closeness and love, yet another attempt to control the rudder of his life.

While he tried to find a response, Simon signaled with his right blinker and took the exit ramp, tightly curved and narrow. They merged right onto the two-lane blacktop road that would soon become Main Street, and a green highway sign flashed past them. WELCOME TO HARBOR VALE.

Rachel whimpered. The car slowed until Simon began to pull away from them.

"Hey," Zac said.

"I can't," she whispered. "The people."

He pulled from every experience he could — walls, ceilings, stairs down into old buildings with low overhangs that shut his lungs down the moment he had to duck. None of it seemed to apply.

"I thought I could do it, Zac, but I can't."

The vehicle was drifting below forty mph, and cars were flowing past them in a rapidly perilous river.

"Okay, listen, pull off here. Put your flashers on."

She obeyed, her fingers fumbling. "The people, they know. Cady knows. And Finn. And David Galloway."

"And I know."

Her eyes locked on him, too wide, unblinking.

"I'm like you. I know who you are and what you did, and I'm still here."

"You're still here."

"And Simon knows too. We want you here. You're safe with us. That's true, isn't it?"

"With you."

"And with Simon."

"And with Simon." Wooden repetition, but she nodded slowly.

"You'll be safe with David too. And with Cady and Finn." He prayed the last promise was true.

Simon's car pulled up behind them. He had circled back. The headlights shone in Rachel's rearview mirror, and she gasped.

"Who is that?"

"Simon. He's making sure we're okay. Will you stay here if I get out of the car and talk to him for a minute?"

"No."

"No?"

"I'll drive away. I'll go to Arizona. Or North Carolina."

And take the cure and breathe her last in a hotel or in this vehicle. Alone.

"Okay," Zac said. "Then we'll wait for him to walk up."

Simon approached the passenger side and motioned for Zac to roll down the window, as if this were a traffic stop and their vehicle had registered as stolen. Zac complied.

"Hey," Simon said, eyeing both of them. "What's up?"

"A little anxiety," Zac said.

"Don't make me do this." Rachel's voice inched toward shrill.

"No one's going to make you do anything." Simon rested his arms on the window frame.

"I can't look at Cady."

"Okay," Zac said. "What if I make you a promise: you don't have to see Cady tonight. And in return, you make me a promise: you won't disappear tonight even if you have the opportunity."

Her bottom lip wobbled. She held on to the steering wheel as if one of them might try to drag her away from her home.

"Okay. I won't disappear tonight."

"And one more promise, a permanent one."

"What's that?"

"You won't take the cure in the form it is now. If you're tempted, you'll tell me. You won't end your life."

Still gripping the wheel, she rested her forehead between her hands. "I don't understand why it's so important to you."

"I want your word."

"Fine. I give you my word."

"About what?"

"I . . . I won't end my life."

"Okay." A sigh built beneath his ribs. He let it out slowly. "Good. Now, we need to switch seats."

"But Simon said you can't drive."

Oops. Well. "At the moment I'll be steadier than you will."

Still half leaning in the window, Simon shook his head. "Can't be helped, I guess."

Or maybe he'd believed it when he said it. Moron. "It's fine. Rachel, you get out first."

She walked around the back of the SUV as Zac walked around the front, both of them keeping close to the vehicle, as many inches from the road as possible. The speed limit here hadn't dropped yet the way it would in another mile or so, when they reached downtown.

Zac was opening the driver's door when, behind Simon's car, another pulled up. A cop car.

"Who is that?" Rachel stood beside Simon, and her arms crossed in an X over her body.

"Looks like an officer making sure we're okay," Simon said.

The squad car's door opened, and out stepped Jacob Greene. Zac's shoulders relaxed. The man was in uniform of course, as Zac had seen him around town about half the time. The other half, he was in civilian clothes and walking hand in hand with his young daughters into David's bookstore. He set them loose, and they went after the books like seagulls after bread. The oldest, Elise, never returned to her dad without a towering armful. Zac had never yet seen Jacob deny her a book.

"Hi, Zac. I saw it was you." Jacob raised his hand in greeting. "You guys okay? Need any assistance?"

"Jacob. Thanks for stopping, but we're good. Just switching drivers."

"Sure. Little narrow here for that." He gestured to the shoulder and the curve of the exit ramp emptying cars less than a hundred feet behind them.

"Fair point. Oh — Simon and Rachel." He nodded to each. "Guys, Officer Jacob Greene. We've chatted some since I've been lurking around his town."

Jacob chuckled. "Some. Welcome to Harbor Vale, folks."

Rachel nodded. She didn't speak, but her expression looked more shy than fearful.

"Thank you," Simon said. "Figured we

might as well see one of the Great Lakes, as long as Zac's here. It's beautiful country this far north."

"Isn't it? Be sure to take a drive along the lakeshore. There's an old lighthouse about ten miles up that's worth checking out."

"I still haven't stopped there," Zac said. They'd passed it early on during their drive tonight.

"Don't miss it." Jacob half turned back to his car. "Good to meet you. Hope you enjoy your stay."

"Just get out of the road in the meantime?" Zac grinned.

"Exactly." Jacob offered a smile of his own, reserved but real. "People take this ramp too fast. I'll pull out first and give you time to accelerate in front of me."

"Thanks."

As Jacob walked away down the length of their cars, Zac caught Rachel's gaze. She wasn't blinking.

Simon saw too. He opened the passenger door. "Get in, Rachel. It's all right."

"Yes," she said, but her eyes remained wide.

Hopping into the seat and fastening her seat belt seemed to take immense effort. She flinched when Simon shut the door for her. He set his hand on the open window frame.

"You're doing fine."

"Yes." Her voice had grown small.

"I'm going back to my car now, and I'll follow you and Zac. Everything's fine."

"Yes."

The squad car still waited behind them, Simon's car blocked in between. When Simon looked ready, Zac flashed his lights once, and Simon did the same. Jacob pulled out, giving Simon and then Zac time to enter traffic ahead of him. Zac hit the gas, and in a minute, Jacob's car turned right when he and Simon continued straight. Jacob was the kind of guy to whom Zac could almost imagine telling the whole truth.

"Where are we going?" Rachel said.

"To my place, I guess."

No answer, but her shoulders hunched, and her breathing deepened with a strained control. She stayed quiet, but it was a reprise of the sound he knew too well. A battle for air when terror crushed everything inside, lungs included. He took his phone from the center console and dialed. Rachel didn't look up.

"Zac," David said from the other end of the line.

"Hey. We're about five minutes from my place. You still there?"

"I and Tiana. Finn and Cady are settled in their hotel room."

Zac's hands tightened on the wheel and the phone. "Sure about that?"

"They won't leave us. I have Finn's word."

A lot of that going around tonight. Zac cleared his throat. "How are they?"

"As expected." David's voice hushed. "Cady is consumed in anger."

"Yeah." And not only anger.

"You were right, my friend. Had I not stayed, we wouldn't have heard from them again."

"Thanks for doing it."

"They are cast down but not destroyed." A long, depleted sigh came over the phone.

"I know the feeling."

"Aye." A pause, a shift of the mood that filtered through the connection. "Do you indeed?"

"Well, I know Corinthians, anyway."

David chuckled. "Of course."

"And both of them are following the same Way."

"You would call yourself a follower now?"

Beside him Rachel had dropped her chin to her chest, and her breaths weren't easing.

"We need to postpone the topic," Zac

said. "See you in a minute."

"Aye," David said.

Zac ended the call and dropped the phone back into a cup holder.

"Was that David Galloway?"

"It was."

"I'm going to keep breathing until we get there."

And then? Despite all, a smile found his mouth. "Good plan, kiddo."

Minutes later he parked in his apartment lot beside his favored tree. David's Jeep sat a few spaces away.

Rachel pressed her spine into the corner of the door frame and the seat. If only she might know the sanctuary of family. Was that God's plan for her? Zac unbuckled his seat belt and leaned to set his palm on her shoulder.

"I can't do this," she said.

Simon was out of his car, striding up to the building's main door. It opened, and David and Tiana stepped out. Rachel stared at all of them, whimpering between breaths. Zac got out of the SUV, pocketed the keys, and walked around to her door. She cringed away from him when he opened it.

"Okay," he said quietly. "I know you're scared."

Her eyes were fixed on him. Pleading.

"I told you I'd help you."

A single blink.

"When a room starts shrinking on me, if I can't get out and go somewhere else, I try to imagine what the sky looks like right then. So here's what I want you to imagine, Rachel. You're in your car, driving. It's quiet, just the wind around you. No one's looking. You can sing as loud as you want to, and no one hears. It's just you."

She shut her eyes. "Just me."

"Now, if I was in the car with you, would that be okay?"

"I — I think so."

"Because you know me."

"Yes."

"Okay, now. If it wasn't me in the car, maybe it would be David or Tiana instead."

Her breath caught.

"David was alone like you, even longer than you were alone. When he meets you, he's going to understand."

"Now?"

"They'll wait until you're ready."

She sat another minute, breaths slowing and steadying. Zac looked over his shoulder at the three standing just outside the door, not approaching, and Simon nodded. Bless the man; he'd explained everything. David stood to one side behind him, arms folded but loosely. Tiana stood on his other side. Their positions weren't an accident, would allow Rachel space when she approached. At last she climbed out of the vehicle and looked up the long walkway to the porch.

"Cady and Finn?"

"They're not here."

Side by side they walked up to the apartments, until Rachel stopped at the bottom of the entryway steps.

"Hello, Rachel," David said.

"Hello, David Galloway."

"Hi," Tiana said, her tone warm but reserved.

"I don't know you." Rachel backed up one step.

"Tiana Burton."

"You're not . . ."

"Ageless? Nope."

"No." Rachel eyed her. "You wouldn't be."

Tiana's eyebrows arched. "Oh?"

"Doc never would have given you the serum."

In the air around them, the sudden thickness felt tangible. Tiana's shoulders drew back, but she didn't otherwise move.

"I see," she said.

Zac hadn't thought of it before, but Rachel was right. An old anger pulled his face into a grimace. *Times were different then* was both fact and excuse. Tiana's gaze remained on Rachel, a flicker of vulnerability there until she blinked it away.

"I'm here because I'm with David."

"I — I'm sorry," Rachel said. "I'm not good with people, and there are so many of you."

Tiana stepped down off the porch and held out her hand. "I'm glad to meet you, Rachel."

Rachel stared at Tiana's hand and hunched her shoulders.

Tiana lowered her hand, a wrinkle forming between her eyes. If Rachel didn't explain, Zac would later, but he hated that, hated the hurt in Tiana's face and every experience that put it there.

Rachel's breathing evened as her focus was pulled from her anxiety to Tiana's misinterpretation. "I'm sorry. I can't touch anyone right now. It isn't you."

Tiana's eyes cleared, and she nodded.

Zac motioned them all forward and addressed Rachel. "Can we go in?"

"N–no. Too many."

David and Simon stood back too far to hear her splintered words, but at Tiana's pointed look they descended the stairs.

"Let's part ways for tonight," Zac said.

Rachel's breathing grew strained as she

looked up at David. "I made the cure. I gave it to them, all four of them."

Zac darted a look around the lot, past the end of the porch on either side. No mortals anywhere around. Still, her words caused his stance to shift, one foot to the other.

And she kept going. "They weren't supposed to die, but —"

"Enough," Simon said.

Rachel gave a start. "I just wanted David to hear it from me."

"Then we take the topic indoors."

"It's a grievous thing that's happened," David said. "I know that, Rachel."

She looked up and met their eyes, each of them for a long moment, the seeking gaze she'd given Zac a few times before. "It is grievous."

Bare trees rattled in a half-hearted night wind, distant traffic whirred along the highway that led to Harbor Vale's main street. They stood there together, and no one had words to throw off the weight of Rachel's.

Zac wanted to invite them in, all of them, but Rachel needed a chance to calm herself. Standing under their gazes seemed to be eroding her from the outside in, a tide against which she was too frail to stand. Zac stepped past David to the heavy foyer door and tugged it open; someone had propped it with the wood-block stopper.

"Come in, Rachel."

She gaped at him.

"We'll see the rest of you tomorrow."

Light poured from the two-level foyer onto all of them, warmer than the white porch bulb. Rachel took a few steps nearer, stopped, and stepped forward again like a fawn venturing from thicket to clearing.

"Yes," she said. "I'll come in."

"Thank you," Zac said to the others. "For everything you did today."

"Anytime," Tiana said, and David nodded.

Zac's throat closed around his gratitude, and a pang of fondness hit his chest. He smiled and ignored Simon's frown.

"G'night," he said, but when he turned to follow Rachel inside, David caught the door. "What?"

"Do you plan to stay awake all night?"

"Coffee." Zac shrugged.

"Right," Simon said. "And when you doze off, she injects you and drives away and in the morning we find you bedridden with gray hair."

"She's not going to —"

"Zac." Simon's voice lowered. "Would you leave one of us in the position you're trying to put yourself in?"

"I . . ."

Tiana propped her hands on her hips. "Let me tell you something, Zac Wilson. I could knock you flat right now with one finger. That woman is unstable, and you know it, and I get that you're trying to help her, but you don't get to risk your life to do it."

He looked over his shoulder. Rachel stood watching through the glass door. He turned back to his friends. All three of them were glowering at him, and a smile tugged his mouth.

"You should see yourselves."

"We're right, and you know it," Tiana said.

"Right," Simon said. "So, couch again for me. We'll stay awake in shifts. She's to be guarded around the clock until I'm satisfied she's not a danger to herself or anyone else."

Zac sighed. "That'll take you a decade at least."

Thirty-Three

Rachel drew back when Simon followed Zac inside, but before Zac could attempt an explanation, she nodded.

"Smart. I might be lying." She took a few steps farther into the foyer. Then she froze. Her arms tightened around her body. "Could I stand here a minute?"

"Sure."

Her gaze roamed from nineties gray-and-teal carpet to cobwebbed vaulted ceiling. She stepped to the center of the room and looked up at the chandelier. Its bulbs were yellow incandescent, the fixture made before the existence of LED.

She seemed inclined to stand there all night, so after a minute Zac said quietly, "How you doing, kiddo?"

"Petrified. Both definitions."

"Turned to stone?"

"And extremely terrified."

Simon hadn't moved. He stood just inside

the door, watching, and an old thought returned to Zac that on a battlefield, in a flood or fire, trapped or stranded, he would choose this guy to have his back. It was a truth he'd known while lifetimes passed, while he went skydiving with Colm, while he met Colm for drinks and idle philosophizing. In a catastrophe Colm would be for himself. Simon and Zac would be for each other.

Whether Simon was ready to agree or not, David had joined their team. The Three Musketeers. Zac buried a grin. Before Simon could demand to know what was going through his head, he made a motion of welcome.

Simon shrugged and approached, eyes on Rachel.

"Let me show you my place," Zac said, and she nodded. So far so good.

She stared at everything, starting with the mat she stepped onto, gray and unremarkable except in the world of Rachel. She shuffled through the doorway into the living room, gazed up at its high ceiling, gazed out the big windows onto the porch. She touched the back of a kitchen chair, the edge of the counter, the light switch by the door wall, and each graze of her palm seemed reverent.

She was too quiet, so Zac spoke up. "I guess it's been a while since you were inside a house."

"James and Anna's, briefly."

"Before that?"

"My own house, 1949. A friend's house, 1955."

His chest hurt. He rubbed his knuckles against it.

"Is this where I'll sleep?" She pointed to the couch.

"You'll get the bedroom," Zac said. "One of us will sleep there."

A slow nod. "And the other will keep watch."

"Best for everyone."

"I get it. I've been erratic since you met me."

Zac nodded her toward the couch, and she sat. He sank beside her, waited for Simon to take one of the chairs, but of course the man stayed on his feet.

"We should get some sleep," Zac said. "Anything you need?"

"I need to know what you're going to do with me."

"*With* you? Nothing. You're a person, not an object."

"Will I be sent away?"

"Not by me."

"You make very little sense." She stood and picked up her duffel from where she had dropped it. "Good night."

She retreated to the bedroom and shut the door without looking back. Clean linens apparently did not concern her. The door locked with a soft click. Zac looked up. Simon was starting to seem like a bodyguard, but he couldn't tell for whom.

"Thoughts?"

"Get some sleep," Simon said. "I'll wake you in four hours."

"I mean about Rachel."

"What's stopping her from slipping out the window in there?"

Zac nodded at her car keys resting on the kitchen counter. "Keep an eye on those. I locked the vehicle."

"So she leaves with the duffel."

"Her car is her life. She loves the thing, and she was careful with her possessions, even cheap stuff. Every last thing matters to her because things are all she has."

"Hmm." Simon strode to the table, picked up the keys, and shoved them into his pocket. "Fear of reprisal is a strong motivator."

"You heard her, man. She thinks she deserves whatever Cady dishes out."

Simon paced in the stretch between living

room and kitchen. "And she wants to keep you."

"Uh, sure, I guess."

"Don't tell me you missed that part."

"Well . . . wait, you mean . . . ?"

Simon gave a quiet chuckle. "Platonic, I think, but she won't throw away the first human bond she's experienced in sixty-plus years."

Zac pushed his knuckles against his chest.

"Yeah," Simon said. "I can't feel it like you do, but I can see it."

Zac nodded, words blocked by the cracks in Rachel. He had to help her. He had to pray for her.

An unexpected thought.

"Enough chitchat," Simon said as if they'd been debating restaurant options. "The faster you get to sleep, the faster I get to sleep."

Zac lay down on the couch, found the flattest throw pillow to support his ribs and another for his head. He tugged the afghan over him and closed his eyes, and Simon switched off the lamp.

Hours later Zac lay as still as possible and drifted up from the tunnel of slumber for what had to be the tenth time. Rib pain had its pros and its cons. The main benefit was shallow sleep, which kept his mind from the grasp of a nightmare. The main drawback was shallow sleep, which kept his body from restoration.

Something moved near him. He pushed up on the couch and listened. Simon? The toilet flushed down the hall. Papers rustled in the kitchen. Where they'd left the research folder. Zac was on his feet without conscious thought, flipping on the lights.

Rachel stood with one hand thrust into the folder. She was shaking so hard she could barely stand.

He was going to punch Simon's lights out. He rushed to her and grasped her shoulders, and the physical touch brought her agony into him with no less force than he'd felt Ruth Wister's joy. This too was a waterfall.

"Did you take it?" His voice rasped with her pain.

"Zac, please." It was a wail. "Please, I need to."

"Why?"

"The picture at the fair, when they were laughing, when they were living."

Zac sat her at one of the chairs. Rachel brought her arms up to hide her face, and he kept his hand on her shoulder though he needed for his own sake to pull away from a darkness so thick he could choke on it. Rachel lived in this. He didn't intend to pray aloud, but the need was too raw for silence.

"Help us, Father. Bring Your light."

"God? You're talking to God?" Rachel's words came out like sobs. "What, you're worried I'll go to hell? Hell would be a reprieve from their dead eyes."

"No," he said.

"Let me go find out for myself."

He didn't know what else to do. He crouched by her chair and wrapped her in his arms, and she caved into him and let him carry her like a child back to her room. He sat with her on the side of the bed until she stopped shaking.

"I'm not conflicted," she said at last. "I swear to you, Zac. There's no part of me that wants to live with what I've done."

"I know, kiddo."

"But you won't let me go."

"I won't."

He hugged her, expecting her to push away, but instead she clung to him. He closed his eyes and prayed. Part of Rachel could still cling. Part of her knew she needed help.

When she sat back and met his eyes, hers were dry. "I have to be alone now."

He got up. "I won't be far."

He shut the bedroom door softly and made it all the way to the kitchen before his legs gave out. He caught himself on the table edge and lowered his trembling frame into a chair. In the opposite chair Simon sat waiting for him.

Zac lowered his head to his arms on the tabletop. He spoke into them. "Some bodyguard you turned out to be."

Something glass rubbed over the surface of the table. Zac looked up. Simon positioned the vials in a row, as Rachel had done in the cottage.

"What . . .?"

"I kept them with me. She would've figured it out in another few seconds if you hadn't flipped the lights on."

Zac buried his face again. "Oh."

"Go back to sleep."

"What time is it?"

"Around four."

"It's my turn for watch anyway." But he couldn't lift his head.

"You're done in, Zac. Go on."

"Maybe another hour, if you don't mind."

"What'd I just say? Go."

He trudged to the couch and lay down, certain he wouldn't sleep. When Simon shook him awake, he couldn't force his eyelids open. He groaned.

"Come on, man."

"Tired," Zac slurred.

"Join the club. Come on, wake up."

Zac blinked a few times and rubbed a palm down his face. Dawn was in the room, gray and reticent, withholding sunshine from behind low, cold clouds. He pushed himself up. Ouch.

"Just let me get a couple hours, and I'll be fine."

Zac got his feet under him and threw the pillow at Simon. "G'night."

"Thanks for nothing, pillow skimper."

"Whiner."

Taciturn and macho, right. Cady would learn differently.

He shuffled into the kitchen, the scent of coffee luring him. Simon must have made a whole pot, judging from the recent dark line on the carafe. He'd drunk half of it. Zac poured himself a mug and sat at the table.

He hoped Cady was sleeping or at least had been able to at some point. Hoped she could feel God near her tonight. That her soul belonged to Him filled Zac with thankfulness. Ironic, given his reaction to the fact a few days ago. But she might feel He had left her in her grief. Zac didn't know what determined something like that, why his memories in the German grave still festered with separation. With desertion.

He sipped his coffee. Good stuff. His own

never turned out this palatable, though he'd never stop denying spurious longevite claims that his efforts tasted worse than an alkali spring. Rain began to patter the roof and drizzle down the sliding glass door across from the table. He sighed. Rain was a cheerful thing when he was cheerful too. Today he wouldn't mind the comfort of sunshine.

Bare feet scuffed at the edge of the kitchen. He looked up. Rachel was mussed with sleep, especially her long hair, which she'd braided but not carefully. She wore modest blue cotton pajamas and looked innocent as a baby rabbit, her eyes only half open and foggy with sleep.

"Good morning," she whispered.

"Hey. Come in." He kept his voice as low as hers, though Simon likely wouldn't wake for anything now.

She sat across from him, watched him sip his coffee, watched raindrops trickle down the glass door.

"Hungry?" he said. "And Simon made coffee."

"In a little while."

They sat and watched the rain. Minutes crept by, and neither of them spoke. At last he leaned back in his chair and closed his eyes. Motrin. That's what he needed. He'd get up in a minute and take some. Most accident-prone human being alive. Statistically, compared to every other human being alive . . . but his stats weren't fairly matched.

"I'm not sure what happened last night," Rachel said quietly.

He sat up carefully and waited for more.

"I couldn't think anything except *If I die, I won't have to face any of them ever again.* It was playing like a record loop in my head."

He waited, but she was quiet again. At last he said, "Was last night the first time it's happened?"

"I told you I'm tired."

"Yeah, but this was different."

She gave a slow nod. "I was safe before. By myself. I keep picturing everyone there on the steps looking at me, knowing me. Last night with the cure right there if I could just get my hands on it . . . It was the best solution."

"Do you still believe that this morning?"

"I don't think so. But I asked myself just now, sitting here, if I'd rather have stayed alone forever. Years and years of more and more aloneness. And the answer is yes."

"Okay."

She blinked, maybe surprised at his acceptance. "I think I want it to be no. But today it's yes."

"You've got time to figure it out."

"I never wanted time, Zac. I wanted a husband and children and a few good horses and land enough to ride fast and far. That's all I ever wanted."

He had no answer for her. That God's ways were higher would be no comfort to a soul who had begged for hell less than twelve hours ago.

"I'd like to keep talking," she said at last. "But I can't take any more hard things right now."

"We could turn this conversation upside down. Truly flippant. If you want."

"I would relish something truly flippant."

"Then it's time for This or That."

"Um, what?"

He explained the concept, then asked, "Book or film?"

The shadow in her eyes half lifted. "Film."

A glut of words was stored up in her, and he'd tug until he freed a few more. "You might be the only one of us with that preference."

"Oh, I've been crazy for motion pictures ever since we got sound."

"When you were, what, twenty-six?"

"Mm-hmm. Two years after the accident, still thinking I was mortal."

"I was seventy-two."

"Oh my."

A smile tugged his mouth from deep inside, and she smiled back.

"My turn," she said. "Do you prefer live music or recorded music?"

"I love both. But recorded, I guess."

"Why?"

"I mean, now that we can get it. Performance can be captured in something more solid than a memory. Live recordings are the best."

Her eyes lit. "That's like my photography. So much beauty everywhere that I never want to forget. I didn't really get into it until the sixties, but even since then the advances are amazing — digital storage of course, but also quality, sharpness, contrast, filters — there's so much to do with it these days."

Aha, there was the word glut. "You'll have to show me your work sometime."

"Oh yes." But the lightness left her in a moment, and she reached out and gripped the table edge. "I was berating myself last night for leaving a trail."

He stood and came around the table to sit next to her. "Why did you?"

She flattened her hands on the tabletop as if to plant herself there. At last she looked up. Her eyes held youth and age in equal measure, a longing for contradicting things.

"I made the cure with me in mind," she said. "All the time passing, all the people walking past me all the time, just walking past while their hair turns gray and their skin turns to paper and they have spouses and children and grandchildren and friends and it hurts *so* much the way they keep walking past."

He nodded. It did hurt. The Life Buoys accumulated over a century testified to that. He prayed for help, kept praying for it. He was only a man. A flawed and wrung-out man. Bungling this was practically inevitable.

"Cady thinks it would be justice. Doesn't she." Triumph lifted a corner of her mouth.

"I haven't asked her."

"Victim's next of kin. She chooses my fate. That's in the Old Testament, isn't it?"

"Um, not exactly."

"Close enough. How about this: if she agrees, you let me die."

"Rachel." He dropped his voice even lower than they'd been speaking for Simon's benefit. "I think you ought to see her and Finn."

"Wh–why?"

"Because you're dreading it. Wouldn't it be better to face them and have it done?"

She ducked her head. "I don't think so.

But you can tell them for me . . . that I know it was grievous."

"Okay." He wouldn't push. Not about this and not about the question she'd left unanswered a minute ago.

"And tell them I stayed. With James and Anna. In case something went wrong, I stayed. They weren't alone."

She'd said she didn't want any hard topics, but hard was all they had. "I went to Missouri. To their home."

She seemed to shrink deeper into herself. "You saw their graves."

"Yeah."

"On their own land, beside their family. It was all I could do for them."

"I'm sorry it was on you."

"I deserved the task." A few quiet minutes, and then she sighed. "I don't think I can get back to flippant."

"There's another thing we need to do," he said.

"What is it?"

"Let's take a look at what's left of the research. If you think you can deal with that right now."

Her posture relaxed, and he wondered what she'd expected him to say. "Of course."

He had stowed the research folder in his bedroom, on the closet shelf above a rack of hangers he hadn't put to use. When things calmed down for a full twenty-four hours, he would take a few days to drive to Denver and back again. He would ship his nonessential belongings including the rest of his clothes. Maybe he'd quit apartment living altogether, sell the RV, and buy a house here. A house with a beach for a backyard.

He resumed his seat across from Rachel, opened the folder, and drew out the contents. Pages spread over the tabletop. And then the vials.

"You drew their blood," he said. "James and Anna."

"With their permission. After the cure, when it became clear they . . . I hadn't had the opportunity with the others. I thought it might help somehow. But they went too fast."

"Have you analyzed it?"

"There was no point."

"And this stuff," he said with a gesture at the remaining vials. "Did you pour any out?"

"No, just burned the notes. The serum itself, I was saving for last."

He examined the three vials more closely now than he had back in the cottage. The clear liquid was tinted a sort of amber. In the other two, the liquid was a similar color but milkier.

"Which is which?" He'd never seen the serum before. A slight chill overtook him. The power in these vials was too much. Maybe no human should have it, mortal or longevite.

"The clear is the original," she said. "The cloudy is the cure."

"Two vials of the cure?"

"One for you. One for me." She ran her thumb over one of them with a wistfulness that shook him.

He cupped them in his hand, slid them into the folder, and stood. "These are going back to bedroom storage."

"Please," she said.

There it was again. Whether she knew it or not, a sliver deep within her wanted life. He had to breathe a few times before he returned to the kitchen, and by then Rachel had begun perusing the notes.

"What are you seeing?" He studied the page she ran her finger over.

"Doc's stuff is gone."

"All of it?"

"I guess it was on top. What's left is mine."

A loss, deep and permanent. History destroyed. "Doesn't seem to bother you."

"Oh, I have a lot of it memorized."

"But the physical archives . . ."

"Can't cry over spilled milk."

He had no words.

"So, practically speaking, here's what we have left. See these formulae here, these are copies of Doc's work. Until I decided to destroy everything, I worked from my copies and kept the original separate, for safekeeping. Anyway these equations got me the version of the cure we have now. I had started tweaking the proportion of ingredients, but one problem of course is a viable control . . ."

Her hands went still. Her eyes lifted to Zac, and in one long exhalation she surfaced from the science, transformed from settled lake to agitated stream.

"Hey," Zac said.

"If I get it wrong again, this time it will be David Galloway who shrivels to death."

"You have time. Years. No one's going to rush you."

"It should be destroyed. All of it, right now."

Zac felt again the dragging weight of David's burden, the expected sorrow of Tiana's casket lowered into the earth. So many caskets had lowered while longevites stood watching.

"No one else is going to take it as it is," he said quietly. "If you pour it out now, you're as stuck as the rest of us."

She shuddered. "I don't know that I can create what we want."

We. Thank God. He set his hand on hers and knew what he had to say — to her alone, surely never to Cady, but if he didn't say it, Rachel would soon brim over with rancid guilt.

"Rachel, listen to me. You did not kill Anna."

Her back pressed against the chair. She shook her head.

"No," he said. "You told her, 'This cup is poison.' She drank it anyway. Knowing. She was broken inside, and that was not your fault."

Not until he spoke the words aloud did he fully see. Every *if* in Anna's letter was a lie.

"The poison was my brew," Rachel whispered.

"So you remake it. However long it takes, you keep trying."

She stared down at the papers, the work of her own mind. "Holly and Sean got no warning. I told them they could be mortal again. They thought it over and decided it would be an adventure."

"You made a mistake," Zac said.

"I was arrogant." She looked up at him, and her lip trembled. "I'm not any longer."

He squeezed her hand. When he began to let go, Rachel grabbed hold and squeezed back.

For an hour she pored over the information that had escaped her pyre. She broke it down for him, and he understood most of it, but his own mind never could have conceived it. This woman was a science genius possibly matching the caliber of her father.

She watched while Zac took pictures of every sheet of paper and sent them from his phone to his laptop. Then they put all of it away, returned to their seats at the kitchen table, and for the next hour used This or That as a loose model for conversation. They discussed books, music, movies, food, history, technology. The upheaval in Rachel began to calm again. She seemed happy to discuss comic book characters for the rest of her life. She had no concept of home cooking, but her favorite restaurants numbered in the several dozens. She knew cars. She'd done minor repairs on her vehicles for years.

"But Stormie, she's been a good girl. Hardly anything wrong with her since I bought her."

"Stormie?"

"Oh, grin if you want. I always name my

cars. This one's Stormie. With an i-e."
"I guess your first was Tin Lizzie?"
She rolled her eyes. "I don't do clichés. Anyway, I was a kid, remember? The automobile wasn't in my scope of life then, except to ride in one occasionally."
"I waited to buy until 1915. Of course the cost dropped again after I took the plunge."
"But you'd have been wealthy by then."
"Not really." The past wrapped him in soft tendrils of story, details twining. "Just a guy in his sixties who'd done a good job saving money. I didn't have the combined lifetimes of squirreling away gold and cash, not yet."
Around eight, Simon lumbered into the kitchen, straight for the coffee. He prowled for breakfast ingredients, and Rachel took over, mixing up thick batter and pouring small circles in the skillet.
"What are those?" Simon pointed.
"They're called silver dollar pancakes."
"I hope you plan to make at least thirty."
She laughed.
"Can you make crepes?"
"Oh no. If Zac didn't have the boxed mix, I couldn't make these either."
They ate Rachel's pancakes with butter and syrup, a few with peanut butter at her suggestion. Not Zac's usual eggs-and-bacon preference, but he'd have let her serve him

steamed shoe leather if it kept her thoughts away from the vials in the bedroom.

When she left to "freshen up," using the term as if it were still common vernacular, Zac gave Simon a quick summary of their conversation. "She's got to talk to Cady and Finn, but somebody needs to prepare Cady and gauge her response."

"She might not appreciate that."

"I'll text first."

"So I stay here and play warden while you go play mediator."

Oh . . . he hadn't thought to ask. Only assumed. He scrubbed his hand through his hair. "If you don't mind. I don't know what else to do, to keep the family together."

More than he'd meant to say. Simon went still, his attention notched up to laser-pointer intensity.

"I guess you didn't hear a thing I said last night."

To the casual observer, Simon's tone would sound indifferent, which meant he was keenly invested.

"I heard you. I don't agree, that's all."

"Hmm."

"And I'm going after them."

Simon huffed. "Fine. I'll stay with Rachel."

When Zac left, she and Simon were in

search of a checkerboard he was fairly sure lay around the apartment somewhere. If not, Rachel said she had a deck of cards in her car.

Sitting in his car in the apartment lot, Zac began a text to Cady. Hey. He stared at the word. What else? She'd know he wanted to discuss Rachel, and she wouldn't want to. He wished he didn't have to push. CAN WE TALK? he added then hit SEND.

He began driving, but not toward the hotel. She and Finn could be anywhere around town, and anyway, he had another matter to deal with. He coasted down the narrow streets toward Cousin Connie's.

At nine in the morning, the bakery bustled. Connie manned the counter alone and barely looked up when he walked in. He slipped into the back, washed his hands, donned plastic gloves, and came out behind the counter. Together they weathered the rush, while Connie said not a word to him and he bent and straightened at the glass cases, fulfilling orders. Spots were dancing in his vision by the time the last customers left, smiling and waving as they passed through the door.

Connie turned to him at last, hands on hips. "All right, Zac, I . . . Oh, for goodness' sake, look at you. You came to work sick? And handled people's food?"

"Not sick," he said.

He braced his right hand on the counter and pressed his left to his side. He'd forgotten how much movement was involved in this job because it was never more than ten feet in a single direction.

"I, um, broke a couple ribs."

"You ridiculous boy." She brought a folding metal chair from somewhere in the back kitchen and pointed down at it. "Sit."

He eased down and hunched forward a little. "Thanks."

"What are you doing here with broken ribs?"

"Wanted to explain."

"And took on the midmorning rush instead."

"You looked stressed. And I owe you no-show time."

"So you came in two hours late."

"I'm sorry, Connie. This isn't how I usually behave on the job."

She was studying him hard. "I think I believe you."

He lifted his hands, palms up. He had no excuse he could share.

"I saw a rather disturbing picture of you yesterday, online. Looked like David Galloway's bookstore in the background."

Agh, this. Of course, this. He blotted his forehead with his right sleeve. The spots were lifting from his vision as the pain in his side faded. "Yeah."

"Care to explain?"

"I don't do drugs. It was . . . I had a panic attack."

"Because of your fall?"

"Not exactly. There are some old things I can't talk about that mess with me sometimes. David's a friend; he covered for me best he could. Didn't know someone snapped a picture."

"It's unfortunate." Her expression was shifting from one form of consternation to another; this one was on his behalf. "Even celebrities should be able to keep some things private."

"I've done fine until now. Well, you know." He gestured to the bakery's main space, where mercifully no new customers had entered to see him hunched in a chair pale and sweating and being stared down by Cousin Connie. "I can work for hours without being recognized. I'm not Tom Cruise."

"I'm sorry for the added stress. And I'm sorry you're hurt. What happened?"

"Fell." He grinned. "I mean, how else would I do it, right?"

She gave a deep guffaw. "At least you can laugh at yourself."

"One thing I'm expert in."

"All right, son, the deal stands. Someone else comes along to answer that sign in the window, no hard feelings between us. Until then you're still employed here, but today you're going home to ice and rest."

"I can do something."

"I need you for the counter, and we've just seen how that went." The brusqueness faded, and she stepped close to pat his shoulder. "Listen, Zac, a car accident broke one of my ribs in 1989, and I remember it like it was yesterday. Go home."

He pushed to his feet. "What about the next six weeks?"

"Let me think on it. Maybe I can come up with a job that'll help me out and not strain you too much."

He rolled his eyes.

"Go on, get." She shooed him out from behind the counter.

He turned and held out his hand. "Thanks."

She shook it. "Rest up and heal up. I want you back here as soon as possible. They might not always recognize you, but they buy more from you than they do from me."

He winked, and she laughed, and he

squeezed her hand before letting go.

His phone buzzed before he reached his car. Cady. MEET US AT THE LIGHTHOUSE.

Thirty-Four

He had to go to them. He had to listen. Maybe speak too, but if so he had no idea what he was supposed to say. The drive gave him twenty minutes to formulate his thoughts, but they refused to fall into a manageable line.

At some point he emerged from under the rainstorm into an overcast chill. The two-lane blacktop road trailed the coast of Lake Michigan in the direction he and Simon had driven last night to Leahy. Zac was driving up a slight incline now, which made sense for the location of a lighthouse.

Brown park signage ensured he couldn't miss it: *Historic Lighthouse 1.3 miles,* then in 1.2 miles an arrow turning right onto a dirt driveway. Long and winding, ending at a blacktop lot with no more than a dozen parking spaces, empty but for Finn's and one other car. Zac parked, got out, and looked around. A tiny visitors' center with a restroom off the back. A trail of rough cement steps leading up and around a tree-covered hill. He tilted his head and could just see the blue-and-white tower. The beacon still resided there, no longer lit except on holidays, so David had told him.

Okay. He was in for a hike.

First he poked his head into the visitors' center. The paunchy bald man behind the brochure counter grinned at Zac's entrance and told him there weren't tours in the off season, but he was welcome to check out the lighthouse on his own. Good to know. No mortals would interrupt on behalf of the historical society.

He headed outside and started up the steps. The divide felt wider today between them — mortals and longevites. The counter-minding guy had been sixty or nearing it, just this side of the Vietnam generation. So young. As Zac climbed, his purpose solidified. The longevites must not remain divided.

Any normal day, he would have welcomed the exertion. If Connie could see him now, she'd call him a ridiculous boy. He couldn't argue as he panted and winced along his way. The clouds overhead drooped like sodden wool but spilled not a drop. The wet grass and pavement, the dripping trees, warned him rain could return any minute.

The main floor of the lighthouse, the living area, was no larger than Rachel's beach cottage. Zac stepped inside, crossed the floor to the stairs, and called up.

"Hello?"

"Zac?" Finn called from somewhere above him.

"Yeah."

"Come on up."

The staircase was a narrow spiral with a wrought-iron rail. Zac stood at the bottom and tilted his head to look above him — straight up, close walls, daylight streaming from somewhere high and out of sight. Maybe he could make it if he focused on the light. He gripped the rail and climbed, counting steps. He froze on eight, and at least twenty remained. He firmed his grip on the rail, but his feet refused to move. Tingling traveled from his clenched hands up his arms.

"I'll wait for you outside," he called.

"Oh, it's too close in here," Cady said, her voice quieter, not aimed at him. Then she raised it. "Give us a minute."

Zac turned and forced his feet to move, though now the low ceiling from staircase to cottage brought tension into his shoulders. Still no other tourists. He went outside and paced around the lighthouse, not much area to circle. The structure was sturdy old brick, weathered gray. He ran his thumb over mortared edges smooth with the years. A good old place, faithful to its work, casting its light to prevent the loss of ships and people. He wished he could go up and study the beacon, see the lake and the horizon as the lightkeeper once saw it.

Finn and Cady approached from the opposite direction. They were dressed for warmth and walking — jeans, sweatshirts, sneakers. Finn was fathomless as ever; Cady betrayed little more as she nodded to Zac.

"Hi."

"Hi," he said.

"I guess you found her alive."

Zac blinked, unprepared for this Cady. A shade less antagonistic than she'd been last night, terse and locked down instead.

"Yeah," he said.

"Finn said we should hear you out."

He spread open hands to them. "Mostly I came to hear you."

"I think my viewpoint is pretty clear."

"And I came to . . . to find a path."

"I know what my path is, Zac. It's the path of the last ones standing after attempted extermination."

He didn't realize he was shaking his head

until Cady's hands sprang to her hips and her voice lashed between them.

"Don't you dare tell me this was an accident."

"It was," he said, trying to gentle his voice, but those two words were a barb under her skin no matter how he said them. He knew that. He should have held his peace, heard her as he'd said he was here to do, without remark.

But Rachel.

"She made the serum deliberately," Cady said.

"Not to do what it did."

"To do exactly what it did!"

"Not in that time frame, Cady. Not —"

"She killed my family, Zac. There is no other point to make. She killed them and —" Her hands fell to her sides. A shudder ran over her. "And she buried them."

Something he could answer. A way to help. "Yes."

Cady's stillness held potential not unlike a box of dynamite's.

Zac measured his words one at a time. *Let this be a binding, not a new wound.* "She performed their burial. She left you the letter. It's all been Rachel; she confirmed everything to me."

"Anna," Cady said.

Zac nodded.

"And James."

Another nod.

"She presented them with a cure and they chose it."

He didn't know what else to do. He nodded again.

"She was in their house. Finn said the bed wasn't made. Anna wouldn't have left it like that."

"Rachel stayed with them," he said.

"She watched them die."

He hadn't brought a binding of wounds. He had brought something else, something he had not prepared for and couldn't yet name, but it was coming, he sensed it, with the next word he had to say.

"Yes."

Cady's frame seemed to split down the middle, an invisible outpouring of shock and pain.

"I'm so sorry."

She turned to Finn as if Zac had become invisible. "She really did it. She chose to go. And not tell me she was going."

Finn clenched his left hand. "Cade."

"And James. He didn't warn us. He didn't warn you."

"Cady," Finn said, and this time his voice was sharper.

Cady covered her mouth with both hands and bent over, fast as if she would fall. Zac surged to her side and caught her shoulders, but she wrenched away from him, stumbled, straightened up. Finn made no move toward her.

Her mouth twisted in a grimace that might be nausea. She turned on Zac and snapped her hands to her hips again, but the defiance of the posture was belied by the torn sense of her that was seizing hold of Zac's chest. She wanted him to think she was angry. She didn't know she couldn't fool him.

"You hear this if nothing else. I want her to pay for their lives. She has to pay for every one of them."

God help him with the words to help them. The words to help Rachel. He had to advocate for them all, even Finn who still hadn't moved a step or shown a flicker of feeling. Zac's spirit bent to the assault, Cady's silent screams too like Rachel's, grief like a shadow over her, though not so thick as Rachel's lost despair. He drew a long breath until the stabbing of his ribs jarred him, brought him out of the spiritual hurt at least slightly.

Father, I can't keep carrying all their pain. Please take it.

His voice strangled as he said the words he thought he was meant to say. "She is paying."

Cady's shiny eyes grew cold and hard, emerald ice where vulnerable pools had been a few heartbeats ago. "With what?" She spit the words like a mouthful of vinegar. "With remorse? You're going to stand there and tell me she's *sorry*?"

"She's suffering. That's what she is."

"I certainly hope so! I hope she's a shattered wreck!"

"She's that too."

"Do you know what I am, Zac? Do you even want to know?"

The sky itself seemed to lower toward him, boxing him in. He reached out. Touched her shoulder. Cady punched his arm away.

"I'm left behind." She covered her face. "Dear Jesus, help me. I'm the one that's left."

Now Finn moved. His arms enfolded her, and Cady fell on his neck and clung to him.

"They're all dead," she said as if no one had told him before now.

Finn held her up and baby-stepped her across the wide grass lot to the curb of the parking lot. Zac stayed where he was, his chest wrung out like an old dishrag. Finn and Cady hunched together on the curb, his arm around her motionless form. After a few minutes, Finn looked back as if unsure Zac would still be there.

He should go, but Finn beckoned him over. Zac shook his head, and Finn beckoned again. Zac shuffled to them and sat on Cady's other side. He looked around for witnesses to her distress, but the place remained empty of anyone but them. Grace? Had to be.

He hoped God would give grace for the rest of it. For his coming here, which might be all wrong. This thing was so muddy and muddled, and he had no idea how to make it clean again, if it ever could be.

Arm around Cady, Finn spoke close to her ear. "Not the best place."

"I can't stand it."

"I'm here."

"It doesn't help."

"I know. But I am."

They sat a long time. At last Cady lifted her head. When she caught sight of Zac beside her, she bristled.

"You didn't go."

"I . . ."

"You said you came to hear us." She drew a long breath as if to belay an outburst. "There. You heard us. There's no path. No path I would step foot on if that creature was walking it too."

He nodded.

She leaned her head on Finn's shoulder, turning her back. "Go away, Zac."

He pushed to his feet. "I'm sorry."

Neither of them acknowledged him.

He turned toward his car. Stupid. Mistake. He had caused more pain. He might have just splintered the family forever.

"Zac," Finn said.

He turned back to them. "I'm sorry. This was . . . ill-advised, chasing you down."

"We need time. We're . . . Well . . ." Finn shrugged as if no words fit.

"Cast down but not destroyed."

"Reciting that a lot."

What would they do now? Where would they go? He wanted to ask, but he'd lost the right, if he'd ever had it. If Finn read the questions in Zac's face, he gave no sign. His gaze moved from Zac to the cars in the lot. Dismissal.

"Bene vale," Zac said, the farewell he extended never to mortals and never casually. They nodded to each other, and he went to his car.

He had come to be a bridge and opened a divide instead.

THIRTY-FIVE

When hunger finally grew loud enough that he couldn't ignore it, Zac went for lunch at Salsarita's, halfway between the lighthouse and downtown. His solitude at a table for four normally wouldn't have fazed him, but today he could hardly stand it long enough to finish his enchiladas.

Around one o'clock, waiting for his check, he texted Simon. HOW GOES IT?

Simon's response was prompt. SHE'S THE WORST CHECKERS PLAYER I'VE EVER SEEN.

HOW'S SHE DOING?

MAJOR ANXIETY, WENT OUT AND SAT IN HER CAR FOR ABOUT 10 MIN. CAME BACK IN WITH A JAR OF SEASHELLS. COUNTS THEM WHEN SHE GETS WORKED UP. SEEMS OKAY NOW.

THANKS.

HOW'S YOUR PEACE MISSION FARING?

FAIL.

GIVE THEM TIME.

Platitudes were no help. He pushed the phone away from him across the table.

A minute later, another text came through. YOU COMING BACK?

Right. Simon didn't even like checkers. Zac would bring takeout tacos in thanks. He was typing a response when his keypad disappeared, overridden by an incoming call, and his tapping thumbs accepted it before he could see the area code. It wasn't a number in his contacts.

Solicitor most likely. Well, whatever. He raised the phone to his ear. "Hello."

"Zachary."

He leaned forward in his chair as if he could bring himself nearer to the voice. "Moira."

"It's me. How are you?"

He'd thought he would be joyful to hear her voice, if only for proof she was safe. But there was no room in him for joy right now, and something else clicked on inside him like the flame of a lighter. He didn't know what it was.

"I'm okay," he said. "What about you?"

"Fairly well, all things considered."

The server brought the check, saw he was on the phone, and smiled with a gesture of *anytime.* Zac held up a hand and dug his credit card from his wallet, passed it to her, and waited for her to walk away.

"Zac?" Moira said.

"I'm at lunch, just paid the check. Waiting for my card."

"Oh. I'll let you —"

"No." He rubbed at the tension in his jaw. "Stay on the line."

"Well . . . all right."

"Will you tell me where you are?" Around him, the restaurant droning seemed louder while he waited for her to speak. "Okay, just stay with me until I'm out of here."

No response, but no dial tone either. He'd count it a win.

The server returned, smiled, and walked away quickly as if Zac's expression gave away the intensity of the phone call. He gave his usual tip and left, all the while waiting for the dial tone. His heart was pounding. Moira. She might be in the diner across the street. She might be in Australia. The door shut behind him, and the background of voices and forks clinking on plates was replaced by distant traffic and autumn breeze in dry leaves.

"What are you up to?" Moira said.

"Still in Harbor Vale."

"I figured you'd stick. For a while anyway."

"Oh yeah?" He got in behind the wheel

but didn't start the car.

"It's a pleasant place."

He nearly told her Simon was here too, but if she wanted Simon's location, she could call him herself.

"And you and David seemed to get along, and he's so new to us. I'm sure you've dragged his entire life story out of him by now." A smile lifted her voice.

After this week, David felt like a sturdy old friend. "He's a good guy."

"Yes." She said it as if she knew firsthand some piece of the man's character Zac wasn't privy to. Maybe she did. Or maybe she was just talking the way Moira always talked, assured, especially of people.

Well. Not always.

The silence had already knotted itself up like a necklace chain left in a pocket. Untangling it would require more energy than Zac had — this moment, today, this week. He leaned back in his seat and closed his eyes.

"I was thinking," she said after a while, "about that little mutt we used to have, when we were living in the house on Riverton Avenue. How he used to eat our slippers but nothing else in the house. How funny his little scruffy face was."

He couldn't lose himself in a blissful

memory. Not today. Anyway, their time in the house on Riverton hadn't been blissful, and they both knew it.

"Henry, wasn't that what we called him?"

"You know that's what we called him," Zac said.

She was quiet.

"So that's why you're calling after four weeks without a word. To reminisce about Henry the dog."

Still nothing.

"Moira, I can't do this with you." He tried to keep the bite from his words then decided to let it in. "I can't sit here working your puzzle. Let's see, Henry the dog — are you saying you want a dog? Meaning you're coming home? Or let's see, Riverton Avenue — are you saying you miss the styles? Meaning you feel old today?"

"Zac —"

"Or maybe you're bringing up Riverton to remind me of the traumatized ruin I was in the twenties. Maybe you're letting me know you don't want to hear anything inconvenient. I hope you've noticed I'm more careful about that these last couple decades."

Her faint cry stopped him. His pulse was pounding in his ears. Adrenaline tingled in his fingers. Look at that, she could send him into fight-or-flight with a phone call. And shoot, he hadn't meant to say that last part, hadn't meant to bat at her with claws.

But this was what they did to each other now.

"I'm sorry." He'd said it often enough today.

"No."

No, he wasn't sorry? No, he shouldn't be sorry? She exhausted him. "Why did you call me?"

"I thought you wanted to hear from me."

"I did." Desperately, until a few minutes ago. "Just talk straight. Please. Tell me where you are and how you are."

"That's not why I called."

She wouldn't give him anything. He had to stop letting it hurt.

She made him wait half a quiet minute then said, "I saw something online yesterday. A picture. Of you."

Curse that picture. He gritted his teeth.

"Some of your silly fangirls are saying it's drugs, but of course I recognized . . ."

"Yeah." He managed to say the word through his tension-locked jaw. "It was an attack."

"In Galloway's?"

"Yeah." The shame burned in his face, in his stomach.

"But, Zachary, a public place like that.

It's been so long."

Ah. Riverton Avenue. Blinding panic in the middle of the afternoon, a sunny day, at the market in town. Witnessed by the store clerk who had lowered the window shades to keep out the heat, not realizing how dark the store would become when the final shade went down. Zac's scream had terrified the woman. In the middle of an aisle, Moira had held him through it, both of them huddled on the floor.

The behemoth had battered him so many times in the Riverton house. Different triggers, same response. Usually nights, Moira holding him through it, her tumbled brown curls against his bare chest, yet he had never told her what the others now knew.

"I'm working on it."

"Does David know?"

He closed his eyes and tried to feel again the prayers of his friends. The care of his friends. A spill of warmth seeped into him. "Yeah. They're really good to me."

"They?"

"Tiana and David."

"Good."

The quiet pushed back in. He shifted in the seat. A phone connection didn't allow him to sense if she was okay, but it was Moira, so he wouldn't be able to anyway.

"I'm glad you called," he said. "I guess you're overseas somewhere."

This silence was empty and arid.

"You might call Simon. Give him some peace of mind."

"Oh."

"We can't just shut worry off, you know."

The way you can. He'd nearly said it.

"You need to learn."

Yeah. Okay. He sighed.

"I'm . . ." The word seemed to choke her.

"Moira?"

"I'm not overseas, Zac."

A clue. "Okay."

"I — I feel like anything I tell you, he might find out and use against me. Against us."

He. Zac grew cold. "Colm."

"I'm not overseas," she said, desperation in the repeating.

"That's good."

"I'm in Chicago."

The cold gripped harder. "Why?"

"I had to see if he was coming back."

Oh Moira. "We severed his brain from his body. We buried him in the ground, separate tarps, separate — You were there, you saw."

"But we don't die, Zachary. Perhaps Colm didn't. Perhaps he dug himself out of the ground and went home to Chicago. To murder again. More mortals dead. And to come after us."

"That's not possible."

"How do you know?"

His kept his breathing level as false sensory input flooded him. Buried alive. Dirt on the grave. "Moira, listen to me. Colm is dead. He can't hurt you."

"I know."

What? "Good. You're safe from him."

"That is true, isn't it?"

"It is."

"I — I didn't call for this. I called because I saw that picture, and I thought you might be in trouble."

"I'm doing okay. And when I'm not, I've got support."

Whether he wanted it or not. An image flashed in his mind, David and Tiana and Simon lined up between him and the behemoth, wearing armored vests and brandishing firearms. The image drew a smile.

When Moira wanted to know a thing, she asked. Telling her the deepest parts of himself didn't feel safe anymore, but if she asked what had been happening to him, what the family was doing to help . . . If she said something to contradict her old words . . .

"I'm glad to know that." Calmness cloaked

her voice again as if it had never slipped from her.

So the subject was finished. Okay.

"How long are you staying in Chicago?" he said.

"Until I'm satisfied."

"And then what?"

"I haven't decided."

He ought to tell her to come home. When she asked where he meant, he ought to say her home was all of them — Simon, David, himself — not a place. And look, here they were in one little town. *Just come home to us, Moira, and we'll turn a new corner, get on with life and stop hearing Colm's voice in our heads.*

She wouldn't listen. But that wasn't the reason he didn't say it.

"We don't have anything left to say to each other, do we, Zac?"

How many times he'd rehearsed this phone call. But no script would ever do Moira justice.

"I do have one thing," he said. Her silence didn't justify his. "I'm sorry."

"You? For what?" The words held a mockery that might be forced. He hoped it was anyway.

"I didn't protect you from him."

She made a scoffing sound. "You didn't

know what he was."

"And I'm sorry for that too."

"He was a psychopath, Zac. He mimicked normal flawlessly. No one but a mind-reader could have seen through it."

Which was why she should have told him. Seventy years ago, she should have told him.

"He was bored, you know."

Zac's fingers were freezing to the phone, starting to cramp. "What?"

"The kills were losing their luster, so he created the story he told me. My fear became his new hobby."

He leaned his forehead on the steering wheel and fought the urge to punch out the car window. Seventy years of fear. "Moira."

"This isn't why I called either."

"No, but I'm sorry. I hope you'll forgive me."

"I need to go."

"All right. Take care."

"Likewise." A long pause during which he thought she'd hung up. Then, quiet and hard, "You've gone back to God."

He blinked. "I have."

"I always knew you would. You took longer with it than I expected."

He had no idea what to say to that.

"Goodbye, Zac."

Now the dial tone. He checked the incoming number; it was an Illinois exchange all right. And it was a burner. He knew that the way he knew all her old names, the shape of the birthmark on the small of her back, the girlish sparkle and grin that happened to her face when she was painting. The way he knew she would call him again though he didn't know when — a day, a week, a month, a year.

He drove home, aching, pondering. Not once had he wished he could hold her.

Thirty-Six

He'd forgotten takeout tacos. He'd forgotten to respond to Simon's text. Moira's call had burrowed under his skin and latched on with teeth, and the deepest bite was the last thing he had expected. Colm. As he drove, the muscles in his legs grew twitchy.

Simon met him at the door. "Tell me you brought lunch. Your cupboards are bare."

"I meant to."

"I can't eat intentions, idiot."

"Sorry."

"I'll grab something while I'm out. I have an errand."

"Here? In town?"

"Just keep an eye on the kid."

By *errand,* Simon meant *mission.* He'd already put on his shoes, and his expression held his signature crinkle-browed irritation when delayed by questions.

Zac gestured to the door. "Have fun storming the castle."

"I can't believe you just — Never mind."

"Classic."

"Cheese. I'll see you later."

"As you wish."

"Idiot."

The door shut. Zac gave it a pat. "Curmudgeon."

On his kitchen counter sat a mason jar filled with seashells. Scallops, spirals, cowries. Pinks, peaches, ivories, a few pale grays. A limpet showing its white underside. A pearlescent flat thing he didn't recognize. As he picked up the jar, a knock came. Zac set it down and went to open the door.

"Forget something?"

Simon's expression was withdrawn. Mission face, and not a taco run sort of mission. No jesting this time around.

"I was going to get it done and then tell you I'd done it," Simon said. "But it should be your choice."

"Okay."

"I figured you didn't have a good shovel, apartment living and all, so on my way from the airport I bought two. They're in the rental."

Shovels. A cold finger traced Zac's spine. Folly to think Colm had orchestrated this from beyond the grave, yet the coincidence of Moira's words followed by this . . . No, it was not a coincidence. No, Colm had nothing to do with it. Zac had to stop thinking in the old ways.

Okay, Father. I'm Yours.

The chill sluiced off him in a warm shower of kindness. His Father was here.

" 'Course I didn't know then how it's been for you," Simon said. "And why. You don't have to go, man. But it needs to be done. I'm sure the grave's settled by now. Could be obvious, if someone spotted it."

"I'll go," Zac said.

"It might set you off."

"I know."

Simon shrugged. "Your call."

"Rachel," Zac said over his shoulder. "Field trip."

Simon frowned.

"Can't leave her here."

"Guess not."

She came into the room wearing leggings and a red tunic top. She'd always worn jeans before, and Zac hadn't noticed how thin she was; the leggings clung and the tunic hung too obviously for him to miss it now. Her frame might have been recovering from long illness, might have belonged to the Dust Bowl days, survival on flour and grease. He had to find a way to ask. Money wasn't likely the issue, given her hair and color contacts. Then again, people prioritized strange things sometimes.

Zac locked up, and they left. Rachel didn't ask where they were going, seeming to pick up on the gravity of the trip. Simon's face was hard as he motioned her to the back seat and Zac got in on the passenger side.

"You're not doing this to verify anything, are you?" Zac said.

"Such as?"

"He's not a zombie."

Simon gave a mirthless laugh. "That hasn't been one of my concerns."

"This is about concealing the grave. Nothing else."

"If you've got some other item on a Colm's Corpse to-do list somewhere, say so now."

"I talked to Moira."

A long moment passed, and then Simon sighed. "Could've started there."

"She said something," Zac said. "About him. I had to tell her he's dead. She said she knew, but some of what she said — I'm not sure she does."

"And you're surprised?"

"No, Simon, I don't mean the way we don't believe it. The surreal sense of it, the forgetting he's not going to respond to group texts. I mean something in Moira still believes Colm is in Chicago, in his apartment, planning his next victim."

Simon was staring at him, gearing up. "Where is she?"

"Eyes on the road," Rachel said from the back seat.

Zac turned his face to look out his window and bit down his laugh. His shoulders shook with it.

Simon growled but refocused on the road. "Where is she?"

"She didn't want to tell me."

"Meaning she didn't tell you? Or meaning she told you anyway?"

Zac shouldn't have brought her into this. "Come on, man. You know it's up to her."

"Old custom. Those days ended."

"Oh? And when did that happen?"

"When she withheld information that resulted in an untold number of murders."

Zac pressed his palms to his eyes. Shook his head. Yeah, Simon deserved to know. But as long as he wasn't endangering her or anyone else, Zac had to respect Moira's confidence.

"Take me back to Zac's," Rachel said. "This is between you."

"And you'll stick around?" Simon said.

She flinched at his bark. "I'll try to."

"Not good enough."

Her head bowed.

Maybe it was new tensions piling onto earlier ones that made Zac's right hand clench with an urge to deck something. "Rachel."

She looked up.

"I'm not risking coming home to an empty house." For all he knew, she was skilled at hotwiring. It would fit.

"This is a murderer's grave."

"Yes."

"A necessary grave."

He started to turn in his seat to make eye contact, but he couldn't manage it without urgent warnings from his ribs. He leaned a little to find her in the rearview mirror. "This grave exists to prevent more graves."

"But you've shown me mercy. Why not Colm?"

He could parse the difference between the cure serum and Colm's methods, but he didn't know what those were. In his nightmares, Colm most often strangled his victims with his hands, but he'd also stabbed a few, shot a few. In the worst of the dreams, Colm tied up scores of mortals and threw them into mass graves, leered at Zac while he shoveled dirt onto them and Zac stood paralyzed beside him.

"You didn't intend them to die," Simon said.

"But they did. That's the relevant fact."

"To determine a sentence? No." Zac straightened in his seat as they neared the park. "No court would convict you of first-degree murder, and that's what Colm was guilty of. Many times over."

"I see," she whispered.

"What're you going to do?" Simon said to Zac. "Take a picture of the settled ground and the weeds and text it to Moira?"

"I would if I had her number."

"It would be overgrown by now even if a zombie dug its way out."

Zac shuddered at the image.

"What was the burner's area code?"

"Simon. No."

"She wouldn't have called you if she wanted to keep it from me."

That held a certain logic.

The park backed up to Galloway's Books, but Simon didn't use David's parking lot. Trekking through the park in the middle of the day was risky enough; they wouldn't allow the possibility of David's being connected to said trek if something went wrong. Instead they would leave the car at the lot behind the corner market. Still small but larger than David's and unseen from the street.

When Simon turned the car off, Rachel said quietly, "I'm staying here."

Simon scowled.

"I will not steal the car. I'll be here waiting for you. But I'd be an intruder at the site, and you know it."

Maybe she was right. "Your word?" Zac said.

"My word. I can pretty much always wait calmly in a car."

Simon hooked the keys to one of his belt loops. He and Zac set out, each carrying a shovel, Simon swinging from his other hand a ten-gallon plastic bucket he had bought as well.

Of course, as if they'd never been interrupted, Simon said, "So Moira's location is need-to-know."

"Yep."

"Which means she isn't in Europe. You think I'd hop in the car and drive after her."

Zac grinned. "Nice try."

"I'm right."

"You could go after her just as easily in Europe. You'd book a flight as fast as you'd fill up a gas tank."

From the market, their path followed the sidewalk for two blocks and then cut through a vacant residential lot. From here they would end up on the east end of the park, with the bookstore somewhere to the north. If they veered northeast, they would find the half-cleared area chosen for Colm's grave. Burs and sap clung to their jeans. Zac didn't bother to brush at them; he'd only collect more on his way back.

He knew the place the moment they emerged through knee-high weeds and brush. He stood looking over the sparse woods. Sunlight filtered through the canopy of foliage, catching the underside of cottonwood leaves and turning them silver as the breeze tossed them. None of this had been visible in the night.

Their mission was needed. The dirt over the grave had sunk, air pockets releasing from the disturbed earth as it settled. Weeds had sprouted, which helped but didn't fully camouflage the six-foot length of ground. Did the serum's organisms continue to live in that soil, feeding on plant nutrients as they'd once fed on Colm's vitality, giving that vitality back to the microbes around them? Or had the death of the host organism precipitated their death as well?

"No evidence of zombie activity," Simon said.

Zac shook his head. He saw this place the

night he'd last been here — the only other time he had been here. Each of them pale in the flashlight beams. White hands wielding shovels, white faces with wide eyes. David's somber, hushed voice: *"It's time."* Their nods. Permission. The glint of the saber coming down. The blood on the dirt.

And then the digging, and then the dirt turned over onto Colm, and Zac lay there in the grave and couldn't get out —

"Zac," Simon said.

He blinked again, but a gray haze crept over his mind. He was slipping as if the ground beneath him had tilted.

A quiet curse, a hand on his arm. "Idiot."

Zac grasped his will in both hands and drew himself up from the depth of the haze. "The idiot can hear you."

"Good," Simon said. "I'll get started. You just stand there."

"No. Let's do this."

"That's a terrible idea."

"It's not. Trust me, man."

Simon's scowl hadn't let up since they'd gotten in the car. It didn't now either, as they trekked deeper into the park and chose a place to fill the bucket.

"Should've brought a wheelbarrow," Zac said as he shoveled.

"Yeah, I thought it might be a little conspicuous sticking out of the trunk."

Zac grunted in what he hoped sounded like protest or agreement or anything other than what it was. His ribs were killing him.

The bucket didn't take long to fill, but ten gallons wasn't a lot of dirt. They team-carried it back and forth. Either could have lifted it himself, but something ceremonial had overtaken the moment. They were here together. They acted together.

When they had a satisfactory dirt pile beside the grave, Simon set aside the bucket and Zac angled for his first shovelful. And froze. He was already sweating; now he went cold. He couldn't look away from the exposed soil, crumbling and brown-black and mingled with tiny rocks and earthworms and roots and weeds overturned by their digging. Digging. Clawing. Fighting for light and air. Fighting to see the sky again. He got a shovelful, swiveled, and dropped it onto the sunken grave. One down.

He kept shoveling. He didn't know if Simon had joined him or not, if Simon had spoken to him in the last few minutes. He covered the grave with dirt and more dirt as the past played in front of his eyes and weighted his chest. The terror and the fight. And then the escape.

The second day. His fingers sinking into horizontal ground. Pulling himself up. Rolling limply onto his back. Coated in mud and blood, hungry, exhausted, but so anguished in soul he hadn't noticed any of that for another twelve hours. Breathing and crying and breathing some more while the sun poured light down on him. Light that had guided him up, that had let him believe he wasn't going to be trapped there for undying centuries.

The shovel fell from his hand.

The first sunny day in weeks. The promise of the sky if he could persevere long enough to reach it. If his second day in the grave had rained like so many before it, if the sun had never come out for him and the dirt had sunk on him like this and kept sinking while he despaired in darkness, might he still be there now? Would he have lost his will until it was too late?

He was on his hands and knees in front of the other grave. Colm's grave. Firm hands held his shoulders. He tried to come back, but the past still hung on hard. Ground crumbled under his palms as he heaved himself up and out. To lie in sunshine.

"God."

I will never leave you nor forsake you.

"You brought the light to bring me

strength. To bring me out."

His hands were covered in dirt, as if he'd been digging with them, scooping handfuls while he knelt there. Maybe he had.

"Come on, Zac. You need to come back, man." Simon's voice was shaking.

Zac looked up. Simon knelt at his side, both hands still gripping Zac's shoulders. "Here."

A hurricane gust of a sigh. "Don't do that again."

"That's the goal." He shut his eyes. "You're right. I'm an idiot."

"Should've stayed in the car."

"I said I dug myself out alone. But it was grace. It's all been grace."

Simon shifted on his knees and looked away.

"God. He didn't leave. He gave the sky back to me."

"You're not making sense, Zac."

"With all that's been messing with me, my head keeps forgetting I'm not still in the grave with those other bodies. Or with Colm. I got out, man." He looked down at his hands, and the dirt caking them made his heart hammer. He scrubbed them on his jeans. "No. I got out."

"Okay." Simon's voice was cautious. Worried.

Zac kept scrubbing at his hands. Dirt had worked in under the nails, which didn't help his pulse. He tried to keep talking. "It's like my mind stayed behind somehow. Here. It's why I can't sleep."

"And why you blanked out that night."

"Yeah, I guess."

Deep breaths. Aching ribs. Zac could have laughed. Those were grace too. Grace that grabbed him by the collar when nothing else would stop his prodigal stupidity. Because he had always been a son. The kind that relinquished a rebellion of silence only when pinned to the floor of a barn in the dark, yet still called a son by the Father.

"He did get me out." Zac's eyes burned. "If He hadn't gotten me out, I'd still be there."

"Okay."

"It's not going to make sense, Simon. Until you can see grace for what it is."

His brother wouldn't respond well to that, but it had to be said. Zac waited for the dismissive response, but Simon gave none at all. After a moment his hands lifted from Zac's shoulders.

"You good? Not going to slip off somewhere again?"

Zac used his shovel to stand. "I'm good."

"Maybe you should sit while I finish this."

"No. I'll be slow with the ribs, but I need to keep at it."

They resumed their task. New dirt fell on the old and slowly covered it until only the new could be seen, level again with the burgeoning forest around it.

THIRTY-SEVEN

The car was still there when Zac and Simon made it back to the market lot, and Rachel now sat in the passenger seat. She had locked the doors and tilted the seat back, and her eyes were closed. She must be as tired as they were, after all the upheaval of the last twenty-four hours. Asleep she looked no older than eighteen.

He tapped on the window, and she jarred awake then relaxed at the sight of him and Simon. She unlocked the car and stretched as they got in.

"Time?"

"For food," Simon said.

"Oh, good," Rachel said. "Zac, I don't know if you're aware of this or not, but the only edible things in your house are pancake mix, bacon, and assorted candy."

He jabbed a finger at her. "Hyperbole."

"Barely."

They went to the Harbor Vale Family

Diner because it was close and incapable of disappointing. Zac went straight to the men's room and washed his hands. Twice. Back at their booth he was still hungry after his burger and fries, so he ordered a cup of chili. He rolled his eyes at Simon's approving nod.

They talked little while they ate, and Zac mapped the rest of his day. He'd stop at the bookstore tonight, but he had a few hours before David and Tiana would close up shop. He needed to know Rachel was ready to be left alone. If so, he would drive out to his dunes. A yearning built in him to soak up the wide-open beauty for a few hours.

Before he had to ask, just outside the diner, Rachel halted and squared her shoulders, facing them both.

"Okay, guys, I need a break. I haven't been by myself in almost eighteen hours — no, sleeping in the car doesn't count — and it probably doesn't sound long to you, but it's taxing. For me."

For Zac eighteen hours with people was only the beginning of the party. On the other hand, eighteen hours in a locked closet would leave him catatonic. He nodded his understanding. Simon frowned at him.

"My word isn't worth much yet," Rachel

said, and Zac's heart lifted at her use of the last word. "But I wish you'd let me drive around for a few hours."

"You'll come back?"

"I will."

"And not head straight for Zac's apartment to break in and steal the cure?" Simon said.

Redness rose in her cheeks, but it didn't look like guilt. More like indignation. "I wouldn't do that."

She wasn't lying. Didn't mean she wouldn't change her mind.

"I'll go back to the apartment," he said. "And I'll collect the cure and the notes and keep them with me."

"That's fair," Rachel said.

"I'd feel better if you walk your way to solitude and let me hang on to the car keys for a bit."

This drew her brows into a scowl. "I need my car."

"To be alone?"

"To recharge."

He couldn't keep her keys forever. Did it follow that he couldn't keep them longer than eighteen hours?

"Oh, for pity's sake," she said, betraying her true years so unconsciously he could have laughed. "I want my car, Zac. If you have the cure, what can I possibly do to myself?"

Well, true.

"You can take off and disappear so we never see you again," Simon said. "Develop some more of the cure and take it then."

"No, I can't. The cure can be derived only from the serum itself, and what we have is the last of both."

That felt like a gift. And a responsibility. Both of which Zac would have to process when he could sleep again.

"Fisher Lake's little pond can't possibly still exist. Even if someone's kept it dug out for the last century, imagine trying to find it now. Imagine trying to identify the organisms in their original form, if they're still reproducing in the water. Only Doc ever saw them, and now his sketches are gone."

"And you wouldn't recognize them based on his sketches?"

"I might." She shrugged. "Again, though — how many ponds would I have to analyze to find the right one? What are the odds a little body of water like that hasn't filled in and become a field by now? Or an industrial zone? I'm telling you" — she turned to Simon — "if I wanted to start developing from scratch, I couldn't do it."

"Okay," Zac said.

She must have read uneasiness in his face. Well, he wasn't trying to mask it. "Zac, really, I won't go far. I'll be back in town by nightfall."

She didn't hold her hand out for the keys. She stood waiting, frustration pulling at her mouth.

"You understand my caution?"

Her frown relaxed. "Because I'm supposed to live."

"Exactly."

"I'm getting there."

Zac dug in his pocket and produced her two-key ring, plain and fobless. Rachel held out her hand and let him drop the keys into it.

She gave him a true smile. "Thanks."

"And let's exchange contacts, in case you need anything."

"Contacts?"

"Numbers."

"Oh. I don't have a phone."

He was pretty sure he blinked at her for two or three seconds.

"Well, who would I call? I have a tablet for internet access and photo storage. I use free Wi-Fi when I need it."

"Ah." It should have been enough, but he wished he had a means to talk to her, to gauge her well-being in her voice. He nearly offered to buy her a phone, but it seemed patronizing. "Do you check your messages often?"

"I'll make sure to check at least once while I'm out. Okay?"

He nodded.

"And maybe I'll get a phone at some point."

They drove back to his place, and she left in her SUV, eyes bright, breaths seeming deeper, rising into her shoulders. Simon watched her pull out of the driveway and fade down the street.

"You didn't give an opinion," Zac said.

"She worries me."

"Yeah." He sighed.

"Then again, you worry me. Moira worries me."

"Sounds like she's all set to join the family."

Simon's mouth tipped up on one side. "Persistent cuss."

"We've got to stay close."

For a long moment Simon stood quietly, watching the direction Rachel had driven away. "It's a nice thought."

"It's not original. Remember which one of us called a Life Buoy yesterday."

"Sure, but there's you and Moira, and then there's all these new old folks. I would've been fine and happy with just the three of us for the rest of our years."

"And David?"

Simon shrugged. "What about him?"

"We needed him, man. When it all came out. We needed support and an objective voice, and he was there."

"Hmm."

"He's solid, Simon."

"Oh, fine, David's worth admitting. Doesn't mean the rest of these folks are."

"You won't know until you try them. If the rest of them come through the way David did, why not have a family of seven?" He grinned. "We'd be magnificent."

Simon gave a theatrical groan. "I don't need cinema references. Or feminine adjectives."

"Say that again when my ribs are mended."

"Looking forward to it."

"But you won't be here."

No matter where or when they met, an impending farewell rested between them from the first moment. Florida must hold charms beyond what Zac had ever experienced there. Simon wasn't the type to be crazy for home, but Zac couldn't remember the last time he'd left for more than a week.

"I'm not going anywhere as long as the

Life Buoy's in effect."

"Only you can lift it." Zac shrugged.

"When I'm good and ready."

"What do I have to do, sleep through a night and eat three square meals?"

"That'd be a start." A current of worry ran under the words.

"What's the rest of it?"

"Rachel." Simon folded his arms, planted his feet. Expecting resistance. "You can't be her lifeline, Zac. It'll wreck you both."

"I know that."

The stance did not relax. "You've actually taken it into consideration?"

"In the sense that I'm likely to screw up? Yeah." He lifted his hand as Simon's mouth opened for rebuke. "I'm hearing you. I don't *want* to be anybody's sole link to humanity, okay? I'll work on it."

A moment of scrutiny, and then Simon uncrossed his arms. "Good."

"Yeah?"

"Well, forging links among humanity is sort of your thing. Just, you know, don't shift your overinvesting madness to that job instead."

Zac grinned. "Noted. So. Life Buoy lifted?"

"There's still the matter of sleeping through the night."

As if Zac were some infant. He scrubbed a hand through his hair and hoped the motion hid the heat in his face. He gestured in the direction of town. "Go forth and enjoy our town then. You've hardly seen David and Tiana."

"Maybe we'd have time to make real acquaintance if we could get through a week without a crisis."

"There weren't any crises last week."

"Not here maybe."

"Oh?"

Simon waved a hand. "Forget it. I'm going to drive around for a bit. I'll see you tonight."

At last, the dunes. He'd take it slow. If he could make it to the top, he'd lie at the base of those ancient poplars and stare up through their branches to the sky. It could rain on him for all he cared. He needed to spend some time beneath its dear expanse, and cloudy or sunny didn't matter.

He'd been driving only ten minutes, halfway to the national park, when the clouds opened. He switched on the windshield wipers and pressed onward. Maybe it would be a quick shower. Regardless, he was going up there. Did he have a raincoat in the car?

His phone began to ring. He fished it out of the middle console. Finn. "Hey."

"I want to talk to her."

He felt his eyebrows go up. "Rachel?"

"Before we leave. Are you with her?"

"Not at the moment."

"But you know where she is."

"I can get in touch with her."

"I'd be obliged."

"Where do you want to meet?"

"Doesn't matter." The edge in Finn's voice might be impatience, or it might not. "You tell me the place and I'll be there."

"Just you."

"That's right."

He'd been so quiet at the lighthouse, no hint of his opinion. No telling, even now, what he wished to say to Rachel.

"I'll call back when I get an answer from her," Zac said, signaling for a turn and notching up his windshield wipers. The shower was becoming a downpour, beating on the car roof.

"Thanks." Finn hung up.

Zac pulled over at the next stop, a corner market and gas station. He parked on the side of the building, tall old pine trees forming a partial shield from the rain, and brought up the app he'd used before to communicate with Rachel. The unread notifications were overwhelming. The bookstore pic and his last post to Doc were still generating replies and reposts. He ignored it all and thumbed out a private message.

HEY. NEED TO ASK YOU SOMETHING.

In seconds, his message bore the check mark of having been read. Rachel's tablet must be in Wi-Fi range. Her reply came through in less than a minute. HI. GO AHEAD.

FINN JUST CALLED ASKING TO MEET WITH YOU. WHAT DO YOU THINK?

Again, she saw it immediately, but this time no reply came. A knot formed in Zac's gut. He might have just sent her on a path as far from Harbor Vale as she could drive. Five minutes later, he was wishing he'd bought her a phone.

He sent another message. YOU OKAY?

A last long minute and then a new message pinged. SORRY. NEEDED A MINUTE. GOT COLD.

Cold? What was she talking about? NO PROBLEM.

REALLY PETRIFIED.

THIS IS 100% UP TO YOU. YOU CAN SAY NO.

IF I SAY YES, WILL YOU BE THERE TOO?

Finn might not care for that idea. Well,

Finn could go jump off a tightrope. IF YOU WANT.

HE WANTS IT TO BE TODAY, NOW?

WHENEVER YOU CAN.

I DIDN'T GET FAR. I'LL TURN AROUND. And then a few seconds later: WHERE?

Nowhere public. Depending on how things went down, even Zac's apartment might not be safe. HEAD BACK THIS WAY AND I'LL SEND YOU THE ADDRESS WHEN I'M SURE.

OKAY.

In the last seventy or so hours, Zac had scorned David's prayers, taken a swing at him, ruined a piece of his antique merchandise, and been rude to his girlfriend. Everything in Zac cringed as he called the man. What time was it anyway? Not quite three.

"Hello?" Of course David answered his phone as if caller ID hadn't been invented yet.

"Hey, I could use a favor. If you don't mind."

"What is it?" David said, not as if preparing to refuse but as if preparing for action on Zac's behalf.

That brought on another cringe. "I'm mediating a . . . I don't know. I hope it's a truce, but I don't know. Finn and Rachel. Your place would be an ideal location. You don't have neighbors on the other side of your walls."

"Ah." A door shut from somewhere close. David might have moved into the stockroom for more privacy. "A good plan, good to be cautious."

Zac nodded, a futile gesture, but he didn't know what else to say. An apology would be fitting, but he wanted that to be in person. Tonight, he hoped. Barring new crises.

"No key under the mat, though," David said. "You'd have to come by the store. I've a spare here."

The man had not hesitated for a moment. "Thanks."

"I will pray for you and for them."

"I'm much obliged," Zac said. "I'll be by in a few minutes."

"Very well."

Zac ended the call and thumbed a message to Rachel. DAVID'S PLACE. 902 SOUTH ST.

I'LL BE THERE.

Zac sent her a thumbs-up, called Finn and passed on the information, and drove to the bookstore.

The shop was mid-rush. Tiana smiled from behind the counter when Zac walked in. He stood to one side while she rang up several customers, chatting and laughing, commenting on their book selections. From every customer's pile Tiana had read at least one book. Zac shook his head. She and David were a true match. Her last customer was an elderly woman with a stack of picture books, and Tiana gushed over these the most, praising the artwork of one, the verse of the next. After the woman left, Tiana ducked behind the counter and emerged with a gold key in her palm.

"Here you go. David briefed me."

"Thanks." Zac added the key to his own ring and looked around. "Is he here?"

"Embroiled in inventory."

Another customer walked in. Tiana smiled a welcome, and the young woman called out, "Hey, Tiana!" on her way to the nonfiction shelves in the back.

"I'll let you get back to work," Zac said. "Hey, did he also brief you about the cost of that book?"

"Which?" She gestured around the store with a little smile.

"The one I ruined."

"Oh, you mentioned that before. I don't know anything about it."

"It was in the stockroom. I . . . um, caused it to fall. It was an antique."

"Well, he's not likely to charge a friend. He'll say accidents happen."

But a friend wouldn't accept that. A book that age, that pristine until he'd wrecked it, would be pricey. And there was the principle. "Tiana, I want to pay him."

"Fine, fine. I'll ask him when he comes up for air. What was the book?"

A pang passed through his stomach. He was no relic like David, but he ached to see the destruction of old things. "*Dealings with the Fairies.* Dark blue, gold script on the spine."

Tiana went still. "Oh. *Dealings with the Fairies.*"

"Yeah. What's wrong?"

"I'll let him know you asked about it." She tried to smile. Failed.

Shoot. It must have been worth a fortune, one of those rarities that went into the glass case behind the counter, handled by request only. "Don't go all mysterious and dramatic. Just tell me what's up."

"I . . ." She sighed. "He wasn't going to sell that book, Zac."

"What do you . . . ?" But then he remembered. The library in David's house — bookshelves lining all four walls, except an open space where a glass case stood, filled with . . . "Tell me it wasn't a first edition."

She didn't answer.

"Of course it was. And it was going into

his personal collection. And he's been searching for it for years."

"Mm-hmm."

"Crap."

"You're sure it's broken? Maybe it didn't fall far."

"The binding broke, Tiana. Pages were falling out of it when he picked it up."

"Oh." She blinked away tears. Yeah, actual tears. David must have been as thrilled as a little kid about that book.

Zac scrubbed at his face. He was an even bigger jerk than he'd thought.

"I'm sorry, Zac. All the things going on right now — It's only a book."

Insight cast a ray of light. "A book by MacDonald. Crying out loud, I bet David reveres George MacDonald. Our contemporary, pioneered genres, poet and novelist, onetime minister. The guy was even Scottish."

Tiana swallowed.

"Just say it."

"MacDonald is his favorite author."

Zac threw up his hands. "Of course he is."

"Zac —"

"Don't. I can't fix this. Money would insult him. That was probably the only one for sale on the entire planet."

"It seemed to be."

"I'm an idiot."

She stepped closer and set her hand on his back. "You're a friend, and it's still only a book."

He shook his head.

"Please, Zac. Go and do what you need to. I think maybe it's something God gave you to do; I don't think anyone else would do it. And in the meantime don't stew about this."

He tried for a smile. "I never stew."

"Don't even." She nudged his arm with hers.

"Thanks, sis."

She blinked. He blinked back. The nickname had been unplanned.

"Well, David is kind of my brother, so . . ." He shrugged. "And one of these days I expect him to make it legal."

Tears sprang to her eyes, wholly different from those for David's book. "I hope so, Zac."

"I'm counting on it."

"I try to. But he's very scared."

Ah. He nodded.

"Sometimes he . . ." She bit her lip and looked away. Looked around the store for anyone to overhear, but they were alone at the front.

"You can tell me, unless he wouldn't want you to."

"He needs to talk to someone who's been through it. I'm a mere mortal."

Zac passed his palm over her shoulder. "I'll keep an eye out for an opening."

"Thank you." She smiled. "Brother."

He couldn't keep from grinning. He gave her a hug, quick and impulsive, and she laughed and hugged him back. He said close to her ear, "I never had a sister."

"I never had a brother." She nudged him again, shoulder to shoulder. "From fangirl to family."

He left the bookstore and drove two blocks to David's home. He got out of his car and stood in the rain, looking up the porch steps. This house had served the longevites often in the last month, become a sort of haven. A house owned by a lonely old man, now open to the family he never knew before last month. Divine irony, no doubt. The trim bungalow was a thread in the fabric of them. And this afternoon would make a few more stitches in that thread.

He mounted the steps and let himself inside and waited for his guests.

Thirty-Eight

While he waited, Zac dealt with things that mattered less than the meeting facing him. He got online and deleted the post to Doc. Yeah, deleting it would garner more speculation, but he felt easier about that than about the post staying up. And maybe some of the new speculation wouldn't tag him. He needed a break from app notifications.

Next he opened his email and typed a message that might be deleted the second Nate opened it, but he would send it anyway and hope Nate passed it along at some point to his son.

Lucas,

Hey, buddy. Your mom told me what's going on in your family. I'm really sorry. My dad died when I was nine, and I remember how confused I felt and how I missed him. Things like this are hard. You already know hard; you don't need more of it. But you're one of the warriors, and I know you've got it in you to press on.

I hope this email gets to you and I hope to hear from you again whenever you're ready to talk. You're a supremely cool young man and I'm glad to have met you.

Keep reading and keep living strong.

Zac

One final thing to do. The dreaded thing.

Zac opened his main app and flinched. New questions about why the post about "Anders" had vanished.

He focused on what he needed to say. Some of these fans were thoughtless; some of them were dirt-grasping gossips. He envisioned the others, the ones Tiana had described. He envisioned her and Jayde and others whose days he had brightened without knowing it. He envisioned the kids watching his videos, the mortals with fragile hopes and fragile health whose needs were met by fund-raisers he could bring awareness to simply because he had the online followers and they did not. In this new world of thumbs up and thumbs down, those icons over a wireless connection could make or break one's social life; and people put almost as much stock in this as the gladiators who had once awaited those same signals.

The digital world was a weird one, but Zac would use it for good as far as he was able. And that meant reforging trust where he had lost it.

He began to type. This would be too long for a simple post. He'd save it as an image and attach it.

To the fans:

A picture was taken of me a few days ago. Public place, glazed-eye face. Yep, that was me. Yep, I was a mess. No, I am not a drug user. But I know it's not enough merely to deny. If it wasn't drugs, what was it?

His mouth dried. He looked up at the ceiling.

"What if I let them think what they want and fade off the scene? Couldn't I do that?"

It would be wrong. Maybe not wrong for someone else, but wrong for him. His visibility could still accomplish good for others. He wasn't free to relinquish it yet.

He scrubbed at his face, pressed a hand to his ribs, and shifted on the couch. "Okay, Father. I'm Yours. Help me get this right."

In that pic, I'm experiencing a panic attack. That's all I'm going to say for now. This is personal stuff, you guys. If you've been through something like it, you know. But here's the thing: it's not something to hide. It's something to go to your loved ones with and ask for help. I've had to do that this week. I wouldn't have shared publicly if not for that pic, but, well, now you know.

And listen up: if you suffer from something like this, don't suffer in the dark. Step into the light with that crap. Talk to somebody. Talk to a lot of somebodies, until you find the help you need. The talking sucks, especially at first, but if I'm worth it, so are you.

I'll do a video soon. Still kind of raw over here, but getting better. It does get better when you step into the light.

Zac

He formatted it as a screenshot image. He attached it to a new post. His finger hovered over the Post button. He cleared his throat and fisted his hand.

"You really want me to do this?"

No voice, not even words the way he'd felt them recently, from scripture he'd known since he was truly young. But certainty. And a gentle push.

Zac posted it.

Then he logged off everything and put his phone away and settled in to wait. He lounged on the couch, half dozing. One day he wouldn't be tired.

Finn arrived first, which wasn't optimal. If Rachel had beat him there, she and Zac could have worked on her calm. But when Zac studied Finn, his focus was forced to widen. Finn's T-shirt was rumpled, his jaw shadowed with black stubble, his eyes flat as ever but bearing deep creases around them. Zac led him to David's living room and offered him a chair, but Finn walked the perimeter of the room. He stopped at the turtle's habitat. She wasn't visible at the moment, burrowed somewhere beneath the wood chips and peat moss.

"Box turtle," Zac said.

"Huh." Finn halted in front of the piano. "Are you sure Rachel's coming?"

"She said she was." He ought to offer something; David had coffee and probably wine. But Zac hadn't asked and didn't have the right to assume, especially not lately.

"You'll leave when she gets here." Finn's flat stare expected cooperation.

"No."

"This is private."

"Rachel asked me to be here."

"I'm asking you not to be."

Zac tried to picture Rachel's reaction to his disclosing something personal about her. He imagined her nodding permission. It would be the first thing she told Finn anyway; she couldn't hide it.

"Rachel is afraid of people. Literally."

Finn continued to stare at him. Skepticism? Hard to tell.

Zac spread his hands. "It's real; I've seen it. And it's compounded with you because of what she did to you."

"She told you this."

"She's starting to trust me. I'm telling you, this is going to be hard on her, and she's going to need a stabilizer in the room."

"Guess it's true I'm not much of a stabilizer."

"Is this going to be a problem?"

"Guess I don't have a choice." Finn tugged the piano bench out a few feet and sat. If he made any explanation, Zac might consider his request. *I'm here for peace, not war,* or however Finn would say it. But he said nothing more.

A soft knock came at the front door. When Zac opened it, Rachel stood with her arms in an X, breathing long and deep through her nose.

"Hey, kiddo. You made it."
"Don't go anywhere."
"Not a chance." He ushered her inside and shut the door behind them. "Need anything?"
"To be somewhere else."
"That's an option, remember?"
"Yes. But no. Where is Finn?" Her gaze darted around the foyer and snagged on the doorway to the living room.
Zac nodded. "Right in there, when you're ready."
"Finn who I bereaved."
She shuffled toward the living room, and Zac walked beside her. She froze at the threshold as Finn rose to his feet.
"Hello, Rachel."
She took a side step closer to Zac and grasped his shirtsleeve. "Hello, Finn."
Zac guided her to the sofa across from Finn then sat beside her. He wouldn't speak unless they spoke to him. Not that Finn was likely to forget his presence as long as Rachel clung to him.
"I have things to say," she said. "But you should speak first, since you requested the meeting."
Finn nodded. "It's not much. But it needs to be said face-to-face."
"Thank you for seeing me. I — I know I

don't deserve it."

"Well, that's what I wanted to say." Finn got up and walked the perimeter of the room as he spoke. "I've got experience with violence. A lot of it. Some of it I did, and some of it done to me."

He looked across the room at Rachel. She was staring at him, and in a minute she'd tear a hole in Zac's sleeve.

"You don't talk much about forgiveness when you're living the life I was. When we were young, you know." He cleared his throat. "But I needed it bad. And I needed to give some too. And not either one of them things happened. Then the folks were all aged dead and gone, and me still this young self here that you see."

Words unleashed, as they'd been on the drive from the St. Louis airport. His accent hadn't changed, but the rhythm of his speech called up old days, old regions no longer existing though the geography was the same.

"Sean and Holly and me, we fell out. Don't matter why, but it was bitter. Thought I had time to settle with them. Thought I had another hundred years if I wanted to drag it out."

"Oh," Rachel whispered.

He held up an open hand. "What I'm saying, roundabout — I know you were trying to cure yourself. I know Zac here stopped you."

She nodded.

"I'm grateful he did. I'm grateful not to number you among the departed, Rachel. It wasn't your time, I don't believe."

Her hands began to shake, jarring Zac's wrist as she held on.

"It breaks me down that they're gone, that I can't make things right with Holly and Sean. That I can't see my good old ones James and Anna, not anymore."

Rachel's lips were pressed hard together, but a faint moan slipped past.

Finn raised his hand again. "I've got to say all of it, and then I'll go. Part of me wants to let it eat me up, thinks that would be justice somehow. Never seeing you nor speaking to you. But I can't take more of that. And you don't deserve it."

"I . . . don't?"

"They knew what could happen, and the risk was worth it to them, and so we lost them. And wasn't none of that on you."

Rachel hunched forward on the couch.

Finn crossed the room and came to crouch in front of her, hands dangling between his knees, the classic pose of the cowboy before the cook fire. "That's what I had to say.

Now if you've got anything, I'll hear it."

"Forgive me?" she said.

He frowned, gave a short nod.

"That's — that's all I had to say." Her free hand clasped Zac's sleeve too, both now clutching side by side. "I'm so sorry. I beg your forgiveness."

"You can stop begging. I forgive you."

"I'm so sorry, Finn."

"I don't see much in people, but I see that."

"Cady?"

He stood. "I don't speak for Cady. I told her I was coming here. That's all I'll say."

"I understand," Rachel whispered.

For the first time, Finn looked to Zac. "We'll leave in the morning, I guess."

Zac nodded.

"Now I've got to go." He strode for the front door.

Zac set his hand over both of Rachel's and nudged. "Let go, kiddo. I want to see him out."

But her fingers seemed to be spasming around his shirt. She whimpered when he pried them loose.

"Hey, I'll just be out on the porch."

"I'm cold, Zac. I'm a deep freeze."

And no jar of seashells in the room. Zac looked around and brought her a striped throw pillow. "Count the stripes until I come back. Sound like a plan?"

"Y–yes."

Finn was halfway down the porch steps when Zac burst through the doorway. "Finn."

He turned back, his face as flat as always.

"Stay in touch."

"I will. Won't speak for Cady."

"She can take all the time she needs. We're not getting any older."

A quick squint, a turning up of his mouth that held nothing pleasant. "But sometimes we do."

He turned and jogged down the steps and out to his car. Something had surfaced in him in those last seconds, something of who he had been the first time Zac saw him, under a parking lot floodlight with a gun in his hand aimed at Zac and David. The Finn Zac had just glimpsed was the one who had pulled the trigger and left David with a scar along his temple. Maybe it was the head injury, as Zac had thought before. Or maybe it was a past of bitterness and violence, chasing Finn's heels like baying hounds. Running him down.

Zac shut the door and returned to the living room. Rachel held the pillow on her lap, her finger touching each stripe.

"Ten. Eleven. Twelve. Thirteen."

Zac sat beside her. "Hey."

"I thought it would be a relief."

"Well, let's give you a minute."

"Zac, do you know what's wrong with me?"

He couldn't tell if the question was rhetorical or not. "You're afraid."

"Look at me. This isn't normal, and I know that, and I can't make it stop."

"You came here and talked to Finn. That's a step."

In a few minutes her shaking lessened. She squeezed the pillow and then set it aside. "I need to drive some more. I didn't get far."

"And you're okay to do that?"

"It'll help. I'll stay in touch and come back by tonight. I'll park Stormie somewhere out of the way and sleep in my own home. You can have your apartment back."

"Sounds good."

Not entirely to himself as long as Simon deemed the couch his designated spot. But maybe Zac didn't mind that after all.

THIRTY-NINE

Rachel left, and Zac sat alone in David's house, loath to leave. Hard things happened here, yet safety enwrapped him. Companionship lived here, and the behemoth did not. He padded into the kitchen, looked around without knowing what he sought, and returned to the living room empty-handed, restless. In the turtle habitat, a hollow half log rocked and bumped a glass wall. A head with cunning reptile eyes emerged from hiding and stared at Zac. The rest of the turtle remained in her burrow.

"I think I've got it figured out," Zac said, and she stretched her neck to watch him sink down on the couch again. "He chose an introvert pet."

She blinked at him. A definite confirmation.

To his right stood a coffee table stacked with books. Zac lifted the whole pile, tugged it into his lap, and set them aside one by one. The complete poetry of Frost. A Western novel, of course. A young adult fairy tale retelling Zac had heard Tiana recommend. Ah, love. Here was a biography of T. E. Lawrence, and beneath it an antique clothbound edition of George MacDonald's *A Book of Strife in the Form of the Diary of an Old Soul.* Zac turned its pages with care. Penciled words nearly crowded MacDonald's poems off the pages. He shut the book before he could trespass on it further. When he set it aside, the final volume in the stack rested alone on his knees.

A Bible.

Well, of course.

He hadn't touched the Word of God in one hundred years. He reached out slowly, pressed his palm to the leather cover, let his thumb caress the spine.

"I guess You planned this too." His throat tightened. "What am I talking about, like there's anything You haven't planned."

He opened the cover. The binding had been reinforced too many times to count. A line of glue, aged brown tape, another line of glue, all beneath several layers of clear packing tape. He chuckled. David wasn't trying to keep the book pristine, merely functional. Zac turned a page to the family blanks. Ah, this was old indeed. Faded calligraphy: *Weddings: John and Sarah Russell, July 13, 1870.* On the next page: *Births: Michael John Russell, February 6, 1872. Kathleen May Russell, January 21, 1875.* Other births a generation later, David's grandchildren. A few great-grandchildren too, judging by dates. And then their deaths. Each and every death was recorded, and drops of moisture had blotted this page several times. Zac set his palm on the account of his friend's loved ones, on the imprint of his friend's tears. The he turned more pages.

Genesis. In the beginning. Formless and void. And God said . . .

"Let there be light," Zac whispered.

He drew up his knees and cradled the book in both hands and began to read. Words that lived in him though he had not read or uttered them since the Great War. He breathed deeper when he read of God breathing life into Adam. He touched the pages again and again, his fingers running along the words, stuffing himself with every line, a starved beggar at last willing to taste the feast.

"Order and beauty from chaos and nothingness." He bowed his head over the book. "Oh Father, do that with me, will You, please?"

He kept reading. He marveled. When he reached Exodus, he closed the book and pressed it to his chest.

"Thanks, Father."

He set the book on the table, stacked the others beside it. He would read Exodus tomorrow. His body drooped. He stretched out on David's couch and shut his eyes. A minute of rest. No more.

He woke with a start and found a clock. It was an antique, its pendulum ticking away seconds in a way that made him too aware of them. David, on the other hand, chose to live with that ticking despite the digital options everywhere.

Five after six. The bookstore was closed. Shoot. He got up and hustled for his car, locking the door behind him. David and Tiana would still be there, closing out the register, straightening the shop for tomorrow. He selfishly hoped they had no plans tonight.

First he stopped at the bakery. In minutes he had bought a few end-of-the-day specials from Connie and headed for Galloway's. The bookstore was lit when he arrived, but the door was locked. He knocked and showed his face in the window, and Tiana spotted him and hurried over.

The door opened on her smile. "Well,

hello again."

"Hey." He shifted his weight from one foot to the other, looked past her into the store, tried to see if he was interrupting. "I, um — well, last week before the chaos set in, David asked me for help with a project. Blind Date with a Book?"

She motioned him inside while he was still rambling. "And you're here to lend your hands?"

"If you're not otherwise busy."

"No way. I've got hummus and chips. Let's party."

"Party? With hummus?"

"Well, we'll have to keep refreshments away from the books."

"That's not what I meant." He held up the brown paper bakery bag. "Anyway, I brought the real food."

She snatched it from him and peeked inside. She nudged items aside and listed them as she went, as if he didn't know what he'd bought. "Mm, lemon zest scone — for me, of course. Pecan cinnamon braid — for David, of course. And three cookies — all for you?"

"That's the goal."

She laughed. "Too much of a good thing?"

"A myth in this case."

She kept the bag, swung it at her side, and

tugged his arm. "I've set aside the books I want. Come on." Her voice rose in a singsong. "Oh David! Look who's come to wrap books!"

Zac followed her to an alcove at the back of the store, a corner framed with, of course, more bookshelves. On an old library cart, Tiana had stacked about thirty books.

David emerged from the stockroom. A smile warmed his eyes when he saw them. "I knew it was inevitable."

"Because it's a great idea." Tiana grinned and turned to Zac. "I can't take credit. I saw it on a bookstore-ideas thread online. I can't believe we've never tried it before."

They got to work and soon discovered an assembly line expedited the process. Zac cut squares of the thick brown paper and lengths of twine for decorative bows, which Tiana insisted on. David wrapped, and Tiana tied the bows and wrote messages in black marker. She embellished her capital letters with curlicues. *Read Me at the Beach! Read Me with a Friend! Read Me to Chew on Some Deep Ideas! Read Me Late into the Night! Read Me and Laugh!*

"These books are mostly new," David said.

"Several are big sellers from the nineties," she said.

"The nineteen nineties."

"Oh, for the love. If you want to wrap a Dickens or a Twain, fine. I'll write *Read Me with a Dictionary.*"

"Aye, indeed, that's what these young ones would have to do." The brogue that had been weaving into his words over the last hour now fully cloaked them.

Tiana rolled her eyes. Then she leaned over and kissed his mouth.

David startled back from her. "Ach, we're in public, love."

"I'm public now?" Zac waved the scissors at them. "Carry on. I'll gallantly look away."

David gave a huff. "I'd wager you'd not find it fitting either."

"I've told you, old man. The calendar's not the only way I'm younger than you are."

Tiana's laugh was like chimes.

After a while, silence descended, and with it the burden of the last week. The regulator on the wall ticked on and on, seconds gone he'd never get back. The fact usually did not faze him, not with endless seconds before him. Strange that he'd noticed clocks twice today, or maybe not so strange. In the past month, five longevites had come to their final seconds. His scissors rasped against the packing paper, clinked as he snipped each length of twine. Tiana's marker made hushed sounds against the packages as she wrote. No one but Zac seemed to feel the weight in the absence of their voices.

A minute before he would have spoken, Tiana looked up. "How was it today, Zac? With Finn and Rachel?"

"It was good. It was . . ." How to summarize? "Finn made peace."

"Will we see them again?" Tiana said.

"He said he would keep in touch. Cady's been silent. For now I just have to wait and hope. And pray, I guess."

"What about Rachel?"

"I don't know. I mean, I'm going to be her family, but I . . ." *Can't be her lifeline. Can't cut her loose either.* And middle ground had always been beyond him.

"If she'll stay local, we'd like to help her," Tiana said. "We've talked it over."

"Really?"

David nodded.

Zac tipped his head to the ceiling and closed his eyes. "Thank you. Really, you have no idea. I was . . ."

"Stewing?" Tiana said.

"Out of my depth."

"So would anyone be, alone," David said.

A long sigh poured from Zac, a substitute for words. He sat a moment, brimming over inside. At last he looked at David, who had continued wrapping books. Zac owed on a promise.

"About the cure," he said, and David went still. "We looked at what's left. There's a vial of the serum — the original stuff. The last vial left. She could use it to turn a mortal."

Tiana and David didn't even glance at each other. It was true, Zac plainly saw: they had both closed the door on that possibility for her, and they weren't tempted to reopen it.

"Or," he said, "she could use it to try again. For a cure that would allow the aging process but not force it into the body's systems immediately."

"So it is still possible," David whispered.

"She burned almost everything, David. Yeah, she can keep trying, but she expects it would take years for a result, any result. And it might not be the one you want."

The man's hands slipped, dropped the novel he was wrapping. It slid to the floor beside him. He didn't pick it up. His chest heaved with a labored breath.

Tiana was watching him. "Basically, we don't have a definite answer now any more than we did before she burned everything."

"Right." Zac had to tell them the whole truth. Nothing else was fair. "We might be looking at a longer time frame now that she has formulas to rework."

"Okay. Cool."

David pushed to his feet. "I'm sorry. Please excuse me a moment."

Tiana watched him go. Looked down at her hands and set aside the marker as if it were too heavy for her.

"Tiana?" Zac said after a long silence.

She sighed. "This is what I was saying earlier."

"Should I go after him?"

"Would you?"

Zac got up and headed the direction David had gone. He found the man kneeling behind the checkout counter, voice too low to be heard more than a few feet away, the brogue thick as Zac had ever heard it. He stepped closer.

"Ach, please, Lord God. In Thy mercy, provide this cure before her life is far spent. Grant me this mercy, I beg Thee. But if Thy will be something else, grant me strength to trust the plans Thou hast for us. I confess I lack that strength tonight."

To intrude on such a prayer felt worse than sacrilegious, but to watch his friend in pain and do nothing was worse. Zac knelt at his side and remembered David doing the same for him, at a time of distress so great it was all Zac could do to keep the haze from taking him.

David looked up from his bowed posture. Tears stood in his eyes, dripped down his face. "It was too heavy for me. I had to give it back to Him. Again."

"Again?" Zac said.

"Ach, I've given it to Him countless times, but then I take it back." He scrubbed his face and looked past Zac, down the aisles of shelves. "It worries her."

"Because she loves you."

"Aye, she does. Such a woman loves me. 'Tisn't easy to grasp. And I'd wed her tomorrow and most gladly, if I could know I'll not have to —" His words broke in a fresh surge of tears that he swallowed back. "I cannot bury my Tiana. Too much strength left me with the other losses. To endure another — I cannot."

"David . . ." Zac sighed.

"I apologize. This isn't what you came for tonight."

"You don't owe me an apology." He sat back on his heels and appraised his friend. "Didn't peg you as a crier, though."

David's laugh was broken but real. "Ask Tiana; she'll have many instances to report."

They stood together, David a little feeble at first, as if the storm of his emotions had drawn on his physical strength.

"Look, man," Zac said. "I wouldn't survive it either."

David bowed his head.

"It's why I haven't been with a mortal since my wife died in 1892. I clung to Moira because I couldn't lose her that way. We tore each other to pieces, but it felt safer. Screwed up, I know, but that's me. Goodbyes wreck me too hard."

Too hard to speak of his boys at all. Maybe Simon knew him better than he wanted to credit. In his antique Bible packed away in a box in Denver, the death blanks were empty. He'd lacked the strength to write any of them down.

"So I can't speak to this." *Sorry, Tiana.*

"I well understand."

Their pace back to Tiana was slow, as if David had more to tell him before they reached her hearing. Or more to listen to. What else could Zac say?

He did have one thing. "At least you're giving it to Him every time you take it back. I never did that with Moira. I just held on with everything in me."

Until now. Today had proved it: Zac had let her go. He wished he knew when. Maybe it had happened back in 1985, and he'd denied it even to himself until today.

Another slow nod, and David halted mid-aisle, meeting Zac's eyes, studying him hard. Listening. As if this were helpful. Well, okay.

"Look, man. If the cure doesn't work out, and if Tiana quits this place before we do . . ."

The tall frame shuddered, but David held his gaze.

"This time you won't be alone. And it does make a difference. Believe me."

"I do," David said. "And I thank you."

They said no more until they reached Tiana. She studied both of them as they resumed their places in the assembly line and took up scissors, paper, and books. After a few minutes, she nodded to Zac, and he nodded back.

Then her marker stilled as she studied him. "You're cutting with your left hand now."

"Huh?" He looked down at his hands. He was. He shrugged. "I'm ambidextrous."

"I knew it. I've seen you write with both, haven't I? I thought I was losing it."

He grinned. "Multitalented stunt guy." Then sobered. "In an 1860s schoolhouse, lefties got smacked with the ruler until you switched dominance."

"That's stupid."

"Superstitious," he said. "I was stubborn enough to write with my right hand at school and my left hand at home."

"Of course you were." She resumed writing, finished the phrase she'd started, then pointed her marker at him. "You and I have unfinished business."

"Oh?"

"Something you wanted to ask me. You might not remember now. It was at lunch after the barn collapse."

"Oh, that." He cut another square of paper. "I was going to ask you to pray for me."

"Hmm." She penned a swirling underline of the last word she'd written and set the wrapped book aside on the "finished" pile. "Did you think I wasn't?"

It did seem a needless request now. "I don't know what I thought. We could chalk it up to broken ribs and hunger and whatnot."

"That works."

"I suppose it had to do with your breaking silence," David said.

Zac looked from him to Tiana and back again. "You two don't forget a word I say, do you?"

"What's family for?" Tiana's smile held a hint of mischief. Oh yeah, they'd been discussing him at length.

His face heated. "I — well, I'm home. You know, in the formerly prodigal sense."

Tiana's eyes grew shiny. "Tell us, Zac."

He did. He stumbled for words a few times, which for him was strange and humbling. He tried to convey how desperate the night in the barn had been and how God had spoken to his soul. He tried to convey his struggle to talk to God and how the struggle waned with each day. He wasn't ready to talk about the reburying of Colm, but he'd get there soon.

He tried to convey the enormous debt he ought to owe. At that point he set aside the scissors, his eyes too misty to cut straight.

"But you know you don't owe it?" Tiana said.

"Yeah."

"Just making sure." She smiled.

"I know truth. I always did. I just decided not to live by it anymore."

"What brought you back?"

"I don't know." He picked the scissors back up, blinked a few times, and resumed cutting. "I know there was no part of me interested in turning around before . . . well, before Colm was found out. It felt like a community evil, what he'd been doing. Like I could see what God thought of it. How it grieved Him."

Ironic, really. He'd been unconcerned with his own evils for most of his life by then. He tapped the scissors on his knee and shook his head.

"I'm a mess, guys. 'Prone to wander, Lord, I feel it,' except I wasn't acknowledging the wandering. And I wasn't exactly wandering either. I was running full out."

Tiana sat with a wrapped book in her lap, marker poised in her hand as if she'd forgotten she was holding it. She had written *Read Me and.*

"I just wish I could undo it." Words were pouring now. Zac gestured with his right hand, still holding the scissors. "I wish I could be some guy finding Him for the first time, you know? Instead I've read the entire Bible more times than I can count and I still ran away. All those years I knew what I was doing. I wish I could erase that crap. Have a clean slate with Him."

Tiana blinked as if he'd just said something monumentally stupid.

"What?"

She shook her head.

"Well, what?"

"Zac," David said, "what do you think the cross is for?"

They weren't hearing him. "I know, salvation, I know that, but — but I kept on knowingly, and accusing Him, and . . ."

"And what? You wore Him out?"

"That's not what I'm saying."

Tiana sat back on her heels, arms folded, waiting.

"I spent a century in rebellion, okay? I just wish it could be . . . gone."

"Really," she said. "East from west gone?"

"Well, I . . . I . . ."

"Zac," she said, and her voice had gentled. She reached past David's place in their assembly line and touched Zac's arm. "You're being ridiculous."

He blinked. He looked to David.

"Aye, indeed you are. Our centuries are like a day to Him. The psalmist tells us so. In fact, he says a millennium, which I doubt you or I will achieve."

Zac looked down at the scissors in his right hand, the curled fingers of his left. His will rose up in him, resisting. Because he was an idiot.

But even that, his Father did not hold to his account.

"It's gone, friend. It's finished."

"Finished." His eyes burned. Such an obvious thing, but without their words he might have taken another hundred years to put it together.

"And as long as you're wishing for what He's already done, you're neglecting to thank Him for it."

"Yeah." Zac swiped a hand under his eyes. "Okay."

"You might want to try a different hymn when you're bogging down." Tiana finished writing on her book: *Enjoy the HEA!*

"The what?" Zac said.

"Happily Ever After. And no, that's not a spoiler; it's a genre indicator."

"Hey, no judgment here."

She set the book aside. "I'm thinking of a hymn I've heard recently. The solo piano version. Several dozen times."

David waved his hand in a cease-and-desist motion. "Wheesht."

"Mm-hmm. 'The Love of God.' Maybe you need to sing that one for a while, Zac. 'To write the love of God above would drain the ocean dry. Nor could the scroll contain the whole, though stretched from sky to sky.' "

Zac cut the last square and set the scissors aside. "I, um . . . Thank you. Both of you. I know I've been hard to live with."

"We've been worried," Tiana said. "We just wanted you to talk to us."

Zac ducked his head. "Sorry."

"No. This is finished as well." David's

voice was quiet and firm. "You'll not carry it around with you. Only commit to putting away the facade you value so much."

A broken laugh escaped him. "With you people dogging me, I won't be able to maintain the facade even if I want to."

"Good," Tiana said.

He swallowed hard. No crying on them. But if he had to, they'd stick around for it. And they'd stick around after. He knew that much. He grimaced when a tear fell without his permission, but then he gave leave to another.

"With you here, I don't want to, and I don't need to."

Forty

He left his phone's ringer on in case Rachel needed him. In case, against all odds, Lucas called. But his sleep was interrupted only by aching ribs and fear of encountering the behemoth. If he didn't sleep, he couldn't dream. An idiotic and unsustainable strategy, but at this point his adrenal system was calling the shots.

At 5:00 a.m. he gave in. He got out of bed, switched on the light, and muttered nonsensical curses until his eyes adjusted. Then he checked social media, resolved not to stay online more than thirty minutes. His post had been shared fewer times than the bookstore pic, but it was being seen and gathering comments. Sweet comments, supportive comments. The denigrators were there but not many. Maybe he could, after all, keep the respect of most.

If he still had work to do for them, among them, then that mattered. He shut his laptop with a smile. He'd do a video soon, after he had managed at least one full night's sleep.

Only one thing to do at five thirty in the morning. Only one thing he wanted to do. He got into his workout clothes, grappled with his shoelaces, and finally gritted his teeth and bent double to tie them. He sneaked past Simon asleep on his couch. No overnight movie marathon this time; the guy was done in.

Under the conditions of the Life Buoy, Zac knew better than to walk out without a word. He found a scrap of paper and a pen.

> I'm out on the dunes. Can't sleep. Adrenaline, nothing unusual, part of the cycle. No reason to worry. See you for breakfast.
>
> Z

He left the note by the coffee maker and drove out to the park.

Standing at the base of his dune, he nearly gave up before he started. He was in no shape to achieve the smallest hill, much less the summit where his favorite copse of trees nodded their silver-leafed branches to the lake wind.

Well, he was going up there anyway.

Normally the climb took him twenty minutes. Today his time was doubled. Sweat was pouring down his back by the time he reached the halfway mark.

But up there, with his trees and his sky, he could rest. His chest would open all the way, allow the hurts of everyone he cared for to seep from within him like a lanced sore.

He made it to the top with his right hand pressing his side, his feet dragging over the sand. Thank goodness no one else would be here at this hour. Dawn rose over the trees far below, bathing all in pink radiance. Zac looked down the slope at the few cars in the blacktop lot, bug-sized. He stood hunched another few moments, enjoying the triumph, but he needed to sit. He trudged toward his little grove. He would watch the sun come up. He would watch the morning turn the sky blue.

"Oh!"

Zac jolted at the voice. Someone had claimed his spot. The early hour had left her in shadows. He'd nearly stepped on her.

"Sorry." He backed into a tree and let it brace him, hoping the gray light concealed his weakness. "Didn't see you."

The woman raised her face to him. Cady. Of course. Early riser like him, exertion junkie like him, burdened like him though with different burdens. So they sought relief in the same place.

They were staring at each other.

She'd gotten here first. For now the spot was hers. He nodded and turned away, swallowing a bitter taste in his throat at the thwarting. He'd head back and stop one dune lower than this one. God would hear him there as well as here.

He was a few paces from the dip of the incline when Cady's voice came, soft and unsure.

"There's room."

He turned back. She motioned to the space beside her. Like him, she didn't care to sit on the bench. He couldn't explain why that mattered, why it prompted him to approach. He lowered himself to sit in the sand a few feet from where she did, her legs stretched in front of her, her back against one of the cottonwoods.

"Thanks," he said.

"You don't look like you could make the trek down yet."

That's why she'd offered? He looked away over the lower dunes and found the merging of water and horizon. He wouldn't make her talk.

"You must have a pressing urge to be up

here. Or you're a masochist."

Wait. She did want to talk? He met her eyes. They held a depth of raw vulnerability he never would have trespassed on if he'd recognized her sooner. He drew a careful breath and, as he let it out, put away the mask.

"Simon says people are my oxygen. Which is true, if I stop and think about it, but sometimes I have to get away to breathe."

"Of course."

He could leave it there. Maybe he ought to. "Other people's aches soak into me. Accumulate, sometimes."

She studied him as if they'd met this morning, here in the sand before the dawn. "I can't say I've ever felt anything like that."

"It's been called extra empathy." He thought of Moira in a flash of soft hair, smooth skin, and words like fishhooks.

"An Elderfolk gift," Cady said.

"Some mortals have it."

"Probably not like yours though, developed for so many years. You might be the strongest empath in history."

He shrugged. He'd never thought about it.

A minute passed in which she seemed content with the quiet, but one question allowed another. "I thought you'd be halfway to Missouri."

"I couldn't stand the thought of all those hours in a car, not — not with all this in my head. I told Finn I needed the morning to breathe out here. To watch the sunrise."

"Yeah. I get that."

"After this we'll leave."

For a long time then, Cady was quiet. They sat together under the trees and listened to the rasping whispers of the leaves. The pink glow crept toward orange and then yellow, true daylight though shy of itself, the canopy above them still mostly gray. Cady stretched her back and drew up her knees. Zac rested, leaning against a trunk with enough width to brace his shoulders.

It wasn't the same as solitude. He never ceased to sense Cady beside him, still and silent though she was. But his chest began to open nonetheless.

"Zac."

"Hmm."

"I think I understand what you did, why you did it. Advocating for her."

He turned his head and met her eyes. "I bungled that."

"Because it didn't work? You weren't the only factor involved."

"Because in my head, I was advocating

for all of you. But I couldn't keep the balance of it."

She rested her chin on her knees and let the silence settle again. At last she said, "Finn told me about her. His words were, 'Something inside her is all wrenched apart.' "

"He's right."

"But he said, if his brain can heal, why not her mind?"

"I hope he's right about that too."

"And you're going to be there for her."

Zac nodded. "We're all she's got."

"Not me. I can't be, Zac. Can you understand that?"

He tried to. If Rachel had offered the cure to David first, and the man had accepted it. If Simon had too, and Moira. If the ones he held closest in the world had chosen this risk. And died.

"She wasn't glad we came after her," he said. "She still isn't."

Cady looked up. "So you're asking me to be."

"No." He rubbed the back of his hand over his tired eyes. "There I go again, trying to advocate."

"Then you're not going to . . . ?"

"What?"

"Call me a bitter old hag."

"No," Zac said. "You're hurt."

"I'm not hurt. I'm raging. There's a difference."

"There is."

Her lips parted. "You can feel . . . ?"

He nodded. Something between them seemed to writhe and try to hide. "Cady."

She flinched.

"I'm praying for you."

"That I'll forgive her?"

"For *you.* That He'll comfort you and heal you." That one day she would be able to extend grace to Rachel — of course, he had to pray for that too, for both their sakes. But today wasn't the day to tell her.

"And since when do you pray?"

The question should have made him self-conscious, but the settled sense inside him was too complete for such a petty thing. With the tree firm at his back and his Father's hand firm around him — as it had never ceased to be — Zac sighed. "Since I spent a night trapped under a bunch of barn wood."

She was quiet a minute, then said, "I'm glad, Zac."

"It's good to be home."

"So this is a return, not a first-time arrival?"

"Yeah."

"I'm really glad." She turned toward him, and light found her hair and danced in it. "I need to go home too, you know. Missouri, I mean. I need to face what's there."

He nodded. They sat together awhile, and morning inched up the horizon.

At last Cady pushed to her feet. "I've been up here at least an hour. I'll leave you to your getting away."

"If you want."

He stood too, gripping the tree for support until he was more or less upright. Cady jogged in place for half a minute, stretched her legs, and eyed the steep dune with anticipation.

"I ran most of the way up here."

He saluted her. "I did not."

The hint of a smile. "Goodbye for now."

"Don't disappear."

"We won't," she said. "I won't."

She seemed about to say more, but instead she turned away from him. She bounded away down the long hill as sand sprayed up from her heels with every stride. She grew smaller and smaller and disappeared over the edge of the next slope.

For now, she'd said.

Zac took off his shoes and padded barefoot to where they'd sat. He lay down in the cool sand and spread out his arms. The sky had brightened to blue with the new day.

DISCUSSION QUESTIONS

1. This book is a collision of Christianity in the real world with a fantasy story, but *what if* there were longevites living today, unknown to us? In what ways might their existence fit into God's plan for humanity? As a "normal" human, do you ever ask God questions about His purposes similar to those asked by the longevites?

2. The longevites have no way of predicting their life span. How would this uncertainty affect your daily life, human relationships, and relationship with God?

3. If you've read *No Less Days,* you began this book having already met Finn — but barely. Did his true nature surprise you as you got to know him? Did any other characters surprise you?

4. Choosing a book's point-of-view charac-

ter can be a challenge for an author. How does Zac's perspective shape this story? Is he always a reliable narrator? What might the story have been if told from another character's perspective?

5. The characters in *From Sky to Sky* are intended to have strengths and weaknesses, as all people do. What are Zac's greatest strengths? What are his greatest flaws? What about the other characters? Who in the course of the story addresses one of his/her flaws? Who changes?

6. Several of Zac's close friends call him out on the masks he wears. Based on your knowledge of his personality and his past, discuss where these masks might have come from and why.

7. Despite their difference of disposition, Simon and Zac are a strong example of the "friend who sticks closer than a brother" (Proverbs 18:24). Do you have a friend like this in your life, a friend who is the Simon to your Zac (or vice versa)?

8. The longevites as a group don't seem inclined to demand restitution from Rachel for the accidental deaths she caused.

Do you agree with them? Does Rachel owe them, and if so, how could she pay this debt? If you were part of the meeting in chapters 24 and 25, what would you have to say?

9. What are the moral implications of Rachel's serum, of Anna and James taking it despite her warning? If Rachel is able to alter the serum, is David morally free to take it and join Tiana in a mortal life? Why or why not? If you were a longevite, would you desire a mortal life as David does, or would you desire another hundred years as Zac does?

10. Zac tells David that he and Moira stayed together so long because he felt "safer" with her than with a mortal whom he would someday have to mourn. He also admits to himself that his relationship with Moira was an attempt to control his life and resist God's authority. Discuss the many reasons a person might remain in a relationship (whether romantic or platonic) that is unhealthy and/or immoral. What will it be like for Zac if/when Moira comes home?

11. In the final scenes of the book, Zac

hopes for several things: that Cady and Finn will join the longevite family; that Cady will someday extend grace to Rachel; that his place in the semi-spotlight will continue to do good for others; that the support he, David, and Tiana offer will be able to help Rachel. What might happen now with each of Zac's hopes? What is needed to bring them to pass?

12. Discuss the significance of the book's title.

ACKNOWLEDGMENTS

If you took part in the creation of this book, you probably know who you are. Some of you helped unearth the bones; some helped them grow flesh; all were vital to the process, and now is my chance to say public thanks to . . .

My brainstormers and/or first readers, for the vital ways each of you furthered the cultivating of Zac's story. Becky Dean and Jenness Walker, who showed up by God's grace in the "wilderness season" of this book. Kristen Heitzmann, who bestowed on this book a wonderfully shredding copyedit sample I shall never forget. Jess Keller, who keeps showing up throughout the years and who cheerleads my young old guys (especially Simon). Emily Stevens, who put down Michael Crichton (whose work she loves, let's be clear) to read yet another early draft of Zac. Charity Tinnin, who sees characters with such clarity and challenges my early attempts in the best ways. Melodie Lange, who is willing to devote an entire Panera night to brainstorming and character analysis anytime I ask. Andrea Taft, who always knows what I'm talking about, usually before I do.

My agent Jessica Kirkland, for championing me and my stories and believing I can do basically anything.

My editor Annie Tipton, for standalone tips and encouragement. My copyeditor JoAnne Simmons, for showing me where my subtext got a little too *sub.*

My lovely house Barbour, for saying *yes* again. Kirk DouPonce, for creating my new favorite cover of all time.

My Creator and Father, Fount of every blessing; my Savior in whose hand I reside forever; the Spirit who nudges and pokes when I am prone to wander. Lord of every good gift, thank You for giving me stories. Thank You for Zac's story, and may the words of my pen be pleasing in Your sight.

ABOUT THE AUTHOR

As a child, **Amanda G. Stevens** disparaged *Mary Poppins* and *Stuart Little* because they could never happen. Now she writes speculative fiction. She is the author of the Haven Seekers series, and her debut *Seek and Hide* was a 2015 INSPY Award finalist. She lives in Michigan and loves trade paperbacks, folk music, the Golden Era of Hollywood, and white cheddar popcorn.

The employees of Thorndike Press hope you have enjoyed this Large Print book. All our Thorndike, Wheeler, and Kennebec Large Print titles are designed for easy reading, and all our books are made to last. Other Thorndike Press Large Print books are available at your library, through selected bookstores, or directly from us.

For information about titles, please call:

(800) 223-1244

or visit our website at:

gale.com/thorndike

To share your comments, please write:

Publisher
Thorndike Press
10 Water St., Suite 310
Waterville, ME 04901